T0117187

Riot

The Fowl of the Crimson Dawn

By

Isaac Tago

Order this book online at www.trafford.com
or email orders@trafford.com

Most Trafford titles are also available at major online book retailers.

© Copyright 2011 Isaac Tago.
All rights reserved. No part of this publication may be reproduced, stored in a retrieval
system, or transmitted, in any form or by any means, electronic, mechanical, photocopying,
recording, or otherwise, without the written prior permission of the author.

Printed in the United States of America.

ISBN: 978-1-4269-9430-2 (sc)
ISBN: 978-1-4269-9431-9 (e)

Trafford rev. 10/31/2011

 www.trafford.com

North America & international
toll-free: 1 888 232 4444 (USA & Canada)
phone: 250 383 6864 ♦ fax: 812 355 4082

"To revolt is a natural tendency of life. Even a worm turns against the foot that crushes it. In general, the vitality and relative dignity of an animal can be measured by the intensity of its instinct to [riot]."
– Mikhail Bakunin

Life and Instinct

Life.
It's all relevant.
But it's all temporary.
It's malevolent.
But also the contrary.
Its name neither time,
Nor love at first sight.
This thing has no rhyme,
No wrong and no right.
Instinct.

By: Isaac Tago

To my extraordinary family, my fantastic friends, but mainly to the deity of a mother I have, Linda, which without her grounding me this book would have never even started, because I wouldn't have been bored enough to discover my passion.

To God, who always knew.

And to anyone who has ever been bullied, beat down by life, or ever felt like they didn't belong. Just remember, when you feel you can't throw another punch and every inch of you begins to wane, that I believe in you. Keep fighting.

Lastly to Sean Matthew Kerr, who was the first to read this book, my biggest fan, my best friend and the one who kept me fighting tooth and nail for my dreams. You helped me find myself again. You are the best thing that's ever happened to me.

Acknowledgments

To all the main characters in this book, that are actually based off the best friends a guy could ever ask for: Beef, Jake, Anthony, Phillip, Camo, Mike, Kiley, Sean, Corrie, Vianca, Brett, Brett, Matt, Ty, Brooke, Buddy, Josh. Thank you for being in my life.

To those Friday night lights and all my brothers on the football team.

To my favorite only brother, Nathaniel, I love you and I am so proud of you. Keep going hard. To my favorite and only sister, Moriah, the one I can share anything with. You and I are more alike than you know, sis. I love you so much, even if I am incapable of showing it in all other ways; this is my way of expressing it. To my parents, Linda and Roy, for having to raise such a difficult, hard-headed child; Yours truly. To every single person in my family, I wouldn't trade any of you for anything.

To love. To Faith in better days. To Laughter. To Joy. To Passion. To anyone I may have encountered in my entire life span; the good, the bad, the bitches, the idols, and even the assholes, I hope all of your dreams come true.

Contents

1.   Fire Alarm

I sit right next to the fire alarm, in the back right corner of the room. One quick push in and down and I could move the entire school to the football field. Tempted to send my high school into a false panic, the teachers at least—it would be more of a relief to the students, I thought about what could happen if they found the culprit to the false alarm. *"What's the worst that could happen?"* I asked myself, *"A three-day suspension from this dump? That would be a blessing!"* I relished the idea now and was no longer tempted. I was convinced. Biding my time, I pretend to pay attention to Mr. Rusenkell who is rambling on about another biological thing that I had no hope in understanding. But my mind is focused on planning an escape route for after I push the button. Besides, I am not a man of science anyways. I am a man of fate. Not that I'm some psycho religious person, I just believe that the only choices we really have are the simple ones like what to eat in the morning, or what shoes to wear. But even then I think it was fate that that type of food is even available for you in the morning, or that shoe will step into someone else's gum because it is supposed to happen. It's all destinies. And right now it is my destiny to push this button.

"*This is probably not the smartest idea you've ever had, Cale.*" I warned myself.

"*I'm not sitting here for another hour!*"

"*Maybe you should just listen to Mr. Rusenkell. Biology can tell you about your body…and maybe explain why your face sucks.*"

"Bite me."

"Excuse me Mr. Valens?" Mr. Rusenkell projected from the front of the class. A confused look was printed on his face and he was no longer talking about amoebas or whatever the hell he was gobbling about. Around twenty-three other faces followed his voice to me, all of them either smiling or giggling. Lasers shot from all of my twenty-three classmate's eyes hitting the upper left of my torso. Embarrassment caved in and collapsed on me like a hazardous ditch suffocating my lungs. They were all burying me alive with their guilt-trip stares.

It was then when I realized I had said "*Bite me!*" out loud as well as I did in my head. I hate when I do that. Now that I think of it I remember hearing my faint voice over the music I was listening to.

"How embarrassing…" a girl whispered from across the room. I was amazed I heard her even through the chorus of "Feeling Good" by Muse which was blasting through my headphones.

"What a freak." I hear a boy say bold and boringly, but no one else seems to reject his impulsive comment that I had already brushed off. His voice broke my trance though, and I realized Mr. Rusenkell's face was still painted with confusion. I took my headphones out, still hearing the song, and I painted my own face with confusion. The room was completely silent, except for my headphones which fueled the embarrassment even more like a cigarette landing in a trash can filled with kerosene.

"Sorry…I- I was…thinking of something- it made me- irritated." I stuttered.

"*You suck at lying.*" I chuckled in my head.

"*Go lock yourself in an asylum!*"

"*Maybe you should just let me do all the talking.*"

Ignoring myself, I went back to pretending to pay attention. Through my peripherals, I saw twenty-three other students slowly follow my lead. Mr. Rusenkell was already writing something new on the white board.

"Twenty-two," I corrected myself, *"twenty-two students returned to work."* Then I realized I still felt a pair of eyes picking at the hole in my shoulder the others made with their death stares trying to drown me in embarrassment. The pair of eyes kept poking at the hole to make sure I was still alive. I covered up the imaginary hole, which felt so real, in my left shoulder with my right hand. Going against my better judgment, which was to continue on with my pathetic life and not give in, I accepted curiosity's offer and looked to my left, only to wish I hadn't.

You know when you judge someone on the first sight of them and their face seems so intriguing to look at that you know your lives will intersect later on in life? Brett Gooding qualifies in this category. He used to be interesting to me, four years ago when we were freshmen. He was popular coming from Kansas. His first year in a high school and he was loved instantly. If it were me though in his shoes the seniors would have brought back the 70's and paddled me until I puked a kidney. But that's just my luck. Going into Stellar High school, I was a different kind of popular. I was known throughout all of Stellar High as the most hated person alive. It's like there were signs all around me that I couldn't see. And not even pickets or posters. I'm talking about Las Vegas signs that have a large arrow pointing to me saying things like: "FREAK SHOW!", or "Number one Weirdo!!", or "Caution: Vampires *DO* exist!" I guess in a way, I chose to be this way. Why should I change who I am and act like everyone else? *"Friggen chameleons."* Always changing around their surroundings. There aren't any stereotypical cliques anymore like it used to be in the 80's. High school is now one big infestation of chameleons. It makes me sick. Brett, however, was not like most chameleons, he would change to a bold blue in a green surrounding and the green slowly changed to his shade of blue. It was fascinating at first. He even had me change my colors at times. And this is where I began to resent him for it. Heaven forbid if I came into a green surrounding as bold blue, I would surely be attacked by a green predator in an instant. So, I hate him because everyone loves him. I'm a wolf that runs alone, and I love it. I think.

I find myself staring at Brett Gooding now. No, not staring, glaring at him. As if my turrets-like outburst was his entire fault. I had to put the blame somewhere, and I could not fit it inside my full tank of guilt and regrets. So I gave it to Brett via glowering at him. His mouth was open like he was about to say something related to hello. I interrupted his contemplating thoughts on whether he should or not with my own way of saying hello. "What do *you* want?"

"Uh…Huh…Uh" he stutters.

It was hard to believe how pathetic he was. One's weakness is another's strength I suppose. A bit of blood rushed to my head at the fact that Brett Gooding: Mr. All-American football star, slash Mr. Prom king, slash Straight-A student, slash Teachers pet, slash role model, was actually intimidated by me. He ranked way higher than me in all of life's aspects, but I couldn't figure out how he could be afraid of me. Bored of his stalling, I cruelly told him, "Take a picture, it'll last longer", a little too loudly.

"That's the second interruption today Mr. Valens", Mr. Rusenkell scolded, "The next time you are going up to the office."

I rolled my eyes. "No! Please don't Mr. Ruse!" I say sarcastically. I'm such jerk sometimes. Ruse-dog is actually a cool teacher and everyone takes advantage of him. This irritates me because I respect the guy as a human being able to put up with immature, ignorant chameleons all the time.

"Alright then move up here to the front desk." He waves to an empty desk right in the front of the class.

I glance at the fire alarm to my right. My entire plan was now ruined. I glanced to my left at Brett and gave him a death stare. If only looks could kill. I look back up at Ruse trying to plead to him to not make me move only so I could execute my plan, "But-"

"Today please, Cale." He interrupted.

"Damn it Ruse!" I yelled to myself. Unwillingly, I stood up and dragged my feet to the front of the classroom all twenty-three pairs of eyes were on me again. *"Chameleons. Don't they have anything better to do then just stare?"* I suppose it is my fault for making a scene. I sat down and Mr. Rusenkell began to talk again. This time I could actually hear some of the things he was saying. Stuff about extra chromosomes and evolution as time passes. I doze off, and fidget my right heel playing the rhythm of a scared rabbit's heart against the floor.

"Can you like stop?" a girl says with all the sass in the world right next to me, "you're extremely annoying." I turn my head so I could see who she was. She didn't even have the ovaries to say it to my face, she just kept writing like she had said nothing to me. This makes me start to tap my heel even harder and faster.

"No, I can't help it. A.D.H.D." I smirk in the nearly exact tone she had given me. Then she looks up at me as if I had just punched her in the arm for no reason at all.

"Last chance Cale. No more warnings after this." Mr. Rusenkell scolded again.

"She's the one who talked first, Ruse!" I defend.

"What are you talking about, freak? I haven't said one word this entire class period. *You* are the only one, you psycho!" I hear a bunch of 'ooh's' in the background like I just got served, or whatever the hell they call it. "Do you want to know why people don't like you? It's because you always give them a reason to stay away from you!" the girl outburst as if she has been biding her time, waiting to explode her words of fury on me. The entire class was in shock; even I was surprised on how someone so little could yell so loud. But I was not about to take crap from some red headed chick.

My eyebrows squeezed together wrinkling my forehead and I roared back at her, "Well you have red hair!" I can hear faint giggles that didn't want to be shared aloud only because *I* had said something about her rebellious hair color.

"Really? That's got to be the worst comeback I've ever heard."

"Your mom's the worst comeback I've ever heard."

"You're so mature."

"And you've got black hair!" the red head scolds.

"You don't know me!"

"You don't know yourself!" she yelled too quickly. This shut me up. I had been defeated by this red head. The color was not like fire, but it was a darker shade of red. It distracted me from making a comeback. If fire had a night time look, this maroon and dark shade of red would be its color. Her words hit me like a feral wave of truth. I was amazed how true her statement was. I was also embarrassed and disappointed in myself.

"Alright, enough!" Mr. Rusenkell intervened, "unless you two want to settle this up at the principal's office." It was more of a statement then it was a question. I remain silent, so does the red head. "Okay then, let's finish today's lesson off then with a lab." Moaning and groaning follow after he says "lab".

"Someone shoot me. Please God, just smite me right now." I plead. Suddenly I see Ruse pull out a Bunsen burner that reminds me of my plan. I look back to my regular seat by the fire alarm and I see Brett still writing down notes from the board. My eyes dart to the fire alarm again. I so badly wanted to pull the alarm, the thought of it boiled in my mind as I strangely dazed out, not noticing my eyes were directed at Brett. With frustration I turn back to the front and I see Ruse is having a panic attack.

"He seems really worried." I notice his facial structure is full of wrinkles, like he is angry and scared at the same time. Ruse begins to start moving faster and searching more violently. *"Did he lose his marbles?"*

"Why don't you ask him?" I answer.

"I thought you wanted to do all the talk-"

"Shut up." I cut myself off. "Hey, Ruse, you okay over there?"

"Where is it? Has anyone seen a green bottle? Anyone!" He panics, ignoring my question.

"What was in it Ruse?" The red head asked, taking the words right out of my mouth. Mr. Rusenkell doesn't answer her. "Mr. Rusenkell! What was in the bottle?" she yelled again in attempt to grab him out of his furious daze after he doesn't reply. The red head seems awfully concerned to what was in the bottle. I had let it go after he didn't answer the first time and just kept on searching.

"Oh my god!" Ruse whispers full of despair so the entire class could hear how important it was. This made me even less interested now that everyone was intrigued to see what was up with Mr. Rusenkell. "Who-who-… who opened the bottle?" Ruse said in that same desperate whisper. It was like he was dying and those were his last words before his heart stopped beating.

"Pretty lame words if you ask me, Ruse." I think.

"I'd go out with a bang like, I'll be back, *or* Death is only the beginning, *just to mess with whomever's head was listening to me."*

"Answer me! Did anyone open this bottle?" Ruse growled furiously. This surprised me. I have never seen Mr. Rusenkell so angry in my entire life. I didn't even know he was capable of getting mad. He never yells, and now Ruse was livid. "It could be a matter of life or death!" he exclaimed.

I don't quite know why, but seeing Ruse angry made me furious as well. My head began swarming with the frustration I was sure Ruse was feeling. And suddenly, the fire alarm went off. The loud sirens nearly defend my ears. I turned around to my corner of the room and I see Brett holding his hands like he had just burned them over the stove.

"Looks like someone did your dirty work for you, Cale." I suggest to myself.

"You know, as much as I hate to admit it, I think you're right."

The entire school was now on their way down to the football stadium and I could not help but feel angry at Brett. Even though I did not see him, I was convinced he was the one that pulled *my* alarm. Unlike all the other students I did not enjoy one second of this fake fire drill because it didn't belong to me. I had no idea that there was this side of Brett Gooding. He was the superman to our school and for all they know, he still was. As for me, he was a douche bag sucking up all the glory, but now he was much more interesting. This dark side of him proved all my incorruptible theories about him wrong.

"*Check his hands.*" I ordered myself.

"*What! Why?*"

"*Check them to see if he has blue stains on them. When the fire alarm is pulled it leaves an un-washable blue stain on your fingers. So if Brett's hands are blue, then that means that he* was *the-*"

"*One who pulled* my *alarm!*" I cut myself off. Excited now, I searched for Brett as if my life depended on it. Usually picking Brett's face out of the crowd was not hard to do, he was usually surrounded by a bunch of fake, chameleon-like jocks and blonde cheerleaders talking so loudly, our rival school two cities away could hear them. But for some reason finding him today was like finding Waldo. I pushed my way through the crowds of students, all whom were parading down to the football stadium, and found no luck finding him.

"*Ironic.*" I smirked.

"*What is?*"

"*The one day you* want *to see Brett Gooding, you just can't find him.*"

"*Look I don't feel like dealing with you right now, so bye.*"

There was finally silence in my head and caught a glimpse of short blonde hair. My eyes locked on the back of the head.

"*That's gotta be him…right?*"

"*I think so. Is he walking in front of Chris Mannroso?*"

"*Yup, that's him alright. He* would *be walking in front of the tallest kid at Stellar.*"

"*Seriously, that sly little-*"

"*Now's the time. Confront him, or you might not ever get a second chance.*" I half jogged, half walked towards Brett's back and tried to stay under the radar so no one would notice my awkward power walking. Once I reached Chris Mannroso's back I peered around him to see if Brett's back was still there. It was. I awkwardly hopped around the giant in front of me and cut him off so that Brett was on my left hand side. Feeling powerful and confident, I tapped his shoulder blade. Laughter roared in my head when he did turn around. My entire confidence was shattered when the face that turned to look at me was not Brett. It was Shawn Date. Another scholarship bound jock. He gave me a weird "What the heck?" look and the laughter in my head grew even louder. It was then when I stopped in my tracks. And let him pass me by as he kept walking.

"You tool! You knew it wasn't him." I grimaced.

"Ha ha, sorry, I just couldn't pass that up. You should have seen your face!"

"Whatever. Just leave me alone." I muttered aloud to myself. I was pretty sure I got a couple looks from walking students in the vicinity of hearing me trying to figure out if I was even talking to anyone. I expected myself to rebel against my orders but there was no debate in my head. Then suddenly from nowhere I felt a five fingered slap on my back that echoed throughout the valley. It scared me more than it hurt, but my reflexes dragged me around to the source of the impact. And what a big source he was.

Beef was a big boy for his age. He always was on the obese side, but it never bothered him. Beef was probably my only true friend here at Stellar High, and I was probably his only friend here too. Freckles covered his body making his skin look tanner than he was. Beef wasn't his real name either; it was a nickname I had given him when we were twelve.

We were sitting at our little island at lunch, the reject table, and he brought out a Tupperware that contained roast beef in it. I pulled out a peanut butter-jelly sandwich and realized I had taken my little step brother's lunch instead of mine. I was allergic to peanut butter. Beef knew this wonderful fact about me and traded our lunches without even asking and said, "You owe me a roast beef. My mom made that special."

"Ha ha, thanks beef." I stated without thinking.

"Huh? What did you just call me?" he chuckled.

"I think I just called you Beef." I laughed. From then on, he instinctively was to be known as Beef, and no longer Bradley Blandfields.

I think my favorite thing about Beef was that he was always happy.

"It was you, wasn't it!" Beef said through his smile, "I knew it! I could tell it was you! I swear I was just adding two plus two and then…"

He wasn't letting me answer; he just kept on going about how he *knew* it was me who saved him from his math test. As badly as I wanted to appease him and tell him it was all me, I couldn't lie to him. Beef was probably the only human being on this planet that I told the absolute truth to and I wasn't about to break that streak over some silly fire alarm. "Beef, it wasn't me."

"What are you talking about Cale? I know you! I know it was you!"

"Then you also know that I've never lied to you before, so why would I start now. I'm being serious this time. It wasn't me."

"Alright alright, I believe you. Who do you think was it then?"

"I don't think. I *know* who it is." I grimace.

"Oh really? Who then?"

"Are you ready for this?" I ask.

"Ready as I'll ever be." Beef chuckles.

"Brett. Gooding." I pronounce with every single muscle in my mouth.

"No!" Beef gasps, "no way! That's impossible!"

I just grin like I had conjured an evil scheme to rat him out, but what I really wanted was to blackmail him, or make him beg. Maybe even embarrass him, but it was never in my intentions to be a tattle tale. That just wasn't my style. I walked away from beef leaving him to ponder on if I was telling the truth or not. He followed after a couple seconds of him trying to put the puzzle pieces together, like I knew he would.

"So I take it you're looking for him now?" Beef asks.

"Yup." I answer

"Typical." Beef say's stopping me in my tracks, "typical Cale."

"How so?" I say angrily. The fact that Beef knew me more than I gave him credit for bothered me.

"Whenever, or wherever there's something wrong, like trouble or an emergency, you go running towards it like a fireman trying to put out the fire. Except you're not the fireman, you are the arsonist that is trying to feed the fire and make it grow so it can be healthy and strong enough to not only tear down the house you set on fire, but the entire cul-de-sac as well!" He yelled. People watched us as they passed by slowing their pace thinking that Beef and I might get into a fist fight. Even though I would never hurt a hair on the big guy, he was really pissing me off right now.

"What the hell is wrong with you! Are you on your period or what? You're causing a scene for no reason!" Beef and I never really fight; but when we did, even though I wanted to tear his guts out, it was fun. And we were better friends from it. "Have you got something to say to me Beef? Otherwise I believe this conversation is over."

"Well we both know you're as stubborn as an ox, and you're going to search for Brett anyways, even if *my* life was at stake, so let's skip the rest of the argument and find this tool. Okay?"

I just nod my head. I couldn't believe he just threw in the towel like that. I was expecting to fight a lot harder for what I wanted but it all stopped and resolved like I wished it to. *"Today is going to be a good day."* I smile to myself.

"Indeed it may, but that all depends on finding Brett Gooding first."

"I don't doubt that I won't." I had never been more determined in my life. With my bodyguard Beef at my back, we searched through the clusters of students standing around on the football field. Ignoring our principle's attempt to calm and quite everyone down, I shoved people left and right hunting Brett. How could I lose someone who had just come out of the same class as me?

"Yeah, you have to be pretty smart *to lose someone* that *quick."* I snickered.

"Is that sarcasm?" I quickly snapped back.

"No!" I gasp aloud, barely noticing it.

"What?" I hear Beef say, but I ignore him leaving him to ponder if I actually spoke or not which I'm sure tended to happen often when he was around me. It annoyed me knowing I was just as vulnerable as anyone else. *"Even though you play it off like it doesn't bother you, but deep down you know-"*

"Ouch!" A girl screamed. I felt bad for a second until I realized it was the red head from my Biology class. Then I didn't care. "Watch where you're going!" she demanded. I must have stepped on her foot while searching for my runaway convict.

"Get out of the way then." I snapped.

"You think you're so tough huh? You don't know me Cale!"

"You don't know yourself." I mocked. And I kept on walking.

"Ooh, ask her if she needs some ice for that burn." I celebrated.

"I didn't even know that girl spoke!" Beef whispered in my ear as we kept treading on.

"I liked her better when she didn't." I grimaced. I felt a tug on my grey shirt. I turned to find the red head was standing there holding the back of my shirt like I was her prisoner.

"Where are you going?" She scolded.

I practically ignored her after I slapped her hand away from my shirt. "What's it to you? And I don't even *know* you, so what makes you think that *we* talk? And who said you could use *my* name?" I don't care for an answer, I just turn from her and keep walking.

"...because I need your help." She stutters, ignoring the last two questions.

"Uh...*I'm* sorry, was that a question, or do you think you are some kind of royalty around here?" I turn around again, wistful to see her face, but I knew she was going to just slow me down and continue to follow me. "Listen carrot top, if you haven't noticed by now, I'm *not* someone that helps another out of the kindness of my black hole." I signal Beef to follow me and I turn away from her, disgusted.

"It's Amanda." She calls out after me, "my *name* is Amanda. And I know your dying to know what was inside that bottle as much as it's killing me."

"Dang it! The cherry head really caught your interest now!" The sad thing was, it *was* killing me as much as it was killing her to know what Mr. Rusenkell was hiding in his little green bottle but I suppressed it. "Why do *you* care?" I ask.

"Because, he said it could be a matter of life and death." She lied, using Mr. Rusenkell's overreaction as a feeble attempt to suck me in. I've always had a knack for catching people when they were lying. *"Takes one to know one."* I insult myself.

"Ok, so why do you *really* care?" She doesn't answer. I roll my eyes and I turn to walk away again to finish what I started. Even Beef was getting tired of this red head, which made him rather pursue Brett which was at the bottom of his Want-to-do list, so she must not be scoring many points with my best friend. As soon as I thought I had gotten rid of her she came right back into my life.

"I did it!" she yells.

Confused on what she was talking about, I gave her a salute and unenthusiastically said, "Congrats copperhead." And turned around again and was about to march my way out of her sight when she stopped me yet again.

"I opened the green bottle." She whispers.

I turn to her and give her a weird stink eye. *"Well* this *just got interesting!"* I tell myself.

"So what was in it?" I ask abruptly. Beef gives me a look like I had just stabbed him in the back, and I forget he has no idea what we are talking about. It could have been like watching a German movie with no subtitles to him, so I decide to fill him in before Amanda could answer my question. "There was this bottle that Ruse-dog was freaking out about because he said someone had opened it and there was nothing in it."

"Ah…" Beef say's, but I know he still doesn't understand.

"It's nothing really," I turn to face Amanda, "so what was in the bottle big red?"

"That's the thing!" she exclaims, "Nothing was in it when I opened it!"

"Did you seriously just waste your time hunting Brett listening to some crazy spaz!?" I question myself. I squeeze my eyes shut and pinch the top of my nose with my thumb and index finger. "You... might be the most retarded person I've ever met." I insulted. "Why would Mr. Rusenkell get all bent out of shape if the bottle had nothing in it in the first place?"

"That's what you and I are gonna find out." The red head orders.

"Seriously? Who do you think you are?"

"Sorry, I know I can be a bit of a control freak, but I'm being completely honest and one hundred percent serious. I can't tell my boyfriend about this because... well I just have no idea who to go to." She pleaded.

"This nightmare has a boyfriend?!" I scream in my head. I noticed that her dark red hair was covering over some of her midnight black roots. It was weird I didn't notice it until now because of all the time I have been spending looking at it earlier in class. It was almost too red, and it had its own heat radiating off of it. Her hair distracted me from the conversation we were having and I noticed there was hope in her face. Hope, that I might actually help her. False hope. Then I remembered what we were talking about and told her, "No thanks." As if I was interested in the first place.

"Wait." Beef ordered.

Completely disfigured, I look at Beef in uttermost disbelief, "Did I *ask* for your opinion?"

Ignoring me, which I could not believe, he asks "Who is your boyfriend?"

"Ugh! Beef! Who friggen cares?! What is the point?" I shrieked.

"The *point!*" he shrieks back at me. His eyeballs bulging out of their sockets, "Is I've seen this girl holding hands with Brett!"

"You should give Beef a Scooby-snack now." I suggested to myself. I was very impressed with my best friend. I gave him a half smile and turned to look at Amanda. "Well, you heard the man. Who is your boyfriend?"

"I don't see how-"

"Tell you what," I propose assuming Brett was her boyfriend, "you tell me who, and where your boyfriend is. And I promise I'll help you find out what was in the green bottle. But the moment you lie to me, the deal is off and so will be your head. I'll rat you out to your boyfriend, and I'll know if you're lying to me, trust me, I always know."

"Bologna!" I call my bluff.

"Shut up! She wouldn't know." I snap.

"Alright," she says, "Brett Gooding is my boyfriend."

A victory dance explodes in my head. *"Thank. You. Beef!"* A grin spreads across my face. *"And..."* I lead.

"And what?" she asks.

"And where is he!" I demand.

"Is that a question, or do you think your some kind of royal-"

"Quit stalling! You're not funny orangutan!"

She is silent for a moment. Then she lets out a sigh of defeat and says, "He left campus without permission and he told me not to tell anyone. There! You happy now?"

Actually I wasn't. I was even angrier now. My enemy ditched so no one would find out their white knight is actually a demon. *"The ink should be still on there tomorrow right? It's not made to come off in a day, is it?"* I question.

"Well!?" The red head interrupts.

"*Well* what?" I mock.

"Are you going to keep your end of the bargain and help me? That's what!" There is silence between us and I am actually really considering it this time. "You know, this isn't just for me. I know you want to know too."

"Fine. Whatever." I say, "But how are we going to find out?"

"Simple. We ask."

"Oh *that* simple, right? *So* simple that you need me, right?" I rolled my eyes.

"Anyone else would call me crazy." She admits.

"That's because you *are* crazy."

"Coming from a reject like you, I'm not convinced. And it makes it easier to hide the fact that if you told anyone, I'd play dumb so you would look like the crazy one who has some secret crush on me. Which is why I am talking to you now because no one would believe someone like you.

"Well, nobody asked you." I could not believe how angry she made me. The frustration she gave me was burning like resting my forehead on a hot stove for a full minute. She was probably the only girl I'd ever punch in the face and not feel bad about it. I noticed that most of the students were already walking back up to the school going straight to fourth period instead of the present third period we spent on the football field. I was so infuriated with this red head I had missed the principals announcement that there was no fire. *"Big surprise there."* I chuckle to myself. "I'll help you tomorrow. Before Biology." I said without looking at her, afraid she might burn my head ache even further.

"Fine." She said like I knew she would. With a heated attitude and a head bob lifting her nose and chin towards the sky.

I roll my eyes.

"You know," Beef suggests, "I have never seen you roll your eyes so much."

I laugh. "Later Beef." I say over my shoulder and start to walk back up the hill to my next classroom.

Video production was actually a class I enjoyed. Most the kids in here were freaks and nobody's anyways. Except for Britney Wilson, Marcus Moon, and Baley Schottenfield.

Britney Wilson, on first sight, could be stereotyped as a dumb blonde cheerleading tramp. But she was much more than that. Britney Wilson is completely gorgeous and has the entire male population eating out of the palm of her hand. She knows it too. All she ever does in this class is text on her cell phone or log on to a chatting website on one of the available computers.

Marcus and Baley were exclusive. I don't think I have ever witnessed a point where I saw one without the other. *"Teenage love"* I mock. *"How pathetic."* And these two could not be more proof of it. Sometimes I called them Barcus when they were together. Baley was short, with curly, dirty blonde and brown hair. She is the star varsity girls' soccer player as a freshman. Marcus was much taller. He had brown skin with ebon black hair that matched mine. Except I had a streak of blonde on one side of my Fohawk. He was the backup quarterback for the Stellar High Titan Football team. If Brett Gooding ever got hurt, which unfortunately never happened for me, Marcus would be the one that goes in. I think God might have known these two would meet and mixed their appearances up while creating them, because Marcus had hazy emerald green eyes, and Baley had enormous innocent brown ones that didn't match her white skin. They needed to switch eyeballs because it bugged me.

Our teacher interrupted my train of thought with an announcement that we are filming a black and white film and there are only three actors. The rest must work as crew. We were filming a parody of an old movie called *Detour*. The main character was a simple guy who starts off hitchhiking. He then is picked up by some lawyer or successful businessman. Further down the road they are traveling, the successful business man decides to let the hitchhiker drive so he can sleep. The hitchhiker pulls over because he is tired and tries to wake up the business man by opening the passenger door, which he is sleeping against. He falls out of the car because he isn't wearing a seat belt and hits hit head on a rock, killing him. So the hitchhiker is all like "Eff my life" and he hides the body and assumes his identity. Further on down the road he picks up a harlot who is hitchhiking and she asks him his name. Naturally he tells her the business man's name as any good con artist would do. Big mistake there! The girl knew who the business man was; in fact she did business with him. What kind of business? Probably a sinful one, but that's not the point. Basically they stay at a hotel and she blackmails him but he tells her that he doesn't give a hoot what she thinks. So being the snob she is, she calls 9-1-1 and brings the corded phone into the room closing the door behind her. The hitchhiker then realizes he can't go to jail so he starts pulling on the cord and doesn't realize the cord is wrapped around the girl's neck. But seriously! Who the hell wraps a cord around their neck on the phone?! Anyways, he ends up strangling her to death and he gets back on the road and starts to hitchhike again. I could already tell that that part was perfect for me. He never meant to kill anybody that he did, but it happened anyways. For some reason, something pushed me to try and get this lead role. As our teacher, Mr. Ballams, called for volunteers on the crew positions, I waited to volunteer for the main role.

"Alright, now if you're interested in being the main actor in this, please raise your hand." Mr. Ballams announced. I was surprised to see that barely any hands went up.

"*Yes!*" I thought. So I raised my hand like "whatever, *I guess I'll do it*" when really, I felt like *"Hell to the yeah!"* and then, like slap in the back of my head, out of my peripherals I see Marcus Moon raise his hand. *"Really Marcus?"* I grimaced to myself. Then all of a sudden voices from all of the students came forth as if they were voting. "Marcus", "Marcus", "Marcus" and so on. Even Mr. Ballams gave me a weird look. I wanted to pause time and ask God why he hated me so much.

"Okay, well we will have to leave it to a coin toss then." He pulls out a quarter from his pocket," Shall we?"

He was about to flip the coin. I wasn't very motivated to win it, because I knew everyone wanted my opponent to win. But God knows how I wanted to win the gamble more than I appreciated my life. And it wasn't even for the usual bragging rights; it was actually something that I thought might have answers to who I am. Mr. Ballams told me to call the toss. Heads came to mind. I wanted to say "Heads!" but for some reason I kept my mouth shut. I was stubborn and committed to stay silent. *"Heads!"* I called out in my head.

"Heads!" Marcus yelled. The coin landed on Mr. Ballam's hand and he flipped it over onto his forearm. I refused to look. How bad I wanted it to be tails now. I would have done anything now to win this toss. I was about to knock the coin out of Mr. Ballam's hand and start it all over. I would say it was an accident to give me another chance at winning, but it was too late. Mr. Ballams uncovered the result. Still too stubborn to look, I pleaded *"Please be tails. Please be tails"* in my head. The room was quiet. It felt like nobody was breathing. I broke the silence.

"What is it?" I ask.

"Tails." Mr. Ballams and Marcus say simultaneously.

A riot erupted in my head at the word. I had never been more grateful and excited in my life. I celebrated all in my head because I feared if I said one word Mr. Ballams would take away what I wanted so badly. I played it off like I didn't care, but I knew that this part meant the world to me. I felt lighter and I wanted to smile and hug someone, but I did none of that.

"Alright. We start filming tomorrow so bring an extra pair of clothes to keep here okay, Cale?" Mr. Ballams said.

"Whatever." I say, pretending to be indifferent.

"Okay good. Alright everyone, I'm going to call you up three at a time to assign camera and script writers."

That's when I drifted off and it was like I couldn't hear anything else. Mr. Ballam's mouth was moving but I was just thinking about coming in tomorrow and playing a lead role of someone who was much like me.

Then like a needle, Marcus popped my balloon of thought interrupting me, "Hey Cale," he put out his right hand inviting mine, "Good luck."

I smiled from ear to ear inside my head. But showed the exact opposite emotion to Marcus. "Thanks." I say wistful denying his inviting hand by looking away. Then he turned around and walked back to Baley. I popped in my headphones and turned the dial on my I-pod to play *"Life is Beautiful"* by Vega4. I didn't even get to the chorus when I heard a sweet singing voice say something that disturbed me.

"That is probably the kindest thing Cale has ever said!" I look over to see where it came from. I found Baley looking right at me from across the room. Of all the people talking obnoxiously in the classroom, I hear her happy voice compliment me. It didn't sound like she was yelling it, but she had to be if it was to echo across over to me. I looked around to see if anyone heard her, which it looked like no one did, not even Marcus. This makes me change the dial on my I-pod to "I don't care" by Apocalyptica. Then I tighten my eyes as I'm looking at her. My eyes say *"Go jump off a cliff"* , but she just waves. I look away, rolling my eyes and I hear her say something else. "Maybe there is good in him after all." She says. A grin wipes across my face and I look at her.

"Yeah right Baley." I say hopelessly.

And then the weirdest thing happens. I am staring at her hugging Marcus and I hear, "One day, he's going to realize that he won't always be the underdog." In Baley's soothing gleeful voice but her mouth did not move. Her lips made no attachments to the words she had just said, even through the music in my ears. As a matter of fact, her lips didn't move at all, I was sure of it.

"Are you sure of it? Or do you think she's in your head having conversations with us as well?" I ask myself.

"I swear on all that I love and hate I heard her like I was blind."

"What? Does that even make sense?"

"Wait, shut up, I need to-" before I could finish I found myself walking towards her and Marcus who looked adjoined at the hip. "What did you just say?" I ask Baley.

"What?" she says in a respectful, but confused tone. I could tell she wasn't lying.

"Did you just say something about me?" I question again.

"Umm I believe not." She said. Then she reached out her hand and sang, "Hi. I'm Baley, and this is my boyfriend Marcus." As if I didn't know.

"Did she really just say that? An alien could understand they were dating."

"Yeah, and she just said Hi, *and I think she wants to shake my hand."*

"Well, Sherlock, best shake her hand and give her your name too then."

"Cale." I state awkwardly. Then I shake her hand and then Marcus's for a quick second. "Wait, so you didn't say *anything* about me. Nothing about...Hotdogs or..." I lost grip of what she had said. Suddenly it came rushing back to me, "Underdog! Did you just call me and underdog?" I interrogate.

She is quiet for a few seconds and then she starts to sing again, "No... but I *could* I guess if you want?" The bell rings. "Well... we gotta go. Take care Cale. See ya tomorrow." She winks and so does Marcus.

"It was nice meeting you Cale." Marcus calls out before they turn around and head for the door.

I planted my feet until everyone else in the class left, and then I shook my head and walked out.

Beef was waiting for me at his dark azure blue scion where he always parks in the morning. I hop in the car and put my Biology book in the back seat. It's nice to leave after fourth period. All the underclassmen stay for their fifth and sixth period while the seniors get out early. I didn't feel bad at all for them because I had to go through it, so why shouldn't they? Beef and I went to get lunch, then we the park and sat on the swings. He pulls out a cigar, I pull out a cigarette. We light up and we spend from 1:00 pm to 5:00 pm talking and swinging. It was quiet in the car as Beef drove me home, but that isn't anything new. Sometimes when you have said everything there is to say to your best friend, silence is just like talking about another subject. We pull up to my apartment and I thank him for the ride.

"Same time tomorrow." He says.

"Same time tomorrow…" I sigh. I close the car door and walk to my door. I stick my key in the knob and jerk it before I enter. "Ghetto piece of crap door." I mumble to myself.

"Watch your mouth!" Glenda calls from upstairs.

"How'd she hear you?" I ask.

"Maybe she has super hearing."

"Or maybe she's God" I suspect.

"You know, I think she actually could be." I begin to ponder, "Pretending to be all imperfect and poor so we can't live like everyone else at Stellar." I say to myself.

"I am poor, and I am imperfect." She yells from upstairs again. I must have talked out loud again. "And *you* need a job!" she tags on.

"Maybe we can go work at a fast food joint together then mom!" I yell up the stairs. My mother was about to lose her job because of the economic recession. I snicker at my own joke. They say people frown upon that but I don't care. It makes me feel better.

"And if it makes you feel better, it must be good for you!" I giggle.

"Now where's my heroine kit and my bottle of vodka?" I joke.

"That's not funny Cale!" Glenda yells. Then she appears at the top of the stairs and raises one eyebrow and walks away back to her precious T.V.

"Wait, was she talking about the drug joke? Or the fast food joint one?" I ask.

"Who knows? Maybe she can read minds.*"* I chuckle. I wouldn't mind that, just as long as she stayed out of my head when I was thinking about sex, or any naked thing. That'd just be awkward.

I walk up stairs and I see Glenda is watching Television. She was watching a show of another episode of a retarded boss who proves himself worthy at the end of every episode. You have to understand its own breed of comedy in order to get it. "*Stupid T.V.*" I think, "*it's all my mother ever does. Watch her favorite shows, go to sleep. Get up. Go to work. Come home. Find the remote. Press power. Select, and watch T.V. Then go to bed. And start all over again. But every now and then she orders movies constantly and watches those. Some are retarded, others actually catch my interest. Mostly retarded though. Oh the sweet life of divorced woman with two kids...*" I complain.

It was a lot better than living with my dad though. If anyone knew what it was like growing up in my shoes, I'm sure no one would ever avoid me or pick on me. They would all pass me by saying "Hey, that's the kid who get's abused by his dad because he doesn't know who else to beat down in the fit of his drunken rage." Or, "Hey, that's the kid who his dad told him it was his solemn fault for his parents got a divorce." Or even, "Say isn't that the kid where his dad told his younger step brother to never grow up to be a *screw up* like his older brother? Yeah, I think that's him." But I don't complain. I probably stay out of more trouble than most the kids at Stellar. I don't consume alcohol like everyone else. I don't do illegal drugs. I take all my depression out on my notebook I keep hidden in a secret compartment in the floor. At that thought I decide to stop watching the television and I head to my room. "Night mom." I say. She doesn't answer like I knew she wouldn't. If she could, Glenda would spend her entire life in silence. "*She just likes the ambience of it.*" I say. Or at least, this is what I tell myself.

For the rest of the day I write about random stuff in my notebook. Sometimes its poems, sometimes unserious suicide notes. Most of the time though it's about how I feel when I'm around Tianna Lecher. I've never met a human being the made me feel so vulnerable before. Thinking about her makes me exhausted. My eyes grow heavy. Images from the day fly by my mind as my eyelids close. "*Today was ok.*" I say to myself.

"*Yeah. It was different.*"

"*Tomorrow will be better.*"

"*Whoa! Down boy! You know very well good days don't come around often, so don't you jinx this or expect it to happen the same way tomorrow, besides what makes you think that tomorrow will be any different than any other day of your lame life?*"

"Because, I've decided." I reply as I put in my headphones and turn to "Bullet with Butterfly Wings" by Smashing Pumpkins, one of my favorite bands.

"Decided what?"

"I'll pull the fire alarm tomorrow."

2. Quarantine

The alarm clock is my master, and I am his slave. He wakes me up violently attacking my ears every morning at 5:30am. My eyelids feel bolted together and sealed shut so there is no chance for air to leak through my black eyelashes. *"This crap's getting old."* I thought. I sit up with my eyes still closed, and I hear the T.V. is on. I get up and walk out of my room, my eyelids still preserving my eyeballs from any form of light.

"Morning sleepwalking beauty." I greet.

"Seriously? It's too early for that. Don't start my day off like this." I warn.

"Too bad I-"

"Stop! Please. I said Please." Then there was finally silence in my head. Groggy, I walked towards the T.V. noise with my hands out just in case I bumped into anything on my way to shut it off. I pictured myself in my head, and the image looked like the creature from Marry Shelley's cryptic novel, *Frankenstein.* When I couldn't find the button with my hands, I let

21

out a snort of disappointment and squeezed my right eyelids tighter loosening the bindings on my left eyelids. My left eye caught sight of the power button and my hand dived for it quickly. Once the deed was done I closed my left eye again. I turned around to walk back into my room. Slouching my back, I let my arms dangle from their shoulder sockets as I dragged my unwilling feet on. I felt something cold with my right arm as I passed the couch. It was smooth, solid, but freezing. I felt it again, this time on purpose and realized it was a foot. My eyelids flew open like when you open a window curtain. My heart was pounding and I see Glenda is lying on the couch. My head twitches to the side confused on why she is still here. Glenda usually was out of the house on her way to work before I even got up. She didn't look like she was breathing and her posture looked too uncomfortable for her to be conscious. Then I asked myself if I had locked the door when I came in yesterday. Could there have been somebody in my house last night? Then, from nowhere, Love rushed through my bloodstream, making my head throb and all my veins pulse faster and harder than ever. Panicking now, I jump on top of my mom and start thrashing my fists at her yelling, "Mom! Mom! Wake up! Wake up!"

"Ouch! What the hell, Cale?" She cries.

Confused now, I give her a strange look and open my mouth. I was about to say *Wait, so you're not dead?* But then I realized how crazy that sounded, so I said, "Wait, it's not *Christmas?*" instead.

"Are you trying to be funny Cale?" She doesn't even crack a smile, like I knew she wouldn't.

Ignoring her, I interrogate, "What are you still doing here mom?"

She pinches the top of her nose with her thumb and index finger just like I do and says in a raspy morning voice, "I got the day off."

"Sweet!" I yell in a high pitch voice. No longer tired, I jump on the other couch and press the power button on the remote. Glenda goes back to sleep. Then she sits up and is suddenly wide awake.

"Wait! What do you think *you* are doing?" She interrogates as I flip through the channels.

"Staying home with you!" I say, "We can bake cookies, make pizza, watch-"

"I don't think so Cale!" she orders.

"But Ma!" I whine. Then I jump on top of her and wrap her like a blanket. "Can't I just stay home with you?" I whine again. I then burry my face in the blanket between us and mumble, "I promise I'll make your day!"

"No Cale. Stop asking. Do you need a ride or is Beef going to pick you up?"

"Whatevs. I was just kidding anyways. I *love* school." I sigh. Then I get up to walk away back to my room while still talking to Glenda. "I *love* everyone! I *love* you world!" and for the first time, in very long time, I hear my mother giggle. The sweet sound brings a slight grin to my face. But too quickly, like most good things, it fades away.

After I throw on a pair of old ripped jeans and a plain black v-necked t-shirt, I head to the bathroom to brush my teeth. Before I even reach the toothpaste, my eyes were glued to the mirror in front of me. I was staring down an 18-year-old matured, young man. My eyes scanned every inch of what there was to see in the reflection. He looked like he was deathly ill. His skin was a pale olive light brown. More beige then brown. His sickly skin covered a decent set of muscles around his arms, forearms and chest. He was larger than the average person in a strange muscular way. Besides smoking, writing and complaining about his mediocre life to his one true friend, Beef, when he got bored he would work out in his room with his extraordinary amount of painful free time he never seemed to get enough of. It seemed strange to me how I knew this 18-year-old so well as I glared at him, but the moment my eyes left him I was sure I would forget what he looks like and forget he even existed until the next time I saw my reflection to look upon the mysterious man in the mirror. His hair was pitch black except for a stripe of blonde that ran in a straight line from the front to the back. It was cut into a Fohawk, the improved look of the Mohawk. He had a pair of light brown, nearly hazel eyes that were eyeing me down as I was to him. "Don't judge me." He says.

"Who said I was?" I snap back.

"It's not hard to tell with you. It never is."

I scowl at him. His last comment angered me even more then thinking about Amanda. "Screw you!" I nearly yell.

"Who are you talking to Cale?" Glenda calls from the living room. Curse my small apartment.

"I'm on the phone!" I yell back. I brush my teeth without looking straight up, afraid I might make my mom suspect something wrong. And as I am leaving the bathroom, I take one last look at my reflection and pause. He doesn't say anything, and neither do I. We both just exchange an effortless smirk before I leave him closing the door behind me.

I lock the front door behind me as I head for Beef's car and I see he is wearing a bright yellow shirt that reads "100% BEEF" on it. I laugh, "Where did you find that? Fat kids R us?"

"You know, fat jokes are uncalled for Cale. It's just a cheap laugh, just like a kick in the nuts." He snaps back.

"Aw poor baby." I make a sad puppy dog face. Then it fades as I roll my eyes. "Beef, I wouldn't give you up for a million and one cheap laughs."

"Thanks... I think..."

"Maybe a million and two though..." and I burst into laughter.

"You're so funny Cale!" I say sarcastically to myself as we drive off. *"Suck it."*

Stellar High School was created in a ditch. There is only one way in and one way out, and that is driving down or up the ramp. Stellar is surrounded by hills and fields. *"Who the heck builds a school away from civilization?"* I ask.

"It's not a school, it's a prison." Beef and I both sigh at once as we pass the last house before the bridge. After the bridge there is a fork in the road. You can either go straight to pass through this forgotten valley and enter a gated community filled with houses Beef and I could never afford, or you can turn right and drive down the hill to Stellar High. "One day, when we are rich, we'll go straight down this road and stick our middle fingers out of the car, flipping off this prison as we pass it by." I say. Beef doesn't say anything. He just grins and makes a right at the light just like we do every day. When we arrive at school it is still dark and there are about twenty cars in the parking lot. "Why in the world did we sign up for zero period?" I ask beef.

"Because we love school so much that we just want to spend every waking minute of the day here?"

"Rhetorical question Beef. And don't make me barf. School and love don't belong in the same sentence." I scold. He sticks his tongue out at me and we both get out of the car. We start walking to the school from the parking lot when a dark red car nearly runs us over. Screech! The tires had smoke floating around them. The engine was drumming a baritone growl of a bear. It was hard enough to see in the dark, but the tinted windows made it impossible to see inside of the car. If we had took a step further in our path before the car came to an abrupt halt, we would surely be under it. Beef and I exchange looks and then back to the car.

"Can we key this guy?" I begged. I wasn't sure if Beef would be up to it, but I sure was. Then the driver's door flies open and Amanda follows it. *"Oh now we have to key this guy!"* I grimace. I grinned a little at calling her a guy. I look to Beef and say loudly enough for Amanda to hear, "See! I told you the devil drives this car!"

"Very funny Cale." The red head barks, "Don't forget we are going to Rusenkell today."

"Yeah yeah, whatever hot tamale! Now don't you have some souls to collect?" She gets back in her car that shares almost the same color as her hair. The door slams shut and she parks right next to where beef's car is. Before Beef and I could even move three steps, Amanda is out of the car and walking with us. "What will it take to get rid of you?" I ask.

"An explanation from Ruse and maybe one of those memory wiper thingies so I can forget I even met you." She lists.

"Okay, for one *you* are coming to me for help. And *two,* those memory wiper thingies, probably don't exist. So how about a bucket of water instead? Will that get rid of you?" Before she could answer, I turn to Beef, "Can you remind me to fill up a bucket of water when we get to the bathroom?"

"*Ha! Ha!* You are *so* funny! I get it okay!? I have red hair! Whoop-D-Freaking-Do!"

"Actually, I was thinking the water might make you melt, but if you *want* to make fun of yourself, that's cool, I guess. I'll just put those flames out on your head for ya." I snicker. Beef is laughing hysterically and so am I.

"Why is she still walking with us?" I ask myself.

"Honestly, I don't care. She can do whatever she wants." She follows us through the entire parking lot. "See ya Beef." I say and start walking left in hopes that the red head will follow Beef instead. *"Wishful thinking."* I thought. Sure enough I could feel the tension from behind me radiating off its own heat. I turn around to face her. "Quit stalking me or I'm telling your boyfriend!"

"Oh like anyone will ever believe I would be stalking a loser like you!" her breath felt like a wave of heat, and smelled terrible.

"What a turn off." I stated to myself.

"Actually I was talking about the mysterious green bottle, ginger!" I snap. She makes no attempt for a comeback. *"Go in for the kill!"* I thought. "Now," I began, "why don't you go and brush those teeth of yours, before you get ginger-vitas." Then I turn around and start walking again. *"Yes!"* I cry out in my head. *"Red head, 0; Cale, 1!"*

"Whatever Cale." She makes my name sound like its own cuss word.

"Right back atcha!" I say over my shoulder. I knew she was embarrassed. I fed off of it, giving me an energy boost. I walked in to my zero period with my head held high and a glare in my eyes and sat down. I put in my headphones and switched the dial to "Sometime around Midnight" by The Airborne Toxic Event. I extend my left arm across my desk and let my head fall on my bicep. As I was about to close my eyes something caught them.

The sight of Tianna Lecher was like a shooting star, in the sense that every time I saw her I'd make a wish. That one day she would actually notice me. She has dark brown hair, which flows out of her head, each section having a wave of a slight curl. Her wavy silk like hair had the perfect mixture of straightness and curls. The roots of each strand of hair seemed midnight black and it faded into a chocolate brown at the end of each one. She has luminous caramel eyes that glisten, and olive creamy skin that matched mine. She didn't wear any make up, she was naturally beautiful. I could write a book on how beautiful she was. Then she smiled as she was talking to her friend, and I knew I would have to write a sequel. Pink rose lips rested underneath a perfectly molded nose. Beneath the lips were pearl white teeth that created an incredible smile. It was contagious, just like her laugh. Her voice was beautiful. Angelic. It hurt to look at her because she was so striking.

"God really took his time on her, didn't he?" I told myself.

"Indeed he did." I agreed, and I continued to gaze at her. Each time her eyes met mine, I looked away in embarrassment and shame. She could vomit all over me and I'd still kiss her. She could fart while doing a sit-up and I would find it cuter than a puppy in a pet shop. She could have no arms or legs, and I would carry her around everywhere. But she didn't have any of those flaws. She was perfect.

"Fool." I call myself.

"I know."

"You're a fool to fall for perfection."

"I know…" There was a long pause of silence in my head for a while. Then suddenly it came. The memory was lucid and still painful.

It's the end of the year, and next year we all will be eighth graders. It's the last class of the day, science. We already gathered each other's numbers and signatures in our year books. Well, the only person who wrote in mine was Beef, but there was someone else I wanted to get a signature from. Tianna Lecher. She was surrounded by all of her friends and there was no route to get to her. Finally when the vultures that circled her flew off, she was by herself, packing her stuff in her baby blue Hawaiian print backpack.

"Do it." I motivated myself.

"I have nothing to lose…right?"

"*Right.*" *I assured. And even though I tried to search for it, there was no lie, or any form of uncertainty in my voice.*

I never thought I would ever walk a plank like in the pirate movies. The ones where the captain with the eye patch covering one eye and the annoying parrot on his shoulder, or even the odd shaped hat and the wooden leg would be poking me with a sword to jump off the boat. But walking up to Tianna felt exactly like how I would expect it would feel on that pirate ship, except I was poking myself to leap over the edge. Inching towards her was the hardest things my legs ever experienced. Finally, I'm standing in front of her, at the edge of the plank. "Hello." *I say. I jump off.*

When she walked away from me I noticed the words she had said stabbed me in the lower left abdomen. I asked her to sign my yearbook and she did. She left no e-mail address, no screen name, and no phone number like I knew she wouldn't. While she was writing her signature I had asked her if she wanted to go see a movie with me. She was very kind about it, but it felt like she wasn't. "I'll have to see." *is what she said right before she left my sight. It felt like she took the words and gutted me just to leave me bleeding to death. I realized there was a severe wound in the lower left section of my stomach and I sort of knew that some things can't be cured.*

The depressing, painful memory that poisoned my blood, heart and brain, was unfortunately one of the most vivid memories I possessed. As my cryptic mind, which was fogging up with thoughts and ideas about Tianna, decided to reminisce this dark part of my past, I felt the poison start to spread through my veins again, crippling me. The words she had said to me so many years ago; the same words she used to stab me with must have been toxic because the poison seemed to be coming from the wound in my gut. I covered the imaginary wound with both my hands. My eyes squeezed shut and my face wrinkled. My mouth clenched as if I ate something extremely sour. I swear I thought I was losing gallons of blood escaping my body from the wound. My hands couldn't hold enough pressure to keep the blood in me. *"Is this what Superman feels when he is near kryptonite?"* I thought.

"Probably." I replied.

"Then note to self, if I do take up being a hero as a job, stay away from Tianna."

"Okay, you need anything else? Coffee? A bagel? What the hell do I look like? Your secretary?" I scolded myself.

I realize I've spent the entire class bouncing my eyes from my desk, to Tianna, to the wall, back to Tianna again. I had missed everything in Mrs. Di Comma's lecture and I was feeling light headed and weak. The bell rings.

"*Thank God!*" I outburst, "*I don't think I can take much more of your infatuation!*"

"*Then don't. Leave. Leave me alone.*" I ordered. And I obeyed. I spend the next two class periods recovering my strength, cleaning my *wound* and de-clouding my mind.

"*I swear, that girl has pheromones that only affect you.*" I say to myself.

"*She doesn't even know I exist.*"

"*Why don't you stop being such a woos and go up to her and talk to her then?*" I tease.

"*Because! Why on earth would someone like that even think about conversing with someone like me? The last time we have ever talked was seventh grade!*"

"*You're right. I don't even know why I talk to you…*"

"*Right back atcha.*" I say. The last phrase I projected in my head suddenly haunted me. "*Did I just get déjà vu?*" I could not recollect where I had heard me saying that. It sounded so familiar and the answer was on the tip of my tongue. Then it hit me like jumping in front of a train running at full speed. I had said that earlier to Amanda before zero period.

"*By the way, not to interrupt your train of thought, but they should rename* zero period *to* death. *Just a suggestion.*"

I ignore myself now focusing on the memory of Amanda. I completely forgot about it and how bad I wanted to forget again wasn't measurable. My hand reached for the hallway door in front of me and it opened before I could grasp it's handle.

"*Telekinesis?*" I ask myself. Before I could ponder more on the possibility, Amanda was standing outside of the door holding it.

"*Speaking of the devil…*" snickered. How bad I wanted her to hear that. Then from nowhere Beef appears at my side. I grin quickly and look at him. "Speaking of the *devil…*" I say. Beef gives me a confused look. My eyes read *just go along with it* and he somehow understands it. Amanda and I are now staring each other down.

"It's third period." She states.

"Thanks for the update captain obvious."

"*Dude! You are completely forgetting about Brett!*"

"Oh man!" I was right. I wanted him to pop up mysteriously and lay his hands out so I could see the blue stain if it was there or not.

"What a friggen coincidence." I said to myself.

"What?"

"Brett Gooding, 10 o clock." I steer my eyes to the direction I've given myself through my peripherals and I see Brett strolling up to us. He makes a gesture with his finger to his mouth signaling me and Beef to be quiet. Beef and I look at each other like, *"Is he serious?"* and we look back to Amanda. Brett puts his hands, which are covered by gloves, around Amanda's eyes and whispers, "Guess who?"

"Brett!" Amanda gasps. They kiss each other.

"Disgusting."

"Tell me about it."

"He's wearing gloves. It's ninety degrees outside and he's wearing gloves."

"Because he's trying to cover the stains!"

"So how am I going to prove him guilty?" I knew the answer to that. I would have to take his gloves off by force. As they were hugging each other I realized I would probably only have time to pick one hand to uncover because he would only have the stain on one hand.

"Left." I say to myself.

"What?"

"Left. It's on his left hand."

"How do you know?"

"Because left *is evil. And he's left handed."*

"Okay so let me get this straight, you are basing your logic off of superstition?"

"Yes."

"So even though, his right hand was closer to the fire alarm, it was his left hand, because he is evil?"

"No! It is on his left hand because he is good *that is why. Ever hear of the right hand of God? And the left hand of the devil?"*

"No, I'm sorry I don't read the weekly newspaper of stupid."

"Just friggen trust me, it's a fifty-fifty percent chance anyways."

"Fine, but I swear if it's on his right..." I warn myself.

"Or what? You gonna hurt yourself?! Just pick the left one already."

I don't fight back. I almost pounce on top of Amanda and Brett when I grab Brett's left hand. I yank the glove off and before he could even understand what was going on, I faced his palm towards me. There I saw a dark blue ink stain on his fingertips.

"Told you so." I proudly celebrated. My eyes met Brett's. He doesn't even attempt to get out of the position I've put him in. I let go of his hand. "You pulled the fire alarm." I told him. He doesn't say anything. His face is just full of shock.

"What now? You gonna blackmail him?"

"Shut up! I'm trying to think!" I order. I see Amanda's face is completely disfigured and full of confusion.

"Why'd you do it Brett?" She asks.

"Yeah why did you do it?" I put my two cents in.

He takes his gaze off of me and puts it on Amanda. "Amanda," he starts, "you have to believe me. It wasn't me."

"Then how do you explain that?" she grasps his left wrist.

"You guys are acting like he killed somebody!" Beef intervenes, "It was just a stupid fire alarm! Stop being so hostile!" This calms the tension between everybody. Beef was right.

Brett starts up again, "I swear to God, it wasn't me. I mean yes it *was* me but it wasn't."

"What the heck does that mean!?" Amanda, Beef, and I say concurrently; Beef's voice was a little more dominant and threatening. Both Amanda and I look at Beef who is gawking at Brett. *"So much for hostility eh Beef?"*

"It was as if I could see through my own eyes, but I could not control my body. I was trapped inside of me!"

"Bologna." Amanda, Beef and I say simultaneously again. We all look at each other and yell "Stop that!" at the same time. Afraid to say something in chorus again we all focus back on Brett, giving him stares that I was used to receiving.

"My, oh my how the tables have turned!" I smirk to myself.

"Now whose the one picking at the hole?!"

"How does it feel Brett? Does it feel good?!" But I already knew the answer.

"You guys have to believe me."

"Why should I? Nobody would believe me! So what makes you so different?"

"Wait!" I told myself. Part of me wanted to believe him. Part of me wanted to tell the other part of me that that he was telling the absolute truth. *"Brett isn't a liar. Why would he make this up?"*

"Uh, maybe because pulling the fire alarm is a serious crime! And he doesn't want to jeopardize his perfect *record."*

"Wow! One day in detention won't kill you, you *should know that!"*

"I bet you Brett hasn't even breathed the air in the detention room, he probably thinks it's the worst place on earth."

I had to agree with myself on that one. *"Hasn't he seen* The Breakfast Club*?"*

"By the way, great movie."

"Top five best movies of all time for sure."

"Anyways! Back to what I was saying! Brett is your arch nemesis. Why are you fighting with me about that?"

"Because I think he's telling the truth."

"So you're telling me you believe this science fiction crap?"

"Yes. Listen, you asked me to believe your superstitions remember? Now I am asking you to trust me on this one. I believe him."

"Your funeral."

"Thank you." And I left myself alone.

Sirens interrupted our speechless gawking at Brett. We all ran outside the hallway doors and saw giant black F.B.I. SUVs and S.W.A.T. cars speeding down the hill towards us. Cop car after cop car we watched them all race down to the front of the school. They all came to a violent halt and men came charging out wearing all black and gas masks on. C.I.A. and F.B.I. was printed on every single one of their chests. No faces were visible because of their gas masks.

"What's going on?" Beef asks, breaking our frozen shock.

"Is that Mr. Rusenkell?" Amanda points to two gas masked agents arresting Mr. Rusenkell.

"That's him." I say. We start to run towards him to find out what was going on. We were about ten feet from Ruse when both of the cops pull their weapons from their holsters and aim them at us.

"Don't move!" they yell. Our arms fly straight up in reaction to being held at gun point. My heart was pounding. *"Am I about to die?"* I ask myself.

"Screw that! I am not getting shot!" I tell myself. "Don't shoot! Don't shoot!" I yell at the cops.

"Get down on the floor! Now! Get down on the floor!" they reply still holding us at gun point. Beef is the first one on the ground. Then next is Brett, leaving me and Amanda still standing.

"I hate how cops always repeat themselves. It's very annoying." I complain. I don't know why Amanda and I don't fall to the ground. It takes a while before it kicks in that we are actually being held at gun point. Part of me feels like I'm going to die, my heart pounds, my eyes are bulging

out of my head and I'm sweating a river. The other part of me is calm. Confident. It wants to rebel against the officers orders and run up to my biology teacher, take one of the cop's guns and shoot them both letting Mr. Rusenkell free.

"Don't get yourself killed Cale." I warn myself.

"I know what I'm doing." I try to calm myself down. "What did he do?" I ask boldly ignoring the officers' orders.

"Get down on the ground!" They keep yelling.

"What. Did. He. Do!?" I state again. Amanda is still standing with me when one of the officers fires their weapon in the air.

"We *will* shoot!" one of the cops say.

"I want to know what he did right now!" I said furiously. *"What has gotten into you? Are you crazy? Do you have a death wish?"*

"You want to know what he did? He stole government property and endangered the entire human race! That's what he did!" The policeman on the left shouted.

The one on the right let go of Mr. Rusenkell and punched his fellow co-worker in the arm. He whispered in his ear but I could still hear it. "This is a quarantine mission; we are not to give out information!"

"What is going on?" Amanda cries out.

"They said something about quarantine." I reply. I look back at the cop on the left. "What is going on?"

"Just get on the floor, or I'll shoot!" He shouts.

"Weak. Pathetic. If they were going to shoot you, you would have already been shot in the leg or something."

"No." I state.

"Are you stupid Cale?" Beef calls from under me. Then I feel a giant tug on my left leg and I fall forward. I save myself from crushing my face in the pavement with my hands catching me. I look behind me and Beef is holding my calf. I shake him off me and I look back to Mr. Rusenkell.

"Cale!" Mr. Rusenkell yells, "You must run! You are either immune or-"

"Shut up!" the cop on the right interrupts Mr. Rusenkell by slamming his gun in his face. The cop starts to drag him to a white van while the cop who was standing on the left holds us at gun point still. I watch as the cop who was in the right throws Mr. Rusenkell into the back of the white van and slams the door shut. As he was walking back to us I hear a scream. Then another. Yelling. Chaos. After about ten seconds of hearing our entire school yelling, I hear an unrecognizable voice over the intercom.

"Attention all Stellar High School. Report to the gym immediately..." He goes on about how *paramount* it is that everyone head to the main gym, but I don't listen because I am struggling being man handled by the cop who was on the right. He tells us to get up and to start moving to the gym.

On the way I catch a glimpse of something red as we pass by Mr. Rusenkell's classroom. It was the fire alarm. I stop for a quick second before I am interrupted.

"Keep moving!" an officer orders. And I feel a surprising push on my back. I clenched my teeth down, grinding them, holding back plans to turn around and break this cop's neck.

"Don't Cale." I tell myself. Amanda looks back at me and so does Brett. But I couldn't find Beef. He was who I wanted to see. He would convince me that this would all blow over in an hour or so and I would be glad that I didn't go to jail for assaulting an officer. But something did not feel right about these cops. The next thing I know I hear a grunt so I whirl around to see that Beef shoved the cop against the wall.

"Don't you ever touch him!" Beef yells. Another cop grabs Beef from the back. He struggles and tries to escape the cop's grip but he can't break it.

"Leave him alone!" I yell. The cop pushes me again. *"Stop! Cale, don't fight."* As much as I didn't want to, I listened to the voice. Beef stopped struggling and the cop let him go after we reached the end of the hallway. The entire school was crowding around the gym entrances. Most of them were bickering and squabbling like chickens and roosters, asking questions they knew no one had the answers to except for the masked C.I.A. and F.B.I. members and possibly Mr. Rusenkell. The entire school was in a state of panic.

Once everyone was inside the gym we heard the doors lock. The entire C.I.A., S.W.A.T. and F.B.I. were inside with us guarding the exit doors. The gym was stuffed with people. It was almost impossible to move let alone breathe. Sweat dripped from everyone and coughing and sneezing started to erupt in the crowd. It was dark inside, and the only light was from the sun that shined through the windows on the exit doors. A kid coughed on me and I was pissed until I realized there was red goo dripping from his mouth. *Then* I was terrified. He coughed again and it sprayed on my shirt. *"Blood"*, I thought. He fell to his knees and coughed even harder spraying out more blood on the wooden floor. Everyone around him started to back away. Then there was a screeching sound of a bottle break on the other side of the crowd and it echoed through the gym. A girl screamed and I became more scared than I ever have been in my life.

"Where is Beef?" I asked myself. My head was on a swivel searching for him. "Beef!" I cried, "Beef!"

"Cale!" the voice came from the crowd but I still could not find my best friend.

"Beef! Where are you?!"

"Over here!" he cried out. I saw him flailing his arms like he was drowning in the sea of people surrounding him. I pushed and shoved my way through to him and I grabbed his wrist with an iron grip. I pulled him through the gym, full of our classmates and teachers. "Are we being held hostage?" Beef asks.

"I don't know." I tell him as I keep shoving people out of my way.

"Where are you going Cale? All the exits are blocked."

"There is a door that leads to the weight room in that corner." I point to the direction I'm marching. When we get a clear sight at the door there is three police men guarding it.

"Dang it!" I yell at myself.

"Now what?" Beef asks.

"Follow me." I order. Without letting go of my grip on his wrist we head back the way we came from. "There is an air vent behind the bleachers where kids hide drugs all the time. Two of the screws are loose, so it opens easily." I tell him over my shoulder. Faces look up as I say air vent and I feel like someone is following me. I turn around to see that behind Beef is Amanda and Brett in the state of panic.

"Cale! Where are you going?"

"I'm getting out of here. Did you see that kid over there coughing up blood? There's something not right that's going on. Whatever it is, if it's contagious, I'm not going to sit here and just wait to catch it." They don't say another word and they just keep on following us. *"The less the merrier, we don't want to make a scene."* I tell myself. I pass by faces of kids that were just another face in the crowd, but now each face stood out. My memory of each face came back to me reading off their profiles on how I knew each one of them. This would be the last time I see them. I was somehow sure of it. I dragged Beef all the way to the side of the bleachers and I let go of him. "You ready?" I ask him.

"I trust you." He says.

"Okay, follow me close." I direct. I was giving the orders to Beef, but apparently there were a few others who must have caught on to what we were up to and were following us. All sketched out I reach the air vent. *"Oh God, please be open."* I thought. I slipped my fingers under the edges and pull. It opens with little effort. There is a brown bag and I could have guessed what was inside before I caught the smell of weed. I pick it up and toss it behind me uninterested in its contents. *"I don't need drugs to stimulate my mind."* I thought as I climb in the vent and start to crawl on my arms and knees down its path. Further down there is a fork in the vent. *"Right."* I tell myself. I keep going until I have to make a decision and I go right. It's nearly pitch black now inside the vent, so I pull out my lighter and flick it on. I make a left when I can and I see at the end of the tunnel is a bright light. I smile and I start to crawl faster towards it. I never thought I'd be crawling after the baby stage, but here I was crawling for my life. Of course when I reach the vent door filtering sunlight into the tunnel its locked. I shift my body around I lie on my back. I put up my feet to the door and cock my legs back. I release and I launch my legs slamming against the vent door. It flies open and the sun's light floods the tunnel as I fall out of the vent and land on my feet with my back crouched over my thighs. I stand up straight quickly and look around to see if any of the police officers saw us. There was no one in sight. I turn to look back at the vent and I see Beef is struggling to get out. "Suck it in Beef!" I half laugh.

"Oh shut up. I'm scared to death, and this isn't a laughing matter!" He says.

"I beg to differ. He's not watching this."

"Shut up!" I defend. When Beef finally falls out of the vent he lands on his back. I help him up and I notice we aren't alone. Amanda, and Brett tumble out of the vent one after another. Out next comes Britney Wilson. Following her was Marcus and Baley who nearly fell out together. *"What the heck?! Did the entire gym follow us?"* I ask myself.

"It looks like it." I replied as Tianna came crawling out. Now I was thankful that they followed. More people kept coming out of the vent and I lost my patience in waiting for everyone, so I told Beef to just keep everyone here and hide if anyone comes. And I booked it around the corner of the building.

It took me a couple seconds to realize where I stood. I've never entered the campus through the back so it all seemed confusing to where I was.

"Where are you going?" a girl called behind me. I turned to see who it was and Amanda was jogging up to me. As her small image grew larger as she came closer, I wanted to yell at her, but I didn't want to chance someone overhearing me.

"Why did you follow me?" I hissed as she came into whispering distance.

"What you think you are the boss of me? You still have to keep your end of the bargain." She hissed back.

"So you followed me and risked getting caught over some bet?"

"Sounds to me like you *care* about me."

"I don't! I just don't think you understand how serious this is! And if your loud shrill voice get's *me* caught I swear to God!"

"Chill Cale." She pretends to lock her mouth up with an invisible key and tosses it over her shoulder.

"You better." I warn.

"So how do you expect to get to Ruse?" she says almost instantly.

"So much for that invisible lock." I thought.

"How do you know I'm going to Ruse?"

"I'm not deaf!" she exclaims, "I heard him say that you might be immune, that's why your being all freaking *Rambo* and stuff because you think whatever is going on, doesn't affect you. And Ruse has the answers. Exactly what you promised you'd help me get. Except the circumstances are a lot more interesting and there is much more at stake."

"First of all, your being too friggen loud, and second of all, why do you care? Why do you care about what was in the bottle so much?"

"I told you Cale, I am the one who opened it. I went behind Mr. Rusenkell's back and I opened it." she answers.

"Wait, are you saying that whatever was in the green bottle...caused all of this?"

"That's what were gonna find out, right?"

"Just don't breathe your dragon breath on the back of my neck." I tell her as I start to run to the front of the school. Bouncing from pillar to pillar, I peek around to make sure there are no cops around. The campus is vacant and empty. I wasn't used to seeing it like this. I spot the white van that I remember the cop throwing Ruse in and I squint my eyes to see if anyone was in the driver's seat or passengers. *"Nope. Your good."* I tell myself. I turn to the red head and I ask her, "Can you keep up?" and before I let her answer I sprinted as fast as I can to the white van. I am out of breath by the time I reach the back of the van. *"I need to stop smoking."* I thought. I open the back door of the white van right as Amanda arrives. Mr. Rusenkell is sitting on top of his hands which are handcuffed.

"Cale! Amanda!" He yells.

"Ruse! What's going on?!" I ask out of breath.

"You have to go! You have to run! Get out of here! Leave me! They won't hurt me!"

"Who is they? The police?" Amanda asks.

"There is no time! You have to trust me and get as far as you can! You can't run on the roads though, you will have to run through the hills behind the school."

"No! you are going to give us answers *now* Ruse and you are coming with us!" I yell.

"Cale, Stop! Listen to me, this is the only way! They won't hurt me as long as I am never seen with you."

"Just tell us what is going on and we'll be on our way and you can go with whoever you want." I scold.

There is a moment of silence before Ruse shatters it, "Fine!" he yells, "Remember the green bottler from yesterday? Well it contains... contained an airborne toxin that alters your genetics."

"What-"

"Just let me finish" Mr. Rusenkell interrupts, "Not everyone dies from this *disease* but most people do. Others are completely immune to it and it has no affect on them. And others... well... something else happens to them."

"Like what?"

"It's- it just depends on your genes. The human race has evolved over the years, gaining extra chromosomes extra-"

"Speak English, Ruse! You know I'm failing your class." I say.

"Basically it alters your genetics. That's all we know."

"We?" Amanda asks

Suddenly there are screams. We hop out of the van and the screaming grows louder. More screams and yelling are echoing through the air. The sound of an engine growls in the distance and we look towards the hill down to this school. Vans with news logos on the side of them are rushing down the only entrance and exit. Amanda and I exchange worried looks and look to Mr. Rusenkell for help.

"Quickly, reach into my pocket!" He orders. I stand there frozen before he breaks my paralyzing panic. "Cale! You have to do it now!"

"Hurry up!" I encourage. I climb back into the van and I reach into his right pocket. I pull out a hard rectangular case.

"It's a video tape." Ruse explains, erasing the confusion on my face. "There should be a video camera in a black case behind me." When I don't move, he awakens my status of shock again, "Cale! Listen to me! Grab the video camera, and run! Take as many as you can. They are going to demolish this place. The F.B.I. and C.I.A. have no idea what is coming. You must run for the hills! Do *not* go home! Do you hear me Cale?" I fall back into a trance of confusing paralysis. "Do you *hear* me Cale?" I close my jaw which has unnoticeably fallen open. I swallow my own saliva feeling it pour down my throat and I nod. "Good." At those words I realize Amanda has already found the black case that contained the video camera and I jump out of the van. I look back to Mr. Rusenkell afraid to let go of the thought that this will be the last time I see him when he says, "I'm sorry." In a deathly whisper.

Amanda shut the rear doors before I could ask what he was sorry for and we ran at full speed back through the school. We reach a pillar and hid on the other side of it. I creep my head around it slowly looking back at the white van. I see two police officers walking towards the van. They tear off their gas masks and their vests that say S.W.A.T. on the back of them. They both jump inside the van and start the car. They start speeding forward and they come to an abrupt halt when they are directly horizontal with us hiding behind the pillar.

"*Run! Get out of there!*" I yell at myself.

"Did they see us?" Amanda panics.

"Be quiet!" I warn, and then I hear a familiar hostile voice as I hear the passenger door open.

"I think they are over here!" he says.

"James! Hurry up, we have to get out of here before they destroy the city, and before the C.I.A. find out this quarantine is a sham!" the driver yells. And their voices jogged my memory. James' voice was undeniably the cop that *was* on the left of Mr. Rusenkell.

"*The one who gave out the information?*" I asked myself.

"*Yes! And the one who was on the right just yelled at James!*"

"Alright Tom! Stop being all sketched out, they won't let this place blow til' we are out of the area and give him the signal!"

"*Tom.*" I told myself, "*He was the one on the right. I knew those posers weren't cops.*"

"Just grab them and let's go!" Tom yelled from the car.

"We have to run, that guy is coming to get us!" Amanda whispers. We are still hiding behind the pillar holding our breath. Any movements or noises and we were dead.

"*They already know where you are idiot! Just run out there and fight them!*" I tell myself.

Confused on what to do, I tell Amanda we are going to run on the count of three. "One..."

James' footsteps get louder...

"Two..."

Louder...

"Three-"and before I could start running for my life I feel a tug on my shirt, yanking me down to the ground.

"Wait!" Amanda whispers. She signals me to look behind me and I see James' face for the first time, except he doesn't see me. If James would look to his right he would find Amanda and I holding our breath as if we were under water. But he is too busy with some electric box across from us. Amanda crawls to the other side of the square pillar out of James' peripheral sight and I follow. I peek back at him as he is still reaching in the box marked electricity that's connected to the wall. He puts his gas mask back on.

"Got em!" he yells. And he pulls out three empty green bottles that were exactly like the one in Mr. Rusenkell's hand yesterday during third period. He wraps his arm around them like he is carrying a baby. Crack! The high pitched breaking sound, which mimicked the bottle breaking sound in the gym, comes from one of the green bottles James had dropped.

"Remind me to not let him carry my *baby."* I chuckle.

"How can you laugh at a time like this?"

"No!" James yells.

"Forget about it! Let's get the hell out of here!" Tom calls from the van.

I hear James' loud footsteps as he runs to the car and the car door slamming. The tires screech and Amanda and I peek around to see the white van that Mr. Rusenkell was in was now driving up the ramp, the only entrance and the only exit out of this school. I stand up at the same time as Amanda and the news vans are all parked around where the white van used to be. Reporters hopped out of each car all dressed up for a formal occasion, as if this disaster was a business retreat. Hefty men with Giant cameras lodged on their shoulders followed the well dressed reporters holding microphones with logos on them.

"Let's go." I order. And we turn from the commotion and start to run back the way we came. We both glance at the broken bottle that had no form of liquid, or solid matter surrounding it and I stop to get a closer look. "There was nothing in it." I say.

"I told you so." Amanda adds. "What does this all mean?"

I shake the case covered tape in front of her, "That's what *we* are going to find out." And we sprint back to the air vent we came out of.

When we get there, there is about twenty-five kids standing around Beef. "Beef!" I call out.

"Cale!" he yells back. He wobbles over to me and asks, "What the heck man! I thought you were dead! I had no idea what I was going to do-"

"Relax Beef. We need to get out of here."

"No, really?" he says sarcastically.

I turn to the group of students behind him and I yell, "Everyone! Follow me!"

"Why are you helping them?" I interrogate.

"What?"

"Why are you helping these jocks and kids who made your entire High School life not worth living?"

I didn't have an answer. I just turn around and in front of me is five football fields length of tall yellow grass after a steel fence. Behind this large meadow are a couple of giant hills. *"I don't have an answer for a lot of things,"* I say to myself, *"and I very well don't understand why I do the things I do, but all I know is this is my choice. And there is not a thing on this earth that can take that away from me."*

"Alright Ghandi, carry on then." And I do. I hop over the gate in front of me and I run through the meadow towards the giant hills.

Halfway through the meadow I stop running to catch my breath.

"Cigarettes will kill ya." Beef says catching his breath.

I turn to look at him and he is drenched in sweat. "Oh and cigars won't?" I ask. He smiles. "So, how'd you get everyone to listen to you?"

"Same way you got me to stay." He replies, "In the state of panic, people are willing to believe anything if it will save their own life, or a life close to them."

I notice that the kids who were back at the air vent were running to catch up with us. "Looks like they really want their lives if they are willing to follow a recluse." I half giggle.

"You have a plan, Cale." Beef states.

"I don't have a plan, Beef. I'm just doing what I do best. Running away."

"Well, you *had* a plan. And it was better than anyone else's. I swear I heard one of the kids trying to get everyone to crawl back through the vent and take one of the cops' guns and kill them all."

"Who gave that idea?" I ask squishing my eyebrows together.

"Some guy named Max Longo."

"Beef, I don't know what's next after we reach the hills."

"Neither do I Cale. But I'll follow you anywhere. I trust you."

And as if the flashback was a lion prowling in the meadow, it pounces on me at the phrase *I trust you.*

We were camping in Beef's backyard. Both fourteen-years-old and angered about the bad day we had just spent in our second day of High School. I had been dumped into a trash can and Beef, who was trying to back me up, got his lunch fed to him; a smoothie dumped on his head, pizza shoved in face and bombed with paint filled water balloons. This is how we spent most of our Friday nights. Inside of a tent we made ourselves with a box of pizza Beef's parents would order for us, though Beef got most of the slices because he inhaled his food faster than a camel drank water, and a bottle of whiskey I would steal from the nearest liquor store.

"I hate life." I announced.

"Ditto." Beef adds as he gargles down a slice of pepperoni pizza.

Beef and I look at each other after a moment of silence and we burst out laughing so hard I swear I thought I peed a little. I look at him after we finish laughing and I ask him. "Do you trust me Beef?"

"What?"

"Do you trust me?"

"Uh… yea… why?"

"Ok then follow me." I get up and I feel all off balanced and light headed from the alcohol. I unzip the tent door and step out into the freezing cold.

"What are you doing?" Beef calls out.

"Just come out here!" I order, and when he does I face him. "Are you ready?"

"For what?"

"Put your hand out."

"Why?"

"Do you trust me Beef?" I ask again. He doesn't answer and he lays his right hand out in front of me. I pull out a knife and he yanks his hand back in, just like I knew he would. I dig the knife into my right palm cutting it allowing blood to escape. "Hold out your hand Beef."

"What? No!"

"Do you trust me Beef?" I repeat. He holds out his right hand again and he gathers his lips to one side of his face. I smile and I grab his wrist. I prick the knife into his palm until I see blood. I put the knife back into my pocket

and I take my bleeding hand and shake his right palm. The cut burns for a quick second but when I look up at him, I say, "Now, we are brothers." And in that instant, pain didn't exist in my life.

It's dark. And we hiked to the top of the hill that seemed so far away from us not six hours ago. We all are still staring at what used to be our school in awe. Helicopters, and jets soared over it about three hours ago dropping what looked like giant bullets from their missile carriers. When the giant bullets landed on top of Stellar High School there was a massive explosion of red and orange that blinded all of us. All I could think of was the screams that still echoed through the valley. Screams that were quarantined inside the gym we had escaped from. Screams of innocent students, kids, teachers too. I cursed myself for ever wishing a teacher dead for assigning a homework assignment over the weekend. I would have gladly done it now to keep this from happening. I would have done it five hundred times over again. None of us, who witnessed the massacre, cried. We were in complete and total shock. There was no room for tears or bitterness, just unbelievable looks we gave to each other. We just sat and watched our school burn to the ground. I remember wishing the entire school was set on fire so we would have an early summer, but I never expected what the cost would be. Ominous, onyx smoke that rose from the flames burning our school not only levitated off our school but we could see in the distance that there was more smoke that clouded the air steaming off of more flames towards the city. Another set of black smoke was floating over the mansions of the gated community I so longed to live in. Flickers of red, yellow and orange flashed over both sides of the valley dancing with the darkness of the black night, and I knew we were all alone. The air was black and ash rained from the sky. The smell of smoke burned our throats as we watched all we knew burn to dust. All we owned all we have ever loved, all we've ever known was now disintegrating to black solemn dust. From the moment the first bomb had dropped I realized God wasn't present, he wasn't here to witness that hell had come to take over. Somber winds passed through us carrying whatever we had left of ourselves away once and for all. There was no fire alarm to pull for something so breathtakingly dreadful.

3. Salvaging Ashes

Someone sneezes and it wakes me up from my light, half sleep. The red sun behind our hill bleeds its light through the thick black air. This is the first time I've ever seen the relaxed morning sun so crimson and ominous. It was usually bright yellow and orange at this time of the early day, which what *should* be in the middle of our first period. *"Maybe it was all just a bad dream"* I had hoped right before I looked behind me, crossing my fingers, at Stellar High School.

"Nope..." I assured myself, *"This wasn't a dream. This is a nightmare."* I told myself as dying flames still burned what was left of our school. Another sneeze and a rigorous cough sounded and it makes me flinch as it grapples me out of my daze the destruction trapped me in. I turn around and I see what is left of Stellar High's population still sleeping on the same dirt covered hill we found refuge on. There was only one survivor that was awake with me. He sneezes, and I find the source to what grabbed me out

of my half slumber. I get up off the ground, my clothes covered in dirt and I start walking over to him.

"What are you doing?" I ask myself.

"I'm going to talk to him."

"Why?"

"Because, I think he might die."

"So you are willing to risk your own life to have a little chit chat with a sick kid who has some kind of airborne toxic disease that might be highly contagious because he might die? You do realize you *are going to die too then?"*

"We are all going to die! They cracked the bottles while were inside the gym yesterday and our beloved red head opened a bottle the day before yesterday. We are all exposed to this thing, *and it's going to kill us."*

"What about the chance Mr. Rusenkell said you might be immune?"

"So if I am immune, or already dead, then what difference does it make that I go over to this kid and make a new friend before he dies?"

"Touché…I still don't know what has gotten into you. Why are you acting so noble now?"

"Maybe nothing has gotten into me…maybe the bad parts have just gotten out of me."

"No Cale. Don't start making your hero speech now. The bad is still here. Trust me… You are not *a hero Cale."* I tell myself. And I couldn't be sure if I was wrong or right.

I am close enough to him now that when he sneezes I see blood come out of his nose. He coughs five times into his hands and wipes the remaining blood off his face with his sleeve. That is when he looks up and notices for the first time that he is not the only one awake. He looks at me with uttermost fear in his eyes, as if I was coming to him as the grim reaper. The look was as if we were actors in a 1978 horror film, where the guy who was playing the innocent, horny teenager turned around to find his co-worker dressed as a serial killer. It pleased me to know that I was to be taken seriously, but it was also disturbing to know that he thought of me as his own personal view of Michael Myers from the movie, *Halloween.* As soon as I am standing over him, his face still covered with dirt, ash and fear, I recognize who he is for the first time. Preston Queen: Our football teams' star receiver and Brett's best friend, or in other words another popular jock that made my life a reason not to live for a living. Now I understood why he had fear carved into every aspect of his face. He thought I was taking my revenge.

"Which you should," I say to myself, *"Besides, you'll not only end his misery, but our misery as well. His death could be a blessing for both of us."*

"I'm not going to murder him." I scold myself.

"You already said he was dead! You'd be doing him a favor!"

"Not yet he's not! And I'm not having innocent blood on my hands!"

"Technically... it will be on the rocks conscience."

"What are you talking about?"

"Throw him down the hill. Let the rocks kill him."

"You are... truly psychotic."

"I know what you are, but what am I?

"You are what I am..."

"Touché again..."

"Am I going to die?" Preston asks me. The fear was still swirling in his eyes.

There is a long pause before I tell him, "Yes."

"How do you know?" Amanda's voice quietly objects from behind me.

I turn around to face her and I could feel the heated irritation building in my head again. Her gaze makes my skin start to burn which expands my irritation into resentment. I realize that all the anger and repressed feelings I had bottled up inside me was boiling at a Fahrenheit degree that was uncharted to a thermometer. Pop! The bottle cap went inside of me and, like an atomic bomb, I exploded with fury and rage. "How do you think I know carrot top!?" I roared, waking up most of the sleeping survivors.

And as if I wasn't furious enough, she raised my anger to a level I didn't even know existed in me with her statement, "You already said that one, retro fairy!" I wasn't sure if I was angrier at her changing the subject and catching me using an un-original nickname, or if it was the fact that she was now giving *me* nicknames. But both subjects collided with each other in my head blowing up like two rockets smashing together after being launched on opposite ends.

As a reaction to the war brewing inside of me, my arms' reflexes shoved Amanda with all of their might. She flies backwards tripping over her own feet and lands on her back. I point to her face with my right index finger. My elbow is locked and my body is stiff. My voice thunders deeper and louder than any lighting storm. "This is all *your* fault!" I growl fiercely. Now everyone is awake and watching me. "None of this would have happened if it wasn't for-"

I am cut off by a surprising blow to the gut and a feral snarl. There was no air to breathe and I was stunned. I didn't' notice I was flying in the air for two long seconds until I land on my back. The impact my back had with the ground caused a prolonged shortness of breath. Gasping for air, Brett comes into my view rising from where I had just fallen.

"Was I just tackled by Brett Gooding?" I asked myself, still unable to breathe.

"Yup. That's embarrassing…"

Finally, a zephyr flooded into my lungs quenching my desire and need to breath. The cool air rushes through me inflating my chest. I had never appreciated oxygen more than I did now.

"Get up!" I yell at myself, *"Get up and fight!"*

I heed my own orders and I jump up from the ground. Brett is bouncing on the balls of his feet with his fists guarding his face. There is a series of "Come on!" and "Let's go!" that come out of his mouth, but I just evilly glower at him. *"Oh how long I have been waiting for this moment."* I thought. My hands curl into fists, my eyebrows slant down towards each other, and I bite the inside of my lower lip. *"Swing."* I tell Brett in my head. *"Swing!"* I order again. *"Swing at me!"* and as if he heard me taunting him in my head, he takes his right fist and lunges it towards me. Prepared for his attack I dodge his fist by ducking. I am beneath him, crouching, when I extend my legs initiating my body upwards with my left fist in front of my face. Every muscle in my left arm flexes right before I uppercut him in the jaw. I feel the jolt of pain in my knuckles as I make contact. My left arm follows through shooting upwards as Brett flies back. Happiness and contentment surged through me as I watched Brett fall to the ground until I see a large object blitzing towards me. I turned to see what it was to find a huge dark brown haired senior rushing towards me. I recognized his face and the name they called him on the football team. Josh Caball. But everyone called him Cocoa. His shoulders were lowered and his face full of fury as he kept charging towards me.

"Oh crap!" I panicked to myself, *"You ticked off a grizzly bear!"* I embraced myself for the collision that was about to demolish me, when Beef flies from Cocoa's side and wrestles him to the ground. I was only able to watch Beef and Cocoa, who was just a bit taller and bigger than my best friend, for a limited five seconds before I was interrupted by another blow to my gut. This time it wasn't as unexpected and breathtaking. I punched the face that I had expected to be Brett's, but it wasn't him. It was Brody Geldert. A familiar face at Stellar High school. I never had any quarrels

with him in the past, so I didn't understand why he had hit me. I watched him stumble against the hillside after I threw another punch to his face.

"Stop hesitating!" I yell to myself as I stared at Brody's pink, freckled face in confusion. I had forgotten how deep Brett's alliances were. A football team Is like a brotherhood, or cult. If you mess with one, the rest come swarming at you. Brody was the injured tailback on the team. This huge massive bear-man that was wrestling my best friend must have been an offensive guard for the Stellar Titan's football team. Before I could see if any other surviving football players were coming after me; Marcus Moon, who had crept up from my behind, pinned my arms against my back. I couldn't believe how easy it was to escape his seize, but when I did I cocked my fist back. I was about to initiate my fist forward at Marcus' face when I was interrupted by an aggressive tug on my elbow. Behind me, Baley Schottenfield was glaring at me, daring me to hit her. I had never seen her mad, so I wasn't exactly sure what I should do to what I thought was a sweet innocent little girl. She *did* have a full ride to USC for their soccer team though, so she must have had some aggression in her. Suddenly Amanda rejoins the fight and steps in front of Baley and leaps from the ground, springing on top of me. Her legs gripped to my ribs and her hands clawed into my shoulders. Off all ties with balance, I fall on my back, Amanda still clawed onto me. My alliance ran as deep as Beef, so it was almost like us two against the twenty-five other survivors. As Amanda and I kept rolling around on the gravel, I caught a series of glimpses and realized this battle wasn't just between the jocks versus the two outcasts; the entire group of survivors was at war. Everybody was fighting each other. Amanda and I had stopped rolling and she ended up on top, pinning me to the ground. Her hands were still digging into my shoulder blades, and mine were digging into hers. I locked my eyes with hers, both our faces full of rage, when I see her eyes aren't their normal boring brown. They are a fiery crimson red. I am still lost in her intimidating eyes when I feel a scorching sting on the back of both of my shoulder blades. Suddenly, the ground beneath me begins to violently shake and for a rough ten to fifteen seconds I see out of my peripheral view the others trip over themselves. Amanda jumps off of me, her face full of shock and her eyes returning to a boring brown. *"Maybe she felt it too."* I thought as the sting in my back where her talons were locked on to grew worse even after the earthquake had faded. The blazing sting felt like I was being pinched a thousand times and stabbed with needles in the same spot. The pain now spread through my entire back and I was ferociously growling in agony

"Fire!" Amanda cried, "Help! Fire!"

I felt the tension between everybody's fighting fade and their eyes watching me as I rolled around in complete torture. My back was on fire. Beef started to slam his hands against my back and kept me rolling on the dirt. The stinging didn't hurt as much when the fire was fully extinguished, but it still burned against my back when pressure was applied. Everyone was calm now. No longer yelling, arguing and fighting each other off their own alliances. Amanda's face was pale white. I looked at her with a twitch in my eye.

"Where did that fire come from?" I asked myself as I fumbled through my pockets searching for my lighter. Once I found it I looked up to her again.

"Did she just start that…with her…with…" It sounded stupid and cliché when I thought of the possibility, but I finished anyways, *"…Mind?"*

"I think so…" And not only was there silence in my head, but the entire group of survivors fell hypnotized to the quietness. Amanda Robesun was the complete center of everyone's undivided attention until three hoarse coughs changed our focus. Preston Queen was still sitting up against the hillside coughing up blood. He sneezes and I get up to walk over to him again. He looked like he got into a worse fight than I did, and I'm pretty sure nobody had a grudge against him that was so bad they went off to punch the weakened sick kid. I stare at him now in an even worse condition than he was before Amanda and I got into a fight that made everyone hostile against each other. It looked like his brown hair had faded into a lighter, grayer shade. His white skin was insipid, and dried blood trails traveled from his mouth, nose, and ears down his neck. His glossy brown eyes dripped with tears because he knew his fate. His pain was so palpable to me, that I was being tormented with multiple twinges just looking at him. Suddenly the tears in his eyes were dyed bright red and they streamed down his pallid face. He coughs loudly and a small, fragile hand reached out from behind me and grabs mine. The grip felt like a wave of sensation flowing through my veins, pumping my heart faster. I turned my neck and vision from Preston to the person grabbing my hand. My heart stops when I realize who she is. Tianna was staring at Preston at my side.

"I don't think she knows that it's your hand she's holding." I tell myself.
"Maybe she just-"
"No Cale."
"I was just going to say-"

"It doesn't matter what you were going to say. Either way, your hopes are up and it's wrong. Don't get your optimism up Cale."

I wanted to punch myself in the face. How wrong could I be? All I know is that she is holding my hand. It didn't matter that she did it out of fear, confusion or if there was a magnet in her hand that forced itself against one inside the palm of my hand. All that mattered to me was that she *was* holding my hand right now. Preston coughs louder and more ominous now and we all gaze at him in total astonishment. We all are frozen ice sculptures staring at him with no idea how to help him. The grip on my hand starts to squeeze tighter and tighter as Preston's entire body starts to shake. *"He's having a seizure."* I thought gravely. Still no one knew how to help him. Preston's body flails and jolts like he is being electrocuted. He stops shaking after thirty seconds of an off and on jerk. He stops breathing. He no longer moves. The iron grip on my hand slowly fades and an angelic voice asks me, "Is- is he...dead?"

I turn to face Tianna and she is looking at me for the first time. Tears are in her eyes. I didn't know what to tell her. I knew the truth. The three letter word that usually means a good thing, but I felt if I had told her, she would leave me. She would leave me and forget about this moment. I force my lips open separating them from each other like dried glue was sealing them together. I was going to say it to her when I let go of her hand. I closed my mouth and I walked away. I walked back to where I had fallen asleep watching my life burn in front of me, and I sat down in the same spot knowing my *new* life was burning behind me now as well. *"She mustn't be a part of my life."* I told myself over and over again. *"She is too good. I am too corrupt. I have to stay away from her."*

As I sit with my arms surrounding my knees I hear footsteps from behind me. Expecting Tianna, Amanda plops her butt on the ground right next to me, and all my hopes and good thoughts instantly vanish and are replaced with cynical feelings and hatred. "What do *you* want, Carey?"

"Who?" she asks.

"Carey." I state again, "The fire starter? You've never seen that movie?"

"Oh." She says boringly.

"Yeah. So what do you want?"

"I- I'm scared." She says under her breath.

"Why do you keep coming to me with your petty issues? You have a boyfriend for that reason!"

"Who's best friend just died!" There is a pause and I look straight again. Preston Queen was a star athlete. It was ironic to see how helpless he was when all I could remember of him was strength and leadership for the airheads of our school. He seemed so impervious before when he walked the grounds of Stellar High. Everyone knew him. The entire city of Irvine knew who he was. Irvine had their own magazines and propaganda of Brett Gooding and Preston Queen together on the cover page of magazines and on the billboards that followed the nearby freeways. Not only did they make Stellar High School, and its home city Irvine famous, but they just *had* to make the entire Orange County and southern California eminent with their own television show.

"It's retarded really, just a cheap show of fake drama and scripted lines that try *to be funny."*

"But they aren't funny at all."

"It's about absolutely nothing, but it's one of those shows where it's so stupid that it's addicting to watch and you can't turn the channel."

"Yeah, but everyone else in the world thinks they are the best thing that has ever happened to this city."

"Now he is dead. What do you think will happen to us?"

"Do you think there is a cure?"

"There is an opposite for everything Cale. That is how we are kept balanced. Sane. For every bad, there must be good. For every wrong, there is to be a right. And for every death, there comes life."

"Do you think if we had a new life…this would be it?"

"You have to die to become reborn." I lecture myself.

"I'm a freak." Amanda whispers. I had forgotten she was still sitting beside me.

"What?" I replied back to her.

"Where do you think that fire came from, Cale?"

I was pleased that she had called me by my name again and not some nickname. I was also intrigued by the subject she had brought to my attention again.

"That's a first." I snicker to myself.

"Tell me about it." Watching Preston die in front of me and the love of my life holding my hand was the perfect combination of events to fog up the memory of the spontaneous flame that set fire to my back. "Fire doesn't just instinctively ignite." I tell her.

"That's what I'm saying…I mean, I- I think I did it."

"Oh don't feed me that supernatural bull crap." I stress, even though I actually believed she might be some kind of fire starter.

"How else do you explain your back lighting on fire?!"

"Look, if this is about me calling you Carey, forget about it! Alright? It was just a joke that happened to fit for the scenario, but obviously you're a little bit more sensitive and dramatic then the act you put on."

"Act?! You are ridiculous Cale. Don't even get me started on *your* 'act!'" I ignore her for a good ten seconds before she brings my good mood back down again with her voice. "We have to watch the tape."

At the phonetic sound of 'tape', I start to shuffle through my pockets for the tape Mr. Rusenkell had given me, which supposedly had all the answers to this catastrophe. My eyes widen in fear when I can't locate it. *"where could I have put it?"* I thought.

"Did you drop it on the way up here?"

"I have it." Amanda confesses, holding the tape out in her palm.

I look at her with complete dysfunction. "How did you get that?" I interrogate. *"I could have sworn I put it in my pocket."* I say to myself. She doesn't answer and I ask her again, this time more clearly.

Fear was in her eyes when she told me she had stolen it out of my pocket while I was sleeping. Anger started to grow again in my head, and silence followed. "I was only trying to figure out what was going on." Amanda pleads, "Plus, you were asleep-"

"So that gives you the right to go through my pockets?"

"I don't know if you *remember* correctly, but that tape is Mr. Rusenkell's and it supposedly has the answers to save *all* of us, not just your sorry butt!"

"Tell me, hot tamale, would you even be alive if it wasn't for me? What would you have done? anything that helped?" I say staring her down. She doesn't make a sound. *"Thought so."* I thought. "Where is the video camera?" I demand.

"I- uh…"

"What now! Did you burn that too?"

"Shut up! I have it. Its- just… damaged."

"What are you talking about!" I yell furiously. I felt like I was going to shove her off the hillside and watch her tumble down do her demise.

"I must have hit the video camera against something on the way up here."

"Great. This is just fantastic!" I sarcastically thought. Now I was even closer to shoving her off the edge. "Are you kidding me?!" I yell at her. "Everything you touch just turns to crap doesn't it?"

"Well it's not *completely* broken." Amanda defends.

"What the- ugh! You just *said* that-"

"I *said,* that I might have hit it against something and cracked the viewer screen. The audio doesn't work either."

"So it's still completely useless then."

"Well…yeah, but at least we have the tape."

"This is just wonderful. So what do we do with the camera?"

"I guess just leave it. It's useless."

"Not exactly." A voice interrupts me and Amanda's arguing. We look over and see Britney Wilson is standing across from us with her arms folded across her chest. There is a scratch in the shape of a crescent adjacent to the outside of her left eye. I could tell it was still a fresh wound from the vividly bright red color that was painted on it.

"What happened to *you*?" I ask her.

She motions her head to Amanda giving her one head bob and an evil glare. "Ask *that* witch." She growls.

"Bite me." Amanda barks.

"No thanks, I don't want to choke."

"Better if I choke *you, Britney*!"

"I dare you to try, fire crotch!" Britney yells back.

"I like her already." I thought to myself changing all of my judging thoughts about Britney in an instant. It looked like Amanda was ready to pummel on her when I intervened. "Were you just eavesdropping on us?"

"Indeed she was and she needs to stick her pimpled nose out of my business." Amanda answers for her.

"If it wasn't for me, you would be ditching that video camera right now. What are you going to play the tape with *then*, fireball?" Britney snaps. Amanda was speechless. I completely misjudged Britney. Not only did I take her for a dumb cheerleading blonde, but I had no idea there was this antagonistic side of her. "I checked the black video camera bag you brought up here; and yes, the viewer screen is broken, but there is also a cord in the bag that can still link the camera up to a T.V. or a computer."

"What good is that going to do?" Amanda shouts.

"Listen you ditz, we hook the video camera up to a T.V. or something, we play the tape and we find out what is happening to us. Did you get that all, Carey?"

"Carey?"

"Don't play stupid, you mean to seriously tell me that Cale's shirt spontaneously combusted? I don't buy it. We all were there, and we all saw you clenching on to him just moments after you through that rock at my head!"

"You deserved it you little-"Amanda screeches.

"Anyways! As I was saying, I watched your assault on Cale-"

"And you didn't help get this demon off of me?!" I interrupt.

"Can I finish? I watched her digging into your back and all of a sudden, red flames ignited from her hands."

"Shut up!" Amanda bellows.

"You know it's true, that's why you're not denying it."

"You're just still bitter because I was voted captain of the cheer team and you're just holding a grudge."

"As if!" Britney shrieks.

"This is just getting annoying now." I thought. "Enough! Britney is right." I exclaim. Amanda shoots a look at my face that reads: *What the heck?* at me. *"As if I would ever take* your *side."* I roll my eyes. "We need to find something to hook this camera up and watch the tape now."

"Oh! Okay! Let's just go down to the T.V. and electronics store and ask for customer service!" Amanda says sarcastically. "Uh, Hello!? Are you *not* on the same planet as us? Did you not witness the city on fire?"

"Is *your* plan to stay here and rot? We have no idea how far those jets and helicopters even went. My house is farther away from where we can see, so I'm sure we can just call for help and watch the tape there." I scold.

"If we even make it there." I told myself.

"Whatever." Amanda says as she gets up to walk away. She stares Britney down as she passes her by. Britney returns the same unfriendly look almost mirroring her.

I shove the tape deep down in my pocket so it couldn't accidently fall out or be stolen again without me noticing. I grab the black camera bag and I walk towards the rest of the survivors as they all gathered in a circle around where Brett had just buried Preston Queen. The only noise that was being made was Amanda's voice whispering into Brett's ear about our travel plans. Nobody else seemed to hear her though, even though I was farther away from the circle then any of them. I figured they were all still in shock. After about three seconds of stillness, I broke the quietness. "We need to go." I announced. One by one, everyone in the circle turned their heads back towards me. All of their eyes were full of rage now instead of the sorrow looks they put upon the burial site. "We should all-"

"Screw you!" a voice calls out. My head jerks to the speaker in reaction. Josh Caball was looking me dead in the eyes. "*You* are the reason why Preston is dead! We should have never come with you, whatever happened to him, *you* probably did it!"

"Learn your facts before you point your judging Sasquatch fingers at me! I didn't do anything! This is all *her* fault!" I bellow as I point at Amanda. Amanda is shaking her head motioning her lips to the word *no*. "Yeah! That's right; Pandora over here opened the green bottle and unleashed some kind of airborne toxin into the air. We are *all* nothing but zombies now. We are just walking dead. So don't be putting the blame on to me, when it's Pandora's fault!" Everyone is noiseless. They all looked back at Amanda at an extreme loss.

"I don't buy that!" Josh Caball yells.

"He's right." Amanda confesses. Now *Cocoa* was giving her a confused look as well. "I opened the green bottle."

"What green bottle?" Someone asks.

"There was a green bottle that Mr. Rusenkell had in class the day before the...Quarantine." Amanda gulps. "And before class, I went in to turn in some absent work. Mr. Rusenkell was in a hurry out the door when I approached the door handle. I-"

"Will you get to the point already?" Britney hollers.

"I am! Anyways, I was told to stay inside the classroom and not let anyone in while he was out. He told me not to touch anything by his desk. So I waited, and I saw a green bottle standing on the edge of Mr. Rusenkell's desk. With no intention to touch it, I walked over to it because I saw a little light glowing inside of it. It looked like a firefly was trapped inside. It was then that I opened the bottle and I looked inside, and there was nothing. The light that was floating inside wasn't there anymore. So I assumed that it was just a reflection or something. Anyways, I put the cap back on and I walked back to the spot where it had caught my attention to see if the glare was still there and the green bottle was duller than ever. There was no light that bounced around in it. I walked back to it to pick it up and shake it to see if there were any contents in it when I heard the door handle jiggle. I hid the empty green bottle underneath Mr. Rusenkell's desk and I sat down in my own desk before he came in. Later on Mr. Rusenkell started to freak out because he noticed the bottle had been open. I tried to get it out of him then and there but the fire alarm went off.

Then, before we ran for the hills yesterday, we went to see Mr. Rusenkell to get some answers. He was vague but he told us that there was a highly contagious airborne toxic disease preserved in the bottles. Some police officer cracked one in the gym right next to my feet before we evacuated the gym. I remember screaming. Anyways, Mr. Rusenkell gave us a tape that supposedly has all the answers to our questions on it, and-"

"Where is this tape?" Cocoa interrupts.

"I have it." I state.

"And you didn't think that it would be a good idea to share this information with the rest of us? Or were you just trying to save yourself?" Brett antagonizes me.

"Here!" I yell, "Take it!" I toss the tape to the back of the circle where he was standing. "What are you going to do anyways with it? The video camera is broken."

He waits for a couple moments as I have everyone looking at him instead of me now. He looks to Amanda and she nods her head. "We need to start hiking back down. We need to find and save what we can use. We'll head north until we find some surviving houses. This tape is still playable Cale. We can play it at someone's house."

"That harpy!" I thought. Obviously Amanda had already claimed me and Britney's idea and gave it to Brett to take as their own. He wasn't informing me of anything new when he said the tape would still play. He was taunting me. Sure enough once Brett was done giving his heroic speech everyone started gather around Brett except for me. Even Beef was standing around him as he looked at me with eyes that read: *Come on Cale, this is the best idea…* *"I can't believe Beef just went rogue on me! He betrayed me for Brett!"*

Brett's pack of followers started to follow him and Amanda down the path we hiked up yesterday and I remain standing, my feet cemented to the ground. Beef stops moving in the direction of the pack, and so does Britney. They both start walking to me now. "Come on Cale, it's our best chance of survival." Beef says. "I hate it as much as you, but we have to move sooner or later."

"That's just how they are, Cale." Britney utters, "Well… how *we* are. We take and never give back. Who do you think everyone is going to follow? Someone like you? Or someone like me?"

As much as her cocky little statement angered me, I knew she was right. "Whatever." I state. And I follow their backs down the hill in last place.

When we arrive at the ruins of Stellar High School, I turn the dial on my I-pod to *Hide and Seek* by Imogen Heap and there is a shriek of agony after a series of morbid thoughts all about the surreal destruction around us. We all turn our heads towards what used to be our basketball gym and Britney is huddling over something on the ground. Considering Britney as a new ally, I am the first one to find myself standing over her back. Two blonde twins with freckled faces lay underneath Britney's clasp around their shoulders. Black stains were smudged on their faces, and their eyes were closed. Both of their lips were slightly ajar when a tiny drop of water falls into the mouth of the twin on the right. Britney is cursing God and crying hysterically with her face buried in between the two lifeless bodies. "No!" she screams, "Why? Kristen, Kelly...Come back! Please! Come back!" she repeats, each time more stuttering and gasps for air intervening her solemn tears. "I promise-, I promise. I promise. I love you I-"She isn't able to hold her voice anymore when she bursts into tears again. Her crying was infectious to nearly everyone in our group. I looked up from Britney holding her dead siblings and everyone was crying as if Kristen and Kelly were their sister's as well. Even Beef had tears streaming down his face. I wiped underneath my eyes and I found no trace of any moisture. I didn't know if I felt sad for Britney, or not.

"Proof of the black hole keeping you alive, instead of an organ connected to your most valuable arteries." I thought. Beyond Britney and the rest of the group that now circled around Britney was a large land mass of black, onyx rubble, ash, and patches of fire. Large broken pillars that once erected from the floor upwards now lay horizontally on the ground. Chairs with steel frames stood naked without any padding or cushion on them. Half demolished buildings of the three hundred hallway and the five hundred hall still positioned themselves up somehow. All of them had black stains on the grey walls and vacant space filled with white ash and black wreckage preceded them. It looked like a scene from a war movie. Everything seemed like I was looking out of the eyes of a color blind person, it was all just plain black and white. I hadn't even noticed I was walking around the graveyard of Stellar High until I turned around to another scream. In my sight was the remaining Stellar High School students all scattered along the debris of the campus. Some were looking straight down and walking slowly. Others just kept swiveling their heads leisurely from side to side and turning around gradually. And few found closure to the presuming outcomes of their friends and fellow classmates. Most of the corpses were

unrecognizably burnt, but others looked as though if fire did not even touch them.

Even through the song playing in my head I heard a soft, quiet cough. My eyes darted around and found something in the rubble was moving. I took my headphones out and shoved my i-pod in my pocket. I jogged across the wreckage, climbing over broken building parts of the old cafeteria and I hovered myself over where I saw the ground move. Underneath the part of the wreckage that moved was another student. "Help! There's someone alive here!" I called out. Not checking to see if anyone heard me, I started to shift around the debris and ash that rested on top of him so he was on top of the earth again. Not only did black stain his face and clothes but light blood paths pursued out of his nose, mouth and ears. He was a chubby, freckled red headed kid gasping for air. He tried speaking but vomit came out instead. I back up and away. His eyes turned red and blood started to drip out of them. He was choking on his own throw up that kept spilling out of him. His puke was bloody and disgustingly green, I determined shortly after I looked away in disgust. He seizures just like Preston and looks like he falls asleep with his eyes open. A sleep he wouldn't be waking up from.

A boy's voice from behind caught me off guard when he said, "Tyler."

I turned to him with no pity for the dead portly red headed kid and looked at the boy next to me who seemed to have appeared from nowhere. He was short and had straight brunette hair. He had immense light green eyes that caught my attention instantly. "What?" I whispered.

"Tyler. His name was Tyler. He was in my math class." The boy answers.

"Does it look like I care who he was to you?" I almost said out loud.

"Never liked him anyways." He says apathetically, "I'm Max." he holds out his hand making it available to shake.

"Cold." I thought.

"I like him." And I shake his inviting hand. When my hand made contact with his a frigid, wintry coldness numbed my hand. His arctic hand felt like I was shaking hands with dry ice. He made no emotion that pertained to any chilliness at all though. I let go of his hand quickly and told him, "Cale. Cale Valens."

"Did you just give him your full name? Who does that? Is this some sort of interview?"

He chuckles a little bit. "Max. Maxwell Longo." he mocks me. His sense of humor was astounding to the fact that we were still in the middle of a crisis. I noticed that no one had come towards me when I called for help as *Tyler* was dying. Max was the only one.

"I heard about you." I tell him.

"What?"

"You were the one trying to get everyone back inside the vents to kill the police officers."

"How'd you know that? I don't remember trying to recruit you." He laughs.

"Beef told me."

"Ah. Yeah, your butt buddy."

"What?" I say with a little tenacity in the layer of my voice.

"Oh come on. You two are butt buddies. Inseparable."

I stick my middle finger up at him and I walk away. He laughs as I leave and makes no attempt to apologize. *"Not that I care."*

"Right…" I extend the phonetics of the word so they last for a good five seconds in my head as I turn my i-pod dial to the song, "Colorblind" by Counting Crows. I walk into a half constructed classroom pondering if I should consider these buildings like a half empty glass of water, or a half full when I spot it. The only thing a different color from the entire black and white aura that surrounded me. The red, square object stood out like a stain on a white shirt. Vast white letters read: *FIRE* on the label. I walked closer to the fire alarm and followed its instructions. I pushed in and down…Nothing. No sirens, no movements, no help, no instructions followed. The waste of effort brought me to my knees. I punched the wall the fire alarm rested on and my fist went effortlessly through the weakened barrier.

"Everyone," Brett calls out from afar, "we need to keep on moving. We have to find help."

I start walking towards Brett as people gather around him to start moving again. "What if there *is* no help." I bellow fifteen yards away from the circle. "What if *this* is all we have left." My questions sound more like statements then possibilities.

"Then we need to find what we can to survive. We'll need to work *together.*"

"I hate that kid for always having an answer to everything." I told myself. Brett makes another inspiring speech to the group and I find myself following them in last place again up the ramp. We walk across the bridge

that segregates us from the city and we find vacant, destroyed cars on the road. The islands that were located in the middle of the road contained burnt trees and bushes. There was no sign of life. This could have been the rapture and we were the only ones left behind. Beef falls behind the crowd, even behind me and I am the only one that waits for him.

"I'm tired." He says.

"When are you not when it comes to any physical activity?" I half laugh.

"Cale. I'm tired of being the follower. There is only so much I can take. And I've reached my limit."

I couldn't tell if Beef was trying to disown me as a friend, or if he was just expressing his hateful feelings for Brett. I prayed for the second one, but I deep down I knew where he was going. I was selfish. Too selfish to ever think about the only person I really care about. Too selfish to care. All I wanted right now was to switch places with him. I wanted him to feel like he had me under the leash now, but knowing my stubborn pride I knew I would never let that happen. All I could do was wish for it.

Behind Beef a black burnt bush shook out of the corner of my eye as my wishful thinking continued to instinctively prey for Beef's forgiveness. It shakes again, and I hear growling. Beef turns around at the intimidating grumble and becomes aware of the black bush shaking as well. The growling turns into an undomesticated roar and a large object leaps out from the naked bush onto Beef making him fall on top of me. My legs are trapped underneath Beef when he lets out a cry for help. "Help-"he yells, but he is cut off.

"Beef!" I screech as I try to assemble my feet. I crunch my stomach up and I lean forward to fight off whatever is latched onto my best friend when I see a golden haired dog licking the skin off of Beefs face. Beef starts laughing and my face is still full of worry. The worry slowly fades to an angry mood and I scowl at Beef. I yank my legs free from Beefs back and I lean down and hit Beef in the shoulder, feeling stupid about getting worried over what I had secretly thought a monster had attacked him. *What are you, like eleven?* I ask myself, criticizing my imagination.

"Twelveteen actually, I'm twelveteen." I fire back, not realizing I had combined the numbers twelve and thirteen.

"That's not a real age."

"It is now."

Beef laughs even harder now and it makes me wonder if I had spoken out loud while arguing with myself, so I strike him in the same spot three more times.

"Cale!" he laughs, "Stop! Ha! It tickles!"

I couldn't be sure if he was talking about the nonstop licking of his face or if he was making fun of my punches. No longer could I hold my anger as I realized how helpless Beef was against this golden dog, so I cautiously exploded into laughter and lightened my face. Beef and I were laughing uncontrollably. The sentiment and excitement of laughter rushed through me like a dive into a deep, chilled pool, surrounded by the aurora of sunlit glimmering water, like a blanket of a thousand blue diamonds. I was happy. I grabbed the dog off of Beef to let him stand. All the while the golden haired dog kept trying to escape my clutch to jump on Beef again. When Beef finally rose to his feet, I let the dog loose and it surged swiftly towards him for a second round. Beef knelt down towards the dog and starts to pet him wildly. The dog's tail wags rapidly from side to side and his forearms kept paddling against the pit of Beef's large stomach, as if the mutt was swimming for his life with its tongue out. Beef imitates the happy creature and sticks his own tongue out. "Beef, don't lower yourself to a dog's level." I sigh as the ember of positivity in my light head dwindles to a serious darkness, but he ignores me and keeps on mimicking it. Laughter erupts in the crowd ahead of us who was now stopped and looking back at Beef, the dog, and I.

"He has no collar." Beef says.

"So?" I tell him. "Come on, let's go I don't- they are all laughing at us."

"Since when do *you* care?"

The sad thing was, he was right. *"Why* did *I care?"*

"Maybe because one of the people laughing at you is Tianna Lecher." I answered myself. "Seriously Beef, we have to keep moving."

"Let's name him."

"What?"

"Name him. Let's name him. What's a good name for an Australian Sheppard Golden retriever mix?" He asks keeping his eyes on the dog.

"Beef seriously, Buddy," I say. Then I start to murmur with my lips closed, "Tianna is watching…"

"That's perfect!" he exclaims.

"Actually it's not."

"Buddy! His name is Buddy!"

"What? How do you even know it's a boy?"

"Trust me Cale, I know a lot about dogs. I saw his privates when he leaped on top of me." He says.

I had forgotten what a crazed freak Beef was about dogs. He knew every species. If he was to be reincarnated into an animal, it would be a dog.

"Probably a chow." I snicker to myself.

"Why?"

"Because! Have you seen the rolls and fat on those things? It's disturbing!"

"Shut up! Fat jokes are uncalled for." I defend.

"Come on Buddy." Beef signals and the dog follows. I drag my feet back to the group and we start walking again, except this time with a dog at our sides.

Even though we walked through demolished houses and destroyed playgrounds, Buddy seemed to lighten everyone's mood. He came to visit everyone in the group except me. He mainly stood by Beef's side and never left unless Beef ordered otherwise. Beef now kept a stick in his right hand that he would chuck far ahead of his tracks and Buddy would fetch it and bring it back. Everyone seemed to laugh at Buddy and recognize what a good dog he was. Even Britney, who had been mourning over her dead sisters, seemed delighted Buddy was around. It was like nothing had happened yesterday, we just got lost on a nature walk for school and we were now going home.

When I recognized the destruction was my house my heart sank. I didn't breathe. Buddy didn't bark. There was no movement besides the wind carrying off ashes of the apartment complex I lived in. I stood there like stone. The song I was listening to faded and a new song started to play "My Immortal" by Evanescence. I gazed at what used to be my house in complete trepidation. The only thing that came to mind was my mother. Glenda. The thought of her was all the motivation my legs needed to move forward. I stumbled over stones and wreckage towards what used to by my home. "Mom." I gasped. The strength inside of me felt drained. I felt the muscles of my body loosen themselves like strings being pulled apart. My body was vulnerable and weak. Invisible bruises and gashes started to twinge all over my body. Covered in imaginary wounds, they became infected and my skin felt itself flay off my bones. I couldn't imagine what was holding me together. Glenda, my marionette had met her demise in the middle of the puppet show and the strings attached to me fell on top of me like walls. My head started to pulse with fear and pain. Memories of my mom came rushing back like feral waves to my mind. Each glimpse of her face started to hit me like bullets. I grew weaker as I started to throw debris and wastes from side to side. My heart didn't beat. My fingers started to tremble and shake like a nervous player unable to control himself during a game of poker. I felt myself falling apart. My senses started to diminish. I couldn't hear, see, or smell. The only thing I could feel was the love I had for my mom. Every breathe I took hurt my chest, because I believed my heart was crying. "Mom!" I cried out. "Where are you, Mom? Mom… Mom!" I tried to think of the last time I had told her I love you, and now it was too late. She would never know that those three words were eating my insides away like somber acid. "I love you!" I whispered, and an eruption of molten magma started to flood inside of me when I found a burnt picture of my mother and I lying on the ground. "Mom." I whispered. How could I be so close to her, yet so far away? The one human being on this earth that I loved unconditionally and I trusted was gone. I didn't think that losing my mother would hurt me so bad, but it did. There was no more of myself left inside of me. I didn't think the helicopters and jets would have gone this far out of the school's radius to cover this all up, but I saw no end to the wreckage. Everything was on fire. There was nothing left. We were the last people on earth, slowly fleeting into nothingness. Slowly dying of an uncharted disease. Slowly disappearing.

I started to think about if only I had stayed home to die with my mother before I saw it and tears started to flood my eyes when I caught site of it. My mom's T.V. It was half buried underneath the rubble of my house, but it was still on. We had been salvaging ashes and parts that were paramount for our survival, and this was the only thing that mattered to me. The only thing of my mother that I had left. I walked over and knelt down next to it. She had left this for me. I was convinced that she knew I would come, and this was her final gift to me. I stared deeply into the television and I put my hand up against it. "Mom." I whispered one final time.

4. Hunting the Hunter

Watching the void blue screen on my mother's television set broke my heart. Even though I knew it could be healed, it would never be the same again. It was as if my heart was a vase and it shattered when it dropped a freefall into my gut. I started to replace each piece, gluing them together with what energy I had left back into a replica of what it used to be but somehow I felt it grow back a little crooked. The low screeching tone the T.V. made nearly chased away all of the sanity left inside of me. *"Who's to say I was sane in the first place."* I thought. A hand lay firmly on my right shoulder. Curiosity wasn't appetizing enough to look behind me to see whose it was. Plus, I didn't have the energy or the strength to turn away. I have stopped my depressing thoughts by now, and swore myself to never reveal such weakness again.

"I'm sorry Cale." Beef's voice softly whispered. I now knew he was the one taking my shoulder as his prisoner with his hand. I don't reply or acknowledge his feeble attempt to make me feel better. I just keep staring a hole through the television. He removes his hand from my shoulder at the same time I finally look away from the blank T.V. screen. I stood up with fire burning in my eyes. I turned around to see Beef standing in front of me. I walk around him and the entire group of survivors stood in a cluster watching me.

"What are you all looking at?" I shout. Nobody replies, like I knew they wouldn't. "The tape." I command. Nobody moves. "Brett! Give me the tape now!" I yell. Everyone looks to Brett, who is still gawking at me, to see what he was going to do. "Did I *stutter*?" I roared. This shook him up a bit, and he pulled the tape out from his pocket. Britney snagged the tape from his hand and yanked the black camera bag from Amanda's shoulder. She walked over to me with both objects in her hand and got started on hooking the camera up to the television without me even asking. It both irritated and excited me a bit that she knew what I was thinking and followed my unspoken orders without rebellion. The loss of my mother's life drained so much of my energy and will, that I became restless. I didn't feel my heart beat. No emotions besides anger projected from my body. And no remorse second guessed my actions.

It took Britney less than a minute to call out, "It's ready." And I am standing over her. I can feel the presence of the others walking slowly towards my back gathering around the T.V. Amanda is the first one to approach.

The television flickers from the blue screen to a black and white view of frenzied static. Britney hits the television on the side of the box and an image of Mr. Rusenkell appears on the screen. It seems as if he was adjusting the T.V. from inside as the motion picture wobbles into place. He stops altering the screen and he exits the scene. About two feet away from where Ruse was standing stands a table that had three cages on the top, each labeled with a number. In the cage to the left, that was labeled "1", a white rabbit with dark eyes starts to quiver in fear. In cage 2, the middle one, an all black cat with green silvery eyes starts to hiss. Cage 3 contains a dog that starts to bark strenuously. Buddy starts to bark back at the screen until Beef muzzles him with his hands. Mr. Rusenkell re-enters the screen except this time behind the table and wearing a white apron that has three dark blue letters on the top right corner of it: M.S.C. As he puts black gloves on he starts to speak to us. "We have finally been able to capture the raw essence of substance 36 via forcing its pressure into these glass containers." He holds a green bottle up that seemed to be empty except for a tiny bright glare that started to rotate in circles inside the bottle. "It was not easy securing these minor particles from its source, but we managed to grasp what we could before the source merely disintegrated into the air. We aren't exactly sure why it happened but we have come to conclude that the source had some kind of hypersensitivity to a human trait, such as our smell, or the way our skin feels. All of us wore suits when we gathered the thick liquid substance into the bottles, but as soon as we concealed each bottle the liquid evaporated completely leaving nothing but a tiny light that floats around looking for a host. The host this source was using was the molten lava from an uncharted volcano in the Pacific Ocean. Whatever substance 36 is, it has been using the lava of the newly found volcano as its own personal host. The weird part is that when lava cools it hardens, or so we thought. The magma that rested on the side of the volcano that we found had elapsed for over ten decades. We measured the molten rock's temperature and it was at a cooler 273.15 kelvin degrees, which is the temperature at which ice melts. The volcano is surrounded by a small undiscovered island. No signs of life seem to inhabit the habitat. No signs of bugs, birds, or any organism. Just mere exotic trees and simple plants that-"

"Get to the point Ruse!" Max yells on my left.

"Yell louder..." I thought mordantly, *"Maybe he'll hear you."*

"What is this thing!" he yells a bit louder

"I wasn't being serious." I told him in my head as I rolled my eyes at the fact that he misinterpreted my sarcasm; Even though I never had spoken out loud.

Ruse continues on about the island which he found no forms of life, besides the agriculture and this volcano that seemed to be active. Then he begins to pull out a syringe and instructs his motions, "I am now going to take this syringe and extract as much of substance 36 I can from the bottle. I will only be able to take one sample because the substance will escape and split up as soon as I take the needle out of the tiny hole I'm about to make in the cap. Let the record show that this is the first time anyone has conducted with such unknown particles. We believe that since substance 36 has controlled the oxidization of hot magma, it can control the overreactions in our body creating an indestructible immune system allowing us to live longer and without illness." Ruse becomes silent for a minute and he gulps. A tear starts to build in his eye, but he holds it back as his voice cracks when he explains, "Also...If mixed with the radio activity of-" he struggles to find his words. He sighs and finishes, "chemo therapy...and it could lead to the long wanted cure for-" he struggles again. "C-cancer…" he whispers. He struggles to start up again, "We have diagnosed cancer into specimens 1, 2 and 3. I will now attempt to cure them with substance 36." He clears his throat and throws his gas mask on securing it tightly so no skin or hair was visible. He picks up both the green bottle and syringe. The syringe dives its pointy needle into the cap of the green bottle. The glare on the bottle disappears as Mr. Rusenkell extracts the air inside the syringe. Once it contains as much substance as it can, Ruse dumps the bottle into a trash can near him. He leans forward over cage 1 and finds the rabbit's neck with the syringe. The rabbit doesn't move or try to get away like it was trained for this. After he gives the rabbit about a third of the substance he leans into cage 2 for the cat. The cat is more defensive to the intrusion but Ruse makes sure the needle is stabbed into the cat's neck. The dog gives Mr. Rusenkell the hardest time, but he finishes the rest of the syringe off on its neck. All three of the animals fall asleep after they are given the shot of substance 36. When he is done, Mr. Rusenkell throws the needle away in the trash can and walks up to the T.V. again. The screen fumbles around as he reaches out towards us and the image of Mr. Rusenkell is overcome by a violent snowstorm of white and black static.

"This had better not be it!" I yelled. "Are you kidding me-"but before I could go onto a rampage, Mr. Rusenkell is back into the picture without his gas mask. He stares right at us in complete discontentment and starts to speak.

"Substance 36 has failed to cure the cancer of all three specimens, but something has happened to them. Something extremely different and unexpected to our knowledge." He moves away and behind the cages again. This time we see the rabbit and dog are still asleep, but the cat is wide awake. The cat stares its green silver eyes straight into the camera right at us as if it knows we were all staring at it, its posture in stone. "Both specimen 1 and 3 have died. Specimen 1 oddly did not die of cancer, but died of rapid growth that it did not have the chromosomes to adapt to the change, so it bled from every hole of its body. It's own essence attempted to escape its natural habitat because it's body did not have the support to keep itself alive." That is when I notice the rabbit's white fleece coat of fur is covered in some red, as if someone had spilt red punch on it. "Specimen 3 however was completely unaffected by substance 36 and shortly died of the cancer we had put in it. Specimen 3's death made no connection what so ever to substance 36 even though we injected it into their main air stream." Buddy whimpers at the sight of the dead canine, and so does Beef.

"It's just a stupid dog." I thought. Buddy looks at me when I look down at him.

"What are you *looking at?"* Buddy doesn't stray his eyes from mine when he gives me a bark.

"Don't judge me you mutt!" I yell in my head, and buddy barks twice more as if he heard me. My eyes roll back to the T.V. and Mr. Rusenkell is now talking about specimen 2.

"Specimen 2 however, showed a complete reaction to substance 36. We have discovered that the cancer still circulates in the blood stream, but so does the substance 36 we injected into it three days ago. Specimen 2 oddly enough has an extra chromosome in its genetics that we discovered. Most of the feline species do not carry this chromosome, but unknowingly specimen 2 does. Let the record show that we did not know this feline had evolved into its next stage of the evolution. It seems that evolution like this only occurs when-"Ruse is cut off by a shaking image of black and white static.

"What the heck!?" What's going on?!" I yell.

"The battery is dead." Britney says as she holds up the video camera to prove it.

"Well find the outlet this T.V. is plugged into!" I order.

"That won't do us any good." She replies.

"Why! You can charge the camera-"

"That is exactly my point. The case the camera came in contained no extra battery or charger cord that could revitalize the battery." Britney says.

"Dangit! What now?" I howl.

Cough! Cough! The deathly sound captures everyone's attention to its starting place. A girl with short black hair starts to cough up and sneeze out blood. We all start to back away from her except for two other girls who are at her side. "Bianca!" They cry out in sync. They start to shake her as her eyes roll up and back. Bianca starts to do all the shaking herself and blood slides out of her ears, nose, mouth, and eyes just like Preston. When she dies, the two girls at the corpse's sides are crying nonstop. They moan and wear out her name. Bianca, Bianca, Bianca.

The dirty blonde haired friend on the left stood up as if she was going to throw up when she falls back and faints.

"Kristen!" the dark brown haired girl leaves Bianca's right side and attends Kristen.

It was silent for a moment before the sound of a chopper pervaded through the air. All of us look up towards the sky to find the helicopter. The sound grew louder and louder but we still didn't find any sign of a flying mobile. Suddenly the chopper finally made appearance in the sky and we became relieved that help had arrived. *"Finally!"* I thought as everyone else and I flailed our arms in the air calling out for the helicopter. Cheering erupted in the crowd of survivors. Help was here. *"I guess we aren't the last humans on earth."* I thought.

"I wouldn't be too sure about that." I grimaced.

"What are you talking about?"

"M.S.C." I thought.

"What?"

"You see the giant letters on the side of the helicopter?"

When I read the initials I stopped my entire "Save me!" parade. This wasn't help coming to rescue us. This was *them* coming to finish us off. Another Helicopter came into view behind the first and following that one was another. The three of them circled us in the sky above us like vultures, and that's exactly what they were. These vultures were here to finish us off. Everyone still jumped up and down and called out to the vultures asking them to rescue them, except for me. "Stop!" I yelled ending everyone's wanna-be-rescued-carnival. "They aren't help!-"

I am cut off by a loud blast. All of us stood straight and stiff. Scared. An ice shattering scream echoed through the air. The dark haired girl screams again before she is silenced by another gun shot that overpowered her voice. That is when everyone scatters and tries to hide. My heart pounds against my rib cage trying to escape my body as I hop over wreckage. More gun shots are fired and I run faster than I ever have before. I hear the ground directly behind me explode with each bullet that covers my tracks. Ahead of me is a spot of shade that is covered by a couple of destroyed walls. I dive into the darkness when I hear the gun shots explode against the half ceiling above me. I stand up in the shade I found protection in and looked out into the daylight. The gun shots quit firing and a helicopter started to prepare itself for landing. The lower it got, the more anxious I became. Rage started to flood throughout me.

"Relax, Cale."

"No."

"She is still alive."

"How do you know? And what makes you think that is who I'm thinking about?"

"*Because I know your thoughts. And look behind you.*"

Before I can fully turn around someone wraps their arms around me pulling me deeper into the shadow. "Cale!" a velvet voice cries, "What's happening to us?" When my pupils finally adjust to the darkness I notice Tianna is gazing at me with fear in her wide eyes.

"*She knew my name.*" I thought. I was astonished.

"*Are you going to answer her? Or are you going to continue gawking at her.*"

I had no idea where to begin with her. I've haven't said one word to her in over four years and here we were hiding for our lives. So many things came to mind but I could not find one word to answer her. "Okay." I say.

"*That's it? That's what you held yourself back for?* Okay?! *Wow you're a real smooth ladies man aren't ya? It doesn't even make any sense!* Okay? *Are you serious?*"

I ruined another chance to gain influence with Tianna when I turned my back on her and faced a helicopter landing right where we gathered around my mother's television. I turn back to Tianna and I order her, "Stay here. Hide. I'll come back and get you."

She grabs my shoulder and stops it from turning on her again and tells me, "No. I'm going with you."

"No." I command, "You'll be safe here. Just stay here."

"What if I don't want to be safe? Who are you to tell me what to do? Where are you going anyways? To get yourself killed? Then what? Whose orders do I follow after you die? No it doesn't work like that for me." She scolds.

Her words are fierce and sturdy. There is no doubt in her eyes. "I don't have a plan." I tell her.

"Then do what you were going to do before you tried to stop me from following. Follow those instincts."

"My instincts were to keep you here away from danger."

"Well *my* instincts are telling me not to stay here alone."

"Whatever." I murmur.

"Don't *whatever* me!" She sasses.

"You sound like my-"I couldn't even get myself to finish the three letter word. I stutter a couple syllables before I release a "Shut up!" out of pure frustration of my words being boggled.

"You shut up!"

"You shut up!" I mimic.

"No, you!"

"You!"

"Shut up!"

"I told you first!" I bicker.

"Really? How 'bout you both shut up!"

"Shut up!"

A piercing explosion startles both Tianna and I from our nagging and we fall to the ground in sync, searching for refuge on the dirt ground.

"What happened to the nice, innocent Tianna I thought she was?"

"I don't know but I think I like her even more now. Strangely."

"Quick!" I hiss under my breath in fear of being heard, "Let's get out of here!"

Tianna and I start to creep out into the sunlight to get a better view at the landing helicopter. Before it even touches the ground, five men in black uniforms and gas masks jump out of the sliding door each of them carrying large guns in their hands aiming them wherever they looked. "Stay close" I whisper behind me. I look back at her to make sure she was ready. She was. I was about to make a break for it with Tianna at my back when I turn around and I jump backwards, knocking Tianna to the floor, as I see a face directly in front of me.

"Holy Batman! You scared the hell out of me!" the face hissed.

"What the-? Who- the- Who are you?" I hiss back.

"Brian, what the heck are you doing?" Tianna whispers.

"What's it look like I'm doing? I'm hiding like you two pansies." He replies.

"Get down! Be quiet!" I quietly order as we move back deeper into the shadows until we reach the dead end. The engine to the helicopter cuts off and it is silent throughout the ruins of my apartment complex. The silence ruined my escape plan. If we were to run now, we would surely be heard running across the remains. "Where are the other two helicopters?" I ask quietly.

"They started heading east as that one out there started to land." Brian answers, his voice carried the volume of a normal conversation.

"Be quiet!" I whisper, "East? What are you some kind of Boy Scout?"

"The sun is setting directly opposite from where they went, so that makes it east. Common sense." He says in the same tone as last, ignoring my last attempt to quiet him.

"Do you think this is some kind of game Boy Scout Brian? Do you think that in this version of Hide-and-Seek, when they shoot you that you get to start over? Pipe down before you get us killed!"

"First of all, Don't call me that. Call me by my last name, Bozzo. Alright? And why? Are you scared?"

I was about to quiet him down again when I hear footsteps approaching our haven. All three of us stopped breathing and moving. The footsteps crunched louder against the dirt and the sound stopped. I gaze at the end of the entrance to the wreckage fort and a man dressed in a black combat suit with a black gas mask aims his gun directly at me. Tianna and I start to move towards the back right corner of the wreckage fort and *Bozzo* silently shuffles to the left corner. We don't make any movements or sound but the man keeps creeping closer to the back of the shadows. He edges closer and closer towards us. I realize soon his eyes will adjust to the darkness even through his gas mask and it was only a matter of time before he found us. The sound of rocks tumbling against each other echoes from the light outside and the man swiftly turns around aiming at the entrance, finding no one. That's when Bozzo leaps on the man's back forcing him to drop his gun. *"Crap!"* I thought as I got up quickly to fetch the gun the man had dropped. Bozzo wrestled the man to the floor throwing punches at each other keeping their grunts at a minimal volume. *"Oh* now *he listens."* He tears off the man's gas mask and immediately covers his mouth. The man reaches for a knife that was hidden in his boot and stabs Bozzo in the left leg. Bozzo quietly grunts in pain and slams the man's armed hand down sending the knife flying. I pick up the gun the man had dropped and I aimed it at the man's face. But he kept on struggling as Bozzo was pinning him to the ground with one of his hands covering his mouth. "Who sent you?" I order quietly. The man stops struggling and he looks up at me with hate in his eyes. "Who are you people?" I ask even quieter. Bozzo doesn't let his mouth loose when the face of the man starts to deteriorate. The flesh of his skin starts to decay and his eyeballs melt like a fast paced decomposition. Bozzo instantly jerks his hand away from the decomposing man and backs away frightened of the sight. I drop the gun when I see the man has rotted into a skeleton. Not six seconds ago he was a man maybe in his mid thirties of forties, his face flushed with fury, and now he was a mummified corpse that looked like it belonged in a museum. "What did you do to him?" I ask Bozzo hesitating to look at him.

"I- I- Don't know- I- just tried to keep him- from yell-yelling…What just happened man?" He says as he raises his hands. Both Tianna and I flinch back. "I swear, I- don't know what happened, I just… was so angry and… all of a sudden he just- he just…"

Gunshots interrupt him and I picked the large two handed gun up from the ground out of instinct to survive. I snatch a shiny hand gun from the side of the decomposed corpse and stick it in the back of my pants. *"Might come in handy."* I thought. I grab Tianna with my free hand and pull over the skeletal corpse outside towards the light leaving Bozzo behind. I admit I was afraid of him, but not nearly as afraid when I heard a thundering voice boom, "Hold it right there! Put your hands up and walk slowly over here." I don't follow the order and I just stand there in shock looking for where the order came from. "That's it, come closer. Get down on your knees and put your hands up!" The voice orders again. I do nothing the voice tells me to do when he commands, "Good, now where are the others?" I realize he isn't talking to me now and I slowly creep closer outside of the fort into the daylight.

"I don't know!" Amanda's voice pleads. At the end of the fort I peek my head around the edge to see Amanda in the middle of the open on her knees with her hands behind her head. "What do you want from me?" She cries out.

"Shut up! We will ask the questions!" a new voice comes in. I peek my head out further and I see two men dressed symmetrically aiming their guns at Amanda. "Where are the others!" the man jabs the end of his weapon into Amanda's jaw and she falls on her face. Her head jolts sideways quickly whipping her dark red hair around so only half her face was visible and from a distance I could see a shiny red flicker in her eye that flashed the area around her. The man dropped his gun and started to shake.

"What is it? What's happening?" the other man asks.

The only reply that is being made is the muted screaming underneath the man's gas mask. He tears his mask off and his screaming volume shoots up about twenty notches. His head was on fire and it spread on to his entire body. He startled the other man as he yelped and shrieked in torture on the ground until the other man shot him three times. He no longer wailed in agony but his body kept burning like a bonfire pit.

"We located another hybrid." the other man says into his intercom calmly, "what shall I do with her?"

"Kill her! Kill her now! That is an order!" The static voice replies.

"Copy that." He holds his gun up to Amanda's face.

Bang! Bang! Two shots were fired. Tianna's grip on my lower back tightened, digging her nails into my skin. My finger slowly let go of the trigger as the man fell to his knees. He dropped his gun and falls on Amanda. Amanda shoves him off of her legs and gets up and starts to look around her. This was the first time I've ever killed someone. The feeling brought forth a lob in my throat like I had just swallowed a big pill.

"I just killed a man." I thought. *"I just murdered someone."*

"Better him, rather than you."

"This can't be right." I reflected, *"This feeling…what's happening to me."*

"Don't run from it. Embrace it. You can't hide from it, it's who you are."

"No its not." I assured myself even though I didn't fully understand the concept of what I was thinking about. Amanda still searched around her for the gun that saved her life. Slowly I walk out into the light dragging the heavy gun by its end. The barrel created a dirt line that followed my tracks towards Amanda. I stopped walking when she finally found me with her confused eyes. She glanced down at the gun in my hand, then back at my face. The silent stare we shared was understandably enough gratitude, so there was no need for the words we both couldn't find under our stubbornness and fear. Bozzo came out of the debris fort shortly after and walked right past me as if it were just another day at Stellar High.

"There were five of them." A new voice breaks the silence. Cocoa walks from behind a broken wall that no longer supported its brothers around it. "That's two down, where are the other three?"

"There's one of them in there." Bozzo points to the shaded fortress. "Two to go." He says. I raise an eyebrow at him.

"*One* to go." Another voice enters. Max carries a severed arm holding onto a small gun in his left hand and in his right; he carries a gas mask that drips red goo. Amanda gives him a disgusted look when Max dissembles the gun from the amputated hand. "What?" he asks her. "Self defense." He assures while he flaunts the hand and mask like trophies in front of her.

"Why are they doing this?" Tianna whispers even though she knew we didn't' have any answers to that question.

"Why don't you ask *him!*" A short, black haired boy yells as a man dressed in a black combat suit and gas mask tumbles in front of him. My gun aims for him until the boy says, "He's unarmed." Then I lower my weapon.

"Who are you?" Brett orders from Amanda's side, stealing my line.

"Where did Brett come from?" I asked myself.

"That coward just likes to bask in his own arrogance." As much as I hated to admit it, Brett had assumed the position of an unofficial leader to our tribe of survivors.

"He's my brother!" Marcus called out from behind me holding Baley's hand.

"Where is everyone coming from?" I thought.

The short boy looks up over my shoulder and watches Marcus walk slowly towards him. "Jonah…you're- you're alive!" Marcus yells. "How?"

Jonah doesn't break into tears or smile at his brother. He simply kicks the man on the ground and shouts in a very boring tone, "Let's deal with the now." He glares at me as if that statement was meant for me. I glare back.

Brett takes initiative and starts to walk over towards the man injured on the floor. He takes the gas mask off the man calmly and sets it down next to him. "Who are you people?" He asks. The man spits in his face and I nearly laugh out loud. Jonah kicks the man in the back and he grunts. Brett asks again, "Who are you people?" after he wipes his face dry.

The man is quiet for a solid four seconds before Brett asks again, this time more thorough, and he finally answers, "You guys are-"he is cut off by the sound of a gunshot. My eyes dart around to see where the bullet had been fired from as soon as the man's face plummets into the ground. Another blast is sounded through the air and we stop looking for whoever is shooting and run again. Tianna and I dive for the shaded wreck fort again. Peering out of the shadows into broad day light we saw another man dressed in all black shooting his gun from inside the helicopter that landed. His familiar voice called out, "James hurry up! Get out here and cover me!" All while he kept shooting. The gun in my hand raised and aimed for him but missed when I pulled the trigger. I shoot and miss multiple times as he backs away from his post further into the helicopter.

"Keep firing and move closer!" I ordered myself.

"What? No! That is suicide!"

"Suicide will be to remain here until the other helicopters receive the emergency call. Then what will you do?"

"I- I don't know- I can't!" I scream at myself. Before I could argue myself again I hear a familiar hostile voice whispering something, even over the loud blasts of gunfire, like he was right there in my ear.

"Tom! Abort your post, we need to call for back up!" the voice pleaded.

"Do it now!" I scold and I seal my right index finger around the trigger as I charge my body to the helicopter.

"Who is that?" I hear the familiar voice in my ear again as both men in the helicopter duck for cover to shield themselves from my rapid gunfire. I was so impressed with my hearing I didn't notice how close I was to the helicopter when the worst thing that could have happened, happened. My gun had stopped firing off even though my finger held the trigger back.

"Great job loser, you wasted all the ammo and didn't hit one of your targets. Ladies and Gentleman please give Mr. Cale Valens a standing ovation!" I grimace in my head.

"This was your *idea-"*

"Later, we got company." I don't realize I'm standing five feet away from the black helicopter staring stupid at my gun until my targets arise from their cowering fetal positions and start to take a more aggressive stance. Their guns steer directly at me. *"Oh. Damn."* I chuck the heavy empty gun forth at the two men in the helicopter. Not even giving my eyes a chance to see if my toss had made contact with at least one of them, I dived underneath the helicopter. I flipped over onto my back and felt a pain in my lower back as it hit the ground. Instinct took over as soon as I remembered I had stashed that hand gun behind my butt. I knew it would come in handy. I whirled the gun around and pointed it up at the helicopter above me. Bang! Bang! Bang!

"Ah! God-! Arggg!" a man bellowed in pain.

"Amazing." I sarcastically congratulate myself, *"You manage to shoot three blind shots and hit someone, but you waste an entire round-"*

"Not. Now." I ordered. Through a bullet hole I made in the bottom of the helicopter I see a man securing his knee with both of his hands.

"Tom! Are you okay?" The other man yells trying to calm him down.

"Don't move!" Brett's voice instructs, "Put your hands up where I can see them!" My head lifts up off from the ground craning my neck so my chin touched the top of my chest. I see a pair of legs that were unmistakably Brett's. The gun that was still being held in position with both of my hands was finally put behind me and shoved down my back again.

"Son of a-"I snort as I start to assemble myself to my knees.

"I *said* don't move!" Brett repeats. I crawl out from under the helicopter and rise, my eyes never leaving Brett's face. "You're welcome." He says.

"No." I state, *"You're* welcome."

"I just saved you." Brett yells loud enough so everyone could hear his *good* deed. But I really knew what he was doing. He was trying to make a fool out of me. He was trying to gain everyone's respect. He had no intention in helping anyone but himself. He just wanted the attention. How could I see right through the face of Irvine, but everyone else just fell hypnotized to him? Whatever spell he was trying to cast, he would find me dead before I caught myself under it.

"I don't need saving." I strictly told him turning my shoulder so he was out of any peripheral sight I might have of him. I reached into my pocket and pulled out a smashed carton of cigarettes. Pleading to myself, begging to be at least one surviving cigarette left, I found none that were usable. Even angrier now, I tossed the carton and turned back to the helicopter where one man, whose face was extremely familiar to me, stood on his knees with his hands open in the air. The other man lied on his side grasping on to a wound I was convinced was caused by me. Slowly, one by one Stellar High survivors crept out from their hiding places and walked towards Brett. I could feel them moving behind me. I jumped up into the helicopter and grabbed the man who was on his knees with his hands in the air by his shirt. Not caring for his personal space I pulled him in so close to me that our heads almost banged against each other. It was unclear to me if I was mad at not having any cigarettes left or if I had grown weary of getting shot at and wanted answers. "Why are you-"Bam! For a moment my eyes had closed and I felt a swirling pain in my forehead. When I realized he had hammered me with his head I took a step back and pulled out the gun behind me and shoved the end in between the man's eyes.

"Tom! Stop!" the injured man wails.

"Tom." I thought, *"Tom!"* I finally recognized the man's voice. My eyes looked at the injured man like he was crazy. *"That must be the weak one... what's his name..."*

"Shut up James! I won't let this little kid strip me of my dignity!"

"Ah! James! Thank you Tom." I thought. "Well, if I'm the little kid that has you hostage, what does that make you Tom? Looks like jerry wins again eh Tom?" His face made a sign like he was either confused or pissed off at my last comment. "Tom and Jerry?" I asked. He doesn't change the confusing aura around him. "The cat and mouse? God! How old *are* you?"

"I got it the first time, runt." Tom hisses. The gun in my hand presses against his face harder, straining his neck back even further.

"Where is Mr. Rusenkell, Tom?" I interrogate.

"You know these guys?" Brett asks still pointing his gun at James.

"Remember the two *police* officers that arrested Mr. Rusenkell yesterday?" Amanda interrupts entering the scene, "Well these two posers would be them."

"Where is he?" I inquire again, daring myself to pull my index finger back.

"He's at headquarters under solitary confinement." James answers for Tom. Tom shoots him a glare.

"Where is *headquarters*?" Amanda asks, trying to take over my interrogation. I roll my eyes and almost backhand her until James decides to give her an eager answer.

"I-I can take you there."

"Does it look like I was born yesterday? I'm not that stupid to just fall into a trap." I scold. Even though demanding him to take me there was my first instinct and intention, I would somehow rearrange it to make it look like I had come up with the idea all on my own. "Why are you people trying to kill us? Where is everyone else at? Where are the police? The government?"

"We were ordered to eliminate the city so there wouldn't be another incident. You guys are not even supposed to exist. They have reported no survivors this morning on the news, we came to make sure of it."

"Whoa! Slow down!" Brett orders stepping up into the helicopter next to me, "First of all, what incident? And second, where are the police? Why haven't *they* been the ones-"

James doesn't even let Brett finish before he quickly answers, "Because the *police* are clueless. MSC is an undercover organization that deals with scientific methods and uses to modify the human race into a more perfect state, now please help me stop the hemorrhaging."

"Hmmm let me think," I tell him, "I'm trying to think of the last man who said he was trying to make the world a perfect place with only perfect humans… something to do with a final solution… Oh yes! Hitler! That's right! The last time a man said that, millions of people died!"

"Please, it isn't my fault. I'm just a pawn. I'm losing too much blood here; I need help taking the bullet out."

"What makes you think I'm going to waste my energy on someone who tried to kill me? Pawn or King, it doesn't matter to me. The only thing that matters now is that *you* are playing on the wrong side of the board!" I kick Tom back and aim my gun at James.

"Cale! Stop it now!" Brett commands as he scurries over to James to help him. Of course he would try to act like the bigger person in front of everyone. Punk. I felt everyone's eyes on my back daggering me, waiting for me to make my next move. I wasn't about to let Brett start calling the shots. And I was not about to be made a fool out of either.

"Get up!" I yell at Tom, "Now!" I lift him up by his suit, tear off the intercom device latched on his shoulder and throw him out of the helicopter. I pick up the gun that was next to him and I shout, "Where's Beef?" praying that he might still be alive as I waited for an answer.

"Right here." Beef shouts back from behind Cocoa. Cocoa steps out of the line of sight between Beef and I and I see that Beef is kneeling down next to Buddy.

"Think fast." I say as I chuck the gun at him and with a great attempt, he doesn't catch it like I knew he wouldn't. "He," I point to Tom, "Doesn't move."

"And where do you think *you* are going?" Amanda inquires.

"I'm going to find Mr. Rusenkell."

"Not without me." She arrogates.

"I hope to God without you." I say.

"She comes." Brett assumes winning back his artificial leader role.

"Who said *you* were going?" I challenge.

"Who said *you* were in charge?" Brett mocks. I could see what he was doing. He was trying to play it off like we were all in this together, but I knew deep down he was still the same arrogant, egotistical Brett Gooding I fell in hate with. Of course everyone would side with him, he was a natural leader.

"A deceptive one." I add, *"He can't fool me though. I know what lurks in his dark heart."*

"Do you ever grow weary of being negative all the time? I mean how do you know that Brett is trying to harm you?"

Astonished with myself, I couldn't believe I had actually admitted that Brett might be the slightest bit right, *"Please tell me your kidding. Please tell me you are* not *becoming another one of Brett's drones. I thought you were better than that!"*

"Quite honestly, I am just fed up with trying to sabotage his every move. I obviously do not have the timing down." I expected myself to argue, but I felt no compelling irritation in my head. Just silence. I wasn't sure if that was a good or bad thing. "Fine. Whatever. Why don't we take everybody then." I suggest entering back into the real conversation.

"We can't do that. We can only take five." Brett says.

"Why?"

"There are five suits back here. Five suits. Five disguises. Unless you *want* to go in and give them what they want." Brett enticed.

Why did this kid always have an answer to everything I threw at him. "Then that leaves two left."

"I'll go." Cocoa quickly announces without hesitation.

"You know we aren't going on a food run, right?" I joke, but no one besides Beef chuckles at the fact that I was subtly calling Cocoa fat.

Cocoa just gives me a repulsive stare when Brett says, "Cocoa is more capable then you could imagine."

"Count me in." Britney snaps.

"I don't think so." Amanda denies.

"*Britney* is more capable then you can imagine," I mock, "after all she was the one who figured out how to play the tape after *somebody* decided to be a klutz." Britney gathers her mouth to the left side of her face and smirks at Amanda as she hops in the helicopter. Amanda smirks back.

"You five aren't going anywhere without me." A new face interrupts.

"Why does everyone want to get themselves killed?" I thought.

"I am coming too." He says. A blonde hair, blue eyed boy walks up through the crowd of survivors. A girl with dark brown hair follows him tugging on his shirt trying to restrain him. I was positive this boy and girl were not with us when we escaped Stellar High. Then suddenly Jonah came to mind.

"Sorry, we're full." I said.

"You have room for one more." He replied.

"Actually, if you can't count, we have five already. Five suits. Five disguises." I mocked Brett.

"*Actually,* there's six suits." He corrects as he stares at Tom who is lying on the ground as Beef kept him at gun point.

"Phil! Stop! Stay *here*!" The brunette girl behind him begs as she keeps pulling on his shirt. He shines her off and keeps his gaze on me as if I was the one recruiting people to come on our suicide mission to rescue Mr. Rusenkell.

"Sorry. Any more will just slow us down." Brett says. Phil, never takes his gaze off of me.

I nod my head upwards, lifting my chin. "Grab his suit and gas mask. You're coming with us." I order, defying Brett's orders. I was not about to be tamed, and I had a sensuous feeling about this Phil. Something in me wanted to respect his wishes. Tears start to erupt out of the brunettes eyes, whose hands are still clutched on to Phil's shirt, wrinkling the front of it. Phil gives me a tiny smile and turns around to the girl latched onto the back of his shirt and starts to whisper into her ear, but I could hear him as if he was whispering into my own ear.

"I'll be back so soon, you won't have time to miss me, Laura." He whispers, "I'm doing this to protect you." Phil then gives her a kiss and I roll my eyes. He doesn't look at her again as he takes the suit and gas mask that Beef had stripped off of Tom and hops into the helicopter with us. His intimate affection with Laura made me search through the crowd of survivors. Straining my eyes for Tianna. When I found her, she was standing all alone. Staring at me. She mouthed "Come back for us." and I could hear her sweet voice in my head.

I look down in embarrassment and refused to blush, but before I let it get to me completely I turn to injured James and order, "Take us now" rudely.

It was a risk taking a joy ride in an enemy helicopter dressed as one of them. James, could have set a trap for right when we landed. If he was smart enough to know I would never pull the trigger to the gun at his head because I still needed him, he probably *would* have set us up. But James was weak; I could feel his weakness throbbing with the mask of fear. I don't understand how anyone could fear an 18-year-old. Even I don't find the adolescent at all related to intimidating. But as long as I had the upper hand, I was going to soak up as much leverage as I could get. We were now hunting the hunter, who had been trying to eliminate us, as James said they were ordered to do. So many questions still hanged on the end of my tongue but my thoughts interfered with every question I created by creating a new question. There simply was not enough time.

"We're getting close." James announced after a two hour period of silence. We would have fell asleep if it weren't for the racket the helicopter was making. I could tell the only thing on everybody's mind was food. We all were starved.

"James, do you have any food?" Brett asks.

"Of course, we weren't expected back at base for another three days, so we stocked up on-"

"Food!" Cocoa yells, "Tell us where the food is!" I chuckle and he gives me another one of his famous *I hate Cale Valens* stares.

"Behind the net, in the back." James calls over his shoulder. Cocoa is the first one to stand up and search for the food behind the black net.

He pulls out a wooden crate and starts to claw at whatever was inside. I give him a disgusted look at the fact that he doesn't even think about sharing.

"Every man for himself." I thought.

"Oh, you're back. Yay..."

"I've decided to forgive you for your treason."

"I didn't think forgiveness was in your vocabulary."

"Hungry?" a small hand holds out a golden biscuit in front of my face. I look up to where the voice came from and Britney is looking at me with hope in her eyes.

"No thanks." I state without taking another whiff of the sweet bakery smell the biscuit possessed. Britney sits down right next to me.

"Thanks for sticking up for me." She says before she takes a bite of the biscuit she offered to me.

"Mm-hmmm."

"It's okay to be approved and accepted you know. You don't always have to wear a mask."

"How would you *know?"* I thought.

"I know, I know, how would I know right? Well we all can't be popular, otherwise I wouldn't have people like you to pick on."

"Good to see your ego hasn't faltered."

"It's a joke."

"Popularity is just a state of mind." I tell her.

"Wow... That's deep."

"Well when you spend your life in the shallow end, you never find the treasures hidden in the deep."

"Wow! You just keep them coming don't you?" she laughs. Contagiously I laugh too. Usually I can't stand to be around people, but the similarities between me and Britney, made it tolerable to exist for once in my life. "I found this." She murmurs as she pulls out a pack of cigarettes and hands them to me.

"You know, a true good friend, would have handed me a pack of nicotine gum, help you quit stuff." I half laugh as I receive her gift and pull out a cig.

"Well let's just say I'm not a *good* girl." She says as she steals the cigarette in my hand and sticks it in her mouth. I light hers and I light one of my own.

Britney passes out on my shoulder after a half an hour. Across from us Brett and Amanda are mirroring Britney and I in almost the exact same position. Both of them slept as well. Cocoa was too busy still eating out of his third crate. And Phil sat in the corner away from us all.

"If you miss her so much, why are you risking your life?" I ask. Slowly he turns his head and looks at me.

"Because." He answers.

"Because…" I lead.

"Because I'm a freak."

I burst out into laughter almost waking Britney. "God, if I had a dime every time I heard that one. You don't know what it's like to be a freak, Phil."

"You wouldn't understand. You weren't there."

"Oh? Alright then Dr. Phil, enlighten me." I say widening my eyes and raising both my eyebrows for a quick half a second. I stick another cig in my mouth and toss the carton over to him. I pass him my lighter after I light myself up. He hesitates before he falls into temptation just like I knew he would.

"There was this girl" he started, "she-she was looking for some girl named Jane. Anyways, this was in the gym…the day of the quarantine." He takes a deep breath as if yesterday's tragedy was years ago. "She came up to me and Laura-"

"Laura who?"

"Laura Forkner? My girlfriend. She was there before we-"

"Oh right, right carry on."

"So this girl, she came up to me and Laura asking for help, blood running down her nose and mouth. Afraid, I stepped away from her at first. I remember hearing a scream and a bottle shattering. She just kept asking for Jane, and I told her I'd help her. I asked her what her name was. She said her name was Ellie. I asked her who Jane was to her and she said she was her sister. So we started searching. Hours passed, and it started with Ellie coughing. It took hours before it started to get really bad and more blood came out of her nose, ears, and mouth. Then she collapsed. And more and more people just started to fall over. Nearly all of them fell down. Puking, coughing, sneezing. Laura and I had tried to pull her up but all she could do was point. We looked to wear she was pointing and we finally found Jane. A dark haired girl with snow white skin. Jane rushed by us to hover over Ellie. Tears in her eyes as she screamed. All kinds of screams started to echo through the gym. Some of the police who took off their masks started having the same reaction that Ellie had. I was afraid I was going to lose Laura. Three boys backed up into us by accident and all of a sudden there was this green light that circled us. A half circle that only covered us six and Ellie. We fell to the floor and couldn't escape the bubble that had us trapped inside. About a minute after trying to escape the bombs came. Explosions of heat and fire incinerated everyone around us. There was no way out of this bubble and no way in. The explosions did not reach us and we survived. We thought we were the only survivors... but apparently we weren't. Jonah helped us get through the city, salvaging what we could. Jane never said a word after what happened. I tried to get her to talk, but she was incapable of doing so."

"So how does any of this make you a freak?" I interrupt.

"I'm getting to that."

"Well sometime today please!"

"Whatever, it's not even worth it."

"Aw sure it is, Dr. Phil." He doesn't answer. He goes back to being alone in his corner and throws his cigarette out the window. I feel a little bad for being a jerk, but it was just my nature. And it was also not in my nature to keep badgering at unhealed wounds. Phil would need to learn that on his own, and if it was none of my business, then less business for me to take care of.

"We're here." James yells. Everyone wakes up and snaps back trying to find themselves again after the long helicopter ride. I tell James exactly what I want from him, and that if he doesn't cooperate, Beef will shoot Tom on my orders even though I was completely lying and had no way of contacting Beef because I had no idea how to use the intercom. A thought of Britney might be able to figure the intercom out came to my mind as the helicopter slows down. And we can feel it lowering like an elevator slowly plummeting down from the top floor to the lobby. We all throw our gas masks on at the same time covering all traces of skin on our bodies. A pinching pain in my gut evolves into a flock of monarchs fluttering around tangling up my intestines. My mouth begins to run dry. My throat is clogged. The helicopter lands and the wings slow to a halt. "Here we go." I mutter. My grip tightens on my gun. The door flies open. And light flashes through making the silhouetted shadow that opened the door impossible to describe the details. The silhouette steps back and the blinding lights make it impossible to see.

"Welcome back red pumpkin crew members." A familiar woman's voice greets. "I trust you found my orders completely executed?" She doesn't let me answer before she announces, "Follow me." I hop out into the light and I follow the silhouette down a narrow white path. Footsteps follow behind me. We were in a white room. Only the helicopter was visible in this room of white. I look up to see the blue sky in the shape of a circle above me, everything else was white. The circle above us slowly began to diminish making it smaller and smaller until the blue sky was no longer visible. Along both sides of the narrow white path the silhouette walks down is a pond on each side. In front of the shadow I was following is a set of double doors. The outline of the woman types in a few buttons on the side of the double doors and enters the room. I follow and hear "Ca- I mean, Tom! Wait!" coming from the helicopter but I don't listen. I walk through the double doors passing the silhouette on my right without looking at her. The others follow close behind me and I see James is still by the helicopter, running frantically towards us.

"He is trying to trap us!" I thought as I watch him hustle to catch up to us. Both of my hands grip the gun tighter. Then I look at the woman who is standing by the double doors still. The details on her face, hair, skin come into perfect view and my heart stops. I almost drop my gun. When I see who the woman really is I freeze and almost start to quiver in fear, as if I was staring at a ghost or a monster I assumed to be fake. She was without a doubt the woman I was sure wasn't really standing there. She couldn't have been. There was no possible way it was her, but my voice cracked when I said her name anyways. She doesn't turn, or acknowledge me when I ask her, "Mom?"

5. The Cure

"Pardon me?" my mother asks. I knew she wouldn't recognize me underneath the gas mask and combat suit. James is still hustling over to me to the best of his ability to run, let alone stand. The wound in his knee handicapped him from making a full sprint. Still too confused on why my mother was here and alive, all I could do was wait for James to catch up to us. He was either going to explain this situation or turn us in. I couldn't help but feel rage building inside of me when I saw Glenda. How could she have lied to her own son? Did she know what was going to happen to Stellar High that morning she forced me to go to school? So many questions started to explode in my mind, until James limped his way into the double doors to answer them.

"Hello Irene." James gasps for air as he salutes my mother.

"Irene? What else did she lie about?" I asked myself.

"Hello James.   Welcome back to headquarters." *Irene* politely welcomes.

"Could I ask that my crew and I get a few minutes in the briefing room? Alone." James asks.

"Certainly. I will meet you at the elevator when you're ready to see Mr. Hamilton." My mother robotically says and then turns from James to walk down a hall that I saw no end to.

When my mother was out of hearing distance, my head jerked towards James. He was still out of breath and leaning against the wall. "Explain to me why my mother is here." I demanded.

"Your mother?" Britney asks, "Why don't we start on why my sister's are alive and acting like robots!"

"What are you-"

"Enough! Quiet!" James whispers. "Follow me." James limps towards a door behind Cocoa that is labeled 'Briefing Room'. Everyone walks into the room after he opens it and takes off their masks, including me. The door closes after James enters and we find ourselves suddenly squabbling and bickering like chickens with questions and demands aimed at James.

"Just let me explain!" James yells to calm us down. "Irene is one of you."

"She's my mom you ignorant-"

"What are you talking about? That's who he called my sisters-" Britney argues.

"Please! There is no time. No more outbursts. Irene is neither your mother or your sisters or anyone else's family member or friend." James explains. I can feel everyone's confusion, including my own, start to cloud around me. "Irene is one of you," He starts again, "she was a victim in our European studies. Do you remember the Bird Flu? Where there was this whole montage about everyone getting sick and dying from the diseases birds would carry?"

"Yes, I remember." Brett says.

"You would." I say to myself shooting Brett an *'I hate you'* look.

"Well let's just say, there was no Flu. It was just a cover story for M.S.C.'s mistakes. What happened to your school was not a first incident. Irene and Aileen are the last two survivors of batch one."

"So we are cookies now?" I suggest, "And you still haven't' answered why my mother is-"

"For the last time! Irene is not your mother! She is a sixteen-year-old girl that was a victim of our first testing series of substance 36." James disciplines.

"So why does Irene look exactly like my mother then." I ask.

"Am I the only one seeing my twin dead sisters walking around and talking in sync? He called them Irene! Is anyone seeing this?" Britney gasps.

"Listen to me, Irene is technically not human." James teaches.

"Oh! That makes total sense now! I have no more questions!" I sarcastically state. Everyone begins to wildly bicker and argue again.

James murmurs, "Damned teenagers," under his breath but I still hear him even through everyone's arguing like he whispered it into my ear. "There is no time for a dispute!" James roars, shutting us all up. I wasn't used to seeing James as someone in control, or someone with authority. "Irene takes the form of the last person, which you might have been close with or in love with, that you've come to know as deceased. She shows you what you've lost in her image. Her twin sister is Aileen. She is also… Different…"

"What do you mean?" I ask in monotone.

"Well, both Irene and Aileen have an extra chromosome in their genes, which was very rare back when we did our first testing. The chromosomes were completely dormant until substance 36 made them active. Adapting to the substance, they gained some side effects."

"What kind of side effects?" I ask. A flash back of the deteriorating man under Bozzo's grasp and the spontaneous incineration that kept following Amanda landed in my hands like the most valuable piece to a puzzle.

James is silent for a minute. He wears his face like he is embarrassed about saying the next thing. Then he utters it in half of a second. "Super powers."

Laughter erupts from within me at the cliché subject. The contagious sound makes Britney and the others laugh just as hard.

"It's corny but it's the only word we can use to explain it."

"So what you're saying is that this substance 36 thing makes people have super powers?" Brett suggests seriously.

"No. That's not what I'm saying."

"Then what *are* you saying?" I intrude.

"Listen! I don't know anything really about the whole power thing. You're going to have to take this up with Mr. Rusenkell if I can get you inside to see him."

"You mean *when* you get me inside to see him." I correct.

James doesn't reply to my statement which sends a jolt of worry through me before he orders, "Put your gas masks back on. We are going to see

Mr. Hamilton." And he walks out before I could ask who Mr. Hamilton was.

The short ride in the elevator couldn't have lasted more than five seconds, and I was sure we hadn't moved. But apparently we were already on the bottom floor when Irene informed us where we were. She signaled us to leave the compacted elevator and James was the first one off. I followed his lead acting like I've seen all my surroundings before. We walked down a narrow hallway and I felt my throat start to swell up. My breath shortened and I could hear myself wheezing a little bit. Cough! Cough! There was no way to cover or cough any more discreetly. James whirls around stopping me in his tracks. He pulls his finger up to his mouth signaling me to be quiet. I retaliate with a finger of my own; my middle one. At the end of the hallway I felt my stomach start to feel a little queasy like I had just drank expired milk. James waits for Irene to open the door at the end of the hallway that had no handle. Irene stands to the right of the door while a silver machine drops down from the ceiling above her. The machine dives down in front of her face and scans her eye with three blue rays of light and the door opens when the machine returns to the ceiling.

We follow Irene through the handless door into a massive white room. Bulky book shelves stretched around both the side walls and a desk was placed directly in the middle of the room. The faint smell of the room made me sneeze and my eyes water. Above the desk hung a large glass rectangle and straight back behind the chair owned to the desk was giant window that extends to each back corners of the wide room. The view outside the window was an endless amount of menacing trees and looming bushes that created ominous shadows.

When I softly spoke, I felt my throat slightly tighten together in a mild pain and an automatic inhaling through my nostrils proceeded after. "I thought this was the bottom floor."

"It is." James assured.

"Then why is there a scary looking forest outside?" I whispered.

"What are you talking about? There is no window." James whispered back obviously trying to shut me up, but I couldn't help but give into my cat-like curiosity and asked another question.

"Are you blind?" I hiss, "At the back of the room-"

"Greetings Gentleman." A voice thunders through the hollow room. Soon after we swivel our heads, minus James, looking for where the voice had come from, a picture of a man is displayed on the large glass rectangle in front of us. The grey-haired man seemed pleased at the sight of us, as if we had just fulfilled his expectations. "Welcome back."

"Hello Mr. Hamilton." James greets back after he bows before the digital man.

"By your arrival here, I am guessing you have completed your mission?" Mr. Hamilton assumes.

"Actually," James stutters, "The navigation system on the Red Pumpkin must have fried and sent us in a different patrol then the Black Fox and the Blue Trigger."

The smile on Mr. Hamilton's screened face faded quickly. "I sent all three crews at the same time, captain James." Mr. Hamilton says, annoyed. "Exactly how does one, with such qualities as a *pilot* such as yourself, lose sight of their own mission?" Mr. Hamilton scolds. His last question sounded as if he wasn't interested or wanting an explanation from James.

"Well when we split up after-"James tries to defend himself.

"Excuses, James, are for the incompetent. And I do *not* employ the incompetent. Do not forget your debt to me, James." Mr. Hamilton roars. "Remember that it is *you* who needs me. Not the other way around."

"I am sorry sir." James apologizes. Watching James lower his head before Mr. Hamilton felt like watching a kid getting scolded at in front of all of his friends; Embarrassing. There was no place and no words of comfort that could be given from the friends to the boy to patch up and heal the awkwardness that misted around each person present. You could only watch the humiliation and choose to feel bad for him, or try to think of ways to encourage his downed hopes after his parents have stopped lecturing him. But I felt no sympathy for James or that imaginary little boy. I was the kid across the street by himself laughing at the kid getting yelled at in front of his friends. I was the recluse who leeched off of that kind of drama for reasons unknown.

"I will deal with your failure later, James. As of now, I must contact Black Fox and Blue Trigger to make sure both crews have done what I've asked and have already searched under every piece of gravel left in Irvine city. I will not chance another incident." Mr. Hamilton scolds.

"I understand completely, Mr. Hamilton. Allow me to redeem myself and contact Black Fox and Blue Trigger for you." James pleads.

It is quiet in the room now. As if James had offended this Mr. Hamilton on the highest level. "Agreed." Mr. Hamilton breaks the silence, "I am too busy to be dealing with these petty issues that should not have happened in the first place. The press and the President of the United States are going to need a lot of convincing. Aileen will direct you down to the holding cells." At his last statement a girl in a navy blue suit walked into the room from a hidden door that was camouflaged in the long book case on the left side of the wall. "Contact Both helicopters, then I want you to pay a visit to Brian Rusenkell. He is under serious guard for his treason and mistake. As punishment he is to be injected directly with substance 36. And if he does not hemorrhage out of every hole in his body, put a bullet in his head."

"But what if he's harmless? He *could* have no-"

"I'm not taking any chances. He made his choice, and now you have to make one. Either kill him, or Aileen will kill you and your failure crew for me right here, right now." The second time he says *kill* the girl in the navy blue suit whirls out a large handgun from behind her, aiming it at James. I can hear the tightening grips on everyone's guns tense all around me. "Which is it, James? You're lucky I'm giving you one because normally there are no second chances."

"I will see to it." James says firmly.

"Indeed. Aileen, please lead James and the Red Pumpkin crew down to the holding cells and make sure my orders are executed. If anything should go wrong, preserve it until I get back. I will be meeting the President tomorrow, so I will be inaccessible for the next forty-eight hours."

"The President? Who is this guy?" I thought. But all I really wanted was to find my old biology teacher. I already had too many questions in my head as it is. I swallowed a gulp of saliva as the man on the screen gave Aileen more detailed orders. When the saliva took a dive down my esophagus, I felt a stinging down my throat. It made me cough. Again. Once more. I hadn't noticed the man on the screen was now looking directly at me with his digital brown eyes and artificial glare and was no longer telling Aileen what to do.

"Crap." James whispers, loud enough for Mr. Hamilton to hear, or so I thought.

"Tom. Are you alright?"

"Er- it's just a cold." James answers for me.

"Indeed." Mr. Hamilton says after a pause. "Clean it up. I can't have anyone ill in two days from now. And you know what happens if you quit or if you give me reason to fire you."

"Far too well, Mr. Hamilton." James answers for me again. James must have had a death wish to continue on helping us. He could turn us in any second. We'd be outnumbered and we'd surely die. I could not define his motive to help us. All I knew was the tense urge I had for James to get us through and the constant hope for us not to be discovered underneath our *hunter's* disguises.

"Do not fail me again James. Aileen will be watching you every step of the way."

"I won't-" James tries to appease him, but the screen flashes off leaving the glass blank again.

"This way." The girl in the blue suit demands. She didn't' look a day over sixteen-years-old, even with her hair perfectly slicked back into a pony tail.

Aileen leads the way down many stairs and through many code-locked doors until we arrive to a door labeled 'Holding Cells'. My fingers squeeze tightly over one another. I am a little more than shocked that our cover was not blown, so the adrenalin charging through my veins started to amplify more and more.

"Do it." I tell myself. Without hesitating, I was either about to do something dramatically stupid, or courageously tactful. Like a western quick draw, I threw my gun up so the barrel was staring down Aileen's eye. Expecting a shocking expression on her face and her arms to soar straight up towards the ceiling, she did nothing that related to my educated guess of her reaction. Instead she whipped out her own personal hand gun and faced it directly between my eyes. It was like a staring contest for the next few moments before I started to feel weak. My gun started to weigh more and my eyelids became heavy. My neck grew weary of holding my newly profound head and started to drift from its stabilization.

"Stop Aileen!" James calls out as he pulls out his own gun at her. She mimics her last movement instantly and flips out another gun from her free hand and faces it towards him. Suddenly I felt like a weight had been lifted off my shoulders when our stare contest was interrupted.

"The penalty for treason is death, James. Mr. Hamilton may have spared you but I *promise,* I will not be so merciful." Aileen scowls. "I sensed the change in you the moment I saw you. I smelt the wound in your knee. I should have trusted my instincts and revealed you imposters when I had the chance." Aileen glares at James. "You have been tainted. One of these zombies have left their mark upon you!"

"Zombies." I tell myself. My swelled throat starts to burn until I release a coughing explosion from my mouth.

"We were all just sitting around waiting for another one of us to start infectiously coughing and puking up blood to our untimely demise."

"What are you talking about?" James shouts.

"The sad thing is you don't even realize it. You were trained to defend this sort of mindless suspension and you have failed to prove that training worthy."

"I can't believe I didn't notice it either." My mother's voice states as she walks in the room from the door behind us. She has two of her own guns held out, aiming them at Britney and Brett.

"I can feel the others stench off of you now. It's so thick and palpable I can almost taste it." From my peripherals, Cocoa lifts his arm up enough to attempt to smell his armpit. I chuckle and Aileen starts another staring contest with me. This time her face was deadly. If looks could kill…

"Don't even try it." James yells as he moves in closer with his hand gun.

"Interesting." Aileen says.

"Very interesting indeed." My mother agrees.

Brett takes his gas mask off and lowers his gun. "We mean no harm. We are only here for answers."

"God, I hate him." I mutter underneath my breath as I take my own gas mask off. So does everyone else.

"But *we* mean harm." Both Aileen and my mother say in sync. They were like robots. Mindless. Lethal. A funny smell tickles my nostrils and I sneeze. I try to quickly open my eyes again to readjust my aim, but shots were fired and doors were open and closed too quickly to comprehend what was happening. I looked around me but both Aileen and my mother had vanished. Amanda and Brett were trying to open the door we came from and Cocoa, Phil and Britney struggled to get the Holding Cell door open. James lays on the ground with his eyes wide open. Two bullet wounds were engraved with dark red, both on his forehead parallel next to each other. My head started to feel like it was floating and I was off all ties with balance.

"The gas masks!" Cocoa yells, but before I could fully put mine on, my eyes rolled back and I black out.

My eyes burn when I open them. The pure white light is all I can see.

"We died, didn't we?" I tell myself assuming this was heaven.

"If it is, then heaven feels like the world's worst hangover."

"I guess that makes life one giant party then, eh?"

My eyes are even harder to open the second time I try and the light is blindingly painful. Even with my eyelids and eyelashes shielding my vision, the whiteness continued to bleed through. Squinting my entire face together, I forced my pupils to accept the light. Through what seemed forever, I found myself lying down in a pure white room. The walls and floor were cushioned just like a psycho ward. There was a door that had a tiny circular window on it. A syringe with black liquid contained inside of it lay right next to me. The pure white floor made the details on the needle endless to describe. My clothes were changed; I was wearing white sox, white jeans and a white T-shirt. My sickly skin seemed to contrast with the white giving me a tan I was not used to. I reach for the syringe before a voice thunders from behind me, "I wouldn't if I were you." I turn around to see who was there and I see Mr. Rusenkell curled up in the back right corner of the room. It was quite ironic actually. It was exactly where I sat in his class when I attended Stellar.

So many things were built up in my head just waiting to come crashing down on him. And me not taking the syringe put the catalytic cherry on top. "What. The. Ef." I state exhausted from my dehydration of answers.

"I know." He calmly says, "I know." He repeats. "It all just got so out of hand."

"Why don't you start from the beginning." I tell him.

"Did you watch the tape?"

"Yes, but it cut out after the rabbit and the dog died."

"Has any strange things been happening since I last saw you?"

"Nope, just the usual school bombing, spontaneous combustions that follow you, people puking out their intestines and blood everywhere, and people trying to kill me every waking second. Oh! And how could I forget the normal-"

"This is no time for sarcasm, Cale!"

"Sarcasm is my specialty."

"Like do you feel different?"

"I feel like a train hit me. Where is this going? And what's in this syringe?"

He pauses for a second and then he sighs, "It's the answer."

I completely stop my body, freezing my face like I was watching the most boring, pointless T.V. show ever. "I'm a stupid teenager. I enjoy no interest in and about everything. So stop speaking in riddles and give it to me straight-" My voice cuts out and I hoarsely cough into my hands. When I pull them away from my mouth, I can see blood is stained on them. I look up at Mr. Rusenkell with fearful eyes.

"Inside the syringe is the cure to Substance 36." Quickly I fumble for the syringe desperately trying to believe in life. "But." He says flatly before

I grabbed the needle completely. "Once you inject yourself... it will kill you."

"How is that a cure?" I ask furiously.

"It cleans the Substance from your body, but your body depends on it now, so once the Substance is eliminated, your body doesn't function anymore. They left it in here for you to kill yourself." I am in shock and confused on what to do. The needle rolls out of my grip and slides across the cushioned white floor. I can feel my own helplessness burden my muscles. I look up into my old biology teacher's eyes and he solemnly says, "I'm sorry." And this time, I finally understand why he said it in the back of the van the day of the quarantine. It seemed so long ago what yesterday had in store for us. The track of time was lost and the care for time was forgotten. I would just sit here and enjoy what was left of my pathetic life.

"I'll miss you." I tell myself.

"I'll miss you too."

6. Fire Alarm

Jonah Moon

Mr. Rusenkell is talking about some evolution thing. I drift in and out of his lecture to keep myself from dying of boredom.

"Bite me." are the first words I hear that can occupy a fraction of my interest in this lame class. I turn my head around thinking someone was about to fight. That would be bomb! Following everyone's heads like a chain reaction we all find ourselves staring at Cale Valens stuttering for an excuse for his outburst and an answer to Mr. Rusenkell's question: "Excuse me Mr. Valens?" I can see his constant recycling rejection of potential friendships diminish in his eyes. He was very interesting. He could run this school if he wanted to, but he chooses to live in solitary confinement. Cale usually keeps a low profile and steers himself away from society, but today he seems a bit more active. Wherever he goes that fat kid just follows like a puppy. The closest thing to friends he has was that fat freckled kid.

I just don't get why he would rather have people hate him then get to know him. But then again, I don't care enough to waste time thinking about it. *"What a freak."* I thought plainly. I folded my arms over each other and rested my forehead on top. I close my eyes and try to sleep because nothing is enticing enough to stay awake for.

I awake several minutes later and Cale is sitting one seat up and left from me getting yelled at by some red headed chick in front of me. She never talked in this class before, I don't think, or I don't care to think. Not even to her boyfriend, Brett, who ironically sat way in the back. Her nagging attitude and her frail voice annoyed me so much that I began to search for scissors in my back pack. The dark red in her hair was beginning to anger me even more. So I went out on a limb and started to cut her hair in stealth. Unfortunately when I was done, her hair looked a lot better. The black roots beneath her fiery hair gave it a nice touch. This infuriated me.

I was just about to try and mess her hair up completely by cutting more off, when the fire alarm rings in my ear. Bomb! The scissors dive into my back pack and I am the first one out the door.

While the entire school starts to herd themselves down to the football field, I walk the opposite way towards my car. I was only five-foot-four so it was easy to hide and move through and behind the mob of people.

"Hey Jonah, where are you going?" my brother's voice calls out for me. I roll my eyes before I lazily turn around to face him.

"Find a ride home. I'm outtie." I call out to him. Baley smiles from his side trying to appease our antagonism, I don't. Their relationship with each other was very tiring for me. I turn back around and I start heading for my car again.

When I get to my destination, there aren't any teachers or proctors patrolling the one entrance to Stellar so it was all clear to ditch. Bomb!

I was about to hop into my car when I see movement in my side view. My head whips to the movement to make sure it wasn't a teacher or anything and I see the last person I'd expect to be getting in his car to drive away from this dump. Goody-two-shoes-Brett-Gooding. But I shrug and lose interest right before I hop in my car and drive away.

Wherever there's a rule I break it. Why does everything have to be so vanilla? I run a red light and speed home.

"Minimum day." I lie to my mom as I walk through the door.

"Where's your brother?" she asks.

"He's at Baley's house." I lie again. She makes a face that reads 'why am I not surprised' and I retaliate by raising my eyebrows and leaving the scene into my room.

A can of sunscreen stands on my drawer. An idea pops into my head and I grab the can and a lighter right before I leave my room.

I'm out in my backyard in a flash and I set up some rocks in a circle, and start a fire in the middle. The blue sun screen can falls in the heart of the fire I created once I let go and I take a couple steps back keeping my eyes locked on the can. Pop! It explodes and a rush of excitement covers me like a wave. That was bomb! A couple seconds pass and I'm over it. Bored again. I take my keys and I hop into my car and start to drive around drowning my ears with music.

The day gets later and I randomly stop by a park. I *was* initially going to see if the swings had some kind of interest saved in them for me, but I find them already occupied by Cale and his fat follower, ham or something. Some sort of lunch meat. They were inseparable. It was just annoying. Since they ruined my plans I just turn back and head to my car again.

I pull in just in time to see Mrs. Schottenfield dropping Marcus off. Bomb! I get out my car after I park in my driveway and I see Marcus hugging Baley goodbye like he was leaving for the army or something. I wish. That would be Bomb! I lose patience waiting for him. I reach into my car again and grab a napkin from an old, empty fast food joint bag. I find a pen in my glove department and I start to write:

Tell mom it was minimum day today or I will kill you in your sleep.

I leave the note on the front door step for Marcus to find. He had to come in sooner or later. Probably later. I'm not afraid of my little brother to not face him when he was awake, although he clearly looked older and was completely bigger than me. Even his brown skin was darker and more healthier looking than mine. I was white and short. Pretty ironic. I walk inside and head for my room again to try to force myself to fall asleep so I wouldn't be bored anymore, when I decide to play with my lighter for a bit. The small flame reminds me of that red head's hair I cut earlier. I wonder if she has noticed yet. I debate whether I should go to school or not tomorrow and I resolve in a must because I have a project due in English. Stupid school. Maybe someone will pull the fire alarm tomorrow to make it easy for me to ditch again. That would be bomb!

7. The Green Bubble

Jonah Moon

The fire alarm did not sound today. So after my second period, English, was done I bolted out the door to try and ditch without being under the cover of the protective sound of the fire alarm. No teachers stood in my way or patrolled the ramp to our school for the second time in two days. Bomb!

A large white van was parked right next to my car. It was strange because I specifically remember arriving thirty minutes late to school today and I parked next to a small silver car. It sort of annoyed me that someone had left earlier than me. I was always the first to leave and the last to arrive. The closer I got to the large white van the more suspicious the van seemed to look. Any student who drove this piece of junk would have surely been torn apart by popular stiffs at our school. I press the unlock button on my key and my car does one of those automatic honk beeps that alert me that my technology on my key worked. I lock the car again, still walking towards it, until it makes a double honk and then I unlock it again just so I could hear the beeping sound and obtain the satisfaction that my key technology works. My life is average. Around the third time I make my car honk, a face comes into view from the large white van. The furious face stops me in my tracks to my car and sends me into a daze of confusion. The face turns from my sight releasing me from my stone position and puts on a gas mask. Interesting... Suddenly the roar of an engine sounds and the large white van pulls out of the parking space and drives right past me towards the school with two gas masked people inside the driver's and passenger's seat. If they were here to penetrate the school's defense for whatever reason, they picked the perfect school, because Stellar had no defensive positions against anything hostile to it. Those fire and duck and cover drills are just lame excuses used by the district that are labeled as *defensive strategies.* I forget what brought my attention to the useless thought of our school's useless defenses and I turn from the school back to my car and start to walk again.

I was just about to clench the handle of my sanctuary that could lead me to my haven (my messy room), when a sound that always captures your curiosity, but is usually rare in the city of boring-old-Irvine, pervaded through my ears. The sound of police sirens caused me to stop what I was doing and look up to the ramp only to see police squad cars speeding down it. Interesting... Now I didn't want to leave school. I wanted to see who was getting arrested and why, so I started to march back towards the campus. The tense air already screamed serious and curiosity with the first five police cars, but then vans and S.W.A.T. cars kept pouring down the road towards Stellar High School and rose the seriousness of whatever this situation was to a brand new level of worry. My pace automatically quickens and I start to jog back to my school.

Cale, his fat friend, the red head, and Brett launch out of a pair of double doors and start sprinting left towards the front of the school. Interesting... I follow from a distance behind so it wouldn't look like I was stalking them. I figured by their fierce running, they would know where the arresting was. Right before I turn the corner I hear my name being called out from behind me. Camo started to wobble over to me with Anthony and Ty at his side.

Camo, Ty, and Anthony were three of my good friends from Elementary school who stayed friends with me through the altering changes of High School. Camo was a plump, white skinned, blue eyed, blonde. I have no idea when or why I started calling him Camo, when his name was Cameron. All I remember, or care to remember is that he preferred it.

Anthony was taller and lanky. His brown hair was cut into a bowl cut which I thought had died out in the eighties; Not that I was alive to know. And Ty, was a bit taller than Anthony with nearly white hair. His skin was pure white and his eyes were dyed blue. The thing I loved about him the most was how unexpectedly funny he tended to be.

"Hey Jonah!" Anthony mimics Camo's beckon for me when I don't acknowledge them. I stop my stalking and I wait for them to arrive in conversation distance.

"What's up guys." I say plainly.

"We were just going to ask you the same thing." Camo says, "Of all people, we thought you would know."

"Well, I don't. But I have a hunch on who might."

"Who?"

I don't reply. I just resume my panther like pursuit towards the direction Cale went. When I turn the corner I see two police officers holding Amanda and Cale at gun point, so instantly I back up and hide behind the wall. Precisely at my moment of reaction I feel a tug on the back of my shirt. "I'm fine, get off me." I order as I turn around to who I thought was Camo. But neither Camo, Anthony nor Ty was to blame for pulling of my shirt. A black suited police officer kept insisting I followed him as he shoved my three friends down a hallway. Disappointed in myself for following his directions, I continued walking through the mob of students all walking in the same direction. A voice over the intercom instructs all students and teachers to report to the gymnasium. Interesting… I've never heard of a lockdown like this before. Usually it was just to lock the classroom doors you were in and hide underneath a desk after you turn off all lights in the room. As if that would stop anyone from breaking an entry. Our school's pathetic defense system was as useful as a mesh jersey being used to cover one from the rain.

Once we reach the inside of the crowded gym, people start to panic and yell at each other. At first I thought they just needed to get over their claustrophobia problems but then an ice shattering scream erupts from the other side of the gym. More screams occur and I realize we are locked in. Some man with a bull horn is trying to calm everyone down, but he is drowned out by his own failure panicking screams.

I am shoved in the back left shoulder and I turn around fiercely to see who it was. Cale and that Ham kid passed me by without any concern of who he just pushed out of his way. This made me livid. I started to follow the trail he was making with Cale's shoving and throwing people out of his way when coughing and sneezing start to sound throughout the gym. Each cough seemed to act like it was being contagiously passed off to the next person closest to the hoarse throat singing sound. Camo, Ty, and Anthony stayed with me the entire time, hugging my back with their presence. I was beginning to think why someone as short as me would be looked up to for answers by my three friends when a boy falls over directly in front of me and vibrates recklessly. Blood trails from his eyes, nose, mouth and ears. Interesting... I bend over and curiously look upon his face as he still shakes. I can hear Camo asking me what I was doing, but I just keep luring my neck closer to the boy who seems to be having a seizure. My nose can almost touch his when he stops shaking. His eyes are wide open with fear and he continues not to blink. Interesting... I recognized his face as all students would have. Chris Manroso, our school's star basketball player. *Was* our school's star basketball player.

Over the next three hours, a couple more start to fall over and seizure just as Chris did, but the majority of the gym continued to show they had no control over their coughing and sneezing. Allergies was a possibility, but what could have been exposed in this gym that everyone seemed to be allergic to? The wooden floors? Not likely.

Two more hours pass by as we started to rot in this god forsaken gym. The police officers give the same excuse: "We have orders to follow." After every time we try to rebel against them. A kid who has been holding his stomach for the last hour finally pukes up a mix of food and blood. I back away. Then he vomits again, more blood then food this time. Still backing up, and he throws up a third time, this time just pure blood. Interesting... I back up further and I feel a thud against my back. I knew I had collided with someone but something catches my eye before I turn around to see who it was. A green light divides the air between me and the red vomit that leaked closer towards me. I turn around and I see Phil and his girlfriend, Laura curiously looking around them. Camo, Anthony and Ty were doing the exact same thing. The green light surrounded us like half of a sphere. As I kept exploring the luminous green light that surrounded us I barely noticed there was two more people trapped underneath this round half orb thing. One girl lay on the ground like she was sleeping and another was on her knees staring into the eyelids of the sleeping one. I reach out to touch the green light surrounding us slowly. The texture of the light felt almost gooey, like a bubble. A bubble that couldn't be popped. I tried to poke it so it would, but it wouldn't even budge. Interesting... I walk around the green half sphere and I see the vomit still oozing towards us like we were standing on a gutter. The puke slides closer and closer towards the green light that was imprisoning us in, as if we weren't already imprisoned, until it finally reaches the light. When they contact each other the liquid like throw up burns like acid against the green light. Steam and smoke rise from where it starts to sizzle. The green bubble we were surrounded in did not falter as the vomit continued to boil into nothing each time it slid into the exterior of the bubble.

I realized we were under the radar of the entire gym because we were trapped in the corner of the gym where nobody was. A police officer finally spots us and marches over questioning his sanity every step of the way. I could tell, even though I couldn't see his eyes behind his gas mask, that he was questioning if he was just seeing an imaginary green bubble or if it was actually real. "Get out of there!" he demands. I press against the green bubble to prove that we couldn't but he wasn't convinced. "I said get out of there!" he orders again, this time raising his gun threatening our lives. But I didn't back away. I wanted him to shoot. I wanted him to test the bubble. Pop! Pop! Screams of uncertainty cry out at the sound of gunfire. Zz! Zz! The bubble sounds as it absorbs and dissolves both bullets. Interesting... The police officer lowers his weapon in astonishment. His body actions were enough to tell his jaw had dropped open and his eyes had widened to their capability. He walks closer to us after calling over one of his patrol partners to check out the mysterious green bubble. I start to back away when he lifts up his hand to reach for it. I had thought this guy can't be that stupid, when he stopped his hand and he pulled up his gun instead. Slowly he forced the gun against the bubble as it made a long buzzing sound. When he pulled the gun away from the bubble the gun had completely been dissolved. The officer showed his patrol partner, and that's when it started.

The first explosion sent the two police officers flying in the air towards the bubble. When they landed on top of the green bubble they dissolved just like their experimental bullets, gun and the dead kid's vomit. It was too unbearable to look for the others trapped underneath, but I stared and watched every second of it. Interesting...

Boom! Boom! Boom! Fire and wind rushed against our own little green shield and it absorbed every bit of heat that touched it. Dying screams of innocent students echoed through the gymnasium as we watched our fellow classmates incinerate right before our eyes. Then we were blinded by a mass wave of orange and red that covered the green bubble. We were drowning in a sea of fiery red. We were protected by this green bubble, our shield, our guardian, our only defense. It was all so very... Interesting...

8. Benefits

Jonah Moon

Gray and black smoke is all I can see through the green bubble that was still shielding us. What was our savior has now become a nuisance to me. I check again, like I have a hundred times over again, for a crack, or a leak in the bubble, but the bubble proved its self impenetrable and inescapable. Interesting... Phil, Laura, Camo, Anthony, and Ty are asleep. I have no idea how anyone could have slept through a night as traumatizing as this. Maybe they weren't sleeping. Maybe they were dead. I crawl over next to Camo who had a light snore going on and I slap in the face as hard as I could.

"Ouch!" he wails, "What was that for?"

"I forgot." I say laughing in my head. "Go back to sleep." I was surprised that he listened and picked up his snoring right where he left off in less than a minute. The only person awake with me was a girl whose posture had not inched from the moment I saw her. She still hovered over the sleeping girl that shared their same hair color. She was a statue of mourning. There was no way the girl could possibly be asleep like that or even be meditating. Her stance was too ridiculously uncomfortable to stay in longer than five to ten minutes. But she continued to prove me wrong by not moving. Maybe *she* was dead. I creep closer to the girl hunched over the sleeping girl and I ask, "Hello?"

Nothing. Not one peep from her. I couldn't even be sure she was breathing. I reach out my hand slowly to tap her on the shoulder when she moves. Too quickly to be possible she grabs my hand with forceful rage and lifts her head up so that her gaze could catch mine. Only one of her green eyes was visible, her right eye was covered by her black hair. She looked furiously at me as if I had wronged her. Her left eye of emerald swirled with signs of wrath. The green bubble seemed to react to her facial structure as well, because once her face squinted, the bubble started to make another buzzing sound as if it was dissolving something. But I was too far trapped in her gaze to look to see if anything was being dissolved into nothing. The buzzing grew louder and louder, deafening my ears. Most people would have been scared stiff at the sight of this girl, but I watched her in awe. She was furiously amazing and threateningly beautiful. "What's your name?" I ask calmly and purely curious.

As if my words were gusts of wind, she blinks for the first time and her head jerks back letting all of her hair cover her face. Suddenly following her jerking movement the green bubble starts to flicker. The lime light of the bubble grows vibrant and feints dull quickly until it suddenly fades out completely. It was gone, our imprisoning shield had finally set us free. Sick! The fog crept in our circle of fresh air and filled it with ashy smoke like a virus. I stand up and I start to walk out of into what finally appeared to be destruction to my eyes.

"Jane." A soft voice murmurs. I turn around to the voice. The girl who assaulted my wrist stands up as her black hair swings down in front of her right eye, dividing her face diagonally in half. "Jane Ledinger." She whispers. Then she turns around and resumes her position next to the sleeping girl, except this time she sits down more comfortably and to the side of her. Jane rests her hand on top of the girl's chest and she looks away. I notice her eye again and it no longer pulsated with green. It was a chocolate brown. Suddenly I had just lost interest in her.

When I turn my view from Jane I find myself surrounded by ruins and destruction. Stellar had been destroyed. Sick! Debris lay under my sneakers and smoke lurked around the demolished school menacingly. This transitioned my unaltered attitude into something somewhat more serious.

Even after the flames of the great fire have died out, in its afterlife form it continued to flaunt its disastrous power by lingering over its victims. Stellar didn't even have a chance. I don't know what infuriated me more, the taunting smoke or the fact that everyone I had ever known had just died. I didn't really share a compassion for my lost fellow students because I did not care to get to know them, but I knew they did not deserve the fate they had been handed. People like Preston Queen and Brett Gooding who were going places in life and were bound to be famous with their faces painted on cereal boxes didn't deserve to be annihilated like this. Even the rejects and the rebels who did everything to make others lives miserable just to make them feel better about themselves, people like me, did not deserve to have their lives wasted. Natural recluse's, like Cale Valens, who have so much potential but they choose to go through hardship willingly – these people had my uttermost respect and they too were wronged in this Armageddon. The only thing that I wanted now was revenge. The vengeance flooding through me did not boil for any sympathy I may have had for any deaths that occurred not a day ago, nor did my heart beat faster for any love that even existed inside me. It all seemed to come from hate. I don't care if this was the rapture, and act of a God that I didn't believe in, or a terrorist attack from another country. Whatever it was, it was the farthest thing from my knowledge of *right*. All I knew is the person, place, or thing responsible would soon be lying lifeless on the floor nether to my feet and that would be all the respect they deserved.

I walk around some more of the new, improved sight of Stellar High and witness small dying patches of flames still burning along the way. Anger started to rage through me like I've never felt before. Prolonged anger. There was a tingling sense in my legs as I grew more and more angry. I must have been too far in shock to really experience the anger before because this lividness was unlike any feeling I've felt before. The rage inside of me kept building and building up inside of me causing my body to start to vibrate. Uncontrollably, I was shaking. Every single muscle in my arms, legs, abs, and neck flexed fiercely. I stopped breathing and my face squished together. I could tell I was going red, but I couldn't stop it. I was too mad to quit whatever I had instinct into doing. I almost couldn't control myself when I finally let it out with a loud war cry that exploded from my lungs and echoed through the valley.

Almost simultaneously with my scream I felt myself start to shake again. But this time it shook from my legs and kept me off balance. I fell on my back and I realized it wasn't me who was shaking anymore. It was the earth. An earthquake that I've never felt before shook me up and down off the earth and back on to it again. The rumbling sound of the hills and the broken walls of Stellar made the earthquake sound even more threatening then it felt. The sound was beautiful; the sound of destruction. It gave me confidence and I started to assemble my legs together to stand up. The entire journey standing up I thought about all those pathetic earthquake drills we practiced when we were freshman at Stellar High...

"Jonah! Get down! What are you doing?"

"Relax, Anthony. This isn't real. It's just another demand this school gives to keep its authority flaunting itself in front of us. I will not be put down by the man." I say plainly to him still sitting in my desk disobeying my teacher's instructions.

"You're going to get in trouble!" Anthony whines still pleading me to crawl under the desk, but I still don't listen. I was small enough to not be noticed by my teacher anyways. This was just another drill. It was just another stupid waste of tact in a phony disastrous situation.

"Mr. Moon, is there a reason why you're not participating with the entire class in this earthquake drill?" My math teacher interrogates me. She had obviously finally realized I was still sitting in my desk like nothing was wrong.

I was about to tell her my reasons. I was going to say something along the lines of: "Yes, Mrs. Brewer, my reasons are my own and you should mind your own business, but I couldn't find the courage to say it aloud. My freshman instincts wanted to reply: "No, Mam." And obey her orders by dropping down underneath my desk, but I knew in my heart that that wasn't me. When I couldn't find the words to explain to her I started to get irritated with myself. I could have slapped myself in the face for taking so long to reply and that would have been a better explanation then still sitting in silence. But all I could manage to do was get more and more annoyed. My leg fidgeted and my fingernails tapped against my desk frantically as if these little movements would help me think. Wrong. They just made me angrier until something shocked me, stopping all my movement and thoughts. Mrs. Brewer had obviously felt it too because her eyes had stopped disciplining me with a confused stare and widened with fear and panic. She dove under her desk and a few girls in the class screamed from surprise. It was an actual earthquake. The irony of it was infatuating. Anthony gripped his panicking hands onto the poles of his desk, squeezing them so his knuckles turned a pearl white that matched his scared face. This made me smile. Adrenalin rushed at the feeling of being shook, but I was not about to sit there and take the beating from this force of nature. So I started to gather my inner leg strength to stand up. A smile was wiped on my face and I launched myself up off the floor on to the top of my desk and rode this earthquake like I was surfing a wave. My arms extended and horizontally aligned themselves with my shoulders as I hunched over my back treating my desk as a surf board. I was riding this earthquake like a feral wave. Sick! This was by far the stupidest thing I've ever done, but it's where my heart was at. Taking the risk of falling off my desk and breaking my neck was my calling and I couldn't have been happier at this moment in time. Lying in a fetal position under a desk that I've wanted to burn ever since I got to this dump they call Stellar High School just wasn't what I wanted. It wasn't what I merited. It did not and would have not given me the respect as a human being that I deserved.

Too quickly, the earthquake faded and stopped completely. What seemed to have lasted for an eternal minute was only a devastating eight seconds to everyone else in the class. When the earthquake was washed away, so had my happiness and content to be here, had eroded with it.

The memory filed under the section of 'Happiest Moments in My Life' was pulled out and revisited as I still struggled to stand. The comparison was futile to the mixture of the feeling and adrenalin I felt now. The melody of the rumbling mountains made me feel like I did when I was a freshman. I felt so alive and brisk. I finally locked my knees tightly and stood straight up. The earthquake still tried to ravish me off the ground like an unbroken bull would try to thrash a cowboy off its back, but I remained standing, conquering it. This time it did not last for a measly eight seconds. I was counting. Fourteen... Fifteen... Sixteen... Then it stopped at precisely seventeen seconds. This time when it stopped I wasn't disappointed that it had come and gone. I was content. I felt unstoppable. It was as if the earthquake my freshman year took away all I have wanted to live for and it had come back to return it to me. I felt different. Unbreakable. I was angry and happy at the same time.

Suddenly a thought occurred to me breaking my focus. What if this was no serendipity. I was smart enough to know that the thought was cliché and unrealistic, but I wasn't dumb enough to pass up the possibility. "Aftershock." I murmur to myself in subtle secrecy. And I feel my head start to vibrate as I slant my eyebrows downwards. Anger started to flood my insides again and the valley began to shake again. Sick! Astonished, I snapped out of my anger and noticed my stance for the first time. My hands were curled into fists and my legs were shoulder width apart. My arms did not rest at my sides either. They seemed to push away from my sides like two same side magnets pushing off each other. Then the shaking stopped. My next move was what any typical epiphany, which consisted of realizing you were more than who you were, would have you do. I lifted my flexing fists in front of me and opened them. Releasing the grip of air I had under my talon like nails that were cutting into my skin. My fingers slowly were shaking at the amazement of what could have been just another serendipity action or actual power. I leisurely flipped my hands from their backs to their front watching them every move they made.

Underneath my hands I barely noticed something levitating off the debris I was standing over. Three rocks were floating above the ground but below my knees. I blinked a couple of times to see if I was losing my mind, but after blink number six I was sure that Isaac Newton had to have been wrong about his studies way back when. The rule of gravity obviously did not apply for these three rocks. I bent over to get a closer look at the rocks when more movements started to occur. Three more rocks from my side view lifted off the ground. I turned towards them and they started to revolve around me. More rocks and stones of all sizes rose from the ground and revolved around me like I was their sun that they relied on. Sick! I started to wonder what happens when the sun exploded and then I tried to recollect the feeling of how it felt when I was riding the earthquake, but all I could manage to do was get angry. Then I went out on a limb and raised my right hand in the air with my palm facing the gray and black sky. The rocks and stone followed my palm. They stopped rotating around me and raised above me all gathering like a school of fish above my right palm. My eyes rolled up to see what the rocks were doing. Then my eyes dropped back down and I caught sight of a rusted, once white street sign that prohibited any driving speed over twenty-five miles per hour. It did not stand straight. It was bent leaning the side. I grin menacingly at the sign. The same sign I disobeyed every time I left what was literally now a dump. With my entire wrath I pretended to throw something at the sign and the rocks launched at an untraceable speed towards my target. The rocks nearly obliterated the sign, wrecking it completely. Sick! The rocks carried the sign nearly fifty feet back, breaking it from its metal pole that held it up.

"Jonah!" I hear someone beckon my name. Obviously the earthquake had woken them up.

"Jonah!" a different voice mimics. I was sure *that* was Anthony. I turn back towards where I had been protected throughout the night and barely saw pairs of legs through the smoke. I start to walk back towards the voices but before I fully commit into doing so, I turn back and take one more glance at the broken sign and I grin.

"Did you feel that!" Camo asks excitedly.

"Feel what?" I pretend to not know what he was talking about.

"The earthquake of course! What do you think I was talking about?"

"Yeah what did you think he was talking about?" Anthony repeats.

"I dunno, maybe this!" I say as I punch Anthony in the arm.

"Ouch!" He whines like he usually does. He coughs and it irritates me.

"Oh relax you big baby." But he doesn't do what he usually does this time. He doesn't apologize. He just starts rubbing his chest and neck like I had punched him there. Maybe I punched him so hard he felt it there. Sick!

"So what do we do now?" Camo asks me. Jane, Phil, Laura, Ty, and Anthony all look at me confused and lost. Why was everyone appointing me as their leader?

"We go home." I reply in a semi sarcastic voice that told them they should have already knew that answer. "We call the police. We ask for help." Did these answers not make any sense to them? Had they been put in shock so badly that their brains were launched back so they acted like cavemen? They don't answer or say anything, so I turn from them and I take a step towards the demolished ramp out of this dump. I hear them all take a step with me simultaneously and it reminded me of the revolving rocks. Sick! I smile and carry on hiking over the ruins of Stellar.

I order the remaining survivors that kept following me to salvage what they could find after we pass by each demolished house. I wasn't expecting the entire neighborhood to be burnt down as well. I figured it was just the school, for reasons I had no idea. All I could really focus on was rocks and stones. Every rock I passed brought a sense of thrill to my shoulders. Earlier on my way up the ramp I found a gun lying under some pieces of car and pieces of Stellar. I stealthily picked it up and hid it behind my back tucking it into my dirty jeans without anyone noticing. Anthony was being a lot more quite than usual and wasn't repeating after Camo anymore. I didn't expect anyone to be anything related to jolly at the sight of this disaster, but it just felt off without him trying to have a say in my conversations with Camo. It was obvious to me that I had no idea where I was going when I realized that I had no home left. Hours of walking pass by and all I could do was keep walking. No one ever second guessed my judgments or tried to come up with a solution to this huge problem. They just kept following me. Irvine had been completely destroyed. "We'll set up camp here." I say. "I'll be right back. You guys stay here." They all don't say a word. They just sit and follow my instructions like pawns in chess. "Jane could you come here a sec?" I ask. She doesn't say anything, but walks over to me like I asked. I turn and walk pass by three to four razed homes, out of sight and hearing distance from the others. Jane doesn't ask the question I thought she was going to ask, "Where are we going?" She just follows as if she knew she was in trouble and I was angry with her. I finally stop when I know I am out of any sense of range from the others and I order her, "Get angry."

"What?" She asks, surprised.

"You don't ask questions, or bicker when I tell you and the others to follow, stay put or jump, but you ask, let alone speak when I ask you to do a simple task of changing your emotion from your calm subtle self to getting angry."

"I still don't understand-"

"Listen. Get mad at me like you were this morning. That is all I'm asking."

"But I wasn't mad…"

"Don't lie to me Jane. Your eyes were burning with green flames of hatred. I know angry. I know hatred. And *you* were angry. You were hatred."

"I don't know, I was sad, because my sister had died. I was stunned."

"Is that who that girl was?"

"Yes. She was my little sister." Jane chokes.

"Then think about her." I order her.

"What? No… I can't- I can't be like that again."

"Like what, Jane?!"

"Depressed! I hate the feeling! I can't be angry when I have no one to blame, Jonah!" Her left eye sparkled with a lavender purple when she yelled my name. This caught my attention and made me lean my head to the side a little.

"I know who did it." I lie to her.

"Did what." She asks un amused.

"I know who killed your little sister."

Jane's neck twitches backwards, throbbing her head down just a tad as if she had just swallowed a piece of glass. Something starts to glow in her left eye. The only visible eye on her face that was diagonally cut in half by her hair. The color purple glows violently in her left eye. "Who." She demands with a deep threatening voice. Then a wall of purple light slices the air between us in half. The purple wall made a buzzing sound that reminded me of the green bubble, but I didn't dare to touch it. Jane looked shocked at the purple light wall in between us. She was caught off guard and she stumbled backwards away from the see through wall of lavender. The wall faded after a couple flickers and I walk towards Jane whose eye had lost color with any form of purple and scared Jane asks, "What was that?!"

"That was you." I tell her calmly. I figured it all out. I figured it out all by myself. I don't know how it happened, but I knew how to trigger it. I felt anger surge through me as I focused on a nearby boulder outside of the demolished home we were standing in. I reached for the boulder and it grew out from the earth towards my hand. I wasn't expecting earth's surface to reshape at my command so when it did it put a surprised smile on my face. Sick!

Jane did exactly what I did when I found out and looked straight down at her hands with her left eye. "So... we are some kind of super heroes?"

Heroes. The sound of the word brought a bitter taste in my mouth. "Sure. I guess so."

"So that light...that purple light thing, that was- that was me?"

"Well it wasn't me."

"But, how- how did you know that would happen? How did you know I could do that?"

"I didn't."

"What?"

"Well, I suspect you were too traumatized to even remember this morning, but when I first saw your eyes, they were astonishingly green. The same color as the bubble surrounding us. Then one thing led to another and I decided to see if it was just me going crazy... but I was right."

"Is it just us two?"

"Can't be. Why would only us have... abilities that others don't?"

"Plenty of people have abilities. The people who are in the Olympics for example, they aren't normal." Jane half laughs.

"Jane. Does it look like I have all the answers? I just found out myself. Do you seriously believe that we are the only two *beings* on this earth that can do something- something different?"

"No." she states.

"Well then. We'll just have to test the others than, won't we?"

"Why are you being so nice to me? You don't even know me, you're usually a jerk to most people. What's with the act?"

"Act?! Do you think this is some kind of play?" I roar furiously. I thought maybe the others could have heard me so I toned it down a little. But calling me nice was like telling me I was tall, it just didn't work. "You saved my life. You may have done it unknowingly, or with apathy, but never the less, you did. And that is why I'm being *nice* enough to show you your new life."

"*New life?* What are you talking about?"

"Do you truly believe that with this light force field thing you create you can ever be normal again? Or are you naïve enough to talk yourself into living with normal humans and expect them to treat you as their equal?" a sense of foreshadow haunted my words...

"How do *you* know? You just found out about this yourself."

"Because I'm not stupid. Think about it. Our school was just bombed. The entire city has been wiped off the map of the earth! We are the last people on earth for all we know, this could be the end of the world, or another story about an act of God to wipe all the evil from this world and give us two rainbows instead of one promising he won't end the world in fire again."

Jane rolls her eyes and sarcastically says, "Oh, so another story will be added to the bible, 'Jane's Bubble'. We'll put it next to the story of 'Noah's Ark'!"

"I highly doubt this is supernatural."

"Why? We obviously have some supernatural talents. Your rock movements and my color screens that I have no clue what they do!"

"Because we were quarantined remember? Whatever was going on, The U.S. government knows about. And once they find out what happened to us and Irvine, I'm pretty sure they aren't going to be too happy about it."

"How do you know they weren't behind it?"

"I don't."

"Well what if they made a mistake. What if they used Irvine's destruction to start a war on another country?"

"There isn't time for what ifs. And if you seriously believe that, then I don't know what to tell you besides your stupid."

Suddenly her left eye shone blue and I felt a push unlike no other force before shove me backwards. All I could see was a blue see through light shading everything around me a deep dark blue as I flew backwards. "Are you ok?" Jane panics as she runs over to me. "I didn't mean to I just, I didn't know it would- I didn't think that-"

"Just. Stop." I tell her and she stops her stuttering. A few seconds pass while I recover from the knock back and I ask, "Why was it blue?"

"I'm sorry?"

"It was blue this time. Before that it was purple, and this morning it was green. Why?"

"I don't know!"

"And why didn't I disintegrate?"

"Disintegrate?"

"Yeah! Why didn't I dissolve like everything else? What were you feeling when you pushed me back?"

"Annoyance."

"Charming. Try it again."

"What? No!"

"Come on. Just do it." I order.

"I'm not going to do it. Stop asking."

"Now! Do it now!"

"No!"

"Now!"

"I won't! You can't make me!"

"Your fat." I say seriously.

Her eye glows blue again and all I see is a blue light and all I hear is a fierce grunt from Jane when the wind is knocked out of me. I fly back again and I hit an unstable wall against my back, breaking it down. Jane comes over to my side to help me up and apologizes again. But I get up on my feet with a grin on my face. Sick! The second fall was more exhilarating then the first because I was more prepared for it and breaking down the wall made me feel important and strong. I was feeling accomplished. And I started to test her colored light force field things some more. I made her think about her sister even though I knew she did not want to revisit the memory of her loss. Tears came from her face and a purple wall of light started to inch towards me when she mutters. "Back. Off."

But I didn't listen. I kept walking back and forth along the purple wall of light talking over its buzzing sound. "She was your sister."

"Stop it!" Jane screams.

"No! Did they stop it when they killed her?"

"Stop!"

"No. I won't." Then a tear forms in her eye erasing all the purple swirling with wrath and the purple wall of light faded. A hint of green started to glow underneath her left eye's pupil and I knew I was getting to her. "They killed her, Jane. They murdered her." I told her, even though I had no idea how she died. I was convinced it had to do with whoever bombed the school though. And I was going to use Jane to bring whoever it was down. I didn't care if I was going to a burning afterlife, as long as the person or *being* responsible was going to burn in that eternal, miserable afterlife with me.

It worked. The bubble returned to surround us and Jane's left eye was insanely jade. I reached out to touch the bubble surrounding me and it was gooey just like the last time. I reached for a rock that lay outside the bubble and pretended to pull it towards me, when it moved on its own in my direction. The rock sailed at an unattainable speed towards me and made contact with the green bubble. It completely dissolved against the bubble and disappeared at the bubble's buzzing sound. Sick! I launched several rocks from all sides of the bubble towards it and they all did the same thing. Jane watched, me and she held the bubble in place. I turned around so I could get a closer look at the rocks disintegrating against her bubble when I pulled a larger rock towards me so I could have front row seats to its disappearance. It was about to make contact with the bubble when the green light flickered off and the rock kept sailing towards me hitting me in the face. My eyes were shut when I hear Jane laugh.

I drenched myself in anger after being fooled by Jane and I quickly jumped to my feet. Jane was already standing in a defensive stance like she was waiting on me. This angered me even further. I was training *her*. Not the other way around. Five rather large pieces of rubble rise from the ground when I specifically pick each one of them out with my peripheral vision. Jane's left eye rages with purple and the purple wall of light returns. I give a little flicker with my index and middle fingers on both of my hands and the rocks fly towards the purple wall in between us. Sick! One after another the rocks dissolved against the wall. To distract her I kept throwing rocks without actually touching them at her wall, but my focus lied on a certain rock that was on the other side of her purple force field. Out from behind Jane's vision I made the rock jump up and hit her in the back of the head.

"Ugh!" Jane wails. But her eye remained purple when she reached her left hand out behind her like she was directing traffic on a broken street light intersection and another wall of purple rose from her backside. She turned her head back to me and squinted her left eye. She had already adapted and learned to control her force fields. This ticked me off. Rocks started to fly at her from her sides and she reacts by extending both her arms out horizontally and two purple walls rose to defend her. Absorbing all the rocks I was throwing at her, the plum colored walls of beam seemed to have boxed her in. There was only one way to get to her; from the ground. Although Jane and I were clearly sparring with our new found abilities, I took it more seriously. I wanted to dominate her and show her that I was above her. I wanted to prove to her that without me, she was nothing. If she felt she was nothing, like she had nothing, then she would surely depend on me. She would *work* for me. Her force fields would be more mine to control then Jane herself. I stagger my stance; right foot forward, left foot back. My shoulders turn as I focus on the ground beneath her feet. My palm rested open at the end of my right arm that extended before me. Jane's violet eye watched my movements in confusion. She was heavily caught off guard when the ground before her started to shake. My palm raised further to the wrecked ceiling above us, and so did the ground in between the purple force fields. Jane lost all her balance and fell grasping the upward moving ground. Before Jane could even react to what was going on the ground grew to be a pillar in between the force fields that kept rising to the not so distant ceiling. My arm extended as far up as it could and I knew for sure this time that it *was* me controlling the earth. Sick! All my movements and wrist motions were mainly based of my imagination and instinct, and maybe a hint of a mixture of what I've seen in super hero movies. The kind of movies that were always so predictable. Hero loves girl. Hero fights villain. Hero saves girl. Hero gets girl. Hero lives happily ever after. "Just disgusting!" I mutter under my breath at the subject.

"Okay! Stop! You win!" Jane pleads, but I thrust my palm further up and the ground thrashes Jane against the ceiling and following through to the other side. The lilac beams of light flicker off and I stop my angry focus.

It's quiet for a moment and I start to focus on the ground beneath me with rage. The leveled ground creates a platform under my feet as it rises towards a hole in the ceiling directly above me. A hole that was created by the same person, place or thing who was going to accept my revenge without any say he, she, or it had. I was convinced fate had handed me this gift to balance things out between me and my soon to be found enemy. And I was going to recruit Jane as my pawn to do my bidding.

The second floor of the destroyed house was a worse sight then the first floor. Like an elevator I had perfect control over, the platform of earth I was standing over perfectly came to a halt when it was even with the second floor. Dark void shadows were burnt into the corners of the room. The only light there was, leaked in from the holes in the roof above. I took a step off my earthen platform onto the creaky second floor. My sneakers squeaked against the floor as I kept trying to soften the annoying sound. I couldn't see or find Jane, so I could only assume she was prowling in the shadows waiting for her perfect time to pounce me. I knew I was a lot more inexperienced with my new abilities then I pretended to be, but as long as Jane thought otherwise, she would surely swear herself to me with respect. But until then, she was a threat. It was obvious that in her left eye, she was completely playing around with me, but this was no game for me. This was a war. It was brewing. I knew whoever or whatever did this to us at Stellar High School and all of Irvine would not stop here. And one way or another I was going to end up on top.

Whimpering interrupted my thoughts of war. It was Jane. I had thought I had hurt her but I did not know her well enough if she was weak enough to cry over a flesh wound. Slowly, I keep walking towards the sound until my pupils can finally recognize the shape of her back in the darkness of the room. Was she serious? I felt like an older brother who rough housed with my younger sister a little too hard: guilty, but prideful of the fact you weren't to be messed with. "I miss her." She whimpers.

That was it? That was the reason she was crying? Not because I had beaten her or physically hurt her, but she was crying over her dead sister again? It didn't even make any sense. Why would her being thrown through a ceiling even bring one thought of someone she loved. I would maybe have understood if she was talking about an abusive, steroid using boyfriend, but a younger sister? It made no sense.

"I miss Ellie." She continues, "I miss her smile. Her giggle... She was so small for an incoming freshman. Just like she always was. Just like she's always been."

An object comes into view that is barely standing in front of her. It was a burnt, broken cradle. I creep closer to Jane and I notice she is softly rubbing her cheek against a dry, burnt teddy bear. Then I realized it wasn't our sparring that had made her cry. It was the room. A baby's room. An innocent baby that had no defense, nothing to protect her had her life taken. And I was to sit here and stand by to watch? The baby's life seemed even more important to me then all the lives I've ever known. Maybe because of the innocence the baby possessed. But then again, the baby also had the large amount of potential to become a malicious succubus, so it sort of made the baby what I've always been fond of. Not good, not bad, just somewhere in between.

"I don't want this. I just wish I would have died along with everyone else." Jane whispers.

Infuriated, I ask her, "You don't want what? Life? You'd let the only survivors of Stellar High die for your own kin? For your own pitiful search of self righteousness you have left inside you! You would have let future, as we know it, die for your own personal pledges to siblings, family, or whatever excuse of a reason!"

"I would be- *we* all would be in a better place!-"

"And how do you know, huh! Do you think that by your wretched sacrifice, salvation would find you and reward you once you died? That it would give you a second chance? This *is* your second chance. You *have* no sister now. This is your life now. There is no going back." I was hypnotizing her with my confusing words, but I knew I was tearing the strong bond she shared with her deceased sister. She was exactly where I wanted her. I was feasting off of her loneliness and gone-a-strayed-mind and converting it into energy like any good salesman would. I was selling a product of invitation. I was letting her know that there was no one else here to help here but me. I was corrupting her.

It didn't take long for Jane to slowly rise off the floor dangling the teddy bear in her left hand. Her back still facing me, I notice her squeeze the teddy bear. Gripping it tighter and tighter until suddenly a violent red flash of light blinded me, but I kept my eyes as far open as I could. The crimson red light that daggered my eyes came from Jane's left hand which was no longer holding the teddy bear. The stuffed animal had disappeared. No... dissolved. Radiant, violent red light still shun in a medium sized circle that surrounded Jane's hand when she turned her neck to look back at me. Fierce scarlet light of true hatred glowered in her left eye and I knew I had convinced her. I had successfully recruited her and unleashed something within her that would surely profit from. Sick!

When we walk back to where we had set up camp until I found a lead, everyone is huddled around something. Coughing and sneezing seem to be the sound everyone was crowding around. Phrases like: "What do we do?" and "Are you ok?", are tossed around in utter cluelessness.

"What's going on." I demand.

"It's Anthony… there's something wrong with him." Ty replies.

"I think he's sick." Camo says.

"I- I think- I'm… I'm s-sick." Anthony repeats in a deathly whisper. When I finally seen him I see blood stains all over his face. Draining from his nose, mouth, ears, and eyes. He brutally coughs up some blood that the others couldn't bare to watch but I don't turn away and neither does Jane. "Hel-p." Anthony beckons in a soft dying voice. Without hesitating I pull out the gun that was still stashed behind my pants and I aim it right for his face. A quick look of fear races to his eyes when he sees the gun but I pull the trigger before anyone could understand the situation.

Laura screams at the sound. Camo and Ty rush to Anthony's side calling out his name.

"What the-" Phil starts, but I shut him up by pointing the gun at him. "What!" he taunts, "You gonna shoot me too?!"

"Are you angry?" I challenge. He doesn't answer at the understatement. I always loved putting people in awkward situations where they didn't know if they should reply or not. "He was sick. It was either him, or us."

"And how do *you* know!"

"Get mad." I order him. Jane slightly grins from my side view.

"What?" Phil says astonished and confused. He grabs Laura's wrist and threatens, "We're out of here."

Pow! Pow!

Phillip Dirk and I used to be best friends. But like all the best friends I've had in my life, they've always seem to come and go when they disagree with me and I've just gotten used to it. He pretends he doesn't even know me when we pass each other down the hall. It didn't matter to me anyways because I didn't care. We used to make bombs together when we were in fifth grade. That's when I started becoming a destructionist. Whatever I could lay hands on I tried destroying. Lighter fluids and graffiti came after I was already bored of tearing down all the Lego's and the tree house my dad had built for me and Marcus. In a sense, I blame Phil for my obsessed corruption. He was the first one to put an explosive into my life. All I remember him telling me to do was gather rocks and form them in a circle. I did just as any gullible little fifth grader would and he pours what looks like water in the middle of the circle over the twigs and branches he set down. He lights a match and ignites the twigs until a small fire burns with sullen heat.

I wasn't surprised or shocked. I just stared continuously into the beautiful flurry of orange and red. Then he dropped a blue can in the fire and ordered me to run. I do as he says but I turn back towards the small fire we made while Phil keeps running. It exploded and Phil sprinted back to the fire and yelled in excitement. I ran back with him and cheer along.

When Phil met Laura during the summer going into freshmen year, he just stopped talking to me. So I stopped talking to him. But I felt no different when he left my life. No emptiness or anything missing. The only time I ever thought about Phil was the thought if he ever made bombs anymore.

I fired two loud warning shots in the air. "You're not going anywhere."

"Where'd you get the gun?" Camo asks.

"Not now. All that needs to happen right now is you, Phil. You need to get angry now." I knew he wouldn't cooperate if I didn't tell him the reason why I wanted him to get mad, but I also knew that he would never even try to get mad in front of Laura if he knew what he might be able to do. I wasn't sure myself if he could do anything, but it wouldn't hurt to just try. If I hadn't believed or tried anything this morning, where would I be now? Would I have been the same Jonah Moon yesterday?

"What do you mean Jonah?" Phil yells furiously.

"Am I not speaking your language? Get. Mad. That's it. Change your emotion. Become angry. Get animalistic. Whatever and however you want to call it, just do it!"

"Why?!"

"Jane." I say. She grabs Laura away from Phil and yanks her loose from his grip. Laura struggles but doesn't put up much of a fight against the new, remorseless Jane. Phil backs away and stops trying to reach for Laura when I shove the gun against his chest.

"Jonah! What are you doing?" I hear Camo yell.

"Now." I say completely ignoring Camo, who was next on my list of testing, "Let's try this again. Get. Angry."

Phil stutters something but already, I lose patience. I try something new with my *abilities* and I focus on a branch to pick it up and beat him with it. But it didn't work. Noticing limit on my powers made me angry and I felt a couple stones rising next to me without me even having to focus. Sick! Phil looks like he's just seen a ghost when he witnesses the defacement of gravity.

"Get angry." I repeat.

Still looking like he's seen a ghost I make a rock hurl itself at him hitting him in the shoulder.

"Get angry!" I repeat furiously. I another rock hurls at him. "Get angry!"

Still nothing from Phil even after rock after rock plunged against him. It was as if he was incapable of getting angry. It was really pissing me off. I tried something different. I pointed the gun at Laura and she screams. "No!" Phil yells.

"Get angry!" I yell and another rock is tossed at him hitting him down.

"Stop!" Phil roars furiously as two rocks are flying for him. Boom! Boom! Both of my rocks had shattered into dust. Quickly I throw a more bigger rock at his furious face without touching it and he reaches out for it when it explodes just like the last two. His face transitions into scared and worry when he realizes what he might have done. I pull the gun down from aiming it at Laura and Jane lets Laura loose. Laura typically runs to Phil's side scared. Who knew a traumatizing event such as our school, city and lives being destroyed would give such benefits. I was certain the rocks I hurled at Phil did not explode at my will and I knew I would have to convince Phil into joining me in vengeance against whoever has done this to us. I let him and Laura ponder on what had just happened because they were shockingly overwhelmed with the floating rocks and the exploding ones. I turn from them and I notice Camo is gone.

"Camo?" I beckon. Silence. "Camo!" I yell.

"Wh-what." Camo's voice replies, clearly trying to shield him from my vision. And it was working, because I couldn't find Camo for the life of me. Ty stood there dumb faced on what he had just seen and I was sure Camo was around here somewhere making the same face as Ty.

"Where are you." I demand.

"I'm- I'm right here Jonah." His voice sounded like he was right in front of me but I couldn't see him. Even Jane was turning in circles looking for the lost image of my good friend Cameron Dark. Then something caught my eye. A glimpse of dull white light kept flickering on and off next to Ty.

"Jane?" I asked.

"It's not me." She replies obviously seeing what I was seeing.

"What are you looking at?" Camo asks scared of my answer. The dull light becomes more and more realistic like a three-D movie until a shape comes in fully. It was a rather large, plump, blonde haired, blue eyed boy. It was Camo. He came into full view like he was camouflaged with the background scenery around him. Even Ty jumped when he noticed Camo in his periphrial vision. "What!" Camo asks, "Is there something on me? Is it a spider!? Get it off! I'm allergic to spider bites! Get it off! Get it off!" He didn't even seem worried about all the treachery I've caused. I could see in his eyes that I still owned his loyalty. Phil however, I would need work on.

I start to laugh and I realize, Camo was another benefited victim of revenge's war. That's what I was going to call it. And that's the only thing I was going to fight for. My own personal revenge. Sick!

The sound of thunder interrupts all of our problems and I turn towards the ominous grey sky. It couldn't have been later than six o'clock in the evening, but the track of time was lost along with all our dependable cell phones. And days were dark enough to realize that it would be a great time before Irvine ever saw daylight again. "Thunder." I grimace.

"That's not thunder." Jane replies. I take a closer look at something moving in the sky that looked like three birds in the distance. The harder I strain my eyes; I realize what the birdlike figures were when Jane announces, "Its helicopters."

"Let's go." I order. Surprisingly without any questions everyone follows my lead again as I head towards the helicopters.

"Do you think they are coming to help?" Jane whispers into my ear after five minutes of walking towards the thundering sound of helicopters. I was glad to see that Jane wasn't as stupid as Laura who wanted to sprint towards the helicopters, but I wouldn't let her. I was glad to see that she was guarding herself and me with other possibilities. She was already adapting to the position I wanted her in. My shield. Sick!

"I don't know." I truthfully state. Jane deserved an honest answer. She had earned at least *that* much respect. I pick up my pace a little and I find myself a bit ahead of the others who seem to have run out of breath after another five minutes of pursuing the loudening sound of helicopters. I admitted to myself that I was nervous, but I wasn't about to let that stop me and show in front of the others. Especially Jane. If she saw any sort of weakness in me she I might lose her allegiance to me. Something in my throat made me bark up a small cough. I covered my mouth to soften the sound and I pull my right hand away from my mouth. Blood was painted on my hand. The irony of the situation made my heart skip a beat. I gripped the gun in my left hand tighter and tighter because I knew I was sick.

9. Restless

Jonah Moon

Only one house looked well enough to walk in as we passed down what we at least thought was a street towards the roaring sounds of the helicopters. Time was of the essence now that I realized I was sick. I would have to pick up the pace with everything I did. I didn't understand why fate had given me such power, or at least showed me through accidental fortune, but why fate was taking it away from me was the new question. Questions, questions, questions; so many questions just kept piling on top of each other. Why, who, what, when, where, how? Exhausting.

The thundering sound of the mechanic flying machine, that gave us signs of life beyond this total destruction we stood in, grew louder and I knew the helicopters were getting closer. Laura was out of her own breath in pursuit of the sound. She should have listened to me and paced herself like I warned her, though I had no concern for her tiresome lack of energy.

I had to look out for myself in more ways now that I realized I was more vulnerable being infected with whatever Anthony had contagiously spread to me. And watching my own back twice as much as I normally did drained me emotionally. Exhausting.

Killing Anthony did not prove to myself that I was completely heartless. I did feel bad for him. Of course I liked him as a friend enough to keep his company, and without him echoing everything Camo says would certainly make the scene less hollow. At times I thought of my deceased younger brother, Marcus and my parents as well but I continued to shut their untimely demise out of my head because I was in denial of the lack of proof. Once I saw their corpse's though… I might have at least tried to cry. I'm sure trying to force myself into crying would feel just as refreshing and terrible afterwards when I was finished attempting it. And I would be tired and ready to sleep from it just as if it were the real thing. Exhausting.

The raging sound of the chopper that continued to grow louder as we approached the one wrecked house on the abandoned street and my mind kept switching subjects from myself, to my deceased family and friends, to these helicopters and its intentions, to my fists full of revenge that were being saved, to my new vulnerability. Back and forth, like a game of ping pong, ideas were tossed around in my head bouncing off the insides of my brain. Exhausting. Chop chop chop chop… Louder and louder, the thundering sound came menacingly closer and closer. Two helicopters flew over our heads and Laura begins to scream at them. Her being the only one yelling at them set off some kind of supernatural psychic scream in my head and I sprinted towards her to shut her up. It was instinct taking place, no thoughts of judgment were being used, no common sense was presence, just a survival gut feeling of trying to be unseen. The thought of silencing my visual appearance made me think of Camo as I kept sprinting towards Laura who was now flailing her hands in the air beckoning the two helicopters that were flying past us. Almost out of breath I leap off the ground after her and knock her to the ground.

"What is M.S.C.?" Camo asks, ignorant of me tackling Laura. Phil however, was anything but ignorant to my actions and was charging at me full throttle. I cover one of my hands over Laura's mouth and with my free hand I pretend raise the earth between me and Phil and an earthen ramp is raised off the ground. If anything was normal nowadays I wouldn't have even second guessed that Phil was to be out of my sight since the ground had miraculously rose between us at my hand motion. But something even odder happened. The earthen ramp that created a barrier between the charging Phil and I had become see through. It was as if I was straining my eyes through a wedding veil. I watched Phil slip and fall backwards before the suddenly new hill in front of him, a furiously surprised look on his face. Even more surprised than I was.

A horrible blast echoed violently in my ears and the memory of shooting Anthony elusively popped in my head for a quick second before I knew wc were being shot at. "Jane!" I command, and like some twin, psychic connection Jane's eye flickers green. More blasts are sounded and I knew the helicopter was above us. I look up through a green view of the menacing helicopter and dark skies. Jane made a larger green bubble that seemed to cover all of us from the rain of fire. Like magnets, Camo and Ty back peddle themselves into me, and so does Phil – except not as clumsily. "Can it be moved?" I roar over the rapid blasts.

"I- I don't- Shut up Jonah I'm trying to focus!" The emerald green dies out a bit and colors back in as Jane speaks.

"Move us towards the house!" I command.

Slowly but surely, Jane was able to move the bubble to follow her steady back walk towards the wrecked house. The helicopter began to land at this point, it lowered down and I knew it was time for my revenge. Adrenalin pumped through my veins and I grew more excited and happier than a college student on his twenty-first birthday. Almost at the rickety door of the torn apart house, I tried to break free from the green cage protecting us but I ended up squishing my face on what felt like a wall of glue. "Jane!" I yell.

"What!" yells back angrily, obviously annoyed of me disturbing her concentration. How hard could it be for her? It took little effort for me to hurl stones and create hillsides. The only thing that drained me a bit was the mini earthquake this morning.

"Change colors!"

"To what!"

"I don't know! Something we can pass through but the bullets can't!"

"Ugh!" Jane struggles as the blasts against her green bubble grew more violent. She bows her head and raises both her hands in the air with her palms facing upwards. It made me wonder if she knew what she was doing. But thinking about Jane's gifts made me think about the more ways I could use mine. Thinking, thinking, thinking. Exhausting. The green bubble faded its jade color and vibrantly shun purple. "Try- n-now!"

I forced my hands through the purple sheath and found its passage quite undetectable of any force. We were free to pass through. "This way!" I yell as I charge into the burnt house. Everyone but Jane follows me through. Laura, Ty, Phil and Camo tried to hide behind the broken walls of the damaged house, Camo being ironically more successful at it. Camo had disappeared completely. "Camo!" I beckon.

"Yes?" His voice squeaks full of trembling notes. I look around. No sight of him, just Laura, Ty and Phil cowering behind half of what used to be a stair case. They all looked at me with eyes that read: *What do we do now?* Having everyone depending on you not to freak out and stay calm was irritatingly tiring. Exhausting.

"Camo!" I yell furiously over the gun fire that Jane's purple bubble kept absorbing.

"Wh-what!" Camo fails to bring any authority into his voice, but he appears from out of nowhere hiding behind Ty. I roll my eyes as he slowly fades into sight.

"I need you." I lie.

"For what?"

"I need your help taking out the helicopter's gun turret. You're the only one who can do it." I lie again. I could have done this somehow if I gave any effort, but this was more than just showing off. This was a game. As beloved as his friendship was to me, Cameron Dark was nothing but a pawn in my game of vengeance, and I am the King.

"Do what?!" Camo panics, "I can't!"

"Camo, shut up. Take a deep breath. Get out there and flank them." I knew he would understand the strategy I had gave to him when I used a military word that involved on attacking one target on two fronts because all Camo did when he wasn't around me was play this stupid war video game that became obsession to every teenage boy all over America.

"Jonah! No!" He gasps with complete confusion.

I grab him by the shoulders and lock my eyes on to his. "Use your invisibility thing."

"What?" Camo says confused looking at me like I was crazy. Maybe I was. Maybe I had been hallucinating rocks and boulders defying gravity and earthquakes and instant earth misshaping. Doubt is such a deadly thing. It sucks you dry from all of your expectations. Doubt plays a big part on why I became atheist. But there was no time for doubt. The helicopter was moments away from landing and it was only a matter of time before the bullets would overpower Jane. I had to get panic out of Camo's head before too much doubt corrupted his self esteem. My right arm fired up with adrenalin and smacked the left side of his face as hard as it could. Plap! "Owww!" he wails like a girl. "What the-"

"You need to listen if you want to live." I threat with the wrath of doom. My eyes burn into his and I know I've got him. I had him locked in my gaze as a fisherman squeezed the life out of a fish caught to pull the hook out of the fish's mouth. "Do this." I whisper. "Do this or you die... We all die." During the state of panic, people become willing to believe anything. They become vulnerable. Controllable. Camo, who was drowning in a sea of anxiety, was all of the above. His eyes told me that he was finally willing to take my hand to pull him out of the quicksand his panicking mind put him in and he nodded his head while gulping what looked like a large amount of saliva.

"How?" he asks almost timidly.

I knew what he was talking about, but I didn't have a straight answer for him. Getting angry seemed to be the only thing that worked for me, Jane, and Phil but Camo never seemed to get angry at all. Even when I shot our closest friend Anthony, there wasn't any anger inside of him, just fear and confusion. "Get angry." I say unsurely going with my gut. He looks at me like he was about to ask me a confused *what?* But he instantly popped back into focus when another loud blast interrupted him.

"I don't think I can hold it up this long!" Jane yells from out front still shielding us through an immense light shield of purple.

Camo begins snorting out of his nostrils and wrinkling the space between his brown eyebrows that contrasted with his blonde hair. He stopped breathing and began to shake his head in a fast vibrating motion. Was he serious? This was his *angry*? I began to think that I might have to teach him how to get angry. Exhausting. The more he tried, the more ridiculous he looked. Finally he stopped, took a deep breath in and popped his eyes wide open only to find the dullness in my blank face. He glanced right, then left. "Do you see me?"

Pow! Pow! Pow! The bullet blasts grew menacingly louder...

Maybe two days ago before this disastrous panic plagued Irvine (and maybe more of California, or the world even as far as I knew) I would have laughed in Camo's face with idiocy for even thinking he could disappear from sight. I might have slapped him in the face too, but because the deafening sound of the bullets I only became more frustrated with Camo for not being able to know his 'trigger' into *inanity*. A broken piece of mirror rested on the burnt wooden floor between me and Camo. I pick it up and show Camo his own reflection. "Yes." I say flatly, "I see you fat and clear." There was no time. I was not one to give up, but if I didn't do something soon about the descending helicopter, I might lose my only other protection than myself, Jane. The broken mirror in my hand carved itself into my palm as I gripped it with rage. I was sure I had begun to bleed, but the vicious adrenalin seemed to have blocked the pain. I launched the sharpened edge towards Camo's neck and held it against his collar as I threatened to slice his throat. "Get angry!" I yell furiously at him. A flashback of me throwing rocks at Phil earlier comes to my mind for a quick second. I figured the others wouldn't approve of my methods to get to them to realize we were more than we know, so I blocked Laura's wailing complaints, Phil's *justified* safety hazardous words, and Ty's worry that might have been sincere but sounded like a joke. Nobody would just take action. I had to do everything myself. Exhausting. Camo's head flinched back as the glass touched his neck. Fear swirled in his eyes and something odd happened to his appearance. He became like a ghost in his facial expression and his body image as well. I could see through him. Whatever I was doing was working. The burnt wall behind him could be envisioned through him. His white skin tone became nothing but a veil the broken piece of glass pressed against. Laura, Phil, and Ty stopped their restraining words and I knew they saw Camo begin to fade so I concurred that I wasn't crazy or seeing things. It's funny how the silence can answer so many questions.

"Jonah!" Jane wails from outside. The purple bubble wasn't glowing with vibrant lilac anymore. Its color was a lot more dull and lackadaisical. The chopper was about to land.

What my right arm was about to do had to be done. I would have to shed a bit of Camo's blood if he was going to fully cease his visual existence. I scratch his neck still holding the glass closely. Camo flinches.

"Jonah stop!" he cries. His appearance was nearly faded, but there was still a piece of his texture still portraying itself in the hint of *reality* we all grew up with. I cast the glass back away from his neck and ominously pretend to coil my arm across my body like I was going to hack at his neck at full throttle. It worked. The last of the fear swimming in his eyes disappeared along with the rest of his body. Fear was what drove him. I had found his weakness and his strength. Although I wanted to relish the fact that I bended reality single handedly, the chopper had landed. My body releases its tense, offensive formation I was using only as a scare tactic and I flip the broken mirror around and face it towards where Camo used to be. The mirror floated away from my hands, and although I wanted to think that it was floating away at my will, I knew Camo had taken the mirror out of my hands.

"Go." I command. I could tell that Camo was in shock and without words, but there was no time to sit and question a bestowed gift. The mirror levitated in front of me trembling in thin air. "Camo! Go now!" The glass dropped from the air, shattering itself once it slammed against the rickety, burnt wooden floor and a slamming door followed heavy footsteps out of the room. I turn to where Laura, Phil, and Ty were cowering behind an empty stair case and made sure their eyes were locked on to me, so they could see what I was about to do. It was my turn. I focused on a spot in between Jane and the now landed helicopter. Men dressed in all black that carried guns bigger than me, which wasn't saying much, began to charge after Jane after they hopped out of the helicopter one after another. My hands laid out straight in front of me, palms up. Before my arms rose up, I imagined an earthen wall rise in front of Jane. I raise my arms, expecting it to be easy, but an invisible force was pressuring me down from raising them up. It wasn't as easy as throwing rocks or boulders, this took a little more effort. The ground shook and a large earthen wall rose to divide us from the chopper. The purple wall of light vanished and Jane fell to her knees squeezing her head with both of her hands like she had the world's worst headache. I ran out front to grab her and drag her inside. The gun fire continued to blast against the wall in between us, but once I grabbed Jane, it stopped.

Weakened somehow, Jane was heavier than I had expected. I began to drag her by her shoulders as quietly and swiftly as I could. The silence of the gun fire confused me on whether I should be hasty or unseen. I thought of Camo. Where was he? Dragging Jane as quietly as I could became more of an effort than it should have been. Exhausting. Suddenly she became lighter when she was lifted off the ground. Phil had come outside and grabbed her legs lifting her off the ground completely. Together we carried her into the house.

I wasn't quite sure what Phil could specifically do, so I wasn't sure how he could help. Something innate in me made me turn to Laura. I had yet to begin my tests on her or Ty. Once in the house, murmurs were picked up by my ears. On the other side of the wall the men in all black were scheming ways to go around or over the newly formed wall. It was only a matter of time, time that I didn't have. A loud, blast shot was fired and echoed through the air. Camo... I thought. They got him. I was sure of it. The gun fire stunned me, along with Phil, Ty and Laura. We all shared the same thoughts. Camo.

A man's voice projected over a bullhorn, "Come out peacefully and unarmed and we won't hurt you!"

"Lies." I muttered under my breath. The gun behind me started to weigh me down a bit and I knew doubt had begun to run its course within me. I turn my head from the wall and realize how vulnerable the sides of the house were. If these men were smart they'd have walked around- spoke too soon. Out of the corner of my eye I see one of them peeking around the edge of the wall I had made in the front yard of the damaged house we stood in. Reaction took over as I started to panic. The vulnerable sides of the house suddenly became defended by two rectangular earthen walls as I imagined in my mind while lifting my arms from my sides horizontally upwards until they created an upside down arc with my head at the symmetrical center point. Gunfire immediately erupted and I found myself out of breath. Weakened by misshaping the ground, I stumbled forward only to be held stiffly up by a firm arm that grappled my right shoulder. Exhausting. I slapped the hand off my shoulder, uncaring who it was, with anger and a bit of embarrassment. I would refuse to show weakness. Rapid gunfire kept on exploding in my ear drums and I figured it was only a matter of time before the men on the other side of the wall would break through and surely kill us all. I had failed. Oh sweet revenge, I thought. How bitter, my craving for it has damned me to utter failure. I would not give in though. My feet dragged myself forward towards and out the broken door to the front porch. The same hand that had helped me stable myself grabbed the same shoulder again trying to prevent me from moving further forward. I strangely recognized the grip of Phil, and shrugged him off continuing my dreadful steps out the door. I take my steps further down the porch and down to the barrier I had convinced myself I had created. The gun fire still firing, it was inevitable the wall in front of me would falter and crumble against the most evil creation man has ever invented, Weaponry. Time could only tell when. Closer and closer I walked to the wall. I could hear footsteps coming from behind me, and I knew Phil, Laura, Jane and Ty were following me. Even at the end of all things, they continued to follow me to our own unjust demise. Camo had been dead for minutes and wherever he was now, I strangely believed I would never see him again. If there was a heaven, the kid would have been there. And if there was a hell, then that's where I would go. If the stories remained true...

Louder gunfire had broken my train of thought. The wall was not going to last any longer. A crow flew overhead. The symbol of death. I cough up some blood discreetly. Even with death waiting in the wings, watching me intently with a bowl of popcorn resting on his hollow lap, I continued to hide my sickness from the others.

A bullet pierced through the wall, frightening me because if I had stepped two steps left, the bullet would have pierced through me as well. What was I thinking? I wasn't going to just sit here and wait for them. I was going to take as many of them with me before a fatal bullet ended my existence. Bile fate had mocked me for the last time. I grabbed the gun stuffed behind me. My eyebrows slanted down and I announced firmly, "I suggest you run if you plan on living through this." It was a warning to Phil and the others to flee, but I ceased to hear any panicking footsteps scurry away. Not even Laura, which frankly surprised me. I used what felt like the last of my abilities to see through the wall, and like I entered an unconscious state, the view became hazy and the gunfire had abruptly stopped. It was absolutely silent.

On the other side of the wall, a spread of bodies in black combat suits lay in random order on the ground. A confused look on my face took over my angry emotion. Was this some sort of strategy? Did they think I would come out and dance over their corpses and chant and praise an inexistent God like some alien or ignorant voodoo witch? Did they take me for dumb? How insulting I thought. This drove me angrier and I began to imagine the wall to return down to the ground. I counted to three before loosening the bindings I had with the three defensive walls, and sent them slamming down even with the ground again. Immediately following I raised my gun and fired at each body once as fast as I could before they could get up, but ran out of bullets before I could shoot at the last three. Fear paralyzed me for a quick second before something fell out of the landed helicopter. I looked up at it and it was a limp body of another black combat suited man. He fell from the helicopter's gun turret which seemed to be vacant. I was at a loss for words. I had no idea what was going on and every wheel in my mind kept churning for answers but kept finding none. Exhausting.

After ten seconds of an awkward silence my eyes caught something moving in the helicopter. I raised my gun, knowing I had no bullets left, and aimed at the movement. The turret moved by itself again. Suddenly Camo fades into sight sitting behind the turret.

"Sweet Jesus, Mary, Joseph and the three wise men." Ty says astonished behind me. I attempt to keep myself from laughing at him, but excitement and victory surged through me like a hurricane. I had felt like I had just won a championship football game. Camo hopped out of the helicopter and kicked the body that had fallen out.

"This one's still alive!" he warned.

And he left one alive for interrogation. He was a natural. Camo was full of smiles and pride. I almost found myself skipping towards him when something makes me sprint. The body Camo pronounced still alive and that I assumed dead next to him began to shuffle out a small hand gun. My eyes widened with fear as I began to panic for Camo. "Camo! Look-" Pow! Thump. The loud sound stalled my propelling feet and paralyzed me. The man had shot himself. No longer smiling, Camo came running towards me frightened for his life. Hurdling himself behind me, Camo and the others all gathered behind me.

As if the suicide didn't frighten us enough, gun shots from further out were echoed through the lackadaisical valley. My head reacted like a cat and whipped itself to the shocking sound. There were more of them? I should have known by how unsatisfying the victory over these predators felt. Perhaps fate had intended me not to die after all. The frightening gun shots not only triggered fear, but it set my vengeful plans back into motion. Things were looking up again, and without a word I start jogging towards the gunfire.

I started to believe the others had given up on tedious questions I didn't have the answers to and started to let instinct take over their mind because not even Laura tried to stop me from running towards danger. Of all the terrible things I've done in my life, I couldn't help but to wonder how anyone could trust me after my killing Anthony. I even found me doubt myself at times. A flashback of carving into Camo's neck with the broken mirror and one of me tackling Laura to the ground crossed my mind as I felt a sweat break from my forehead. Still jogging, I noticed the gunfire had quieted. That's when I stop in my tracks. I can hear Jane and the others mimic me after a three second delay.

It took my mind a while to recognize the pieces of debris used to be an apartment complex next to an elementary school I had attended. Trashed cars and burnt trees made the scenery gloomy and hopeless, but all that was on my mind was where the gunfire had gone. It was one of those moments where someone like Ty would say, "It's quiet...Too quiet..." ominously but sarcastically. I was surprised he didn't. I might have chuckled a bit to break the serious vibe the setting set off.

Suddenly, I felt a warm metal on the side of my neck and I knew I was being held at gun point. Whoever had just went rogue on our little survival clan was now no better to me than the enemy trying to kill us. Anger flooded my emotions and I knew my plan of revenge would have to include killing the betrayer of the last of Stellar high's population.

"Put your hands in the air." An unfamiliar male voice had ordered. Not Phil, Ty, or Camo. It didn't sound like any of them. Had they been disguising their voice the entire time? I subtly hoped it wasn't Camo.

"No." I stubbornly state. I turn slowly to face the traitor only to find I was wrong about there being one. It was another man cloaked in black with a gas mask on that mimicked the others trying to kill us. The others already had their hands up wrapped behind their heads. All of them except Phil.

"Get down on your knees!" the man commanded a little more intensely.

"Which is it?" I sarcastically ask.

"What?" he asks confused. I was biding time, waiting for Phil to jump into the fray at hand. Just waiting...

"Which do you want? You want my hands in the air? Or do my knees on the ground?" I shoot Phil a quick look of hurry.

Angry, the man cocks the weapon in his hands back and pokes the tip of the barrel aggressively at my forehead. "Both." He commands.

Phil was taking too long. I was ready to shake the earth to save myself from kneeling to this ignorant ant, just so I could get to his queen. Click. My eyes widened. There was no gunfire. I didn't know what to feel. Angry that Phil would have just let me die, or grateful that a miracle just happened. My eyes dart to Phil, and I see he is standing behind the man holding me at gun point with his right hand up, palm facing out. A flashback of me throwing rocks at him earlier came to my mind. He was in the same stature when those two rocks being flung at him had burst into pieces. I realized what could have happened, so I quickly dove to my right and I had heard an explosion just as I predicted before I hit the ground. I turned to see the man wailing and grasping on desperately to his right hand that seemed to be fuming smoke. Quickly, I levitate myself off from the ground and grab a hand gun saddled into his right hip hoister and aim it for him.

I cough clarifying my point through sarcasm. He looks at me with hatred, but all I could imagine him with behind his gas mask was a pair of sad puppy eyes begging me for forgiveness. "Yeah. You know what to do." The man, still gripping onto his hand tightly as if it were ready to fall off got down on his knees as I imagined him shooting me looks of stubborn failure on the way down. Phil grappled his gas mask by the front and tore it off. "Hands in the air." I order, only because I could almost feel the pressure he was applying to his hand to suffocate the pain. I knew once he released his grip he would feel the excruciating misery Phil had somehow put him through. My best guess right now was that Phil had made the gun in his hand explode just like he did with the rocks I had hurled at him earlier. I was almost clear now of what he was capable of. I nearly laughed at the thought but I somehow understood the fact that Phil could control explosions. I somehow knew he prevented the gun from firing and forced itself to combust whilst still in the predator's hand. A couple days ago if I had said that in my own head I'd have probably smacked me in the face. What a ridiculous assumption to make. "Did I stutter?" I politely ask. Angrily he gives in to the pain, grinding his teeth together as he releases his grip and puts his left hand in the air. "*Both* of them." He gives me another look of hidden mercy before he raises his right arm as well. I catch a glimpse of his right hand and I see that it had been blown clean off. Well…not clean. Suddenly I noticed how tired the man looked. Was what I was asking at all tedious? Absolutely not. Repeating orders was tedious. Exhausting.

The sound of gunfire from the west had all of our heads react by jerking to the sound, like a siren calling our names. I look back at the man I had just humiliated as he sulked about his missing hand. "How many more of you are there?" I ask belligerently. The man doesn't answer. I roll my eyes. Exhausting. I drag the man up by his collar and his hands go sailing together continuing the pressure I had ordered him from. I squint my eyes at him. If he wasn't going to answer my questions he wasn't going to be comfortable. I poke his missing hand with the gun I stole from him. He yelped like a hurt dog. His pain almost brought a smile to my face but another series of loud blasts interrupted my victorious thoughts. I threw the man forward, towards the sirens of death. He turns back to look at me, my arm locked, gun in hand facing him, face filled with arrogance and confidence. "Take me to your buddies."

It wasn't a long journey at all, but the constant worry my captive was going to lead me into a trap kept me and paranoia best friends. I should have been surprised at what I saw. I should have jumped for joy and yelled for hallelujah at the top of my lungs when I saw them, but when I saw familiar faces I had thought to be dead I became infuriated. I hated them. All of them. I didn't want them to be alive. I wanted them dead. I liked it that way. Something within me was changing and it was overpowering me taking all the strength I had. Exhausting. I grappled my prisoner by the back of his suit and whispered into his ear, "This had better not be a trick." But his posture seemed to announce he was just as confused as I was. Walking more slowly now towards the ghosts of Stellar High I overheard a conversation going.

"There's one of them in there." I recognized together his voice with his face as Brian Bozzo. "Two to go." He says.

"*One* to go." Another voice enters. Maxwell Longo cared for no one, I wasn't entirely surprised to see him alive. The kid was adroit. I was sure he could avoid a few naïve men wearing badges arrogant enough to call themselves police officers. Max carries a severed arm holding onto a hand gun in his left hand and in his right; he carries a gas mask that drips red goo. Amanda gives him a disgusted look when Max dissembles the gun from the amputated hand. "What?" he asks her. "Self defense." He assures while he shakes the objects in front of her.

"Why are they doing this?" Tianna whispers with a voice purely angelic. Too innocent to be found in such deathly settings I have come to inhabit as my new way of life. I was almost sure I was looking into heaven as the ghosts of Stellar were disputing why these demons had purged the gates of heaven like nightmares to the afterlife. Something innate in me decided to intervene the dead spirit's conversation by throwing the bait in the sea of the dead before me, only to demand leadership over these zombies. They could be useful to me if I learned to manipulate them as I manipulated Jane.

"Why don't you ask *him*!" I shout out as I shove the man in my grasp on the floor violently. Like magnets my eyes darted to a movement too quick to be thought possible, well there was nothing impossible now. Cale Valens. I went blank when I saw his determined face aiming a gun towards the man I had captured. I could somehow recognize his determination in his odd face and I inhabited it as my own. It was as I was sensing his emotions. "He's unarmed." I bellow almost wishing he wasn't so Cale would have shot him. Cale lowered his weapon and his tension had released me, leaving me drained somehow. Exhausting.

Another familiar face enters the scene by Amanda's side, Brett Gooding. One glimpse of Amanda's firery red hair kept me strangely on my toes still wondering if she found out I had cut some of it off the day before the quarantine. "Who are you?" Brett orders like he was the one in charge of these ghosts of Stellar High. Did he honestly expect me to answer cooperatively with the tone of voice he was giving me? Instantly

I knew Brett Gooding was going to be standing in my way of taking control of the predicament at hand that I intended to manipulate for my own personal game.

"He's my bother!" A voice that trembled my posture called out. I knew it was Marcus before My eyes caught sight of him stumbling down a pile of broken concrete behind Cale. I was surprised, excited, shocked, overwhelmed and wanted to rejoice at the sight of my brother, until I saw Baley attached to his hand. Real big shocker there. It wasn't that I hated her, just the sight of her brought me back to reality that things were the same as they have always been. Everyone was the same twisted, selfish people they were a week ago, just different circumstances. Quickly the happiness in me flushed out, and I noticed I was soaking up attention from more ghosts that seemed to slowly fade into the scene from their feeble hiding spaces.

"Jonah…you're- you're alive!" Marcus nearly yells, overjoyed, "How?"

I don't acknowledge any form of sympathy from my brother and carry on with the present. Anger took over to kick the man in front of me to his knees. I shout out, "Let's deal with the now." Already beginning my orders I would be soon used to demanding from these ghosts. I stare at Cale, because I knew he would be the hardest to convince, but his antagonism for Brett might be able to work in my favor. He stares back at me as if his answer to my unheard question is an assertive *No*.

Brett takes initiative and starts to walk over towards the man injured on the floor before me. Calmly he kneels down next to him as if he were here to forgive him. "Who are you people?" He asks. The man spits in his face and I almost start to chuckle, but instinct took over and reminded me that I needed the answers this man knew, so I kick him in the gut and he grunts. Brett asks again, "Who are you people?" after he wipes his face dry.

The man is quiet for a solid four seconds before Brett asks again, this time he whispers and I'm sure nobody could hear him besides the handless predator, and he finally answers, "You guys are-"he is cut off by the sound of a gunshot. My eyes dart around to see where the bullet had been fired from as soon as the man's face plummets into the ground. Another blast is sounded through the air and I quickly spot the source. Unlike the others who dove for refuge, I stood there staring at the coward firing from inside a helicopter. Laura had fled my side with Phil attached to her, Camo had vanished discreetly, and Ty seemed to have Followed Jane hide behind a broken wall that stood crippled above the ground.

I wasn't even phased from the gunfire because I had grown a custom to it so quickly. Dumb founded I stood there in the middle of the scene where my captive was shot down in cold blood. I was not trying to be suicidal, dangerous, and specifically not afraid of a pathetic coward that hid behind a helicopter door shooting a gun at me. I was just full of tiresome apathy. Exhausting.

It got to the point where I rolled my eyes every time a gun shot was fired. I did nothing, I made no effort to dodge, hide, run, attack or defend myself. I just somehow knew that this would all blow over too quickly to feebly run from a man with a gun. Plus I was a bit restless and bored to the point where fear was a bickering angel surrounded by a band of bloodthirsty demons scratching their talons on the concrete toying with the angel.

A cough lurked in the back of my burning throat, but my pride wouldn't let it free from my mouth. I refused to think I was still sick. My eyes saw Cale charging for the man in the landed helicopter, but my focus was on training my throat to get used to the pain. I stood there and held the burning sensation in my spoiled throat while continuously bullets ricocheted off everything around me.

I couldn't come up with any explanation for why I decided to not dive behind a wall. It was if I was being caged into my own body. I was being possessed by a death welcoming, suicidal demon. Yet I didn't try to resist its purging. What was happening to me? Exhausting.

Things resolved with the a bullet wound in the man's knee Cale had put in. I continued to stand perfectly still in the same spot. I didn't want to move. I didn't want to do anything. I didn't really even want to exist anymore. I was so tired of everyone. I was annoyed with the fact that I haven't gotten any answers yet. I wondered when would I perish and start to bleed out my nose, like Anthony. Was this feeling death? I was beginning to resent life and all of its aspects. As I ponder I notice the ghosts of Stellar have regrouped by the helicopter and were conversing. My legs propel forward, but I leave something behind as I walk towards them. I could feel it leaving me. The demon that was draining the essence of my life, possessing me to stand in the middle of havoc when my better judgment was to disperse and hide like the rest of the spirits, had dropped off like a heavy suitcase filled with bricks. I was lighter, that was verily. But I didn't understand the feeling. I was somehow…empowered.

I turn my head back after a couple steps towards the undead students and peer at where I was standing not a moment ago. Still standing, an image of me looked down at the ground. I turned more fully towards the alternate me. Quickly he glances up and glares at me. My parents appear surrounding him out of nowhere placing their hands of each of *my* shoulders. They vanished. All three of them vanished into thin air. Confused at what had just happened, I turn back around and believe this omen was a metaphor my mind had created to tell myself that I had been altered, and that I had left Jonah Moon behind forever.

I arrive into the crowd, still dazed, and the helicopter's engine roars. The wings on top of the chopper start, first slowly then violently, to spiral. As it lifts off the ground I take another step forward in front of a bigger kid, which was nothing new, to see who was leaving on the jet plane. I counted Brett, Amanda, Britney, Cocoa, Phil, and Cale. To my right wept Laura, and I admitted to myself that I was shocked to see Phil leave her, or even me rather without saying anything. I roll my eyes to the left and I see Tianna standing silent with a solemn face staring at the rising helicopter. Her eyes began to grow glossy, but never once did she say anything.

As the helicopter faded into the distance beyond the grey skies of omens everyone stood in silence. They were all lost. Without a leader. I already saw what was happening. I already knew what my actions were going to be next. I was bored…but now that these unbranded cattle are beginning to scatter, I grimace. They looked at each other like they were recognizing one another less and less as every moment passed. They were losing themselves. They must have followed Brett here because knowing him, he was sure to have a plan that could easily persuade a bunch of ignorant teenagers who have been brainwashed into thinking whatever popular kids say is right. And now what? What are they to do once their leader abandons them? All they have been taught was to do right unto others and others will do right unto them. I would use Brett's betrayal against them. I knew these headless roosters would follow me. If I possessed that innate fowl siren of the breaking dawn, they would be sure to blindly and thoughtlessly succumb to the alarm like fire tells the mind to panic.

There would be a new leader. Whoever led these poor unjustified, ignorant souls to the middle of this chaos was no longer here to lead them out. Like the devil in white, I would control these ghosts like I had broken Jane. Although drained from the given circumstances that I still was getting used to, I was restless and determined to finish what I had set out to accomplish. I would take down every single one of these men, and I would stay alive long enough to break whoever poisoned me. Even if the mastermind behind it all was the inexistent God himself, whom I don't believe in anyways, I knew this was wrong and the only way to justify what had happened was to get even. I will not sleep, I will not rest, I will not settle.

The sound of thunder ignites the silence. The treacherous sound foiled my thought process and lifted my head towards the sky. The track of time was lost. The thunder didn't fade. I look at Laura instantly as a memory caught up with me. I recognized the sound and I knew this thunder was manmade.

"Looks like rain." Cale's fat friend clumsily holds a gun with wide eyes gazing above. I look to him and almost laugh. He *would* be alive if Cale was.

I answer him, "That isn't rain, pork chops."

"It's Beef!" he defends, not really making his case any better.

"Well." I ignore him, "This will be fun." I smirk at him before the continuous thunder sound grows louder. Beef looks up and I snatch the gun out of his hands with little effort.

"Hey! Cale put me in charge!" Beef says almost convincingly.

I switch off the safety on the gun I assume Cale had switched on before he handed it to Beef. "Well then Jerky, hope you've got good aim." I toss him the gun and scrambles for it in thin air. I turn and walk towards the others and Laura stares at me with vigor in her eyes. She knew the sound as well as I did. I prepared myself for what was about to happen. The helicopter came into sight as a black dot in the dark sky. I braced myself and saved my energy for what was about to happen, but I couldn't help to release the tiniest cough without unsealing my cold, firm lips because I was jaded and utterly exhausted.

10. Vultures

Jonah Moon

Overhead the helicopter drew itself closer and closer to us. The mindless zombies that surrounded me were confused on what to do. Lost. They had no idea where or what they were doing. They had all given up, they realized what was coming for us and they stood around waiting for them to come and finish us off. They had no will and no desire to live any longer. Hell was empty and all the devils were here. Even I started to contagiously believe them that this was the apocalypse. No crazy religious person had to shake me and cry out to the heavens for a higher power to come and smite thee, this was the unexpected truth about the end of life. The corruption of man had finally turned its back on itself. Everyone went rogue.

Nobody deserved what they got. Karma is sleeping on the job.

I shook myself free from the convincing grasp of depression the others seemed to be bathing in, though they had reason enough being unclean with life. I know I needed to pull them out with me, but I was lost on how to motivate such morbid spirits. Confused. The only thing to reinforce them to live now in my mind was criticism. Reverse psychology. They couldn't be any lower than they were, and if I were to try and push them even further down, the only place to go would be up.

Laura wept feebly on the floor. It was then that I decided I would assault her first. "How pathetic." I insult her with a deep voice that captures everyone's attention. Laura stops whining and looks up with tears still streaming down her eyes. "All of you. Pathetic. You don't deserve to live." I point to growing helicopter in the distance that approached rapidly. I would have to convince them even faster now. But how? Lost. "They have destroyed our lives! They have taken our families away from us, and yet they still remain unsatisfied! Oh, but go ahead. Stand down. Why don't we all just lie down together and let them drop one bomb to finish us off! It's what you all deserve isn't it? So come on! Let them come! Let these vultures pick off the helpless prey." I lay down on the dirt with my arms and legs spread like was getting ready to make a snow angel. I was stretching my body to make myself the biggest target possible. Out of the corner of my eye I see someone move through the suddenly still and shocked crowd. The movement walks determinedly closer to me and then plops himself next to me on the ground. Ty doesn't laugh, giggle, or make a comment while he does this. But somehow his action makes me feel lighter. This is something I usually would have laughed at. The ironic un seriousness of situations was usually my weak spot. I was mystified why my taste in comedy had suddenly changed. Lost.

I lift my head up off the ground keeping my body tied down to the floor with invisible ropes attached to my limbs. The others stared at me like I was mad. "Well?" I yell over the growing thunder. They don't move. I had caught their attention, but they still remained leaderless. No one of the crowd tried to contradict my words with a typical war speech trying to rally the troops to defend themselves from the vultures drawing closer ahead. Sick! I was glad no naïve soldier decided to do that, it might have jeopardized my subordinate plan to consume these ghosts' moral judgment and manipulate it in my favor.

Nobody moved. There was no sound but the wind and the mechanical thunder overhead. They all looked at me, waiting, with the virgin eyes of a child. Interesting…had I already convinced them? I quickly jump to my feet and stand as tall as I could. Though was shorter than everyone around me I felt empowered and strengthened. Jane came marching out of the crowd to my side proudly.

"So death then I suppose. Feel free. It is your life. What's left of it anyhow." I state before I walk through the crowd still staring dumbfounded. "Run and hide while you can." I mutter as I exit the crowd.

I start to plot the inevitable action ahead of me in my head. I picture the guns firing at me before they even begin to fire off. Someone interrupts my violent thought process. "It's getting close now." A soft voice whispers behind me while my left ear absorbs most of the sound. I turn my head left and out of my peripherals, Tianna gazes at the growing helicopter. I knew of Tianna, but I had always assumed her to be a stuck up harpy like Britney Wilson, or like all the other girls at Stellar. But from up close there was something about her pretty face. Innocence seemed to dance upon her face lightly, swaying with the breeze. She shun as a beacon of beauty that captured my attention. It made me feel light. I didn't believe in her existence, as I didn't believe in God. I knew what I was slightly feeling. The very look of her drained me. Exhausted. She brought forth in me something that I never knew existed. I knew what pleased me, and I knew what irritated me. Tianna was next to revenge and I wanted both of them. I wanted her as badly as I wanted to squeeze the life from whoever had broken my old life. I was no longer Jonah Moon. I had convinced myself that he had died. I would have to rename myself, what was left of me. But to what? Lost.

"I see that." I say calmly. Apathy was the only thing that kept me from insanity. I felt no fear trying to crawl under my skin every time the helicopter clapped with a thunderous booming sound that kept itself propelled in the air.

"So are you just going to lay down and die? Or are you going to fight?" She boldly states. I completely turned to face her and I could see the seriousness in her eyes. She didn't fear me? Lost. She had the courage to mock me, and yet somehow I was not offended. Interesting…How could someone who looked so delicate and beauteous be so firm and tough?

She walks away from me almost instantly after she mimicked me back towards the crowd of bewildered ghosts. By the looks of their faces they couldn't believe the leadership in her walk as I was unable to. Confused. She pierced through them calling out, "Beef. The gun." In complete monotone. Beef hands her the gun, he was so reluctant to have me hold, readily. She walks over to the knee-wounded pious vulture of the dead and slowly kneels down beside him mocking his pain at the very arch her knees created. Kindly, she tilts her head slightly to the right and looks at him intently through invisible glass like he was an interesting ancient artifact on display. Calmly she gives him an ultimatum. "You have two choices. You can either be good, and attempt to help your friends up in the air." She pauses and looks away from him towards me and grazes her eyes solemnly over the rest of us, "Or you can be bad, and help us survive."

Did she mean to switch those verses up? Why would he be anything related to bad if he helped us live? Wouldn't it be the other way around? Confused. Tianna was indeed more poetic in her speech than her beautiful face. I had to look down out the embarrassment of thinking the word beautiful. Interesting...Tianna somehow made me feel ashamed of my own self. All I could focus on was how I wanted her persona to reach through the wounded vulture and convince him to help us. There was a long pause between her ultimatum and his reaction, a thundering pause. And out of nowhere, I caught it: Tianna's words. I realized what she had meant by being good or bad. She viewed all of us as the bad guys. With the gun in her hand aiming straight ahead for him, she realized he would have to make a choice and remain the hero of this story and complete what he was supposed to finish, or he could join us and betray his own kind. The helicopter grew louder.

"Choose." She demands shoving the gun against his sternum in sync with her words, then retracting the device back a couple inches. "Die like a hero, or become a villain." The man is shocked and in complete silence. I am in shock and complete silence. Lost. Where did this angelic harpy come from? Her words were so...Interesting...they were tragic and strange. She overwhelmed me with surprises of her personality that drained me towards her leaving me restless. Exhausted.

"Ok." The man states. "I'll help you."

Stunned at his compliance to reinforce our dwindling existences, I felt jealousy when I could see in his eyes that he was just as fascinated in Tianna as I was, but more so relief and excitement that these vultures were not incorruptible. Bomb! All I had to do was threaten them with their lives to follow me. If I threatened enough, I could maybe soon have a whole army of pawns working with me to place my unknown enemy in checkmate. Sick!

The helicopter grinded against the wind louder every second. The defening sound grabbed all of our heads and caught our non divided attention. As soon as it became close enough the helicopter began circling us above. It was a game of duck, duck goose as we bided our time waiting to see who would make the first move. Too prideful to admit I was the prey in the situation something held me back from taking the first move. Something naïve and buoyant inside wanted to settle our differences with the vultures democratically. Pow! A Stellar ghost dropped dead right beside me. "Jane, Now!" instantly a purple sheath of light encircles everyone as Jane surrenders her hands above her head with a lavender haze swirling in her left eye. Controlling Jane was becoming more and more easy. Sick!

"What is that?" Tianna whispers with wide eyes.

"Shoot them!" I demand without explaining anything to her.

She doesn't hesitate as she raises the gun Cale's other three quarters had given to her (Beef), and fires at the helicopter. One mere bullet hit made helicopter dip and jerk itself right in the air and down fell a vulture plummeting right towards the purple bubble. On impact with the purple shield, the vulture seemed to cease from existence after his dying scream was cut off. Tianna looked at me like I was crazy. She obviously still didn't believe what was happening. The remaining vultures began to rapidly shoot now, relentlessly.

"An eye for an eye." I mutter.

Thinking the shield impenetrable, the helicopter slowly began to land beside us and the vultures continued firing their weapons as seven of them came hopping out of the vehicle. Distress suddenly came over Jane's face and worry followed on mine. "Oh no." the traitor gasped.

"What?" I say irritated underestimating the seriousness of the situation, still trying to keep faith in the purple shield. He doesn't answer. I furiously grab the collar of his shirt with both hands and threaten, "What is it!"

"They have one of you with them." He barely gets out of his mouth. He was obviously still bitter about agreeing to help us.

"So you agree to help us and you have yet to do anything about it!"

"Jonah!" Jane beckons in distress.

"What!" I yell, taking my fury towards the traitor out on her.

"I can't hold it!"

"Suck it up!" I yell back and face the traitor again. "Now what do you mean one of us?" I interrogate.

"Just kill me. She's going to kill me anyways."

Out of frustration, I yank the gun out of Tianna's hand and kill the useless traitor without thinking twice.

The purple shield started to dull its color as the vultures outside it kept firing the weapons at it. An eighth vulture slowly and majestically floats out of the helicopter, but carried nothing in her hands. She dressed in black, but unlike the others, she didn't have a gas mask. She walked around the other seven who continuously drilled the bubble with their fire arms. She gets almost too personal with the shield, invading its space before she tears a line in it. Jane wails in pain in reaction to this. She grabs each side of the tear like curtains and widens the tear so she could walk through as if she was entering a teepee. A little bewildered, I witnessed her for a couple more seconds, astonished. I knew I had to do something, but she had broken through Jane's shield, which saved us from a million and one bombs and bullets but failed with a simple scratch of this succubus's fingers. She looked around for a slight second before she flicked her wrist and Jane went soaring through the air, and the bubble faded completely. The other vultures didn't quit their siege as soon as the bubble went down. Instinct took over and I began to infuriate myself as I punched the ground. The ground shook violently knocking almost everyone on their backs, everyone except the Snow white of the vultures who seemed to have just noticed my existence. She looked at me strangely with black eyes that matched her short, dancing, black hair. I dug my right hand under the ground grasping more dirt like a controller and I clenched my hand into a fist imagining an earthen pillar just below Snow white's feet. In sync with my imagination, an earthen pillar just beneath her feet shot her straight up launching her off the ground. But she unexpectedly adapted to the unnatural disaster and landed on her feet as any cat would. The other seven vultures started to get back up on their feet. With my right fist still in the ground, I dug a hole with my left hand and used the earth like a controller again to shake the ground violently, knocking them down again. Before I could turn back, Snow white was already in front of me mimicking my position almost exactly. She gazed into my eyes, with her fists in the ground, not saying one word. Confused on what she was doing, I was stunned, unable to move. Lost. Suddenly the earth beneath me shook and I was elevated away from Snow white upwards. Before I learned that she had repeated my very movements and before I could even begin to be furious that my new powers weren't even unique, I was on my back after sailing off the earthen pillar Snow White had created.

She had to die. There would be no way I would allow anyone to live who had the same ability as me. Before I got to my feet, I noticed Jane was back up, fighting off the other seven with Tianna and the others at her side. Too quickly, Snow White was hovering over me just as I stood up. Unafraid to hit a girl, I punched her in the face and we entered a fist combat. My body felt fluid, and light. I was able to leap off the ground to kick her in the side of the face without any effort. She backhanded me in the face then shoved her knee against my gut, before I hit her with excruciating pain in the neck. She flew back, and I realized as I followed through with my punch that I was just as fast as her.

Dodging each other's vicious strikes I can see sheaths of blue light making the other seven vultures look like fools out of my peripherals and I knew Jane was tossing them around in thin air. The others didn't hesitate to defend themselves as they attacked the vultures. Catching sense of me off my guard, Snow White took advantage of the fact that I was exhilarated watching Tianna fight and she drilled her knee in the pit of my stomach again. Rocks begin to fly at us the entire time we dance with each other. I subconsciously command a few rocks out of their offensive mode to defensive mode, encircling me knocking away the stones she was commanding to harm me with. Mirroring me, she took every step I made and failed to fall for every juke I planted. I aggressively threw myself in the air above her as she lunged for my throat and planted my feet in her back propelling myself away from her. Like two snakes I imagined the dirt to coil around her ensnaring her in place, but she failed to seek imprisonment as she flipped out of the trap. The stones still in mid air crumbled into tinier ones and spun at once like a mini tornado and hurled itself towards her at my command. Being abused by stone after stone she was picked up off the ground acting as the core of the mini tornado spinning uncontrollably all while I kept my left hand locked out in place controlling it. She somehow broke free of the imprisoning earthen tornado that turned into a ball of stones that just kept spinning by sending each individual rock in every direction breaking the posture I attempted to keep it in. Once she landed, she didn't breathe before she propelled a blue force field knocking me back. To combo her offensive attack, she mimicked my powers again and propelled me upwards with a giant earthen column. One after another, blue blankets of light pushed me further into the air after I tumbled off the column. To end her continuous pushing of me further towards the sky, I tried to blindsid her with multiple stones I sent from the ground. She caught wind of them racing towards her and developed a purple shield just before her to eliminate the gravel being forced for her. Taking advantage of her distraction I raised a pillar of earth to catch me from a deadly free fall and lowered myself to the ground level safely and quickly just before I sprung after her.

Our movement was faster than I could have thought possible. She leaped off the ground in another attack against me and something leaped after her from behind. Laura let out a girly roar as she caught onto the back of Snow White. With little to no effort, Snow White flipped Laura backwards like a rag doll then continued to come for me. But she slowed to a halt, and her eyes rolled back before she fell backwards on the ground passing out.

Confused, I took advantage of the fact that she was randomly unconscious to kill her. I could somehow hear her heartbeat and still feel a little warmth that her body radiated off even yards away from her. I focused on the ground beneath her and slowly the particles began to melt together as liquid. Quicksand took Snow White under. There would be no prince to awaken her from this eternal slumber underneath the earth.

I looked at my hands. I was growing. My instincts were taking over, almost controlling me, making me into the being I was meant to be. Sick!

The other seven seemed to have been taken care of with no casualties on our side. Jane piled their bodies all in one pile and I sank them to join their Snow White under the earth's surface. I wondered what came over Snow White when she fell, stunned to the floor. I looked over at Laura who seemed to have recovered from being thrown like a dog's chew toy. I shook my head in disbelief and convinced myself that it was just another aspect of my powers that I haven't fully discovered yet.

The group pulled together, all of us drained. Exhausted. And we began to sit and wait. Still leaderless, Tianna seemed to substitute for Brett as she gave everyone a rallying speech that assured everyone Cale and Brett were coming back to save us. Bored, I drifted from the group.

Nightfall came. There wasn't even a cricket to interrupt the silence. A fire was built by Tianna and Jane. But I remained uninterested and unsatisfied with everything. Whoever was in charge of these vultures was still out there. I swore not to rest until I found them. My swearing burdened me as a curse, because although I was completely drained, my pride forbids me to sleep.

Something rustled in the dark and I stood up quickly.

"It's just me." Laura's voice speaks softly.

"What do you want?" I demand.

"Nothing."

"So go away then."

"I can't sleep."

"I'm out of bedtime stories."

Ignoring me she sits next to me, confused as I was. Lost. We remain silent and restless for the remainder of the night. Still in the same position roughly six hours earlier, I could have sworn I heard a fowl crow in the distance. The morning had come and not one ounce of sleep took me over, but Laura seemed to have succumbed to the night. She slept peacefully on the ground. I got up and walked over to the rest of the group whom all slept around the burnt out fire.

Without even the slightest idea of celebration, lightning-less thunder took over the dark grey skies again. Everyone awoke to the alarm and looked at each other morbidly. We knew the sound too well to be convinced of a weather change. More Vultures were coming. Laura had awoken as well and came hustling over to the rest of the group. Black circles enveloped everyone's eyes. How we were going to survive this was completely up to fate. I cracked the knuckles in my fingers hoping to find some form of endurance, because I was, just as everyone else, completely exhausted and lost.

11. New Beginnings

Mr. Rusenkell and I stared at each other for a while, speechless and lost. I would guess it's been two hours since I realized I was dying, but I didn't even remember what waiting felt like, so I couldn't determine the waiting time before he finally broke the silence.

"Do you think you could ever forgive me Cale?"

"No." I say in my head.

"It's not like it's even his fault."

"It's his entire fault." I try to convince myself. My eyes darken and I repeat out loud, "No."

Obviously disappointed, Mr. Rusenkell looks down in embarrassment. Did he really think I was about to accept his apology happily and let go of the fact that I was dying? Another cough takes over my throat. Periodically tiny squirts of blood come out of my mouth whenever a cough is released. Denial and bargaining with life follow shortly afterwards every time the color is seen.

Tap, tap, tap goes the door in front of us and it flies open slamming against the white wall to its side. Boldly charging in Aileen pushes a cart carrying a television into the room. Quickly and without a word, she sets the Television up so it is facing me and she touches the power button before it flashes on and a picture of a man and a woman are sitting behind the desk of the local news station. Aileen turns up the volume and rolls her eyes while she leans against the television.

I start to focus on the television and start to hear a conversation about the city of Irvine. "Well Suzanne, it looks as though this tragedy has ended the lives of many citizens all at once. Police officials are saying this terrorist attack was led by a band of menaces, known as the White Crows. And here we have a government official, David Hamilton with more information on this band of local renagades who seem to be terrorizing the country one city at a time, David?"

"Thank you Chuck." Mr. Hamilton arrives on a smaller screen in the left hand corner. Footage of the demolished city of Irvine is portrayed all while he states, "My fellow American citizens, we are doing all we can to capture these terrorists. What has happened in the local city of Irvine is a utter tragedy and will not be taken ever so lightly. These menaces who call themselves the White Crows have waged a revolutionary war against the United States of America, and we shall not stand down."

"He's very persuasive." I thought.

"Shh!" I hushed.

"Please be alarmed that these so called White Crows are relentless and are showing no mercy as they have demonstrated already. Some agents of the White Crows are these three menaces, who seem to be the leaders of the rest of the group. These delinquents are the ones who are to be blamed for the thousands that have recently died in the Irvine attack." Three different black and white photos of whom all looked no older than 18-years-old flashed onto the screen. There was a girl with short dark hair who seemed confused, and the other two boys looked angry. But all three of them were obviously not ready for the picture, or not expecting it. "Please be aware that these villains are dangerous and I want to remind everyone to be vigilante and alert any authority if they should spot out one of them."

The power shuts off and Aileen starts to explain, "And so on and so on." As she wheels the cart and television out the door. She reenters the white room and folds her arms across her chest as she powerfully states, "So you see now what you've done Mr. Rusenkell? We wouldn't have to take such drastic measures if it wasn't for you, but luckily for you, this is working in Mr. Hamilton's favor." She crookedly smiles and I'm oddly attracted to her for an instant. She looks to the floor at the cure resting in its syringe and puts her foot on top of it before she kicks it light enough so it wouldn't break but with enough force to make it roll to me. "You should think about it, hybrid. You don't want this life." She bitterly explains. Then she storms out of the room.

I look to my old biology teacher wrapped in confusion. I had no idea what was going on, and it was about time for answers. "Are you going to tell me what in the world is happening?"

"Yes." He whispers, depressed.

"Well?" I insist after a pause of silence.

"What do you want to know first?" he asks looking as lost as I was.

"Stay with me Ruse." I say in my head. I could tell he was slowly losing himself. He was falling apart.

Calm and collect, I ask, "Why don't you start by telling me who you are." It was obvious that teaching high school biology was not his profession.

He softly speaks, "My name is Brian Rusenkell. I work for a secret agency called Modified Science Corporation. Here is where we used to test for cures and disease antibiotics and what not. Over generations we've invented many cures but also have created many deadly poisons. There is always an opposite of everything, there is no in between." His words were morbid. "Recently my wife was diagnosed with cancer shortly after our-"he pauses. I give him a sympathetic moment of silence. "-our daughter died from it. I swore I'd do anything to protect her." His eyes gloss over with liquid steel. "That day in class before these animals destroyed Stellar, I went home to find her already dead. I knew it was coming. I knew her time was dwindling. So that morning I took a bottle of this airborne toxin that M.S.C. manufactures. It was the only chance I had of saving her. It saved Jinx, so I hoped it would save her."

"Jinx?" I ask.

"Remember the cat in the video? The only one that survived the disease?"

"Oh."

"Yes well. The cat still remained to show signs of cancer, but it seemed to stop multiplying once substance 36 took over it. Just like cancer the toxin took over every cell in the body and the cat's eyes seemed to glow with emerald. It's pitch black fur was dark and coated with black silk. It somehow enhanced Jinx to the point where he was able to harness an unbelievable amount of agility, speed, and a thought process like a humans. I was sure it would work for her." He drifts his gaze off to the side looking lost again, but still down to earth enough to keep explaining. "When I realized the poison had been released, all hope I had had been lost." He looks down and swallows a gulp of saliva. "She died that day. And I murdered thousands more single-handedly the next day."

"No you didn't." I do my best to comfort him. I catch myself feeling sorry and I snap out of it. "It was those White Crows." I say with bitterness in every syllable of the word to take the focus off of the generosity in my voice when I assured Mr. Rusenkell he wasn't a murderer.

He looks up back at me and is almost shocked. "Don't you ever think that Cale. They have nothing to do with this! They are victims!" he begins to get angry. This is probably the second time I have ever seen Mr. Rusenkell get angry. He never gets frustrated, he's always chill.

"But didn't you see?-"

"It is a lie! *I* killed Stellar! *I* killed Irvine! *I* killed my wife…"

The poor guy was set on blaming himself. Although his speech noble, there was still a tingling symptom of vengeance that lurked in the back of my throat for these so called White Crows.

"They were all already going to die sooner or later." I do my best to bring some sense back into him.

He laughs. "Cale Valens. Always looking on the dark side of things. But somehow justifying the good in it."

"Shucks." I whisper in monotone.

"I see the good in you." He comforts as if I needed it.

Bewildered at his insight, I take the syringe Aileen had rolled to me and I crush it with my hands. "You don't know me." I threaten. *"Because I don't know myself."*

The glass had carved into the palm of my hand as I knew it would, but something in me wouldn't let me feel the pain. I looked at my injured hand and watched as something remarkably healed me. The cuts somehow healed too quickly and my palm returned to normal. There was no sign of injury anywhere. Completely shocked I turned to Mr. Rusenkell in confusion.

He swallowed before he assured me, "You're one of them now."

"One of who?" I demand.

"Them. The next evolution step of humans. You're a superhuman."

With a dumb face and a crooked eyebrow I ask, "What?"

"You have an extra chromosome that was dormant before you were exposed to substance 36. The bane has now taken control of that chromosome and activated it."

"What?" I say again making the same facial expression.

"Did you ever pay attention in class?"

"No, but Brett did."

He rolled his eyes as though he already knew I've been cheating off of Brett Gooding since day one of the semester. "You are the next evolution stage of the human race. Substance 36 can either kill you, do nothing to you or it can almost enhance you depending on whether your genes are strong enough to harness the power your body already possesses."

"So why am I coughing up blood?"

"Because your body is getting rid of the old blood that you survived off of and is generating you into a superhuman, giving you new blood."

"What's a hybrid?" I recall Aileen spitting the words at me as if she was disgusted.

"You are a hybrid. Half of you still remains human, while the other half is purely the poison. Pedigrates are manufactured. David Hamilton creates them from hybrids. They are entirely artificial."

"So what, they are like robots or something then?"

"No, not exactly. They are deceased victims that are revived after they die. As long as the brain doesn't stop functioning, if they are injected with a special serum before the brain fails, they are revived and called Pedigrates because they are no longer human. They don't remember anything about their past life or their present life. David Hamilton uses this to brainwash them, and they are convinced they are stronger than any hybrids."

"Well are they?"

"Unfortunately, yes."

"Peachy." I mutter, a little disappointed I was a hybrid.

"But they lack heart. The human will and the free spirit of choice is unable to them."

"So I'm guessing these two assassin twins are Pedigrates?"

"Them and more."

"How many more?" I ask a little worried.

"Scared?" I tease myself.

"Not on your life."

Mr. Rusenkell's eyes wonder away. "I don't know anymore. I was reassigned when I found out about the effects."

"Are they going to kill us?" I ask.

"I don't know."

"That's a yes." Silence follows my pessimism. Suddenly Tianna pops into my mind. And then Beef. I had forgotten I've left them behind. Soon they would be hunted down. I would never see them again. *"No."* I demand.

"No what?"

"Just no."

"Umm okay." Anger flourished threw me. Something innate gave me strength to stand. A weird flush of lightness took over my head and I felt like I was two pounds. With my hands clamped as fists my eyebrows dive down towards each other expressing my sudden lividness. Something began wrestling with the wind, defying gravity below me but my glare remained on the door in front of me. My peripherals decoded the objects to be pieces of the broken syringe and the actual liquid of the cure to be floating up towards my chest without anything controlling it. There was a small window on the door in front of me and outside of it was a back of a head. I could sense the presence of the Pedigrate psychically. I could smell the stench of an impulsive corpse standing guard outside the door. Somehow I knew I was in control of the world around me. The pallid room pressured me in. It was time to break out. Power surged through me, the extraordinary feeling jolted every inch of my skin. I had never felt so capable. *"Where is this coming from?"* I ask myself.

"I don't know. But I like it!" I almost shouted. Adrenalin didn't even compare to this sensation of intoxication my body was producing. "What happens to a Pedigrate when the antidote is given?" I bellow in a deep, ominous voice that wasn't my own. The instinct to warn Tianna, as a rooster would warn the dwindling night of the rising sun, had sounded like a battle cry in my head.

Nervous, Rusenkell replies being cautious with his words, "They would die, Cale."

At the end of his sentence, my head shivered in slow motion and the syringe had somehow manufactured itself back together containing the cure inside of it again by itself. "Don't be so naïve Mr. Rusenkell." I announced dully after my insight picked up the kindness in his words. He didn't want any more deaths, or violence. Like an arrow, the needle aligned itself to face the door and soared straight for it at an impossible speed, cutting the air in half and impaling through the door at the man standing guard outside. He collapsed, and a force pushed devastatingly against the door and wall in front of me as I released my fists. As any fireless and explosive-less bomb would, the entire wall in front of me was demolished. Familiar debris polluted the air and an alarm screeched through the hall.

"*Whoa.*" I grin with my eyes.

"*Please tell me that was us.*"

"*No.*" I tell myself, "*That was me. Just me.*" I step on the cured, deceased Pedigrate who has pieces of the door pinning him to the floor, and swivel my head from left to right down the hallway. "Are you coming?" I announce back at Mr. Rusenkell without looking back for him. I walk down the hall with clairvoyance that he would follow. It was pure intuition that took over me. All I had to do was imagine ideas, and they seemed to fall under my orders. Rustling footsteps came rushing down steps at the end of the hall and more guards came to heed the alarm's call for help. After all, that's all an alarm is for; to alert the incapable.

There were two doors on the left, and three on the right down the hall. I imagined the walls to explode as I had demolished mine. And with a sonic clap, they were torn from their hinges and forced to collide with each other in the middle of the hallway.

"*Behind you.*" I warned myself.

I turn to see five familiar faces already free, and holding Aileen and my mother hostage with syringes. They don't look like they put up much resistance.

"Cale let's go!" Brett orders.

His beckon almost made me stay behind. But I wasn't going to let my pride get in the way of me seeing her again. "*How did they get out?*"

"*No clue.*" I say to myself, completely disappointed.

Mr. Rusenkell follows swiftly behind the others while I walked casually behind them in last place. Brett forced Aileen to show us the way out, and lackadaisically she pointed every direction out until we reached the elevator. Brett crammed everyone inside the elevator and had to hold the door from closing a couple times as I strolled in with no rush in my movement. The irritation on his face let me know that he was debating on leaving me behind. The awkward elevator ride almost made me laugh. Everyone was quiet and avoiding eye contact while a jaunty tune was played as we quickly moved. I couldn't hold it in. I let out a chuckle, and everyone looked at me with disgusted looks. "*They are taking this way too seriously.*"

"*Tell me about it.*" I concur as the metal doors automatically open up and we pour out of the elevator. Everyone else rushes to the double doors we came in and out towards the white room that contradicted the ebon helicopter in the middle of it. I continue to just walk and call out, "The wonder twins killed our pilot remember?"

They all stop in the amazement of my truth. None of them knew how to operate a helicopter. As they all halt, my peaceful stroll catches up with them and as I pass through I say sarcastically in a low dull voice, "Hurry, hurry!" mocking their rush.

"I can fly it." My mother's voice calls out from behind. I stop, still trying to realize that she wasn't really Glenda, and grew irritated that Brett's hustle came back into motion as they all climbed into the helicopter. I turn to see Cocoa holding Aileen who doesn't seem to be happy with my mom as she glares at her. My mom glares back.

"Hmm..."

"What now?"

"It's just weird. I thought they were supposed to be dominant over hybrids."

"Just get in." I order myself as I climb into the helicopter.

Aviating through the air I feel anxious to see her. I grew worried of Beef. I thought of all the worst situations they could have been in, but they all resulted in death, which didn't make me feel any better.

We began to hover over dead Irvine. "Home, sweet home." I whispered morbidly. Eventually Irene had found the rest of the Stellar High survivors and began to land. I was anxious to see Beef. It was morning, although the grey sky shadowed the sun making it look like twilight. The closer we descended, the more my eyes strained to find Tianna. Beef wasn't that hard to spot out. Every single one of them, their faces pale as if they've just seen a ghost. They could have been cardboard decoys the way they stood so still.

Once the loud chopping of the wings came to a halt, and the engine ended its roaring, everyone stepped out of the helicopter one by one. Slowly redeeming their sanity, the still crowd then realized who we were. Phillip reunited himself with Laura. *"Touching."* I grimace to myself as they hug. Their faces slowly began to regain some of its color.

Buddy barked, overjoyed around Beef. I looked at him and couldn't help but smile in my head. Buddy shared his love with everyone but me. Even when Beef politely ordered him to run to me, Buddy refused and just ignored my existence. "That's fine." I grimace. "I prefer cat's anyways."

Still looking around for Tianna after being rejected by a mutt, I noticed everyone started hugging and becoming all lovey-dovey with each other. It made me want to puke. Someone bumped into me. "Watch it!" we both say simultaneously in a threatening voice. Only to find I've threatened the very person I was searching for.

"I think this is the closest we've ever been." I announce to myself.

"Oh…" we both say awkwardly.

"Wow this is pathetic." I tell myself after yet another awkward silence.

"Bite me." I scowl back.

"Excuse me?" She asks, confused and offended.

"Dang! I did it again."

"Classic!" I chuckle in my mind. "Start over?" I ask almost indecently.

"Please." She confirms.

I take my hand out and offer it to her when I greet, "Hi, I'm Cale."

She raises an eyebrow before she wraps her hands around mine and squeezes firmly. "Tianna." She states. Something in her voice told me like a siren, that this was a new beginning. My head felt light and I started to feel like I did just before the broken syringe was remodeled right before me. Ecstatic and overwhelmed with confidence I had finally met the girl I was going to marry. With my own clairvoyance I was sure of it. All the while I felt an eerie glare gazing a hole in my back…

12. Aileen

Curiosity is truly a deadly thing. It didn't take long for the welcome home to be abandoned and questions erupted through what remained of Stellar High's population. I turned around and almost ran over Marcus' littler, older brother.

"We thought you were one of them." He says. "Could've killed you." He whispers ominously before he walks past me.

"Okay?"

"What crawled up his butt and died?"

Information was transferred over as Mr. Rusenkell warned the remainders about the effects of substance 36. I listened in to maybe catch something about what exactly it was that I was capable of now, but something else caught my ears. It was two low voices, whispering in the helicopter. I strayed from the lecture everyone else gave full attention to, and silently walked towards the helicopter where the voices grew louder.

"Cale?" Tianna interrupts my stalk. "What's wrong?"

I had forgotten all about Aileen and Irene. "We brought back hostages." I explain.

"What?"

"We brought back two Pedigrates from the headquarters after we saved Mr. Rusenkell." I whisper, trying not to cause a distraction from the lecture. I walk into the helicopter and I see Aileen and my mother handcuffed in the front seats. Tianna follows me inside. Aileen looks at her strangely.

"What." Tianna demands from her.

"This helicopter has no gas. We are in the middle of nowhere. Well, now we are...Is this Cale's squeeze?" Aileen deviously grins towards Irene, but my mother doesn't share the same emotion when Tianna punches Aileen in the face. Aileen stretches her jaw like she is yawning and continues to speak, "What's done is done and there's no bringing this place back to life. Besides, I had nothing to do with it, so if you feel like punching me in the face again little girl, you better be prepared-" Pow! Tianna punches her again, but harder.

"Restrain her!" I demand

"No way! This is awesome!"

Again, Aileen seems to shake it off and continue. "Why don't you go fetch your little friend Brett and unlock us, dear. If we make a break for it in this helicopter, have your friend Phil blow it up, ok?" she consults.

"What are you talking about?" I ask.

"Oh I think you know." She glowers at me assuming I should know what she was talking about. I played the look off like I did, but I knew she knew I was ignorant.

"What are you doing Cale?" Brett intervenes.

"None of your business." I state.

"Actually these two are my business. They have answers, and I captured them."

Aileen shoots another look at Irene. Something was wrong. I could smell it. "Well then-" I start before Tianna interrupts me.

"So why don't you unlock them and have them tell the rest of us these so called answers."

"I don't-"

"No time like the present, eh Brett?" She insists.

"Yeah Brett. No time like the present." Aileen agrees as Tianna hops out of the helicopter. I follow her in awe. "Excuse me, everyone!" She calls out, interrupting Mr. Rusenkell's lecture. "Brett would like to share something with us." She turns to pay attention to Brett, and he stammers before he unlocks Aileen and Irene.

He stands up to the crowd and announces, "Here is Aileen and-"

"I'll take it from here turbo." Aileen interrupts. "All of you hybrids pipe down. If you wish to live, it would behoove you to listen up. I want everyone to line up in a single file line. I will categorize you all and separate the hybrids from the regulars."

Rumbling of confused voices started asking questions about what was a hybrid.

"Oh boy." I somehow managed to hear Aileen mutter, "This is not going to be fun." She whistled to silence the rioting crowd. "How about everyone line up and we'll carry on from there?" I looked to Mr. Rusenkell to see if we should trust her. I didn't believe her. Something was going on.

"Don't worry everyone." Brett announces, "It's okay, I promise you." Everyone seemed to start moving when Brett confirmed that everything was going to be alright.

"Hmm…"

"Indeed. 'Hmm' is right."

Of course they would listen and start the line. I remained silent and unsure of the situation, but even Tianna could smell that something was wrong. "Can I talk to you?" She asked under her breath without even looking at me.

"Yes, yes, yes, a million times yes!" I shout in my head.

"Dear God, get a hold of yourself." I bitterly assault.

"Sure." I say following her behind a shaded area away from the survivors. Before disappearing I felt a pair of eyes stare me down again. "What's wrong?" I ask.

Tianna explains how the group was attacked by a group of vultures, and describes a bubble that Jane seemed to be controlling, and how Jonah, who was Marcus' littler older brother, was somehow able to sink the bodies into the earth. I wanted to believe every word she was saying, but I just couldn't see how any of this was possible. A flashback of escaping the very place we rescued Mr. Rusenkell from came to my mind as I replayed the memory of the world around me falling under my control over in my mind. Maybe I would awake in my bed and be off to school like any other day, but no matter how hard I pinched myself, these supernatural occurrences just became more instinctual and real. "Something is happening to me

Cale. I hear pulses, I feel like I can fly, I feel like I can flip through the air above the tallest building and still be able to land safely on my feet."

"Want to try it?" I joke.

"Cale this is serious."

"Of course it is." Someone interrupts.

"Jonah, what are y-"Tianna is cut off.

"I don't need to be judged by this traitor. I know exactly what I am capable of. You're welcome to join us, but otherwise. This is the last you will see of us."

"Us?" Tianna asks.

"Myself, Max, and Jane."

"Where are you going?" I intervene.

"Away from here." Jonah says as he walks away from us.

"These two know where to find David Hamilton."

Jonah stops in his tracks. "And who is this David Hamilton?"

"He's the guy who is in charge of the people that have been attacking us."

"So he did this to us?" Jonah says after a long pause.

"I- I don't know. There are these three. Who seem to be in charge of this group of terrorists called the White Crows who apparently destroyed our lives."

"Well," he says still facing his back towards me, "I guess I can put on an act for now. We leave tomorrow then." And he walks away.

"Regular." Aileen announces. "Get over with the rest of them." Irene seems to be discreetly recording something on a piece of paper from the inside of the helicopter. "Next!" Aileen breaks my concentration as I watch Marcus Moon sit down in front of Aileen who is sitting cross legged on the dirt, ash ground. "Don't move, be still." She orders. All Aileen does is look at him before she announces, "Another Regular." I look over to Irene to see if there was a pattern, but she seemed to have disappeared. I walk closer to the helicopter to see if my mom was still inside, as Baley sits down in front of Aileen. Aileen's voice was more jaunty and pleased to announce, "Hybrid." In a devious tone. "She's a painter."

"Oh, I do like to paint! How did you-" Baley starts in her sweet typical voice.

"No. You paint something, it becomes real. That is your ability. Next please!" Aileen indecently shouts.

Cameron Dark steps up to the plate. "Hybrid again. He's a shade-stepper."

"A what?" Cameron asks.

"You can turn invisible. Next!" Aileen was getting frustrated. She didn't have any patience at all. Next sat down Jonah, whom she called an earth breaker and explained he was able to control the surface of the earth. Jane was called a light bringer who said to have the ability to control force fields of light as Jonah decided to demonstrate his powers in front of the confused regulars. Although Baley was categoriezed as a hybrid, she sat with Marcus who sat with five other disappointed regulars. I had assumed by the looks of their faces that being a regular was what something you didn't want to be.

The gloomy mood seemed to lighten as others started harnessing their supernatural powers. It was as if Aileen was handing them out like candy. People started to have fun. I didn't even remember the word. She instructed that our capabilities were purely instinctual and that we would have to learn how to use our abilities the natural way our mind let us think. Laura was diagnosed as a sleeper, which she said that a certain touch could paralyze or mobilize anything. Phil became a demolitionist which was said to have the ability to allow things to automatically self combust. "This one is a Leech." Aileen announced in a strange voice. Bozzo got off the ground and walked over to the regulars lackadaisically. "No." Aileen says irritated. "You are able to leech powers off of those around you."

"Yes!" Bozzo says excited. "Awesome!" he shouts.

Aileen rolls her eyes and shoots a look at the helicopter. Irene was writing something down with the haste of a jackrabbit behind Brett Gooding. "Next!" Aileen calls out. Amanda walks up and sits down. "Fire starter." Aileen says quickly. The look on Amanda's face was a little bit disappointed.

"I could have guessed that." I muttered.

Cocoa was themed a flea giant, that could enlarge his size to a building, or shrink down to the size of an atom. A kid named Ty became a regular, While Max Longo became a boiler: which apparently, he had the ability to create and control water, and also control the temperature of all mass. Beef's turn was next. Buddy wouldn't stop furiously barking at Aileen when Beef sat down. I was excited to see what Beef would become. Buddy got in the way of Aileen and Beef had to restrain him by grabbing his neck and yanking him backwards. Buddy didn't let up easy though. It was as if Buddy was protecting Beef from her. Maybe she was doing something to us. Maybe she wasn't doing what she said she was doing after all. This could have been a scam!

"Back away from him!" I demand. As Beef and everyone else stop playing with their powers and look to me. The fear for Aileen hurting my only friend gave my voice the authority to control a tank of wild great white sharks. I march over to her and stand between her and Beef. She scowls as if I've spoiled some sort of plot.

"Well, aren't we anxious to cut..."

"I'm not cutting." I state, "I'm telling you to back off."

"And why should she?" Brett interferes.

"This doesn't concern you." Tianna defends as she crosses over to me. Jonah looked infuriated at either myself or Aileen.

"Don't tell him what concerns him or not!" Amanda defends.

"Oh typical! Just typical!" Britney almost screams, "Why don't you go open some more bottles that don't belong to you, Pandora!" I almost laugh at the fact that everyone was catching on to the nickname I granted her.

"Why don't I just light your fake blonde hair on fire?" Amanda fires back. And soon everyone had a bone to pick with everyone. We were all arguing vigorously and relentlessly starting to physically shove each other. Not once did my eyes leave Brett's glower who seemed to have had enough of my rebellious attitude. We both leap after one another at the same time as if we rehearsed this fray over and over again, getting our timing down perfectly. Everyone, including myself, was embracing the fact that the unrealistic idea of obtaining super powers was now a real thing.

Brett and I collided with one another at an impossible speed. *"I'm super fast?"* I thought as we wrestled down from the air. Brett launched me back away from him and I with complete agility I landed like a cat. I sprinted for Brett again and tackled him down too fast to have thought possible.

"I'm super fast!" I concurred to myself, purely excited. The surge of excitement reinforced my aggressiveness towards attacking Brett. Fire and force fields broke out between the group of survivors. The earth began shaking, and the heat of the air seemed to escalate, nearly burning my skin. But the distractions didn't stop me from pummeling Brett. Rolling on the ground, I caught a glimpse of Aileen laughing, like this was entirely what she wanted, and my mother began frantically looking around unsure how to fix the mess at hand. Every element of power the survivors contained was used against one another until a deafening siren echoed through, piercing our hearing, causing everyone to fall to their knees, squeezing

their heads; Everyone except for myself and Tianna. She seemed to be the source of the screeching siren that weakened everyone's mind. Even buddy rolled on the floor in agony. Aileen mimicked the dog for a good ten seconds before the highly pitched roar stopped. And everyone's eyes bulged open in misery. Quietness stirred the air before Aileen disrupted it.

"A siren." She struggles out as she dusts herself off. She gazes into her eyes and looks as though something unexpected had just happened. "The immortal siren…" she gasps almost too quietly to hear. Aileen maneuvers around the others who still seem to be recovering from the glass shattering screeching towards the helicopter where Irene was. She begins to whisper something before a massive body collapses on top of me. Beef was trying to find his balance.

"Beef!" I struggle to keep him up.

"Sorry Cale," he says quickly before changing the subject, "I need to ask you something." He speaks out of breath from trying to recover from the screeching.

"Can you breathe first?"

"I want her to look into me."

"What?"

"Don't defend me. I want her to look and see my powers, I'll be fine!"

"No, it's not like that Beef, I don't trust- Something is going on!"

"Brett-"

My eyes almost pop out of my sockets, "Don't you dare Beef! I'm not trying to disappoint you! I'm only trying to protect you."

"I don't need to be babied Cale!"

"Ugh! Fine! Do what you want."

"Thanks." He says happily as he turns away from me to head for Aileen, I grab his shoulder and face him towards me.

"After me." I demand before I walk around him towards Aileen. Questions about where the screeching had come from filled the mouths of all the recovering hybrids and regulars, but I knew it was Tianna.

"Just what do you think you are doing?"

"I'm going to see what I can do."

"It's a trick! You know it!"

"What if it's not?"

"Are you not seeing all the signs? She is putting some kind of voodoo spell on these idiots and calling them hybrids or regulars!"

"I'm not going to let Beef do this alone."

"Get off your high horse, since when was nobility your best aspect."

"Shut up! I need to know what I can do!"

"You have got to be kidding me."

"You scared?"

I shut myself up and march straight up to Aileen. "I'm next." I demanded. "After Brett, that is." If I was going down, so was he.

"She already did mine."

"Oh? So what is your super power? Super stupid speech giving abilities that make you want to vomit?"

"Very descriptive. I like it."

"Thanks. It's a true story."

"Right?"

"No, actually. He's a flyer." Aileen confirms.

I look to her, then back to him. "Prove it." And Brett takes off before I could finish taunting him, shooting straight up disobeying all of gravity. He shot up like a rocket and came spiraling down faster than any bullet could. When he landed the earth shook beneath his feet in utter seriousness. "Well then Buzz Light-year, I suppose it is my turn." I say unimpressed with his gift.

Aileen tells me to take a seat in front of her. Everyone has gathered around to witness my reading.

"Ha! Don't be so naïve, you know they previously gathered around to see Brett fly. They don't care about you."

"Can I ever have a moment?"

"Nope. But hey. Maybe once you get your super power, you can fit in with the rest of the misfits."

Aileen gazed into my eyes as I gazed into hers. She seemed to be taking longer than any other reading she had already done with the others. She reaches forward with both hands, a bit frustrated and grasps onto my hands. She leans in slowly, closer and closer. "Let's try this again." She says calmly before she jerks her hands back after only a few seconds of gazing into my eyes and jerks her head back as well. I literally saw the light leave her eyes before Aileen collapsed on her left side.

Whispers turned into curious murmurs, and then came Irene's scream. Irene rushed over to her side and lifted Aileen's head off the floor. Aileen's eyes remained open but lackadaisical. Irene checked her pulse and announced, "She's dead."

13. Irene

Words like "freak" and "Murderer" echo through my head. Even in a new world of supernatural events, I was outlawed from my own kind. I was only trying to protect Beef, and Aileen goes all noble and dies!

"Don't you say one word." I warn myself.

"Swordfish."

"I mean it. Nothing."

"Give me a break. Did you honestly believe you could start over anew, make new friends and win the girl of your dreams all before a new dawn?"

I ignore the devious voice in my head in high hopes it would behoove my silence as a warning. But it wouldn't.

"Destined villains, cannot be heroes, Cale."

"I am not a villain." I grimace, unaware I have spoken out loud.

"Oh but you are, you see, you have just murdered Aileen. This is only the beginning. She was merely one of the first."

"And the last. I won't kill again. Even if I have to lock myself up in an asylum."

"But how do you prevent what you have no control over, Cale?"

"You know."

"A remarkable assumption."

"Tell me how."

"Admit you killed her first."

"Don't you imbeciles have anything better to do than just stare!" I roar, walking away from the group of awe-eyed teenagers. I would not admit to something I had no knowledge of doing. How could I have killed her without even touching her, no signs of adrenalin, or anger within me. No marks of struggle upon her skin. Nothing. There was no longing for vengeance lurking in my blood. The air between Aileen and I may not have smelled of a sweetly zephyr the dew spit up from the lush, green grass, but it didn't compare to the putrid smoke that hazed around Brett Gooding.

As everyone decided to finally break from surrounding Aileen, I turned back to look at her. Irene hovered over her, weeping. Seeing my mother cry nearly broke me. There was something devastating about watching your own mother cry. It was a curse they put on all of their children. Like a piece of me was dying and I was slowly fleeting into nothingness. I had to remind myself she was not Glenda. She was just a foolish girl controlled by power. In the midst of her cry, she pulled something out of her black boot. I recognized a syringe with a black liquid in it as she injected it into Aileen. Irene waited patiently for her to awake, as I awaited the same. Everyone seemed to scatter slowly but still remained glaring at me. Irene shook Aileen more violently as if the syringe was supposed to bring her back to life. But Aileen never came back. I backed away, in fear of my mother's wrath, and walked away from a superficial life I didn't want any part in.

Beef had stopped me from wandering too far, Buddy keeping his distance from me.

"What." I demanded avoiding all contact and turning away from him.

"What did you do, Cale?" he accused.

Instantly my eyes became full of raging vigor. "I did nothing!" I hissed. "I sat there, and she did her little gaze thing and just died, okay!"

"Cale, I'm not-"

"Don't judge me Beef! You have no idea what it's like-" Buddy barks defensively at my scolding towards Beef. "Shut up mutt!" I turn back to Beef.

"You have no idea who I am. So why don't you take your little pooch away and leave me alone!" Buddy didn't heed my warning the first time I attempted to silence him. "I said shut up stupid dog!" Buddy silences himself.

"Leave Buddy out of this!" Beef defends.

I turn from him, infuriated, and continue walking. "Dumb dog." I mutter with a hidden jealousy I stubbornly hid from Beef.

"The Cale I know wouldn't turn his back on me." Beef says stopping me in my tracks.

"That Cale died. I never asked for this. I never wanted this. Everything was fine the way it was."

"You don't have to lie to me Cale." Beef comforts.

His words hit me like an unexpected car crash. I hadn't noticed that I had let Beef in. I had become vulnerable and open enough for him to read me like a book. Fear began to encourage me to keep lying to him, but the truth inside my heart wanted to resurrect itself.

"I know how much you hated Stellar. Where were you going to go after you graduated, if you graduated? Huh?" His words hit me like bullets, angering me. "I could have made friends Cale. I could have made other people like me, but I stuck with you the entire way. Because you're my best-"

An explosion on the tip of my tongue blew up as I turned back to roar at beef. "Well consider this the end then! I *release* you from this pathetic life style. Go make your friends you could have made if I didn't hold you back and forget my face! Matter of fact, forget I ever existed!" I snarl in lividness. Beef wears a surprised shock on his face. I turn from him disgusted.

"When's my birthday?" he asks quietly.

"September 22." I reply instinctively.

"Do you know what your abilities are?"

"I don't know." I mock. "Wonder twin decided to die before telling me. So I have no clue what I can do."

"Well there's one thing for sure that you can do."

"What." I reply looking at him with pessimism of anticipating his next words.

"You can read minds." His voice whispers, but his lips remained sealed.

I became paralyzed for a second, and then I pulled away from the idea and brought myself back to reality. "Funny. Did your dog tell you that?"

"That was a bad joke." Beef says again without opening his mouth. I was sure of it this time that he had not spoken out loud, but yet I somehow managed to hear him.

Say something again I had whispered in my head, but commanded Beef.

"Something." Beef announces without any lip movement. My eyes grew a little wide as I realized he had to have read my mind.

"You can too?" I say out loud.

"I don't know. I just heard your voice in my head." He explains.

Excited, I pretend to stay my calm self and ask, "Okay, what am I thinking?"

"Pineapples, venom, gas, computers."

"None of those things go together."

"Fine." I roll my eyes, *"Apples, oranges, grapes, tomatoes-"*

"Tomatoes are vegetables, not fruits."

"So what."

"So that doesn't match with the apples, oranges and grapes."

"What? No tomatoes are fruits!"

"No, you're a fruit."

"Really?"

"I don't- I don't know. I don't hear anything Cale." Beef says, interrupting my argument with myself.

"But you just heard me say-"

"Yeah I swear I heard you say '*say something again*' but that was it."

I started to wonder on how that could be. Then it occurred to me. *Do a flip* I thought.

Instinctively, Beef does a back flip through the air and lands perfectly on his feet. "Whoa!" he says astonished.

"Did you hear me that time?" I asked.

"No, but I just did a flip! I've never been able to do a flip! I've got to show someone! How- how did I do that?" Beef looks at his body with brand new eyes and I strangely look at him with a raised eyebrow.

"I wonder..." I thought. *Do several jumping jacks.*

Robotically, Beef stiffens his body up to do ten jumping jacks before I commanded him to stop in my head. I was controlling him. I made him sing a nursery rhyme, then roll around on the ground. I made him play dead and then I had him do the splits, which I definitely knew he was incapable of. But he remained obedient to my silent call and continued to look at himself with amazement and confusion. He claimed to not hear my voice, so I stopped imagining obstacles for him to go through, and his confidence led him to think he was an all-star cheerleader.

Excited, he shouted for me to watch him while he, alone, attempted to do a back flip. In mid air, I realized he was about to break his neck. He hadn't pushed himself off the ground enough to fully rotate his body so his feet could catch him. A frightening shock awoke in me and forced me to reach for him, debating if I should dive for him, but he froze. With my hands reaching out for him, Beef somehow magically contained himself in the air, without touching the ground. I stopped my pursuit towards him in utter surprise and let down my raised arms. In sync with them, Beef began to descend too, crying out for help all the while. My arms stopped halfway to my thighs, and so did Beef. I raised my arms up again to the same position they were in and beef hovered higher, imitating them. Beef whimpered as he rose higher. He was either unable to move, or too scared to. Buddy heaved Beef's whimpering and came over to lick his face as he remained upside down in the middle of the air. I curiously look upon his back strangely. My fingers took control of the situation and somehow twirled him around to face me. Buddy remained on his back side and kept licking the back of his neck, comforting Beef.

Could this really be happening? "Cale! Help me down!" Beef wailed.

I released my focus on him, dropped my arms completely and looked at buddy who continued to lick Beef as he collapsed onto the ground without injuring his neck.

He arose to his feet, looking all around him. Both of our faces dumbfounded, I admit, "I think it was Me." before he could even ask.

"How'd you-"

"I just do." I interrupt before he could finish asking.

"Cale?" I new voice enters. Buddy, Beef and I all turn our heads to Tianna as she walks awkwardly to me.

Some silence passes before Beef foolishly says, "I'll leave you two alone. Come on Buddy!" Buddy tries to stay but Beef drags him away. Tianna waits until they are out of hearing range before she breaks the silence.

"Why'd you run off?"

"Why do you care?"

"Don't be so rude!"

"Shut up!"

"Well, why not?" she replies.

"Because." I say trying to come up with a quick answer. "No one cares."

"That's not true." She says.

"Did you come here to argue because of what happened?"

"No, I came here to talk."

"Well I don't want to talk."

"Well you should reconsider."

"Why should I? You're not my mom." I scowl.

"Because I said so, that should be enough."

"Well it's not. Thanks for playing. Have a nice day." I say before I turn to leave. Too quickly she arrives in front of me and grapples my shirt.

"I need to get something off my chest and you are going to listen to me even if I have to-"

"What? Let out a screaming siren that'll cripple me down, torturing my ears?"

"How'd- how'd you guess?"

"Guess what?"

"That that was what I wanted to talk about."

"I didn't."

"Then how'd you know?"

"Because I saw you okay? Now get out of my way." I attempt to maneuver around her, but she quickly recaptures the front of my path towards nowhere.

"No."

"Yes." I say as I pick her up and set her aside. She was light, and easier to move than I thought she would have been. I continue walking on.

"Stop!" she alarms as she grabs my shoulder, and I suddenly see my vision fades to black as my body freezes itself unwillingly into place.

I awake from what felt like a sleep, but still standing in the same pose my body froze itself into. As my eyes opened I saw Tianna in front of me, grasping my face asking me if I was alright. My body broke free from the paralysis and I fell on top of her, both of us falling to the ground. She shoved me off of her and dusted herself off as she stood up.

"What'd you do?" I say, laying on the ground with no interest in standing up.

She looks at me, disgusted. "You sound like all of them." She bobs her head as she folds her arms across her chest. "*I* did nothing. You simply froze in place for like five minutes. You were like in some coma or something. And you wouldn't budge."

"Maybe you should start lifting some weights." I joke as I rest my hands behind my head.

"Maybe you should lose a pound, or fifty." I close my eyes and I realize how exhausted I was. "Get up." She demands.

"No."

"Excuse me?"

"No thank you." I say politely.

Some silence passes before she gives up and lies down next to me. The air stood still. I took advantage of the quiet and inhaled deeply. Although thick, I somehow managed to breath in a fragrance of freshness from the ash burned sky. "Stubborn." She states under her breath. This makes me turn my head over so I am looking right at her vertically, and then back up at the grey sky. The verge of laughter boiled in my throat before I started laughing. Breaking all tension, my contagious laugh awoke a song of laughter out of her. There wasn't a reason for it, and there wasn't a reason for it not to happen, but somewhere in between our dancing laughter, I felt a connection possess over me, and then I felt it in her as it continued to swing back and forth like a pendulum. I was sure it was coming from her heart.

We sat there, soaked in silence after we finished feeding off of each other's laughing. It was a comfortable silence, one to be reckoned with in a book or song. For the first time since I could remember, life was peaceful. There were no alarms, no gusts of wind, no bullets, or blood. There was no sound of danger as the fowl of dawn would shriek as a warning to the glowing, solemn moon that the prideful, boasting sun was coming to shine it's glorified candle light amongst the world. When the fowl crows, it is the one moment in the world where there is a neutral red and lavender light that contained remembrance of the beautiful past and the opportunities of the brand new beginning. Half dark and half light; the fowl's rightful place belonged in between the middle of it. Just like good and evil, I didn't belong to either side. I would start a riot where I saw fit and I would be the same one to silence it if I felt like it.

"Favorite color." She mutters under her breath

I somehow know she is starting a series of questions when I answer, "Red. Yours?"

"Blue." She contradicts.

"Favorite word." I mutter in the same tone as her last question.

"Forever." She answers. "Favorite movie."

"The Lion King." I sigh at being honest. She looks at me like I'm lying but my nose doesn't grow any longer. I raise my eyebrows and pressure my lips together while nodding once. "Favorite book."

"I can't read."

"Me neither." I giggle.

"What's your darkest secret?" she asks.

"I'm better before you get to know me."

"That's not true." She says wistfully.

I curl my lips knowing better. "Favorite animal."

"Wolves." She enunciates.

"Why?"

"Because they mate for life."

"So?"

"So? You don't think that's cute?"

"Just because they mate don't mean they fall in love for life. Animals can't fall in love." I say pessimistically.

"They can too!" she defends, getting a rise out of her. Her natural blush bloomed with crimson laced upon her cheeks. She was cute when she was mad. It only made me want to provoke her even more.

"Most of them just have babies and leave. I don't buy it."

"Well I do." She says, stubborn.

"Why?"

She looks at me very seriously with eyes of a pure look. I could see her through my peripheral vision as she continued to softly stare. I turned my head to her and gazed into her eyes, willing to listen. She speaks with a slow grace and sincerity enough to know she was using her words as metaphor's for us. "Instinct. Their natural instincts. Instinct to hunt. Instinct to survive. Instinct to love." She whispers, trying to convince me in a near cruel tone. She was beautiful. She was menacing and malevolent at the same time she was the contrary. She was temptation in human form and she knew it.

A butterfly fluttered above us and I couldn't help but know that it was me that created it. Things were different with Tianna. I didn't have to focus to use my powers. It was as if my subconscious mind was in control, while I got to sit back and enjoy the view as I did whenever I was in the passenger's seat of Beef's car. My eyes contained themselves on it until it reached fully out of sight. I turn my head back towards Tianna and find myself gazing into her caramel eyes. Although we were in the middle of what seemed like a war, there was no need to rush or move, let alone speak with her. Time simply stopped for us. Old feelings came rushing back like looking through an old photograph book. I realized that I was in love with her. I had always been at first sight. And even if she didn't feel the same way, I would keep this memory until my dying day.

"I've always thought you were peculiar." She sort of whispered.

"Thanks?" I say. What was I supposed to say to that? I sit up straight, holding myself up by my arms.

She copies my lazed posture before she says, "I like it."

"Thanks." I say more commonly. "I think you're peculiar as well."

She laughs and punches my arm. Personally I didn't find it funny, so I didn't laugh, which made it awkward for her I supposed when she looked away. "Why didn't you ever talk to me?" She asked after some quiet.

"Because." I said flatly, unwilling to share my answer.

"Because..."she led me on.

"No."

"Why not?" she says, building a little irritation in her voice.

"Because I don't want to."

"Tell me."

"No."

"Look at me." she demands as she grabs my face to look at her, "tell me what's the matter. Talk to me." I don't say anything. We just sat there as she uncomfortably held my face and I awkwardly stared.

"Just forget it okay?"

"You know I won't."

"Because Tianna! The last time I talked to you, you made me look like a fool! You embarrassed me and yet I still had feelings for you! What was I supposed to do, huh? Erase you completely?"

"What are you talking about?"

"Seventh grade."

"Yeah? And?" it took her a moment before she realized she remembered. "Oh..."

"Yeah."

"Well I was young, Cale! " she defends.

"It doesn't matter." We both say nonchalant.

"Jinx." We both say in monotone again, betting ourselves the other wouldn't say it.

"Double jinx?" we both question.

"You owe me a soda if we ever find one." I tell her.

"You owe-" she starts before I interrupt her.

"Nope! You can't talk. Rules of jinx."

"You can't talk either than!"

"No, I can."

"Oh why are you the exception?"

"Because I'm the only exception."

She sticks her finger down her throat and I shoulder bump her off balance, since she left the only other arm holding her up vulnerable. "Punk." She says as she recovers herself up to punch me in the arm. She bit her lip. That was already one of my favorite things she did. It made me want to kiss her. There were a million reasons why I should have, but something held me back. Like there was something that needed to be cleared out of the way before I did. "So, I have a confession." She states.

"Here we go."

"It's kind of a deal breaker." I raise an eyebrow and carry a worried look in my eyes. She takes a deep breath in before she admits slowly, "I sort of, talk to myself sometimes." And there wasn't a reason in the world that could stop me from kissing Tianna that very moment in time. I leaned in with half aggression, and sealed my lips against hers, as they caressed them with care beyond fulfillment.

We walked back, hand in hand under the grey sky. I couldn't help but think that this was all just part of her plan to get me back to the group of people I had run away from. Brett's voice was heard thundering. It didn't worry me, because I never listen to his speeches anyways, but the tremble in his voice alarmed me that something was terribly wrong. I let go of Tianna's hand and raced over, following the trail of his voice. I was amazed how fast I had become. I was legitimately supernaturally fast, and the fact that Tianna was agilely keeping up enlightened me that everyone had become capable of things we weren't before. With the wind dancing upon our face, we reached the others who seemed to be rioting over something. Aileen's corpse hadn't been moved, but everyone seemed to be circling a huge, unnatural fire I could only assume Amanda had made.

Beef came rushing up to us, "Cale, come, quick!" I heave Beef's words to see what the commotion was about.

"Traitor!" people hissed as they threw dirt at Irene.

"She is a traitor!" Brett complies. The group of rioters seemed to have lost all sense of human-like qualities and gained some animalistic habits that were hostile and savage.

"We should kill her!" Shouted some. "Throw her into the fire!" shouted more.

I slithered my way through the rowdy crowd of teenagers into the middle where the attention was.

"Cale." Brett said almost evilly. "So good of you to rejoin us."

"You make *us* sound like a cult, Brett."

"Always the pessimist. We'll deal with you when we are through with this traitor. Cocoa, bind him."

"What do you mean deal with me?" I ask menacingly as Cocoa walks up to my back. I could feel his presence behind me.

"This traitor," Brett announces to everyone, completely ignoring my question, "has been plotting against us this entire time!"

I feel a beastly grasp on my shoulder, and I could only assume it was Cocoa, so I threw my elbow backwards in the pit of his gut blowing him back. He collapsed to the floor as Irene stood up to defend herself. "He lies!" she wails before Amanda back hands her.

"Silence, witch!" Amanda hisses.

"Let her speak!" I demand.

"Why should I." Brett arrogantly demands.

"Because I want to hear her side."

"I have already heard her side," he says to me giving me the nastiest glare I have ever seen from him, and then he turns to rest of the rioting crowd to say, "and she continues to lie to us all!"

"We must end this!" A voice calls out from the crowd. It's amazing what fear will do to someone. It can break their heart, and allow it to grow back crooked.

"I do not lie! It is the truth, he is against you all!" Irene says before being smacked down again by Amanda. Cocoa has recovered and grapples my head as he grows larger past his normal size. A rage within me awoke and turned to Tianna. Something innate in me controlled her with anger and she let out a screeching siren. Cocoa diminished his size to a small child as he squirmed on the floor. They all began squirming, frying against the ground like fish out of water. I could feel Tianna trying to pull away from my control, she was trying to stop the noise, but the rage within me kept her voice shrieking. I accepted the pain and took every inch of sound in as I punished all of those around me. On sight of Beef on the floor, I stopped my focus on Tianna and lost all hope of anger within me. Tianna's siren had stopped.

"Now, you all listen to me!" I roared with fury. "The girl speaks!"

"No one is going to listen to a freak!" A voice cries out. I use my instincts to recollect where the voice came from and my hand reaches for him without looking. Choking, he grasps onto his neck as he floats in the air towards my empty hand until his neck is in my palm. Brody Geldert struggles for air as I hold him up as an example. Before he falls unconscious I throw him into the fire and continue talking.

"Now. As I was saying, before I was rudely interrupted." I politely say. "Irene." I say.

Fear swirled in my mother's eyes as I remained calm in front of her. I realized I had just killed a fellow classmate. It didn't quite process all the way, but part of me was consumed by hatred and was willing to do whatever it took to get rid of Brett. "Would you like an invitation?" I pretend to write on an imaginary piece of paper with an imaginary pen. "Here. Dear, Irene. Please save yourself and tell us your side of the story." I pretend to crumple it up and throw it at her, but something actually launches from my hands and hits her in the face. The imaginary paper became real.

"Eerie."

"Right?" But I continued to pretend I knew that would happen.

Irene starts, "I am not a Pedigrate. Aileen was." Mr. Rusenkell came to mind, he would be able to determine if this was true or not. But where was he? He seemed to have silently disappeared after he got done explaining to everyone about the differences between Pedigrates and Hybrids and how you have to die to become a Pedigrate and Hybrids are simply human beings with a dormant chromosome awakened from the mystery toxin M.S.C. seems to be manufacturing. If I remembered correctly, Pedigrates had no memory of their past lives, therefore they became easy to control. "Brett is a Pedigrate!" Irene states.

"She continues to lie to us! We have to kill her!" Brett interrupts, attempting to rally the rioters again.

"No, we should kill you!" Irene yells. "Aileen has created a monster! This is all a scheme to capture you all! Brett willingly took his life for this fire starter and was revived with this serum!" Irene pulls out a syringe with black liquid that was identical to the one she injected into Aileen earlier. "This serum will allow you to return back to life as long as you are not brain dead!"

"If that is so, why didn't you use it on your sister?" Brett accuses.

"I did!"

"Doesn't the brain continue to work-"

"She is brain dead! Aileen, Brett and I had all secretly plotted to capture the remaining survivors and return you back to headquarters, where David Hamilton would finish you all."

"If I was a part of this conspiracy, then why were you making a list in secret?" Brett yells, holding up a piece of paper with names written on it.

"A list?" someone asks. It only took one interest in what Brett was saying, and it would spread like wildfire. I knew that much about my arch nemesis.

"Yes. A list of the biggest threats she would have against!"

"Quiet!" I yell.

"It's true!" Irene yells, "But this is all a scheme! A Pedigrate will sacrifice him or herself for the cause, so I had to agree! You must believe me! I was only trying to protect my sister! She never knew I was still me! She thought I was pure! Please I beg-"

"Enough!" Brett roars and throws her into the pit of flames as the sea of red and orange swallows my mother.

14. Incubus

Pain and suffering filled my eyes. I could not believe Brett Gooding was capable of something like this. Half of me believed my mother was still inside of Irene, and the other half had been suppressing the old feelings, blocking the pain of missing Glenda. I barely understood what had just happened, but I launched myself at Brett, attacking him! A bestial wrath pursued through my fists as I pummeled him. We rolled on the ground fighting for a position on top of one another. Everyone seemed to just watch in awe as we manually attempted to destroy each other.

On top, I coiled my arm back getting ready to release a perilous plunge down on Brett's face, but something stopped me. Loud vehicles came from nowhere and encircled us. Men in black jumped out of the vehicles and ordered us inside the hummers as the held us all at gun point. Unwilling to fight, everyone complied and was kidnapped into the vehicles. Brett grabbed the list from the ground that he had said Irene was using to determine the most dangerous of us and shoves it down his pocket.

"He thinks he's slick."

"He thinks he's a lot of things."

It wasn't long before I was forced into a car with Brett.

"Just my luck."

I was handcuffed, and so was he. The cars swiftly drove off from the scene, but I turn to look and see that Buddy was chasing us behind. I thought of Beef. How heartbroken he must have been when they tore that dog from his arms. He had to of put up a fight for that to happen. Buddy continued to chase the car, and in the distance I watch the helicopter explode with furious red flames. This is how I knew these men weren't officers of the law. They were too proficient, too clean. I knew where they were taking us. These men must have been with the White Crows. They were cleaning the evidence of our existence.

Find us Buddy. I thought. And I knew, no matter where these terrorists took us, Buddy was going to be able to find us. As Buddy kept chasing us slower and slower, something of me imprinted itself on the memory of the dog. Some form of clairvoyance told me that the next time I would see him; he would inspire something inside me.

"Do you have the list?" A voice in the passenger's seat asked. Brett held out his handcuffed arms and the man in black sitting next to him unlocked his chains so he could reach into his pocket to hand the list to the man sitting in front. "Who's your friend?" the voice asked in the same menacing tone.

"He's number one." Brett said.

The man in the passenger seat turned and leaned over to look at me. I recognized his face right away. I had yet to see him in person, but I was sure it was him, just by the stench of cigars and brandy. David Hamilton. I realized, since I was the only one in the car that was unaware of my surroundings that they were about to knock me out. I had been wrong about these kidnappers being the White Crows. So I continued to stare at David Hamilton when the man in black sitting on my right put a chlorophyll cloth up against my face. I somehow knew the smell and I continued to stay conscious. He held it there for a good twenty seconds, and I didn't allow myself to feel a single ounce of dizziness. I remained focused and awake. I kept telling myself it was all in my head.

"This one's interesting." David Hamilton concluded when he realized I the chlorophyll had done nothing. He takes out a gun and slams it against my head. All I do is readjust my position and stare at him again.

"Aim for the temple." I instruct as I wink at him.

And the last thing I see is his face full of fury before he takes another swing at my head.

I don't know what day it is when I awake. My eyes open and there is a throbbing in my head. I find myself in a white room with blinding white lights.

"If I had a dime every time this happened."

"You'd have twenty cents." I say unimpressed.

The room was much smaller than last time though, it was more of a size of a college dorm. Pristine and pallid, the white walls suffocated me in, but I tried to remain calm. I lay on a white bed in a new pair of white shirt and white jeans. I sat up against the head of the bed and over to the left was a drawer holding three things I've seem to have lost the last time I was here: a ruby lighter, a ruined carton of cigarettes and my red i-pod. I hopped out of bed to check the i-pod and make sure it had my music in it and wasn't just some imposter. It had everything; every song down to the last Incubus album. Overwhelmed with joy I put an earphone in, but before I could choose a song, someone came barging in the room. I threw my i-pod down in reaction and stood up straight to see David Hamilton peering in under the arch of the doorway.

"I would have returned your belongings to you sooner, but you decided to escape."

My eyes searched around the room for an idea to spark on how to escape again.

"Your welcome." He persists. "I hope you don't mind. I drew some blood from you in your sleep. I couldn't wake you, you looked so peaceful."

I look down to my left arm and red dot rested in between my forearm and bicep. My eyes creep back up to him. "What do you want from me?"

He looks down as if he had done something wrong. "I'm terribly sorry for all of the confusion, and for hitting you on the head. I had to take precautions. I thought you were one of them."

"One of them?"

"The White Crows. I had to be sure you weren't under the influence of one of the members of the White Crows as Brett informs me that Irene was. You see, even with training these deviates seek control over us."

"Who are you people?" I say confused.

His smile was crooked as he said, "That conversation is for another time. Come. Dinner is served." And he walks out of the room.

I wait in the room and debate if I should follow or not. My stomach growled for food, but I could never show I was hungry in front of him. After a minute of debating, I couldn't help but succumb to the idea of food and I jammed my belongings into my two front pockets and left the room, closing the door behind me. I followed the memory of Hamilton turning right down the hallway until I saw an open door where light seemed to be coming out of. The sounds of small talk and spoons clanging against glass plates echoed out of the room. When I walked through the doorway there was an extremely large in length dinner table that stretched far enough for fifty persons to sit and eat at. Almost every seat was taken by a familiar face from a recently demolished high school and Hamilton sat at the very end of the table, like he was some sort of royalty. Everyone had stopped eating when they saw me.

"Just like good old times." I thought as they made me feel awkward to be alive. It was quiet, but I remained still and kept a stern face.

"Don't be rude now, Cale. Find your name and take a seat." Hamilton announces from the end of the table. I say nothing as I walk around the table seeing filled seats with people gawking at me as if I had done something wrong.

"You killed Brody Geldert."

"Brett killed Irene."

"They didn't trust Irene."

"Well. I never liked him anyways."

"Excuses are for the incompetent.

"And I will not use them."

When I finally found my seat, it was labeled on the very other end of the table Hamilton sat from.

"You've got to be kidding, right?"

"On top of it, look to your left and right?" I nearly chuckle. Amanda and Brett were the next seats next to mine on both sides of the table.

"Just eat." I told myself, famished. I sat down and looked at a plate full of a rich, humongous steak, a baked potato with melted, creamy cheese and bacon sprinkled on top of the mushy white mountains it created, and crunchy, green asparagus with carrots. I started to carve into the tough steak when I realized I carved threw the plate. I looked up in embarrassment, but everyone seemed to be grappling their steaks and ferociously ripping it to shreds with their mouths and fingers. The table was a mess, and full of animals. Except Hamilton, who just stared at me while he politely ate with all the manners in the book. I decided

to eat some of the baked potato first, so I grabbed a fork and dug in. I was no animal, and I wasn't going to lower myself to a level where Buddy pranced in. I mocked Hamilton and ate politely, the best way I knew how. I attempted to carve my steak again, this time with less strength and I successfully got a piece, even though I scratched the recently broken silver plate with the knife. I look up as I take a bite and the animals at the table are no longer feasting like barbarians, but politely using their manners as well now. Even pinkies flew out as people took sips out of their drink. Hamilton continued to stare at me in curiosity. It made me feel uncomfortable. I returned to looking at my food and realized how hungry I was. I was starving enough to forget every useless manner I have ever used and start grubbing with my hands. I look up as I prepare myself to eat as an animal, just to be different from everyone else and everyone eats like a barbarian again as I rip out a chunk of steak with my mouth as I held the steak in place. Hamilton has a smile on his face, like he had taught the others at the table to eat as I felt, and mock me. I stopped eating. The others continued on their animalistic grubbing.

"Are you not hungry, Cale?" David Hamilton calls from the other end of the table.

"No." I lied. I got up from the table and tried to walk out the door I came through but a man in all black stopped in the doorway, blocking my exit.

"I prepare this meal for you, and I don't even get a proper thank you?"

I turn to him, confused on what I should think. "Thank you." I say somewhat thankful, the other half just wanted to get out of here.

"I'm not hungry either." Tianna says.

"Sit down Tianna." Brett commands.

"Don't tell her what to do." I yell back at Brett.

"I'll speak freely." Brett says as he continues to eat his food like a barbarian.

"Feel free, but the next time you speak to her I will cut out your free tongue and hang it freely on my wall."

"Is that a threat?" He demands as he backs away from the table and stands to face me.

"Think of it more like an ultimatum. You keep your tongue as long as you watch it."

Brett coils his fist back, getting ready to strike when Hamilton shouts. "Enough!" Brett relaxes his position to face him. I keep my back turned.

"It seems as though we are ready for the main event." He claps his hands twice as he gets up from the table. "Everyone, if you will. Please follow me down the corridor to the room a relinquishment." Everyone immediately finishes eating and follows him out of the dining room down the hall. Beef falls in last place, with his head down. I knew he was missing Buddy. Tianna comforts him, as she puts an arm around him letting him know that everything was going to be ok.

Up a couple stair cases, guards posted at every corner, we walked into a familiar room. It was the same room where I first saw Mr. Hamilton on the glass screen for the very first time. The two book shelves on each side stretched along the length of the room and a glass window towards the back gave view to a dark forest, just like last time. Everyone was dressed in the same white clothes. It was as if we were being initiated into a cult.

The glass screen falls slowly from the ceiling at the touch of a button Hamilton presses. And the news starts playing. It was the same subject as the breaking news I watched earlier when Aileen showed me. A band of renegades called the White Crows are to be blamed for the thousands dead of Irvine. It showed the pictures of the three leaders who are supposed to be in charge and I felt a squeeze on my hand. Tianna whispered into my ear, "I know her." I looked at the confused girl on the screen with short dark hair. "She tried to kill us before you guys showed up."

I looked at her strangely and unaware of what had happened. "What?" I ask in shock.

"That girl almost killed us back where we were. But Jonah killed her." She whispered, keeping her voice to a minimum.

Jonah looked back at us after getting a good look at the picture, and I heard him say in his mind, "One down, two more to go." As he grinned.

"So you see," Hamilton starts as soon as the program was finished and the screen is shut off and sent back to the ceiling, "the people who are responsible for all of this trouble, are these White Crows. Again I apologize to all of you for the aggressive kidnapping, but it was the only way I could be sure I could get you safe. It seems as though I have failed you, for I have come to learn that one of you has already been taken by them. A boy by the name of Cameron Dark and also the man who betrayed this facility, Brian Rusenkell. I had foolishly assumed that they had left all of Irvine to perish, so I sent out squads to search and destroy any of these renegades they could find after the incident." He was very persuasive although I could see right through his fake sincerity in his tone...or so I thought. "They are the ones that destroyed Stellar High School and everyone in it.

They murdered the thousands in Irvine and all because they couldn't stand to see others like them."

"Others?" I ask rudely.

"You. You all are the others. After being exposed to substance 36, your lives have changed, have they not?"

"Is he serious?"

"It was a rhetorical question."

"These White Crows are merely, you. They are supernatural beings that have adapted with the toxin. Their leader, Paul couldn't stand the fact that there was going to be others like them. So they tried to destroy you all after learning a couple bottles of substance 36 were stolen by our very own fugitive, Professor Brian Rusenkell, and taken to the unfortunate place they would soon demolish. Think of your families they've destroyed. Your friendships. Your lives are broken, and yet you continue fighting on. You are at the top of the food chain now. It is survival of the fittest and all of you seek to be fit."

His rallying speech convinced me that maybe he was on our side. Maybe we have been blinded to rules long enough for our own internal instincts to take over. Then he brought out a piece of paper. "I have here with me a list, and I want you all to line up on the right if I call your name." he takes a moment to make sure we are listening then begins. "Cale." He announces. I walk up to where he pointed to stand as if I was receiving some sort of medal.

The room is divided into nearly half when he calls the people who didn't get called a bunch of regulars. Baley could barely stand on the side I was on with Marcus being trapped with the rest of the regulars. Hamilton orders the regulars to be escorted out of the room while the rest of us waited in silence. He assures us that the regulars are to be taken to a safe quarter until we can learn to control our powers only to prevent any harm that may be made against them. "The separtion is only temporary. It is not my intention to keep you from your friends."Baley quits her sniffling as she begins to trust Mr. Hamilton.

"Now, before we begin our training, behind this room you will meet a very dark thing. It exists in your mind. The very dark creature resides in your fears and feeds off your doubt. The creature may come off as a persuasive demon, but it is your wisest form of conscious. I cannot go in with you, but the orders it gives you, you must follow. For your own good. You must see past it's devious nature and understand that this incubus is a part of you. That is the name it goes by. Incubus." He gestures everyone with a wave of his arm. "Follow me please." He says as he walks towards the glass wall in the back of the room where the dark forest was. He steps through the glass like it was air and we all slowly halt before he specifically asks me to walk through and no one else. I put my fingers up the glass wall and push through what feels like a breeze of chilly cold air. "You will all experience something different. You will all see what your heart sees. This room is where you will face your greatest fears. The room will empty, if you should prevail, and that is how you will know if you have passed.

"So this is some sort of test?" I ask as I walk through the glass completely.

"Somewhat." He confesses. "In you go." He bobs his head towards the dark woods while exiting the room back through the glass where everyone else stared at me and I walk in without letting myself be afraid.

Deeper inside the woods, I turned back to my only source of light which seemed to be fading each step I took. As soon as it got too dark I pulled out my lighter and lit the darkness. Slowly I crept from tree to tree. A spider crawled onto my shoulder as I leaned on the trunk of a tree. Quickly I brushed it off and stumbled away into another tree. My heart started to pound. Fear was taking over me at its highest peak when I turned around to see a face looking back at me. I yelled something ignorant before the face said, "Hello Cale."

"Who are you?" I asked as I recollected myself.

"Why, I'm you Cale." I shined my lighter up to see the face again and recognized that the face wasn't lying. It in fact was my face. "It's a bit twisted don't you think?" my face spoke as he took a bite out of an apple. "To know that your very worst nightmare is yourself?"

"You're not real." I spoke, like I was talking with a ghost.

"Oh, but I am very real. I'm the dark part of you, Cale."

"Right. Is Santa Clause in here as well?"

"He can be if you create him."

"What?"

"He can be if you create him."

"I know what you said, It just didn't make any sense."

"It makes perfect sense. You have yet to discover your full potential Cale. Because that naïve side of you is holding you back. Don't you see? Life is so much simpler when you are free." My face takes another bite of the apple and I oddly feel the juice and piece slide down my throat. "So, you can read minds. Big deal. That story has been told before. You have some form of telekinesis that is underdeveloped." A flash back of Beef floating in mid air with my arms comes to mind. "But you haven't seen the other side of your powers, Cale."

"How did Aileen die?" I ask.

"If I know the answer, you do too, Cale. You just don't want to hear it."

"I don't know."

"Then I don't either."

"Some help you are."

"I'm here to help you give up your enervating guilt and move on. I'm only helping you to help me." the incubus whispers as he moves through the dark almost invisible. He ends up by my side before he starts again. "Notice anything weird at dinner?"

"No." I lied.

"Hmm…*I* did." My alter ego squints, "the other upside of being you is I know when you're lying. So, let's cut the crap. Notice how dinner was in your control?"

"What?-"

"Did you or did you not notice how those beasts would eat according to your emotions? It's a simple yes or no."

"Yes, but-"

"Did you or did you not notice how quickly Tianna fell in *love* with you?" My twin uses the word love as though it were a last resort and every time he said it he was forced to throw up.

"Yes, but-"

"Hmm…indeed now there is obviously a pattern. Not only do you control peoples actions at times, hence when you made Beef foolishly believe he was able to do a back flip, I mean come on Cale. He was only able to because you imagined it, and commanded it to happen. But also, besides the mind control thing now, you have neglected the most valuable part of your powers…"

My mind was fogged. I couldn't retreat back and convince myself that this was all an illusion. It was as if my final defense was forced to reveal myself. This was the true heart of fear, and I was the artery holding myself together. I knew part of me was bleeding out because I had foolishly thought someone really liked me for who I was. I believed Tianna was running along the same track, parallel with me, but all I was doing was dragging her behind me manipulating her every step.

"You didn't really think she could fall for someone like you, did you?" the devious side of me comforts me mocking my thoughts after I don't answer his question. "She doesn't belong with you." The lighter in my hand went out and it became pitch black in the forest. Snap! A large flame ignites the darkness over a thumb. The image of me lights up a cigarette with his thumb. "Must I demonstrate everything." He says with the cancer stick in his mouth. "Always so naïve and weak, you are the reason we aren't out of this place right now and living it up in Tahiti. I hope you know that." The incubus inhales and blows out smoke while keeping a flame somehow ignited above his thumb. "You know. I don't like the quiet you. It's no fun arguing to something that's broken."

"I am not broken." I say coldly.

"A ha, so it lives. Well then, are we getting back to business? Or are we going to sulk over a dumb girl?"

I was a fool to think that I could ever achieve love. I couldn't even get a dog's love. Buddy hated me. I look in the eyes of my incubus. There was nothing to fear now. I stared right through him with nowhere to run.

He smiled evilly and whispered, "Business it is then." Before he evaporates like smoke and appears leaning on a tree as a small camp fire set itself up bringing some light to the perilous darkness. When he evaporated he became the very smoke he exhaled and traveled with it like a breeze. "You'll learn in time how to do that." He assured as he took a final bite out of the apple he was chewing and threw it into the fire. I stood to face him and he waved his hands so a cigarette appeared on the tip of his index finger and thumb pressing against the bud of it. "Cigarette?" he asked.

"No thanks." I said coldly.

"You won't die from it. Well. Not anymore rather. Since you've got the toxin already carrying throughout your blood, you're pretty much immune to most all sicknesses. Unless of course you try to cure yourself well then, that'll be the end of us both."

"Tell me what I can do."

"Well we both know you can read minds, and control those around you…but what happens when you think of something, when you truly imagine something to appear from no form of reason? Something that is truly related to clairvoyance…" he inhales deeply and then snaps his finger as a carton of cigs creates itself in his hand. "Hmm…" he thinks, "I wonder."

I got what he was saying. I understood that he was telling me I had the ability to create anything I wanted with just a mere thought.

"Not just create either," he says majestically, "but destroy as well." The carton levitates from his hand and bursts into flames. The ashes float around me and I open my palm as they land in my hand. An all black butterfly starts to flap his wings in my hand. "Cute." He says. "But not exactly what I had in mind." The butterfly is sucked out of my hand by some invisible force and he rips the creature in half. With the two ends, he holds out both of his palms and the wings fall spiraling to the floor. "Why do you think Buddy hates you, Cale?" Once the two wings hit the floor, they mold themselves together and grow into something menacing. "It's because you created him to!" The figure from the butterfly grew into a ferocious black dog that barked furiously at me. Drool and saliva oozed from its fangs as it coiled itself back getting ready to spring towards me. "Good boy." My incubus said as he stroked the jackal's back. The demon dog began to whine at its master's touch until the incubus knelt down beside it and broke its neck. I shudder at the sound. "You created Buddy for Beef, to protect him from me."

"This is just a dream." I say trying to close my eyes.

"Really? Don't go back down the road of denial please, it's only going to take longer."

"Longer for what?"

"Longer for us to escape." The incubus proposed. "You don't really want to stay here do you? Serve a master and let him control you? Not me. I don't serve anyone."

"You serve me." I state with confidence. "You need me."

"Ah, so you're smart as well. Sad but true, there are boundaries I cannot cross...yet. Unless, you decide to relinquish me."

The thought intrigued me. I didn't want this demon inside of me, haunting me every breath I took from the cold world. "How?" I ask.

"Story for another time Cale. You see. The one thing you do not have control over, I do. And *you* need me as much as I need you at this point. For you see, I can sense the future. And this is going to all work out in my favor."

"But you are a part of me. I will learn how-"

"Not if I keep it from you."

"Tell me now."

"Tell you what, I'll tell you what's going to happen next and you are going to pretend like nothing is wrong. Very soon, a tiny, goodly girl is going to ask you for help. You will help her, no matter what the task is, but you will leave them once they are safe and return to David Hamilton."

"What do you mean safe."

"Secure, protected, out of harm's way, am I not being clear enough for you?"

"Safe from what?"

"From you."

"What?"

"You will realize that the only place for you is to be nonexistent."

"I don't-"

"If you wish to see her again, alive that is, it's best she thinks you're dead."

And in that instant the darkness became blinded by light and the forest disappeared. I was standing in a enormous white room that held nothing in it besides me. I turned around and there were the others staring at me. I walked back towards the glass and Mr. Hamilton stopped me to ask, "What did you see?"

I looked at him as if he already knew and walked back through the glass. Tianna came rushing to my side asking if I was alright and if everything was okay. I simply ignored her and shrugged her off. I didn't want to lead her on any longer. My feelings were my own, and they didn't belong in someone else's head. I walked back to the hallway where the diner and rooms were plugging in my earphones. I selected a song called "Where is my mind?" from the pixies and turned the volume all the way up to drown the fuzziness out of my head. I stepped in my room and closed the door behind me.

"You don't believe that fool, do you?"

"Part of me does." I explained. That same part of me couldn't help but think that I was being trained for something big. Like I was training for an inevitable war approaching and there was nothing that could prevent it from coming for me.

15. The Great Escape

Days passed and everyone grew more and more impatient as we waited for something bad to happen. David Hamilton had promised everyone that the White Crows were still out there, just biding their time when to strike next. Baley grew sick. She must have been away from Marcus for a week now and all she could do was find new ways to miss him. David Hamilton had restricted her from any form of drawing in fear she might draw an escape route to see Marcus, but he assured her that Marcus was just fine along with the other regulars and she would soon see him as long as she learned to control her powers. He even explained that regulars were merely simple humans able to cope with substance 36, but vulnerable to super humans like ourselves.

"But I wish to see him at least." Baley complained. I roll my eyes as I overhear the conversation in the room next to me. With improved hearing, the conversation was a lot clearer than I wished.

"When you learn to control your powers you will see him again."

"But how can I control my powers if I'm unable to use them! You don't give me any practice."

"Because you are too attached to the human. One slip of the pen and you could destroy him."

"But who said I was going to draw him?-"

"I've heard enough." The deep voice says before exiting the room and slamming the door behind him.

The doors can only be opened from the outside and have some neural pacifiers on them that prevent us from escaping by using our powers. He explained to us that we must live like this until we reach a form of maturity with our powers.

"You mean like prisoners?"

"Apparently." I thought. It was the same routine every day. At precisely eight, our doors would open and we would be expected in the dining room. Breakfast would be served and we would all meet in the room of relinquishment where Mr. Hamilton would instruct our training. I never participated in any of his little reindeer games though. I sat up against the wall and watched as the others dueled against each other. Then he would instruct everyone how to fight. I sat in the corner and laughed with earphones in my head as I watched Brett's face get serious with the combat skirmish against the others. Next came lunch, which I usually substituted a cigarette with. Then after lunch we all went to a part of the facility called the Wash, where we would all be escorted around the gigantic building and learn the functions of the science that went on there, except the west wing which was forbidden. After our daily tour was dinner and then a final training session in the room of relinquishment before we were locked in our rooms for the night. He kept us busy every moment of the day.

Knock, knock, knock. In entered Mr. Hamilton and I, like usual continued to listen to my i-pod while he talked. Unfortunately for me, I haven't learned to tune him out yet since I could hear his thoughts in my head with the door open, disabling the neural pacifier that kept me from using my powers. "I expect you to participate today." He said without opening his mouth before he left.

"That was odd." I thought.

"Yeah, he didn't tuck you in and read you a bedtime story last night."

"No imbecile, he came in early just to tell me I needed to participate. I never participate. He knows that. Why today? What did he mean?"

Unsure of the omen in his message, I decided I would carry on the day just like I had done for the past week.

Eight-o-clock came and our doors automatically open. I can see the others rushing down the hall towards the diner, as I slowly got out of bed. I did a small stretch and someone was knocking at my door. I look up to see Baley standing in my doorway.

"What do you want?" I ask bluntly.

"I need your help." She says. And I hear her words echo through my mind with importance. Something told me that this was going to be an interesting day. I don't say anything and she continues on, "I know where they are keeping Marcus."

"And?" I say

"I need your help to get him out of there." She said.

"Maybe he's in there for a reason."

"Don't patronize me, Cale. I know your allegiance doesn't swear to this Mr. Hamilton and I know you could care less, but I am asking you this favor and I have never asked you for anything before."

"Sorry. We're fresh out of kindness. Try again next week." I say as I push her out of the way.

"They're going to kill him."

I stop. The last of the sprinting hybrids enter the dining area. "How would you know?" I ask.

"I don't know. But something in me is telling me these White Crows are going to find us very soon and finish us off. We have to hide."

"Hide." I thought out loud. I remembered now what the incubus of myself had told me to do when this day came. I looked at Baley up and down. Her eyes changed color to an emerald green. "What happened to your eyes?" I asked. "Weren't they brown?"

"I- I don't know." She said. "It's as if Marcus and I had switched eye colors."

I remembered the day I saw them and I specifically remembered wanting their eyes to switch colors. Naïve and small, Baley stood in front of me, begging me with green eyes to help her. A debate inside me told me that I shouldn't listen, but out of fear of the incubus to return, I heaved the words and nodded my head.

Baley hugged me at my gesture and dragged me towards the dining room. "We can't be late to breakfast. I'll show you afterwards!" she says excited as she good-heartedly skips to the dining room.

"She's delusional."

"Yeah."

"You're not really going to help her are you?"

"I think I am."
"I thought you didn't like her."
"I don't."
"Then why help her?"
"I don't know. It's as if something keeps pushing me to do it."

I realized I would have to watch my back the rest of the day as I strolled into the dining hall for breakfast. The seats never change. I was always stuck in between Amanda and Brett at the end of the table across from Mr. Hamilton. For the past week I've avoided all eye contact with Tianna and completely ignored her in hopes that she would be better off alone. But this morning she kept looking at me from the middle of the table on the right side. I thought maybe it was because I was thinking about it that she kept on looking. So I tried extra hard to ignore her. Beef seemed to alienate himself from me as well, although he gargled down his pancakes like nothing was wrong. Fed up with the lifestyle we all were living I rudely walked out while everyone continued to eat, muttering "I'm not hungry." As I got up.

I walked down the hall to the room of relinquishment. I walked through the glass and into the white room. There was no sign of any leaves, or anything remote to a forest. I had come to see my incubus again and he wasn't here. I wondered around the room waiting for him to arrive, but he never came. Frustrated, I walked back out and before I walked through the glass I noticed there was a room the peered over me like it was station to view over the room of relinquishment. I checked for stairs after I walked back through the glass and thought of where Mr. Hamilton came from whenever someone came out of the room. He would always come through the wall over...

"There." I thought. A red book stood out of place from the rest of them. I walked over to it slowly in fear that I might get caught. I figured I was already caught on camera somewhere. I might as well be quick about it. I took the book out and was about to place it in line with the others before I heard a noise from the door that led to the staircase.

"Curiosity killed the cat you know." Mr. Hamilton's voice boomed.

I turn to face him, hiding the surprise and fear deep inside. "I don't plan on dying anytime soon." I told him.

He smirked and walked into the room. Following him everyone came marching in as usual. They all seemed to have lost a bit of themselves though, like a piece of them had been torn from their personality. "So who wants to be first today?" Everyone raised their hands willingly except for Tianna, who kept looking at me. "How about you Tianna." He announced disappointing the rest.

"Oh, no thanks."

"It was not a request." He spoke with a fake endearment.

"Help me Cale." Tianna said in her mind as she walked through the glass. But how was I supposed to help?

"I think its best you join the rest of your friends Cale." Mr. Hamilton whispers as he passes me. I listen to him, and before I can turn around to see, the red book is in place and Mr. Hamilton has disappeared. I kept an eye on the book at all times, but I couldn't help but wonder what Tianna would need help for. Was she in any danger? Distracted by the thought that she might be I looked into the room of relinquishment and I see the forest that wasn't there a moment ago.

Tianna came out of the forest and back into the room where the others waited to be selected like toys inside a claw crane machine. Before I could look back at the book shelf, Mr. Hamilton was already hovering over me looking downwards. "Next?" he asked. I looked away in disproval. "Baley, how about you." He says as he walks away assuming she would get up and walk through, like she did. I was too concerned about Tianna, that I got distracted when she sat next to me. I didn't see Mr. Hamilton disappear because the look on her face was as if she had seen a ghost.

"Are you alright?" I whispered.

"Oh now you want to talk?" She hissed.

"You don't look so good." I say after a beat.

"Thanks." She gets up and walks away from me to sit next down to Brett. For a moment, I felt betrayed. I felt as though she had stabbed me in the gut and left me to die.

Baley came out of the room of relinquishment with a mysterious glow about her. She came down to sit next to me.

"We've got to do it now!" she whispered.

"What are you talking about?" I say in the same voice.

"You've got to help me free him now. It can't wait. They are coming for us tonight!"

"How do you know this?"

"There's no time to explain, we must leave!" she whispers as she drags me out of the room. She was surprisingly strong and quiet considering no one seemed to notice our absence as she led me up the staircase.

"Odd. There are no guards." I thought. "Wait!" I hissed, trying to keep quiet. "Why aren't there any guards on duty?"

"This is their interchanging shift. They're pedigrates that work for Mr. Hamilton." She explains as she drags me up the stairs again. "The White Crows are going to attack this facility tonight so we must get out of here as soon as possible."

"Wait!" I demand. "How do you know all of this?"

"My incubus told me."

"How does your incubus know?"

"She just does, I don't know! I've been seeing her and she paints the future, she knows what's going to happen next and she warned me that I needed to rescue Marcus from the White Crows!"

Still confused, I trusted her enough to get us to the wash. Things were running smoothly until she said they were in the west wing where two guards stood watching over the entrance.

"Are you insane?" I suggested.

"What are you scared?" She fired back.

"Touché little girl." Although I didn't like it, I read her mind and I knew she wanted me to persuade them to shoot each other in the toe and knock them out. "Your violent aren't you."

"When it comes to Marcus, I'll do anything."

"I can see that."

"They're pretty much already dead anyways." She tried to reason.

"I'm not going to kill them." I say as I turn the corner while they stiffen up straight as they aim their rifles for me, the rifles carrying the logo of M.S.C. neatly printed on them. I don't stop walking when I hush them with a simple finger over my mouth and they drop to the floor snoozing.

"What'd you do?" Baley wondered with amazement, following swiftly behind me after they fall flat.

"The mind is a mysterious place." I said, and I don't explain any more as I walk forward and open the double doors without having to put in a code or touching them. Inside the double doors was a room filled with science stuff. Machines hooked up to other machines and chemicals lay strew about what I could only guess was a laboratory. There were also tanks with naked bodies floating inside them. Baley and I walked through the creepy science lab giving each other weird looks every step of the way. I was just about to ask if we were headed the right way when we found a door to another corridor. Inside the corridor was a prison of people who simply looked like they were dying from starvation. Right away Baley found Marcus and she sprinted to him and hugged him through the bars. Weak and disabled, Marcus looked like he was unable to travel.

"I'm gonna have to end up carrying him aren't I?" I thought as I bent the lock off the gate and opened it. "Let's go." I said in boredom, but Baley and Marcus continued to play the roles of Romeo and Juliet as they wept for their recent long distant relationship that kept them apart. I roll my eyes.

"I need a pen and a piece of paper." Baley gasped.

"You're kidding." I state, "Shouldn't you have his number memorized, already."

"It's not for that, I need to draw us something."

"You're kidding." I repeat in monotone, forgetting Baley even had powers.

"Quickly Cale!" She rushes the words out of her mouth. I hadn't tried creating anything since my incubus showed me how in the room of relinquishment, so it took a second for me to imagine a notebook and a pen to appear out of nowhere. When they did I threw them at Baley and she released her grip on Marcus to start drawing something furiously. "My incubus said we must go here, and we will be safe from the White Crows." She said as she continued to draw something.

"Why not stay here in a guarded facility that even the government knows nothing about?" I ask, thinking my incubus to be stupid for telling me I needed to help this child escape from what felt like home now.

"Because, the other part of me saw them coming!"

"What other part of you?" I ask.

"My incubus, she said that she was a part of my powers and that she knew how to see the future, but she wouldn't teach me how, but she promised that if I was able to get everyone out of these cages and bring them to…" she scribbles the last part of the paper quickly and shows it to me, "Here! Then they would be safe from an upcoming attack from the White Crows." I looked at the picture as Baley held it up. It looked nothing more than a mere street going through a simple town with a clock tower. The sketch was simple, and somewhat good for drawing in such short time, but I was confused on where this place was.

"What is this place?"

"Las Vegas." She said.

"This looks nothing like Vegas- have you ever even been to Vegas?" I ask, completely dumbfounded by the simple street that resembled nothing of the bright lights of Vegas.

"Yes, in fact I have been many times." She says grabbing the drawing out of my hands. "Las Vegas isn't just the strip you know, this is a street a little bit away from the fancy part of the city."

"And this is where we'll be safe?"

"Yes." She sounded so sure of herself.

"And how do you expect to get there?"

"Why, you Cale."

"Come again?" I grimace.

"You. My incubus said you would be able to take us here if I drew it."

"I am not driving to Vegas. I don't even know where I am now."

"No one said drive Cale…"she lingered on to my name.

"How do you expect me to transfer you somewhere that I've never even been to, let alone exist?"

"You've never been to Las Vegas?" she asks in the same tone as I asked earlier.

"Not to the boring part!" I say.

"St-stop f-f-fighting…" Marcus stutters with a chill in his throat, barely keeping his eyes open. Baley looks at me with the solemnest gaze. I roll my eyes before I imagine a canister of water as Baley asked for in her mind.

Footsteps rush up from behind me and I knew we were in trouble. I locked the door to get inside the prison corridor with my mind. "How did she say I would be able to do it?" I asked calmly.

"I don't know." She gasped, realizing this might have been a failed plan as there came a rapping on the door. "She never said how. She just said I needed you."

The door banged harder. "Think, Baley!"

"I'm trying!"

The door breaks open and I turn around expecting to fight for my life, and Tianna comes waltzing through with a disappointed face. She avoids all eye contact with me and marches straight for Baley. "What is going on?" she asks irritated. Baley summarizes the entire plan to escape in less than twenty seconds as she rushes every word. Tianna looks as though she is breaking a promise when she quietly asks, "Let me see the picture." She walks over to the corner of the room with the notebook in hand and waves her arm in front of the wall in front of her. "In you go. Quickly now." She orders.

"In what?" I asked breaking the silence. There was nothing to go into.

Tianna's face, still disappointed, she directed by pointing, "Into the wall." Baley and I looked at each other like she had lost her marbles, then she throws the notebook up against the wall she pointed to and if disappeared through the wall as if it were standing quicksand. "I don't agree with this, but for the past week my incubus has been telling me she was an oracle that could tell the future and that the day would come when the painter would go missing and I was to do everything in my power to stay behind and keep her from leaving if neccessary, blah, blah, blah. So before I get caught, I've opened a rift in time you must walk through to get to the other side." Baley, right away, went inside the cage and tried to lift up Marcus. "Be a gentleman. Help her." Tianna demanded from me. I did so with a bitter look and practically dragged him over to the wall. Tianna bobs her head towards the wall and I toss him through. Baley hugs Tianna and whispers thank you in her head to me before she walks through. "Go." Tianna orders to me, still trying to avoid eye contact.

"Not without you." I said.

"You don't understand Cale."

"Go first." I order.

"I have foreseen nothing but hiding and running and more hiding. That is not the life I want to live."

"What do you mean foreseen?"

"I tried talking to you, but you ignored me. I searched deep down within myself to figure out what I had done to deserve your silent treatment, but nada."

"Tianna, you don't understand."

"Oh I understand just fine. I've seen what you say here. You say stay-"

"Come with me." I tell her. Her stubbornness hid the blood rushing to her head at the thought, but I felt the heat from her pounding heart as I asked her to escape with me. I grabbed her hands in mine and she looked astonished. Images of happiness, meadows and yellow sun filled her mind until her thoughts were broken by an intrusion.

Jonah Moon came around the corner, halting when he saw myself and Tianna holding hands. "Let's go Jane." He ordered as Jane came around the corner with him.

"But Jonah, she said-"

"I don't care what your incubus said; we are hunting them down tonight!" Jonah's glare never leaves me.

"How did you?-"

"When I saw you leave, I knew something was up. I didn't need some vision of myself to tell me what to do. So I killed him."

"What?" Tianna gasps.

"I killed my incubus. Where do we escape now?"

"Through the wall." I say.

"Great." Jonah says as he shoves Jane first through the wall. "How long does this thing keep open?"

"As long as I keep focusing on it, but what of the others?-"

"Great." Jonah repeats. "Close it behind me, I don't want the others coming through."

"What's going on Jonah?"

"Oh did I not mention?" Jonah speaks in a very nonchalant tone, "When I killed my incubus, I grabbed Jane and followed you to the wash, but I'm pretty sure most people saw me, because all the while Mr. Hamilton was throwing a fit about the room or something and yeah. So I'm pretty sure everyone's on their way here because I might have said 'We are getting outta here.' to Jane a little too loudly."

"How sure?" Tianna says a bit scared.

A siren shakes the room with a boisterous sound that makes us flinch.

"Probably one-hundred percent sure now." He says before he disappears behind the wall.

"Cale." Tianna warns.

"What?"

"I'm getting déjà vu. This all happened in a dream before."

"What?"

"I can control time, and sometimes I can see the future, they come in visions and images."

"I thought you did that loud siren thing." I explain.

"I can do that too, but my incubus called me something. She said I was some sort of oracle of eternity or something and that I shouldn't trust my dreams and my visions until I've become fully trained."

"Well what does that mean? Is escaping wrong?"

"I guess. But why does it feel so right?"

More footsteps came around the corner and Tianna tells everyone to go through the rift. Bozzo, Phil, Laura, Max, and two others hesitate before entering the wall in front of them. Max kicks Laura up against where Tianna pointed to go and she falls through. Phil dives for her and disappears through the wall as well.

"Go." She orders me as Bozzo disappears through the wall. The piercing alarm almost grew louder, like it was a title wave coming for us.

"Where to?" Britney strolls around the corner like nothing was wrong, an angry expression upon her face glowered at Tianna. Beef shortly follows her hustling as fast as he could, he leans over, out of breath gasping for air.

"In the wall." Tianna says.

"Mhm." Britney smirks, but keeps walking towards the wall. "F.Y.I. Brett isn't too happy about me sealing him outside the wash with a code locked door." Her blonde hair flips over her shoulder and hits Tianna in the face before she walks through the wall.

Beef struggles to get to me and almost brings me down as he leans against me out of breath.

"I'll see you soon Beef." I said.

I didn't have to read my best friends mind to tell that he wasn't going to leave me. But I was going to leave him. I yanked him off balance and shoved him into the wall where he disappeared.

I turn to Tianna and she seems to struggling with some sort of headache. "What's wrong?"

"I can't keep it open." She says struggling to keep balance.

There was no time to think when I told her, "Close it." and instinct took over as I threw her into the wall. Instantly following my rough goodbye, Brett came around the corner of the entrance and glared at me with perilous eyes.

"Where are they?" He demanded.

"Who might you be referring to?" I politely asked pretending I had no idea what he was talking about.

"The others!" Brett barked. "Where is everyone!"

"By golly I don't know! Oh heavens where, oh where could they be?"

"Don't play coy, I know they were trying to escape."

"And you want to prevent that?" I ask indecently.

"Yes. Only one was supposed to-"

"That's enough Brett!" Mr. Hamilton's voice thundered as he entered the room.

"Yes master." Brett graciously bowed down.

"Master?" I thought. As Mr. Hamilton turned the corner with Amanda, Cocoa and three others at his backside.

"Come." He announced. "It is time for lunch." He spoke as if nothing was wrong. I attempted to read is mind but he broke my concentration by ordering me to fix the gate I had broken on the cage Marcus had broken out of. I looked at the others who lie strew and about on the ground, all of them exhausting what looked like the last of their lives. Their voices yelped "Save me!" and "Help!" inside their heads, but I did nothing. I bent the lock I had easily broken and relocked it all while Mr. Hamilton hovered over me to watch with angry eyes. I wondered if I would ever see Tianna or my best friend again and for a moment, I had suddenly wished I had not agreed to help Baley escape. Some instinct in me told me that I only caused the escapees more trouble.

There were so few of us at the dining table but Mr. Hamilton ate as though there were always a small amount of us. An apple rested on the side of my plate its skin bruised with imperfection the bruise reminded me of my incubus. I had done exactly as he asked…or so I thought.

"Not hungry again, Cale?" Mr. Hamilton says across the table as I stare at the apple.

"No." I half whisper, avoiding all eye contact. I could see Brett and Amanda glaring out of my peripherals. Some time passed, holding hands with awkward silence and I decided to do something bold. "I wish to see my incubus." I demanded.

"But after lunch we patrol the wash Cale."

I realized that Mr. Hamilton must have the ability to operate the room through some sort of control panel since when I crossed through the glass alone earlier the room remained empty for the white walls. Something was wrong in my gut. I could feel it. I tried listening in on Brett's mind, hoping he might have an answer, but all there was to hear was a fuzzy, screeching sound that gave me a brain freeze.

"Something wrong, Cale?" Mr. Hamilton says as I try to hide the pain. My head felt like it was being shook violently repeatedly, rupturing my brain.

"Nothing." I lied. Squinting my eyes. I tried to listen in on Amanda, only to suffer the same throbbing ache my head could barely take. I thrust myself off my seat and stumble out the door. I know I'm being followed, but I keep moving forward.

"*What is my purpose?*" I thought. "*What is my meaning?*" I could feel myself dying somehow. The only thing I could think of was returning to the room of relinquishment. I desperately needed answers. My body began to sweat. "*What am I going through withdrawals for?*" How badly I wanted myself to argue back and tell me how weak I was, but nothing seemed to come. Leaning against the wall, I felt as if I was going to faint. "*Where is Mr. Rusenkell?*" I thought. I started blaming my fatigue on nausea from not eating. I stand up straight, still a little off balance and a hand firmly grips onto my shoulder and guides me into my room. Too weak to search for my recently missing i-pod that would maybe drown some of the pain out, I let my body shut itself down onto the bed, hearing the door close behind me.

My own voice awakes me and I sit up in bed. "Good morning sunshine."

As I sit up, I see an image of myself in a rocking chair that never had been in my room before. "This is a dream." I assumed.

"Sort of." The other me stated. "You're being tricked, Cale. You know it."

"What are you—"

"Just hear me out, alright?" he interrupts. "You know deep down something's wrong. It's eating you alive. Literally. And what's killing you is you. You are using your own powers against yourself. Think about it Cale. This guy, this David Hamilton guy; what exactly does he want from you? He feeds you, he keeps saying you need training. For what? What are you training for? He's manipulating you, you fool!" I the image of me poked himself in the head tapping two fingers against his skull like a woodchuck would drill wood.

"He's protecting us." I say.

"From what exactly?"

"The White Crows."

"Well, if that's true, then who is protecting your little girlfriend from them right now?"

"She's not my girlfriend."

"Will you stop with the nonsense already? She likes you! Like her back. Get married, have little Cale junior baby stubborn suckers, live your life man!"

"She only likes me because I've psychically convinced her too."

"Have you even asked her yet?" I remained silent. "Didn't think so. You don't belong here Cale." The image of me lights up a cigarette. "You're losing your marbles kid. You are unique, Cale. You were made to be an equinox of good and evil. You have your own side to fight. You know what you need to do next." His words were of hidden power and cryptic fortune.

"Who are you?" I ask with all of the curiosity in the world.

The alternate me smiles as if he's been waiting for me to ask that question from the very beginning. "Let's just say, I'm a divine message from your employer." He winks and evaporates with the rocking chair into white smoke, leaving the cigarette behind.

"Can I quit then?"

"No."

"Shut up. I didn't ask you."

"Incoming." My eyes darted to the door as it flew open with Brett's strength.

"Come on Cale, let's go!" he beckoned, trying to keep his voice low.

"Why does room service always come at the most annoying times?" I thought. "Do I know you?" I ask.

"There's no time, come on, we have to go!"

"No." I say after looking at the time the alarm clock read. It was five-thirty in the morning. *"I should be resting peacefully but instead the ghost of Christmas future comes to haunt me and tell me I don't belong where I am, and my arch nemesis is at my door begging me to come with him."*

"Decisions, decisions." I thought.

"Cale you have to trust me, we need to save them!" Brett whispers.

"I think I like my bed more right now, you can try again in a couple hours." I say as I cuddle myself up and close my eyes. Although I was curious on whom he was talking about. But I didn't care for Amanda, or Cocoa or...

"Fine! Stay here!" he slams my door shut. I shiver as I pull the blanket over myself and force myself to fall asleep.

I end up just watching red numbers that influenced the time on my alarm clock go by for the next five hours and no one comes to get me. No call for breakfast, no training sessions or attempts to break free. I was either being forgotten, or left alone.

"Just like you wanted, right?" I asked.

"Just like I wanted." I tell myself unconvinced. I wouldn't let myself miss Beef or Tianna. I wouldn't allow myself to feel the weakness their absence caused me, although the pain had already been seeping through me repeatedly. I felt someone coming. The presence was unmistakably Mr. Hamilton, so I sit up in my bed and face the wall the head of my bed rested against. He knew knocking wouldn't be necessary since I already would feel him coming, so he opened the door gently.

"Cale." He said. I don't respond to him. "Would you like to visit the room of relinquishment?" He spoke in a very motherly, soothing tone. I look at him with apathy written over my face. The incubus was haunting me. He was like a drug I only used once, but somehow managed to make me addicted to him. I had done what he had told me I would a week ago,

and now it was time to see him again. But I knew I was going in to end it.
I wouldn't succumb to its riddles of persuasion whatever he was. Although
it took a convincing human form, I was sure that it was just a figment of
my mind. I needed to break free from his curse. I needed to create a great
escape from his clutches as I led the outbreak of the others. I nod seriously
and follow Mr. Hamilton out of the room as any drone would. It was time
I regained control over myself again. I was going to kill my incubus.

16. The Visitor

"Go ahead and step on in." Mr. Hamilton ordered. I willingly walked through the glass that felt like a cool breeze of air, as it always did and peered into the dark forest. I turn around and Mr. Hamilton is gone, as he usually is once someone stepped into the room of relinquishment.

"Maybe it's more than a power button he presses." I thought.

"What do you mean?"

"It's obvious he overlooks these sessions." I tell myself as I glance up at the window I had spotted out last time. *"Maybe he monitors these incubi."*

"Maybe…" I thought. Leaves rustled under my stalking feet, as I crept into the dark wilderness. I checked my pockets as it got darker and realized I had left my light on my counter top. I remembered how my incubus had created a flame from his finger.

"Strange…"

"You can't do that."

"Amanda can though…"
"She can create and control fire."

I snap my finger and think of a flame to sprout up from my thumb, but nothing happened. For the first time, I felt like my powers were neutered. I just wanted some form of light. I look down to my right hand and my fingers fold over my palm as I think of light. I close my eyes and take in a deep breath until I can feel my eyelids dwindle at something brightly glowing. I open my eyes and in the palm of my hand a bright, white light shun. I gave the light life with a thought of it living and it began to float around me like a light bulb with no strings attatched.

"Put that out!" Something hissed in the darkness. At the voice I could only assume to be my incubus, I psychically commanded the light to shine brighter, and a desperate movement for shelter swiftly gusted itself behind a tree as the white light hovered above me and shun itself brighter. *Brighter* I thought, knowing the light would repel the incubus, maybe even kill it. "Put it out! Put it out!"

"Tell me why you had me help Baley."

"You failed! You let the oracle of eternity go!"

"I did exactly as you told me I was supposed to!" I was in control now.

"But now there is another task you must fulfill." The incubus hissed.

"I'm done with your prophecies." I warn as I make the light shine brighter.

"Bring her back, Cale! Bring her back!" The light glows brighter and brighter until it becomes blinding I can feel the presence of the incubus suffering behind the tree, taking refuge. My hand becomes a vacuum as I imagine my demonic twin to be inhaled into the palm of my hand. I pull it through the tree and bark goes flying in every direction as the neck of what looks like me rests uncomfortably under my right talon and I watch him incubate into ash as the living light purifies all the darkness. The forest becomes no more and I find myself standing in a large white room just as it was yesterday morning when I came wondering in by myself. I turn to look at the window the perched itself over the room of relinquishment to see if I could catch a glance of Mr. Hamilton. But he was already standing on the other side of the walk-through glass. I begin walking towards him when the little light bug-like creature I created, zips in front of me. I snatch it in mid air with two fingers and watch it flay into nothingness in my hand before I crookedly smile and walk through the glass.

Mr. Hamilton looks at me as though I have ruined something valuable, but I walk past him towards the staircases without saying anything. Like sonic radar, I picked up some form of voice coming from him, and I could have sworn it said "Bring her back, Cale." But before I could analyze his mind, Brett came proudly marching into the room with Amanda and Cocoa.

"The word is out." Brett says proudly with a smile on his face. I badly wanted to smack it off.

"Good. And of the civilians?"

"All of them safe and sound just like you asked." Amanda answered just as proud.

"Wouldn't mind smacking her either." I thought.

"Excellent news. And what are they calling you?"

"I don't know, why don't we check the news?" Brett suggests in a goody-two-shoes tone.

"Kill me now God, please! Throw me a thunderbolt!" hearing his daddy-look-at-me-I'm –proud voice was more torture than the raunchy headaches I got from trying to read his mind yesterday. I didn't even want to chance it today.

Mr. Hamilton pushes a button behind his desk and the glass screen comes down from the ceiling. The news is playing and the announcer is saying how a dawn of super heroes is born. As I listen to the story about how the White Crows have attacked again, letting off explosives in Los Angeles, three heroes extinguished the fires of the city and was able to save everyone from any casualties. "Citizens are calling this dynamic trio the Three Wonders."

I almost puke at the cheesy name.

"The Three Wonders have saved the day here from these terrorists, but the real story is, who are they? And are there more of them?" I watched the footage of the three stooges as they extinguished the fire. Brett flew all over the place and Cocoa grew to an enormous size to carry the people trapped on top of the roof down to the floor before he changed his size back to normal. Amanda eliminated the fires by somehow absorbing the heat.

"Could have been four." Brett said as he turned from the screen to look at me with puppy eyes.

"You've got to be kidding me." I thought. "I needed my beauty sleep." I said.

"Is that what this place is? Some sort of toxin manufacturing facility that pooped out super heroes?"

"Count me out." I thought as I turned to head towards my room.

"Don't worry, he'll be okay." I hear Mr. Hamilton whisper as I disappear from the room.

I thought I'd feel more fulfilled after killing my incubus, but now I was just left without a motive. I was positive there wasn't a brick holding my door ajar when I left it this morning to follow Mr. Hamilton into the room of relinquishment, so I paused before entering. I cautiously opened the door and looked around the room for a sign of an intruder. I was caught off guard when something behind the door yanked me in, kicked the brick away and closed the door, locking us both in.

"Tianna!" I gasp. I notice she is wearing different clothes.

"How dare you push me!" She scolded.

"What are you?-"I started with no recollection of even touching her until I remembered shoving her through the wall unwillingly to escape with the others. "Oh."

"Yeah! 'Oh' is right!" she says furiously.

"You are really angry."

"How'd you guess!" she nearly screams.

"Keep it down!" I hush.

"Here." She throws something onto my lap as I sit on the bed. "It's a gift from Britney." She says in a disgusted tone. It was my velvet red i-pod. "She stole it?" I asked

"She charged it. The battery was dying or something."

"She took it just to charge it?"

"She's a techno-path. She controls technology. Anyways, she wanted to give you a card with it, but my dog ate it."

"What's your dog's name?" I ask.

"I don't have a dog." She said.

"Cale," I pretend to read her mind, "I stole your i-pod to charge it, but I forgot to give it back. Follow Tianna through the rift so we can meet up. I'm looking forward to seeing you." Tianna looked furious and confused. "You read the card before your dog ate it didn't you?"

"Don't read my mind." She said. "Now come on. Let's go."

"I must have been accurate to what the card had said." I say to myself astonished at guessing near perfectly. It didn't take super powers to guess that Britney Wilson liked me and Tianna wasn't too happy about it. This made me a bit happy at the fact Tianna was willing to be angry over me. "Where are we going?"

"Through the rift I opened in the dining room."

"Well good luck getting out." I said as I lay back against my bed putting my arms behind my eyes.

Tianna turned to face me, too prideful to admit she had done something stupid by closing the door behind her. "I forgot."

I smile at the irony. I was imprisoned in my room with the one person I wanted most in the world, but could never have the real her. It was like the common honor between writers. True writers never used that of other author's writing, just as I wouldn't ever feel the real her as long as I wanted her. "Might as well stop stressing yourself out by focusing on the rift." I yawn.

"But how will we get back?"

"Can you open a rift to somewhere different?" I ask.

"I don't know." I haven't tried. "I'll give it a shot."

"Good luck." I say closing my eyes. Apparently she forgot our powers were neutered in our rooms.

"What do you mean?"

"Can't use your powers in here. I've tried before."

"What will he do if he finds me here?"

"Let's hope its Brett that comes knocking then, eh?"

"Cale, this is serious."

"And I'm being serious."

Frustrated, she sits on the bed realizing there was no point in arguing with me. I smile at the fact that I won the argument. "Why did you avoid me?" she asks sincerely with a voice purely angelic. I stop smiling. I don't answer her right away. "It's like…" I lean up and lift my feet off the bed so I'm facing the wall opposite from her.

"I don't want to talk about it." I grimace.

"Well we're stuck here, might as well-"

"No."

"You are so stubborn!" she yells standing up off the bed.

"Oh and you're not?" I exclaim mimicking her movement to tower over me.

"At least I'm willing to sacrifice some of my pride to communicate with you!"

"Yeah? Well it's kind of hard to communicate with someone who doesn't know what they want." I scold knowing she was still unaware of my innate control over others.

"At least I'm not broken!"

"Broken?" I ask dumbfounded.

"Yeah! Broken!" she sounds out the word through every syllable. "You know, I don't even know why I came back for you."

"It's because you're infatuated with me."

"Well I'm glad to see your ego isn't broken!"

"You haven't the slightest clue, okay?" I say while I slide over to the other side of the bed to improve my threat.

"I know! That's exactly it!" It didn't work, I should have known she would never back down.

"What do you want from me?!"

"All I want is you!" She yells furiously as she punches my chest.

"Oh yeah?! Well I want you too!" I yell back in the same tone.

"Prove it!" she yells.

"*You* prove it!" I yell back, and before I could finish yelling she grabs me by the collar of my white v-neck and seals her lips up against mine. How badly I wanted to pull her silky black hair as she mauled her nails into my back. The feral tigress sank her teeth into my neck as I swallowed her with my arms, squeezing her precious body. I couldn't resist her mint like breath any more than I couldn't resist the complete her.

"*Incomplete.*" I thought as I remembered the only reason she felt this way was because I was her puppeteer.

"*I don't care.*" I tried to convince myself that the feeling was just too right, I wanted to live in her kiss.

"*It isn't right.*" I couldn't bear the thought any longer as I released myself from her.

"Why'd you stop?" she asked as I backed away from her to sit down on my bed.

I couldn't believe I was about to say what I was, but I did anyways. "Because…" I start. I let the silence take my place, as she sits down next to me on the bed. I had hoped the silence would have said it for me, but I knew I would have to tell her anyways. "Because, Tianna. I love you." I was unable to look at her. I knew I was in love with her the day I first saw her. As crooked as people make love out to be, I knew my feelings for her were love, just as sure as I was about the sun setting in the west. There was no book, or manual to tell me what my feelings were. They were merely titled by the instinct inside. We were all just vessels driven by instinct. I wasn't looking at her, but I could feel the warmth of her smile as she looked at the back of my head. She placed her hand in mine with utter grace, her hand softer than the memory of a childhood bear I used to keep for comfort that I used whenever I was home alone and Glenda was off at work. Like a puzzle, her hand fit perfectly in mine. I turned to face her. I imagined something on her hand, a tattoo of some sort as I gazed into her eyes trying to maintain my breath as she kept trying to steal it.

"Ouch." She whispered as she felt a little discomfort somewhere, like she had been bitten. She looked down and her eyes grew with amazement. I looked down too and on her hand written along the lower top where her thumb sprouted out from were the words "Forever" written neatly in my handwriting. She looked back up at me with a surprise look in her eye.

"I'm- I'm sorry, I didn't- I'm sure I can erase it somehow." I stutter.

"I thought you couldn't use your powers in here?" she asked.

"I can't. Watch." I say as I attempt to unlock the door by pushing my hand against the air between the door and me. Nothing happens. I turn back to face her. "You see?"

Knock, knock, knock. My eyes widen with fear before I direct Tianna to hide under the bed. I sit up in my bed, and in enters Mr. Hamilton. "Hello Cale."

"Hello." I say dully.

"Wow. I got a hello back. Aren't we feeling quite chipper today?"

"Crap." I thought. "What do you want?"

"Look, I know you miss your friends. And I know you don't want anything to do with me, but give us a chance. The world needs you Cale. Those White Crows are still out there. And for some reason, they want to hunt you all down, one by one. Here you are protected. Here you are safe. I hope you consider joining the team." He says before he starts to walk out the door.

"Leave it open, sir." I say respectively.

"Ew what is that awful taste?" I say at the bitterness of the ending to my last comment of salute.

"It's my acting."

"Spare me the righteous respect, please."

"Are you coming to the wash for your daily duties then?" Mr. Hamilton asks.

"Yes, give me a moment though."

"Very Well. I shall expect you there in five." He types in a code that turned the red light green, which meant the next time the door was opened it would automatically lock itself once closed.

As soon as he left my room, I drag Tianna up from under the bed. "You have to get out of here. Go back."

"I'm not leaving you."

"Please. You have to trust me. My incubus wanted you back here for some reason, and I don't know why. I can't risk you getting caught."

"My incubus told me to come to you no matter what it takes."

"I thought you said you didn't believe in your incubus?"

"I don't."

"So why'd you listen?"

"My incubus also told me never to leave this place or I would suffer. And when you forced me through my own rift, I- oh! I almost forgot! There's something you need to know-"

"Not now Tianna! I have to go."

"But it's important!"

I grab her shoulders so that she would listen to me. "Open a rift back up, to that same place in Las Vegas. Go through it and as soon as I can, I will come find you." I don't let her speak as I push her out the door.

"I assumed this brick didn't belong here." Mr. Hamilton says as I close the door behind me. *Run* I pronounced in Tianna's head, and she took off sprinting towards the diner. "Stop her!" Mr. Hamilton ordered. I went sprinting after her in obedience. But by the time I entered the diner, Tianna had already vanished. I knew Mr. Hamilton would not be happy with my inadequacy, and he shoved me inside my room warning me that the next time I was to have another visiting hour, I would report to him immediately. "She could have been an imposter for all I know!" He warned. He was beginning to sound like a step father.

"Why all of a sudden an abrupt interest in my safety?"

"Or maybe he has been concerned of your safety…" He made me feel as though the entire world were out to get me. He twisted my thoughts so I could see his point of view. He left me to the silence of my room while I dwelled the thought if the visitor was actually Tianna or an imposter like Mr. Hamilton had warned…

17. Betrayed

After weeks of obedience, Brett and the others were rewarded to walk around the facility freely. Their doors were ripped from their hinges and personally burned by Amanda while they danced around the burning doors like Indians. I kept to myself most of the time.

"I miss Beef." I told myself.

"Can you do anything else but sulk here and whine about how miserable your life is? You're bringing me down too!"

"I can slit my wrists. Will that make you feel any better?"

"Perfect."

"I hate you."

"Cale! Come out here!" Brett's voice, all cheery says as he opens the door to my room. "I want to show you something!" I heard him even through the music blasting in my ears, but I continued to stare at him like I was dead. He came in to my room leaving the door to slowly fall in place to lock me in and I continued to stare. "Yoo-hoo" he hooted while he waved his hands that snapped his fingers in front of my face. But I never blinked and continued to enjoy Paramore singing "Ignorance" in my ears. gradually the door was going to close, and I grew worried that it would lock us both in here together, so in a flash at the very last moment, with a speed too fast to be human, I zipped out of bed, and out the door leaving my i-pod and Brett Gooding behind as the door locked shut. "Very funny Cale." He said from inside, but I was already speeding down the hallway with unimaginable speed to the dining room. The more the days past, I seemed to have adapted to my powers and lived with them more instinctively. I figured out that I was able to sense the presence of another being and My senses were heightened to superbly devastate a regular human sense. I also figured out how to evaporate into smoke as my incubus once did. I knew I could do more with it but it seemed to only come at times of need. I resented the fact that was able to control people in memory that every time it happened there was something throbbing in my heart as well as in my head that meant a great deal to me. I couldn't remember for the life of me why I resented controlling others with my mind. The only thing I that came to mind was a mere word: Forever.

"Cale." Mr. Hamilton's voice surprised me and stopped me from entering the dining area. I turn to him, already knowing what he was going to ask of me but continued to play stupid. He stood outside my room and nodded for me to unlock the door. I roll my eyes before I start to leisurely walk towards him, soaking up every ounce of my practical joke I had played against Brett. "Faster." He demanded. And before he could even roll the 'r' on the word I opened the door and was back at the entrance to the dining room.

"Cale!" Brett shouts for me, but I continued to ignore him and he continued to follow me around like an annoying little cousin. He developed into this happy child. Everyone did. Even I felt a little bit happy inside. But I never showed it. "Cale I have to show you my room!" he barked at the table as I took a bite out of a slice of pizza. I looked at him with a vividly blank face.

"Is he for reals?" I thought.

"This kid can't be serious." I was sure this was all an act. But sure enough, like a puppy full of love, Brett's incredible strength lifted me off my seat and dragged me to his room. I peered into it, timidly afraid of catching whatever happy disease that took Brett over. His room had more color than mine. The bed rested horizontally against the wall to the right

unlike mine and the walls were painted dark and light blue with images of clouds.

"Tis nice." I said "Okay bye."

"Wait!" he says grabbing my arm before I try to break for it. "You haven't seen the best part yet!" The fool dragged me into the pit of his room and I held my breath in fear of breathing the same air as him. "Look at it!" he said excited as I saw the wall filled with newspaper clippings entitled "Superman exists!" and "Dawn of the Heroes!" spread in black and white across every inch of the wall. Every article was a well written story about how These three Heroes, Brett, Amanda and Cocoa have helped save the world from things as simple as forest fires to the complexity of solving a murder case before the murder actually happened. "You could be out there with us buddy." Brett comforted my back as I continued to hold my breath in. But as soon as he touched me, something went wrong. I let my air out silently and discreetly but I had never felt more hatred towards Brett than ever before. Just from a two-syllable word that labeled us friends.

"I'm not your buddy." I said deathly as I evaporated myself from his room and disappeared in the hallway. Before I could discreetly hibernate inside my room Mr. Hamilton stopped me. "What." I demanded.

"I need you today." He said. Handing me two pieces of folded black clothes.

"For what."

"I'm going to send you on a mission."

"Send Brett."

"No, I'm specifically asking for you."

"Send Brett." I repeat slower and more serious as I walk into my room.

"You will report to me in fifteen at the room of relinquishment in those clothes that I just gave you, where you will be paired up with a partner for your mission. Do I make myself clear?"

"I will do none of those things. Do *I* make myself-"

"You will comply if you wish to see her again."

"Who."

"You know who. I know where she is."

"What are you talking about?"

"After this mission, I'll tell you."

"You can tell me now, or forget it."

"Then forget it." he says and walks away from the door, letting it gradually swing to close itself. I waited to the very last minute to grab it and step outside.

"Alright." I say, admitting defeat. "I'll do it." I was far too curious now to know who he was talking about and plus, how bad could this *mission* be.

"Fifteen minutes." He says as he continues to stroll down the hallway like he knew my answer before I gave it.

I felt as though I had just sold my soul to the devil himself as I walked up the stairs to the room of relinquishment. When I arrived, I see the three stooges dressed in the same black outfit as me, an almost skin tight rubber black combat suit that reminded me of something out of a comic book. "Yeah, there's no way this is going to work out." I say as I turn around to walk back to my room.

"Wait!" Mr. Hamilton Demanded, appearing from nowhere, like usual when it came to this room. "Meet your partner." He said as a short, dark haired familiar girl walks into the room through the glass, wearing the same outfit as the wonder trio and myself.

"Where have I seen her before?" I thought. I was sure I had seen her face before.

"I don't know..."

"I'm Hayley." She introduced herself putting her hand out to shake mine.

"Whatever." I said overlooking her brilliant looks. "So what's this mission thingy?" I say completely ignoring her hand gesture and facing Mr. Hamilton.

"The city of Brooklyn needs our help."

"Ha!" I laugh. "What else is new?" Everyone looks at me indecently.

"Every day the White Crows grow in number, and very soon they will start repeating bigger attacks to repeat the tragedy in Irvine. Our spies have recently detected some stolen vials of substance 36 to be taken to a hospital there. Unfortunately we have no knowledge of which hospital so I'm going to have to divide you all up. Brett can handle his own, so I will send him to take Maimonides Medical Center by himself. Amanda and Cocoa will go as one and Cale and Hayley will go as one. There are two vials total. I ask that you retrieve them with vital care, because if they break...There will be more bloodshed." He warned.

"How were these vials even taken? And why would it be taken to a hospital?" I asked rudely.

"I don't know. We either have a trader in our midst, or someone must have broken in to steal it. Remember these vials contain substance 36 in them so…"

He continues on with the briefing, but I couldn't help but wonder if someone I knew had stolen the missing vials. What would they need them for? And in Brooklyn? Could there be some mistake?

"Do you understand?"

"Yes sir." The others indulge Mr. Hamilton. A simple 'whatever' look from me is all he got as he showed us to our means of transportation.

Two jets perched themselves on an anchor where he informed us that Brett would be able to fly alongside while Amanda and Hayley controlled the Jets. A black bird logoed the sides of the jets. "Are those crows?" I asked.

"They're ravens." Hayley announced a little too quickly. "That's what we call ourselves. Ravens of the night." She stated proudly.

"That's stupid." I said in a moronic tone.

"Why?" she said, obviously butt hurt about my comment.

"Because it's daytime." I say looking above me seeing the blue sky at the top of the ceiling where the jets were supposed to aviate towards.

On the way, I asked questions like where we were parting from, and I figured out finally that the M.S.C.'s base was located underneath Alcatraz prison in San Francisco.

"You're Kidding me." I said astonished to Hayley's reply.

"Afraid not." She sounds over the loud engine of the jet. "Tours go on all day long and you've yet to notice?"

Brett's stupid face smiles as he flies alongside with us in the air. This entire time, we were under water and I had no idea. "The jets come up away from where people can see and fly straight up past the clouds before takeoff."

"Is there an entrance through the prison?"

"Just one. It's off limits to all the pedestrians, and is guarded by Pedigrates. You can't miss it. The base is kept secret. If humans found out about our stationary, things could get ugly." It would take some time to get used to the fact that I was no longer considered a human.

"So that's the base then eh?"

"One of them."

"One of them?"

"There's more across the globe. All run by the infamous David Hamilton." She made it sound like Mr. Hamilton was the bad guy.

It didn't take too long to fly across the United States. We were going so fast, it took barely an hour before we hit Brooklyn. "We're here." Hayley announced proudly descending from the air.

"So what's your power?"

"I'm a leech."

"You don't have any?"

"No, I'm a leech. I leech off of other's powers as long as I'm in focus and in distance. So stay close."

She lands the jet on top of the hospital where the helicopter sign was.

"Won't we get in some sort of trouble for this?"

"Rookie." She said in her mind.

"Yeah, I heard that."

"Rookie." She announced out loud while staring at me before she popped the hood of the jet open and hopped out. I follow her trying not to ask any more questions.

"You can ask what you want. I was only kidding." She says as she breaks into the roof door. Having my thoughts exploited was going to be a little bit annoying. "Just be lucky there's only one of you on chart." She comforts. "For now at least."

"What was that?"

"Nothing." She hushes as we walks down the stairs onto the top floor of the hospital. "Turn your earpiece on." She ordered as we got to the door to the top floor. I turned the device Hayley had given to me while inside the jet on before plugging it in my ear. "Okay, you go left, I go right. Avoid all eye contact, try not to get the cops called. Comprende?"

"Whatever." I say.

She rolls her eyes with a slight grin and busts open the door like she was F.B.I. I act the part as I patrol the busy hospital. In search for two small, green vials. Great. I started to wonder how long this was going to take when a buzzing noise came over my ear.

"Got one!" Hayley's voice alarms in my ear. "I believe the score is one to zero?"

"Bite me." I grimace as I start to search harder. And then something innate hit me. I turned around to see if I could spot out Hayley and found her searching the end of the hall.

"Hmm…" I thought. I crept up slowly to see if I could somehow target my mind reading and listen in on her thoughts. After listening in on several nurses complain about their mean, aged doctors, a dying patient wishing for his last wish for his imbecile family to pull the plug and stop delaying the inevitable and a sick child wanting to go home to play his video games I finally heard something of use.

"As soon as I get rid of this fool, I can take care of the rest of them." She told herself. A flash back of the briefing Mr. Hamilton gave earlier said it was possible that there was a traitor in their midst. She was the traitor. "I'll give him the cure as soon as he turns his back." She says while I see her fondling with a syringe in her left hand as she pretends to look around. "Okay Hayley. Just like she said. Under the body bag in room 36."

"She?" I thought.

"Who might this she *be?"*

"I don't know."

"Her incubus?"

"How would her incubus know where the green vials were hidden?"

I wasn't sure how, but I was convinced that I was dead right about the mystery 'she' being her incubus. "Got it." I heard her voice say as she walked around the corner. "Cale? You there?" she said.

"Oh, yeah. Wait. You got both of them?" I asked. Realizing she was actually speaking into the microphone chip implanted in her ear.

"Yes. Two to zip. Better luck next time chuck." She says as she leans on the door we came through waiting for me.

"Ladies first." I say afraid that she might stab me in the back with the cure.

Realizing I had ruined her backstabbing plan to assault me when I wasn't looking, her face twisted into disappointment as she took my insist on her being a lady, I mean what was a gentleman to do then hold the door for the lady.

"Indeed you are quite the gentleman."

"Crap. She heard me." I forgot about her powers when I closed the door behind me and Hayley sailed through the air to dagger me with the cure. All too quickly I fiercely grabbed her forearm before the syringe could impale me and kick her against the stairs leading upwards to the roof. I charged for her in utter rage, but she was as fast as I was when she grappled onto the bar handles posted on both sides of her and did a back flip kick into my face knocking me back. With an offensive advantage over me, Hayley used it to spring upstairs, knowing I would soon be up on my

feet and on her pursuit. When I reached the roof top her voice echoed for me to stop where I was. I figured she had a gun aimed for my head, but when I found her, she was standing on a ledge of the building dangling the green vials over the edge.

"Don't move or I drop them."

"Give them to me." I demanded.

"Why do you want them? So you can claim the next trophy from your little secret society and become a famous hero just like your little friends?" She mocked.

"Who do you work for?" I ordered.

Hayley laughed and said "You're too naïve. You're playing on the wrong team freak."

"Sticks and stones." I repeated to myself, remembering Brody Geldert's fate.

"You are nothing. Just a useless, filthy hybrid!" and in that moment, she fed a building flame inside my head that innately pushed her off the edge with the force of my palm.

"What happened to sticks and stones?" I asked myself as I summoned the two green vials out of the air to float to my left palm.

"I dislike traitors." Was my excuse. I leaned over the edge of the building to see the plummet Hayley took a free fall from and I was sure she wouldn't have been able to survive it. I look at the vials that I had stolen from mid air as Hayley was knocked off the edge by a forceful psychic blow and something seems to be very plain about them They contained nothing inside them. No form of liquid or solid inside could be measured from even a superb beings sight. They were merely, regular vials. I was sure of it. But why would Hayley sacrifice herself for a pair of fake vials?

"Maybe because that wasn't really Hayley?" Hayley's voice appeared from behind me and she started familiar combat that was obvious to me she had been trained by Mr. Hamilton. "Those vials are fake by the way." She says kicking me in the face. She gains some distance away from me when she dangles the real two vials from her hands. I break the vials against the ground and send the broken pieces flying through the air controlling every piece of glass to follow her like heat seeking missiles. After failing to maneuver her way around the pieces she turns and faces her palm out making them into smaller, harmless pieces of dust. The fight between Hayley and I carries on as we slam each other against the ground without having to touch each other, until she throws both vials off the edge as soon as I start making herself choke. She knew it would break my focus and give her a quick advantage to strike. With my face turned to where the Vials were thrown, I see only one has made it over the edge, the other rolled along the ledge of the building. I'm overlapped with her striking fists as my distraction worries me for the second vial to take a free fall.

A flash back of all that this toxin has caused plays in my mind as I focus on the vial and manage to catch it with an invisible distant helping hand from rolling off the edge. All this trouble over one small dose of a bane that caused nothing but chaos.

Our fight continued to prove itself a useless one as we equally harmed each other, both of us using my powers. With one hand on the floor my foot raised itself high enough to boot her far enough back so I could catch my breath. Too quickly though, she swept my legs beneath me and prepared to stab me with a syringe filled with black liquid. I grabbed her forearm before she could impale the needle in me and we waged a war of arm strength as we pushed each other back and forth like the world's toughest game of tug-o-war. Somehow she was using my power against me by preventing me from launching her off and away from her pinning me against the floor of the hospital roof. She was like the lock on the door to my room that blocked me from using my powers. Every attempt I made, she blocked me like the perfect goalie, until she suddenly lost her strength and bent her neck back. She dropped the cure from her grip and I picked it up as I athletically flipped myself up to my feet, leaving her stunned on her knees. Hayley fell flat, after trying to stand and a forced empty syringe, much like the one in my hand stuck itself in the back of her neck.

Before I can recognize my rescuer, he has zoomed himself up from the opposite ledge, where he was standing, and leaning over Hayley's back. He was dressed in a nice, button down shirt with slacks. I slowly back away, gripping the syringe in my left hand preparing myself to use it on him as he continues to keep his head down while staring at Hayley's back. He flips her over and gestures his hand on his chin, scratching it like he was thinking. "You're not one of them, are you?" He said, finally raising his head so we could see each other eye to eye.

"I know you." I gasp as I recognize his face. "You're a White Crow." I say as I identify his young face to be one of the three leaders the news warned us about. Then it hit me. I realized that Hayley's face matched the female picture on the news as well.

"She was one too." He said solemnly.

Almost intimidated, I lingered in defense and waited for him to spring at me.

'Why was she trying to kill you?" He said looking over his shoulder, paranoid.

"You tell me." I accuse.

"*I* had nothing to do with your assassination."

"Who are you?"

"I am Paul. Who are you?"

"Brett." I lied.

"Are you some form of double agent, trying to take me for a fool?" he says after quickly vanishing himself to the ledge and back, picking up the green vial and showing it to me. "This is fake." He said as he tossed it behind him waiting for it to shatter. "What is your business here?" It was no mistake that he carried all the seriousness in the world in his gaping blue eyes. His blonde, slick hair was combed neatly and not a speck of dirt was stained on his shirt. He was extremely professional. "Speak." He demanded.

"I'm here on behalf of David Hamilton to retrieve some stolen green vials. Happy?"

"So *you* are his new pet. Brett Gooding if I'm not mistaken."

"Who wants to know?"

"I do, in fact. There's a bounty on your head that all the White Crows have been ordered to collect."

"By who's order?" I ask.

"Mine."

"Then come and claim it." I say slightly crouching down, preparing to defend myself.

Paul laughs and shrugs my comment off as if my taunt was the feeble work of reverse psychology.

"Which it was." I thought.

"Hush."

"Chicken."

"So where's the real Brett Gooding." He demanded after looking deeply into my eyes as if he was searching for something in them that would tell him I was lying.

"How do you know you're not looking at him?"

"Don't take me for some sort of fool, Cale." I hid the surprising emotion under the muscles of my face at the fact that he knew my real name. "The benefits of being a profiler. I know everything about you, by just your presence being here."

"That's your power? So what makes *you* so dangerous that the entire country needs to beware of you?" I mocked.

"I'm deadly when I need to be." He grins. "You aren't like them Cale." He says after a pause and another odd gaze into my eyes. "I can see it in your eyes. I don't need to be an earth breaker like your friend Jonah to know that you aren't as loyal to David Hamilton like Brett."

"Jonah? How'd you know about him?"

"When your friends were sent through the rift, Jonah became a mini David Hamilton himself when he realized he had found one of us."

"What do you mean?"

"Your friend Jonah has the ability to break all attatchments between alliances anyone decides to create. You could be completely brainwashed, and he'd have you eating out of the palm of his hand if he wished. The third most wanted male in the world that illegibly is leading the White Crows found that out the hard way."

In my mind I try to remember the faces on the news. I connected the dots with Hayley and Paul, and remembered the third man's picture when I asked, "What happened to him?" realizing the high pitch in my voice symbolized I cared a little bit, so I corrected it by adding, "Not that his fate is of any concern to me."

"Naturally." He says grinning almost like he knew my hostility was a defense mechanism. "Shawn was ambushed by your conniving friend and his band of loyal followers he quickly conjured into slaves of his favor. Shawn was blamed for a wrong he had not done and murdered in cold blood, although he put up a fight. Some of the ones who escaped disagreed with Jonah's ravenous rage in which he started terrorizing innocent civilians. The fool is consumed by revenge and sworn to find me. Luckily some sense of the good in humanity survived in another one of your little friends as she trapped him inside of a painting of some sort. His followers continued to pursue Shawn's group of survivors until every last one was hunted down. Once I caught word of the dent in our numbers, I left my campaign to bring order to Hamilton's disloyal subjects in search of Brett Gooding and his lovely sidekicks. I believe in an eye for an eye. We have remained in hiding for too long. I will not stand and watch the world burn just to smoke us out."

"Have you heard of a Beef?" I asked, worried about his fate. There was someone else I wished to know about but all I could think of was the word 'forever' when I tried thinking about the mystery person that fogged my mind.

"I can't promise you anyone's preservation at this point. I assume the smart ones have heaved my warning and blended in with the rest of the world. The ignorant will eventually be hunted and killed. I only know the fate of the few that caused us problems. Jonah, whom was taken care of already by one of yours, Baley I believe her name was. Britney was sedated and taken to an asylum just west of Las Vegas."

"What did she do?" I demanded to know.

"She is too dangerous, I will not risk my people's lives in a world of growing technology."

"And who are you to control her life?" I ask angrily, "What gives you the audacity to categorize us and ship us off to asylums!"

Remaining calm he continues to explain, "We aren't the bad guys Cale. We are the good guys. We only do what's best for our kind and humans alike. If you are to be mad at anyone you should be pointing your fingers at David Hamilton, not us. He's the one manipulating you all."

"He has done nothing but protect us from self righteous traitors like you!" a fire started to build inside of me for no reason at all.

He pauses and looks deeply into me as if he was trying to hypnotize me. "You don't mean it." is all he says. "The last of my generation is already staking out in Las Vegas where the *sanest* of your friends had escaped to. You can find me there once you've realized we aren't the real enemy here." And in an instant Paul flashes to the edge of the building and jumps off with a perilous dive down.

I was left in complete distraught and frustration. His cryptic words kept my mind in boggle I didn't even notice Brett had landed himself on the edge of the hospital roof behind me. I could sense him walking towards me in shock after witnessing Hayley lying on the floor, but I remained star struck with confusion. "She was going to kill me." I grimaced coldly.

Brett's voice remained calm, even at the betraying situation. "I don't remember you obtaining any cures on this mission."

"I didn't."

"She brought two?" Brett said, clearly examining the deceased body as I remembered she had one coiled in the palm of her fist when she tried to impale me with it.

"No."

"Where did the other come from?"

"A guy named Paul killed her." I confessed.

"Paul." Brett said with utter disgust. "Where is he?" he demanded to know.

"You know him?" I knew I was left out on the loop when it came to the real world after spending weeks in solitary confinement under an extinct prison, but something alarmed me that this conversation was not going to end very well.

"Where did he go?" he demanded with more vigor in his voice. I turn around to face him and saw how serious he was. Timid to read his mind in fear of crippling my head, I waited to hear him out.

"Jumped." I said plainly.

I hear him whisper something ignorant before he interrogates, "Where did he say he was going?"

"Las Vegas." I whispered automatically. "Where the rest of them are." I kicked myself in the gut after answering him without rationally thinking. Part of me wanted to protect Paul's disappearance because as evil as his tactics were, I had some kind of respect for him for saving my life.

"We shall clean the city then." He states.

"Shouldn't we return back to Hamilton first though and tell him about Hayley over here?"

"No." he stated.

"But I thought-"

"Listen Cale, these guys must be stopped. They are the reason we are even involved in this war."

"What war?"

"They cannot be controlled, so therefore they are a threat to us." Brett says completely ignoring my curiosity and arrogantly unveiling at least part of what this whole super hero thing was truly about.

"The vials were phonies." I expressed in a dark tone remembering why I had even come to the other side of the country.

I expected more shock in his voice, but the confidence in his tone confused me even further once he said, "I know."

"What do you mean, *you know*?" I grimaced. He turns his back on me and doesn't answer as he fondles through Hayley's pockets. "What do you mean?" I demanded louder.

"They were planted here by some of our agents to draw the White Crows out."

Suddenly I remembered the fact that Hayley's face remarkably resembled the White Crow leader on the news. "She is a White Crow!" I yelped.

"No she's not." Brett assured. "This *thing* works for Hamilton." I was confused on why he didn't acknowledge her as a person but a thing as if she was a dispensable toy.

"Well, you mind telling me why Hamilton sent *me* of all people to the other side of the country on a fake mission with a traitor who was planning to assassinate me?" I ask as if it wasn't a big deal.

"It isn't really nowadays."

"Nothing is really."

"Been through worse." I thought.

"She was ordered to kill you." He said.

"I can see that but-" I catch myself before I could ask a stupid question. My heart pounded at the fear that seemed to have been a pin shot straight out from his words and pricked itself in the core of my chest where the stunning paralysis bloomed itself inside me like a hurricane of butterflies enveloping the insides of my body, exploring the tracks of unclean guilt and one small butterfly just nicked a chord in my head that belonged to the bile naïve side of me that actually believed David Hamilton, his army of Pedigrates and Brett's fantastic trio were heroes. I had been betrayed. I understood the fact that I was now going to have to defend myself from Brett, but I didn't understand why. Had I done something wrong? I wracked my brain for an answer on why Hamilton would want me dead, but couldn't find one. I dared myself to whisper, "Why."

Brett doesn't answer, but instead leaps off the ground, grabbing me by the collar of my shirt and drives my back into the ground. His unbearable strength forced my back to crack the floor of the roof as he piledrived me towards the edge of the building where I used his own strength against him in propelling my legs upward so my red converse shoes I refused to switch earlier into more *professional* uniform boots could grip his torso and thrust Brett forward, above my sight off the edge of the building before I could fall head first. In realization that Brett could fly and my maneuver wouldn't do much but buy me time, once the edge was close enough to handle with my hands I gripped them tight enough to flip myself up and off the edge of the hospital to diagonally drill myself into a window of the top floor where a patient on the hospital bed was startled with enough fear that I heard his heart monitor flat line on my way out the door into the hallway.

"Sorry guy." I thought.

"He was old, he wanted his family to pull the plug anyways."

"That was the guy?"

"Yupp, think of it as you did him a favor…in a sick, twisted way."

I chuckle in my head at the irony of death before I turn to see Brett hovering out of the window I had broken into from outside the hallway.

An evil grin on his face is the last thing I see before he zips up into the sky, but the last thing I hear is, "Consider them all dead Cale." And I knew who he was going after. Not only was he going to alarm David Hamilton about the rest of the White Crow's whereabouts but I knew he meant he was going to finish the disturbed lives of the remaining Stellar High School survivors.

Infuriated, at lightning speed I zoomed upstairs back onto the roof where I was caught off guard. From behind, something sharp daggered itself into me. I reached back to pull the pain out from me and felt a feather tipped syringe sticking out of my back. Woozy and light headed I yanked the thing out and crushed it in my hand. My hand shortly bled until it healed itself at a remarkable speed. I stumbled to the floor, trying to recognize my surroundings. I grew numb and claustrophobic. There became no air to breathe as I began gasping. The only thing I could feel was Brett's presence stalking me from behind. With what felt like the last of my strength, I listened in on his voice as I collapsed on the floor and heard him chuckle in his head, "The good guys *always* win, Cale." And I realized that villains were not born into this dark world, It was the *good guys* or heroes rather that created the bad guys or as he referred to me, the villain.

18. The Great Escape

Tianna Lecher

I have always secretly been fascinated with Cale, so naturally when he decided to ignore me I felt like I had been stabbed with a pencil in the pit of my stomach where it was left to let the lead poisoning slowly spread through my veins killing me softly. I watched his back exit the room after completely ignoring my question. I was curious to what he had seen when he walked through the glass. I didn't think my purely inquisitive words would be at all offensive to him in any way.

"Tianna." The man who introduced himself as Mr. Hamilton beckoned my name with a booming voice that interrupted the daze Cale had unintentionally put me in. I look over to the man without saying a word. "Why don't you go next." The persuasive tone of his operating tongue made me not want to listen to the man and walk away as Cale had, but I was succumbed and overlapped with the curiosity of the mystery on why Cale completely ignored me and what he had seen. Letting my sight softly fall down and to the side avoiding all confrontation with him, I processed the idea in my mind.

"What's the worst that could happen." I thought. And I walked straight passed Mr. Hamilton and through the glass as Cale had demonstrated into a room filled with tombstones and willow trees perching shading all light away. I wouldn't let the fear get to me as I kept marching through recognizing the names on the tombstones after everyone I've passed. Baley Schottenfield was buried next to Marcus Moon. Even in death those two were never separated. My heart stopped when I saw the two gravesites side by side. I used to call them Barcus because of their attachments to each other. Marching my withered legs through more gravesites I notice more names carved onto more greyer and dark chrome headstones with names like Britney Wilson, Josh Caball, Brian Bozzo, Amanda Robesun, Phillip Dirk, Laura Forkner, Cameron Dark, Bradley Blandfields and Max Longo. Further into the shaded area, the darker it got and more tombstones I passed until I got to one that stopped me. I read his name and I felt the lead poisoning again start to overcome me, crippling my veins and muscles. "Cale." I whispered. As I saw his name, Cale Valens, carved onto a gravestone. For a second I started to believe this was real. Next to his gravesite was an empty ditch, the length of a medium sized coffin. I walked closer and closer, in near slow motion.

"Perfect fit don't you think?" my voice called out from the ditch. Surprised at hearing my own voice, like you do when you hear it backfire over the telephone with delayed signal, I backed up instantly. "Don't worry, I won't bite." My voice calls again just before I see something shaded rise up from the empty grave next to Cale's like a vampire would awaken from a coffin. As my eyes adjusted to the darkness I focused on the shaded figure and recognized that the image was me. This was my incubus, I was sure of it. The devious creature took my form, portraying itself as a part of me.

"What kind of sick joke is this?" I ask.

"Don't like it?" the image of me asks as she seductively walks around me and whispers, "It's the future…beautiful isn't it?" She walks away back to the empty grave and leans on the tombstone of Cale Valens. A sense of protection, like a mother bear protecting her cub, begins to boil in my head at the sight of her defiling his grave. "This is what will come to pass, if you should decide not to heave my words."

"I highly doubt that." I grimace.

She stares at me, as if she didn't understand. "You've already experienced some of your powers, have you not?" I don't answer. "Your innate scream that deafens the ears of all that persist in the radius of the siren. Your freezing touch that with the right emotion can freeze others in time as if they were a video cassette put on pause. And I'm willing to bet that you get flashbacks of the past nearly every hour of the day." The incubus knew more about me than I knew about myself. This frightened me into nodding my head. "But you've yet to discover your true powers." Purely curious, I looked at her and waited for a demonstration of what she was talking about. "Have you had any visions of the future yet?"

"No." I lied, remembering a dream I had the night before Cale and the others came back.

She was dressed in a white business suit that I would never wear, but she continued to look exactly like me down to the last freckle. She smoked a cigarette in broad daylight, which I would normally not do, but I couldn't deny the fact that she was a part of me. For a while she didn't have anything to say to me as she gazed at me with my light brown eyes. It was as if all she wanted to do was stare.

"Who are you?" I had said.

She looked away as if she had to think about it, took a drag and exhaled before she announced, "Let's just say I'm a divine intervention from your boss." Confused, I stood and suddenly realized I was stranded in a meadow of golden rye. The clone of me dressed in a professional white suit sat on top a light grey boulder in front of me. Behind her, a fusion of bold crimson, angelic orange and blinding gold shun vigorously of the breaking dawn. I was surrounded by falling leaves of auburn from the black clouds overhead. The blend of light that nearly pierced through the hills shared its time with the darkness before it got ready to rise toward the heart of the sky to take over. Tree's of autumn carried a barrier on the left and right side of the field. "You will awake from this dream, and speak to no one about it. Do I make myself clear?" she threatened. I nod in compliance before she goes on, "Very soon you will learn more about your powers I have given you from birth."

"From birth? I just recently-"

"From birth." She states. "Substance 36 is a bane. It is simply a substance that enhances your senses. You have always had flashbacks before you wake up in the morning, have you not?"

"Yes, but what-"

"A simple yes or no will do, we haven't got time." She says politely.

"Yes."

"And you sometimes get the feeling of something coming up, like what you are going to get in a class, or signs that let you know what you are going to eat later on, correct?"

"Yes."

"And you have never told anyone about the strangest of the strange coincedences that have happened to you, am I wrong?"

"No." I complied.

"Because you were brainwashed. You were manipulated by society that into thinking these psychic coincidences are merely coincidences and nothing more. The world is programmed by critical thinking adults and scientists who are completely unsatisfied with the life they have chosen to live, so they rely on intelligence and forbidden knowledge to overcome what they fear most: the inexplicable. When you are a child, you let your imagination waltz around your head and steer your life around through barriers and through any obstacle. It is purely sublime. You run off of instinct, and mystery as a phoenix echo of the dawn. This is your chance. You may be evasive and live in critical thinking, or irrational violence. Or you may heave my words and live in sublime." She spoke with such power and awe-inspiring velvet that I remained star struck at the confidence in her faith. "I will show you one power you possess that rarely anyone takes advantage of." She states as she gets off the rock to walk closer to me. "The power of the present." She explains as she waves her arm at the boulder. "This is a rift. Once you walk through it, the rift will close right behind you. No exceptions. You may open one if you can visualize the time and place of an area that you wish to go. This is how you will escape." She explains as she walks into the boulder as if it were an optic illusion. She appears from behind me, frightening me a bit. "Very soon you will be taken captive. You will subtlety listen and follow every direction, but when the signs of escape begin to point, you will follow, no matter what rule you have to break, no matter what, you will escape your captive no matter how much like home you feel. You will leave your heart behind and eventually you will return to mend it, but it will break on the third visit. You will live your life, until your heart returns to you. Don't underestimate the power of love, Tianna. There is no power greater. Sometimes when there is love between one another, no matter what kind of love it is, you can feel that other person. You get to know them, and you see how their mind thinks and how their heart beats. During the process of falling in love, your thoughts intertwine with each other and sometimes you are not two individuals, but one heart, one mind, and one soul. Your powers can be molded together and used as one. But

beware, child, brainwash in its most evil form is heartbreak. There is nothing more devastating than the evil thoughts you think when your heart is broken. Fight. Don't let it consume you." Her voice begins to echo and the sunlight begins to fade. "Don't let it consume you." And in an instant, I wake up to a crowing of a rooster.

My eyelids fly open, and the siren of the rooster is soon overcome by a thunderous sound of a helicopter. I debate with myself if the sound was a helicopter the entire time, but all the while I knew they were coming to kidnap us. I would listen to the dream and I swore not to tell anyone. Besides, who would believe me? I thought of how just yesterday we fought for our lives to defend ourselves from the men and the short haired girl that tried killing us, and how would we know if this approaching helicopter would be charitable enough to spare our lives only to abduct us instead. Jonah would not stand without a fight. All of us were awake now as we all bided our time until the helicopter came close enough to take us. Something told me though before the helicopter landed that this helicopter wasn't here to kill us because I felt my heart innately pounding fast and slow against my chest making my throat throb like the bass of the drums at a rock concert, just the way I felt every time I saw Cale Valens.

"So you mean to tell me that you have had no kinds of dreams or visions from the future?" the incubus asked me.

"No. Not one." I lied again.

"Well, that's because you haven't matured yet, because as much as you will want to fight it, I am apart of you and hold a portion of your powers." She said wickedly. I could tell she was lying, but I remembered distinctly that I needed to remain subtle about being taken until the signs pointed to escaping. I pretended to listen and did everything the incubus asked me to, but I was not convinced that she was even real. The incubus was nothing compared to the dream I had before I had awoken here in a tiny white room with no windows or furniture, just a bed with an alarm clock resting on a tiny dresser beside the bed and pallid walls that screamed of insanity. The incubus told me that I possessed the ability to wipe the memory of others just as long as my presence was inside them. The incubus knew nothing of any power of the present my divine messenger had told me about in the previous dream. She only continued to show me that I was able to travel back in time, but unable to change it. It was already set in stone and that I would be as a celestial phantom in the past, as I would be if I *matured* enough to visit the future. I pretended to cower in front of her, but she ceased to break me, even though I let her know that I was willing to listen.

When she told me she would expect to see me soon, I parted from the graveyard and walked back into the room where Mr. Hamilton awaited me with the others. All of them remained quiet and unsure of themselves. "Well?" Mr. Hamilton said.

"May I be excused to my room?" I asked politely and he nodded. I walked out of the door just as Cale did and ignored everyone as I kept trying to convince myself that the incubus was a phony, but her words kept badgering at my mind and my faith in escaping, like she was trying to convince me that I needed to stay here forever.

One long week passed, every day the same routine and the only thing that kept bugging me like an open wound scratching against every wall and corner I turned on was the fact that Cale would still completely ignore me. I grew more and more infatuated with him as every day passed, I couldn't help but want him even more. Something was different about him today though. I couldn't stop looking at him. His olive skin was glowing with beauty. He barely ate, as I barely ate. I couldn't stop looking at him, as if it was some kind of…."Sign." I thought. I was convinced that I would need to follow him. I couldn't explain it, but the faith in my dream that was dwindling down, being jaded every day from the incubus had somehow refurnished itself into a vivid memory and reminded me that I needed get out of here, and I was going to take Cale along with me. I knew I loved him. I couldn't explain it any better than that. I wanted to just hold his hand, even for a quick ten seconds. I just wanted him, his name, his dark hair, his fresh scent.

"I'm not hungry." He muttered before he got up from the table to walk out the door. An animalistic part of me wanted to clear the table with a cat like spring up and over just to stop him from leaving, but the more civil part of me took over and caused me to remain sitting. I remembered the angel-like creature in my dream, that I started calling my guardian angel, and her words that said we were all brainwashed by society into thinking the bestial judgment inside us was wrong, and the way to live is not to be abstract but alarmed with every point of sloth to be renovated with a proper stance.

Soon after Cale had left the table, a worried look grew upon Hamilton's face. He soon called breakfast off and the next thing I knew, he had said we were going to get a jumpstart on the day and head to the room of relinquishment early as everyone followed him down the hall like slaves to his call.

We arrived into the room where he ordered me first to go in through the glass to see my incubus. I refused politely, but he insisted that I had no choice. Leaving everyone else behind I thought of how badly I wanted Cale's help as I walked through the glass to see my incubus again.

She repeated herself about how she was all knowing about the future and that I would soon get knowledge of the future via dreams. I remained quiet, although I wanted to debate that I was unable to dream of the future with the neural pacifiers in our doors that kept us from using our powers in our rooms when we weren't supervised at night. She was a lot harsher in her speech than the other times. She was constantly repeating how paramount it was to remain here where it was safe, but I remained stubborn to my faith and what I believed was right. There was nothing that was going to strip me from the realest dream I have ever had. I've learned that the more apathy I showed on my face, the more broken I seemed and the quicker the sessions would end. So I brokenly look upon her as I am told that I am free to leave until next time. I walk out through the milky glass and couldn't see anyone else's face but Cale's in the very back right corner of the room. I walk over to him and sit next to him like he had summoned me there, and the first words I heard from him in a week are asked, "Are you alright?"

At that moment a whole flock of repressed woman feelings coming surging out and about through my mind like winged birds flying all a strew. "Oh now you want to talk?

"You don't look so good."

"Thanks." I said, getting up and walking away from him. I sit right next to Brett because I knew how much he hated him. I knew it was wrong but I wanted him to feel a fraction of the silence he had given me as I shun him off.

Thoughts of him start to eat away at my sanity like decomposing insects, but I stubbornly refuse to turn around to look at him. It didn't last very long, and I would have called myself weak for turning my head to see him, but if I had not glanced back to see him disappear down the hall with Baley, I would not have built up enough courage to go looking for him.

"Baley must be looking for Marcus." I thought, "But why would Cale go along with her?" No guards were on duty as I climbed up the stairs. I know I felt an evil glare on my back before I left the room, so I knew I would soon be followed. I had to be quick before I got caught. I came across two guards that lie on the floor, and I couldn't help but think they were dead. They were guarding the west wing, where I knew Cale and Baley had gone exploring into. I physically open the doors into a room of chemicals and lights. Conducted electricity and vials of different ominous colors could only inform me that I was in a science lab. Tanks filled with water had naked humans curled into a ball inside of them. They looked smaller and almost like their skin was deteriorating with the water. I decided to peer closer at a pair of what I thought were familiar eyes of the female specimen in the tank. Closer, I watched. She looked so familiar. I read a label on the machine below her like she was a museum artifact. She had short dark hair and I could barely see her eyes as she covered her face with her arms. "Hayley Owens." I read aloud softly. There was a number next to her name, the number 3. I attempted to look closer at her face as her body sank to the bottom of the tank, drifting slowly. I recognized her in this moment. She was without a doubt the same girl, whom Jonah referred to as 'Snow White', that tried to kill us before we were taken here. But she was dead… Wasn't she? Slower the deceased body drifted further down towards me. I watched her eye as it remained still. Then it boggled towards me and in an instant she was awake and alive with fear as her dreaded face looked at me. Frightened I stumbled backwards tripping over my own feet. I started to push back the fear as I found a pair of closed doors that would lead into another corridor of the forbidden west wing. Quickly I crashed myself into it only to find it locked. I kicked and slammed against the door with my new strength and it flew open after several strikes. I march into a room filled with cages of suffering people. Trying to hide all of the fear and adrenalin boiling inside me, I stride over to Baley without even glancing at Cale. I just knew he was there, I didn't have to look at him to be sure, my heart told me he was. In witnessing to the pain and suffering, I knew I needed to escape this place, but I didn't realize Cale would end up not coming with me.

Remembering how my guardian angel had done it in my dream, I raised a rift, thinking of the place Baley drew. It was a clock tower in the city of Las Vegas. I have never heard of it, but I trusted Baley's artistic description and imagined the place the best I could.

I argue with Cale about leaving this place and going to somewhere safe, but he refused to go in before me for some reason. The entire time others came swiveling around the corner and into the wall I could only think of Cale. His rare smile that was slightly crooked would be the thing most

I'd miss about him. I somehow knew I would have to leave him behind. It was as if I was thinking his thoughts and the thoughts he was going to think next in the midst of the riot of the great escape. Others stampeded through the rift and I continued to hope for Cale to give up his pride and come with me, but he continued to stand still. I saw the hurt in his eyes as he pushed Beef into the rift. He threw me a small crooked smile that I loved so much just before he shoved me in the rift with his masculine strength. A vortex of black sucked me through and spat me out into the presence of shadows holding the rest of the others captive. I knew the rift was closed behind me and there would be no Cale following me into a trap. That's exactly what this was, a devious trap. I began to wonder if my incubus was correct once an unfamiliar face walked up to me with my knees and hands on the floor from the fall I took after being spat out from the rift. I thought of regretting listening to my *guardian angel*, but it was too late. The nervous constriction in my stomach, before Cale pushed me in, grew into an anxious worry of what these shadows were going to do to us next. I didn't blame Cale, he only did what he thought was best in protecting me, but I couldn't help but wish he hadn't.

19. The Last Visit

Tianna Lecher

S hadows of the dark room hold everyone who had escaped through the rift hostage, by grappling their throats and silencing the distance between their backs and them at a perfect zero percent. As the shadow that approached me turned into a face after walking further into the moonlight coming from one circular window above an archway I assumed was the way out. When I didn't recognize his face, I began biding my time, plotting an escape route in my head.

"Hello." He said in a gentle voice, hovering over me. "I am Shawn." He introduced, bowing down and grabbing my hand as he kissed it. He had wavy black hair that curled at every end. It was parted from the right side of his head and combed over. "What is your name?" he asks as he pulled me up with unbelievable strength.

I wasn't fooled by his charming denotations as I glanced around the room to see everyone sweating with fear, but his chivalry was hard to resist. "Tianna." I say plainly.

"Such a beautiful name. Tianna." He fathoms, "Tianna." He repeats. "Tell me, Tianna, how did you come to find us?"

"I just did?" I thought. "How does one find what they aren't looking for." I stated out loud.

"Interesting." He pondered on my reply before he asked, "So how does one stumble across a building that doesn't exist?"

"What?"

"Do you know where you are?"

"Somewhere on the outskirts of Las Vegas." I defined the best I could. There was little I knew about Baley's drawing and I started to wonder if I had opened a rift to a clock tower somewhere else in the world.

"True. It's been an abandoned little village for centuries. And it's been erased."

"Erased." I asked dully, considering this guy was a kook.

Shawn smiled as if he knew I thought he was crazy, "This place was the perfect hiding spot until one of our own went rogue and double-crossed us. A leech known as Hayley Owens used my powers to tear the fabrics of reality and cast herself out into the existing part of the world. She fled the premises, and we knew she was off to tell David Hamilton where we were taking refuge. I sealed the tear she made to escape and realized as long as they didn't have an illusionist, there was no way she could return. I just never knew why she would betray us. But now there seems to be a problem, you see, we have company...we *never* have outsider's company because of our situation." His charming tone becomes more threatening. "That's where you come in. How did you get here?"

I decided the truth might have been too absurd for him, so I started to think of a lie until Baley admitted, "I did it!"

Shawn's face turned to face her as the shadow holding her, squeezes her head up more uncomfortably. I thought, "Now would be the best time to leave with everyone's attention pointed at Baley." But I couldn't leave the others behind while I got my escape.

"Oh? And how might that be possible?"

"I drew it! I drew this place!" she belted out, being squeezed tighter.

Shawn gave the signal to the shadow to let her loose and Baley fell to the ground before him. Marcus struggled violently, but was completely restrained by little effort from the shadow behind him. "A painter?" he asked. And I started to get a grasp on what Baley was capable of. "Who even told you of this place?" he interrogated as he drew himself closer to her menacingly.

"My incubus!" she confessed, "Please, we have done nothing wrong! Let us go! We escaped from that place!"

"Escaped? How am I supposed to believe you are not deceiving me and planning to stab me in the back as soon as I let your little friends go?"

"Because you are the ones trying to kill us, not the other way around." Baley explains.

"Such a determined little creature. What is your name?"

"Baley."

"Baley, who do you think we are that you would even think of accusing us trying to kill you?"

"The White Crows."

"Why, yes we are in fact the White Crows, but I have no interest in killing you unless Paul returns and determines whether you are slaves to Hamilton's call or just a band of misfits that run around with no sense of order, in which that case you all will be taken in and cared for by us. So do not think so irrationally my dear Baley." As Shawn's fingers graze against the weeping cheeks of Baley, Marcus starts to fight again for freedom from his restraint. Shawn notices the struggle. "It seems as if this one is attached to you. Very protective. Feisty. What is your power?"

"He doesn't have any." I declare bringing his attention back to me. I asked myself what I was doing but I couldn't find a reason I had decided to jump in to protect Barcus.

"A regular?" Shawn's face grew more interested.

"Yes."

"That would explain his feeble attempts to escape." Said the shadow holding Marcus.

"Quite!" Shawn ordered. He snapped twice and tiny shadow emerges from the darkness and shows herself in the moonlight next to Shawn. He whispers something into her ear, and I can see the small girl who could be no older than twelve-years-old has nodded her head. It was obvious her approval was of some sort of significance to the others, because the shadows began to gasp as they started letting their captives loose.

"They speak the truth." The little girl says almost in disappointment.

"Riley is a seeker. She knows when someone is lying." Shawn explains.

Riley starts to speak again addressing everyone in the room with her cryptic, booming voice. "The threat of our vulnerability remains though. The painter has exploited our hiding spot, and I assumed this 'great escape' they have made was just an attempt from Hamilton to bring us out of hiding. With the painter, he has prevailed. Tell us again, painter. What was the plan your *incubus* told you to do." The little girl makes the incubus sound like something fake, just as I assumed.

"She was in the image of me." Baley stuttered, "she said that she was a part of-"

"A dark part of you that can foresee the future and that if you didn't listen to her you and your friends will die blah blah blah. It's the same story with everyone." Riley was stern and fierce with her words and obviously familiar with the incubus. "All I want to know is what the plan of escape was and how you were supposed to escape."

After a second of thinking Baley continued on, "She told me that you were all coming to finish what you started in Irvine." I hear a couple of the shadows sigh and chuckle in disappointment as if they heard this story before.

"First off." Shawn starts. "We had nothing to do with the assault on Irvine." I was shocked, but teetering on the fact of whether he was lying or not. Baley's face looked convinced.

Baley continued, "She told me where Marcus was being held captive, in the west wing, and she showed me a drawing of a place in Las Vegas as she explained it. She said I would need to take Marcus there if I wanted to be safe. She told me that I would need some help getting passed the guards guarding the west wing and the only one that could help me was a boy named Cale Valens." At the sound of his name my heart began to race. "She told me that I needed to convince him to help me, because he would be able to create the materials I needed to sketch this place in Las Vegas where I was supposed to go. But she warned me never to draw someone in a painting, otherwise they would be trapped inside until the ink bled from the drawing."

"What is Cale? A vendor? A resource man?" Shawn asks.

"They don't have a name for him." I interrupt as if the question was for me. Shawn looks at me strangely because the tone of my voice became a little harsher and I knew he knew that I was trying to protect him. "He has the ability to create objects with his mind."

"I've never heard of that." Shawn says, "Is that all he does?"

"No. He can read minds, and destroy things by making them dissipate into nothing. He has this aura about him too. He- he just thinks of stuff, and they tend to happen."

By my stuttering Shawn assumed, "Are you in love with him?" he was so bold and unafraid to speak his mind, but at his comment I felt a pair of eyes daggering me from the left side of the room. My eyes glanced just for a second but the darkness covered the face of who was glaring at me.

"Yes." I thought. "As a matter of fact I am in love with him." Is all I wanted to say, because it was the truth. But instead I lied and felt apathy flourish through me where the soft, fresh breeze of freedom could have been pumping through my veins making my head buoyant. "No. I am not." The bitterness of the words that left my mouth felt as if I had done something terribly wrong.

"That doesn't explain how he could help you escape the base-" Riley starts to say but cuts herself off as if a light bulb idea popped inside her puny head. "That's it." she says. "You weren't supposed to escape. Is this Cale here?"

"No." I say almost sadly. "I left him behind." Trying to lie to make the others believe that Cale and I had no attachments for each other, but I knew it was a lie. I wanted to say how he was a hero for saving us all and that he voluntarily left himself behind to make sure that my life was saved. But I knew Cale, and the last thing he would want was a parade dedicated to him.

"Then it is clear." Riley states. "Hamilton has used the painter to make the unseen visible again."

"Can't we just erase it again like you did before?" I asked.

"We could. If she were still alive. Savannah gave her life making this place invisible with me. I could not repeat the power even if I tried." Shawn said morbidly.

"What do you mean?"

"Savannah was my wife." Shawn couldn't be more than 19-years-old, there would be no way I could get married that young. "With me being an illusionist I was able to temporarily make it seem this part of the town had been eradicated into thin air, while Savannah made it permanent by erasing it from the face of the earth into almost an alternate world where we took refuge from the seizing Hamilton. Unfortunately at the last minute, Savannah was shot with the cure in the final seconds where we all evaporated from the world. We buried her alongside this clock tower. We had to use our powers as one to create an invisible refuge. And now it is all for nothing, for surely Hamilton will send his army for us."

"Then we must flee." Riley insists.

"We shall contact Paul, and first thing at dawn we will migrate elsewhere."

I could think of nothing else but Cale as I continued to try to fall asleep in a designated area like a hotel room that Shawn had escorted us to. Shawn warned his personal guards that they would have to be extra careful now that civilians could patrol the small lost part of an old town. Whispering from behind me alerts me that someone is awake. I hear Jonah's voice talking about how these White Crows are nothing but liars and how they are deceiving us all. I try not to get involved as I focus on sleep.

Someone shakes me from my half slumber. "Pst." Her voice says.

"What." I say keeping my eyes closed.

"Here." She whispers. And she slips something presentable on the floor before me with a white envelope next to it. "It's for Cale." My eyes open and I notice its Britney who has lain a dark red i-pod down. "The battery died, so I decided to charge it. Forgot I even had it."

"Why are you giving it to me?" I asked, almost afraid of my interest for Cale being exploited.

"Because you're the only one that can go back to give it to him. Just make sure he gets the card okay?"

"Why?" I said debating on whether I should just throw the card away or not.

"Because. I like him. You got a problem with that?"

"No," I lie, "but why do you even like him. He's cruel, and- he's just a creep!"

"Well maybe I like creeps then. Listen if this is too big for you I can-"

"No, I'll give it to him."

"Attagirl." She says with a wink, and I feel like giving her a black eye but she walks away before I can commit. I open the envelope and read the card stained with a perfume stench that made me want to gag, but as I read the card I had to stop and take a breath after every period trying to hold back real vomit. I stuff the card in my pocket and keep the i-pod safely on my chest. I couldn't help but turn the thing on and scroll though his music. Through every song and every artist labeled, I could feel myself falling in love with him even more. I missed him so much. I dared myself to plug in the headphones and told myself I would only listen to one song but in the morning I would realize I had listened to it through the night. I clicked the shuffle button and it was as if he had chose the song for me when the screen lit up and read "I miss you" by Incubus. With a sly grin I shifted myself on my side and somehow felt the warmth of him embrace my entire backside and swarm all around me like a cozy blanket that allowed me to drift off into a rejuvenating slumber.

I awake at dawn. Everyone is asleep, and I remember my dream. The same guardian angel in the white suit had brought me a sign of the future. She told me I needed to see Cale, and my heart jumped for joy. She explained that I would need to open another rift in a distinct place that I remembered from the facility I escaped from and bring Cale back through it with me. Little did I know he would be too stubborn and not accept my ticket to freedom. I vaguely remembered the dream before we were all abducted, so I assumed it would end well. I awoke with a calling to do something of great importance.

I waited for two hours and the others continued to remain asleep. I quietly opened a rift in the wall, specifically remembering my surroundings so I could return back here with Cale. I walk through the rift into a mall I had remembered visiting in New York when I went one summer to visit my cousins. I needed to change my white clothes into something more me for him. I had hoped that by the time I came back no one would have noticed my absence. As I walk through the busy store, I grab a couple outfits remembering the price of everything I was about to shoplift so that I could repay the store back the very second I could. I opened another rift in the women's dressing room after dressing myself up in a red shirt with skinny black jeans. I let my hair down from the pony tail I had put it in last night before I entered the rift.

I walked into the diner of the base that kept us captive. "I'm getting better." I thought remembering the last time I came out of the rift I nearly scraped my knees. But to be fair, Cale did push me through. This time it felt like I just took one step through the wall and I was on the other side of it where the diner was. It should have been around eight, where everyone would be required to be seated at the breakfast table, so I quietly expected a voice to shout out my name as I came into existence of the danger zone I fled from.

No one was feasting at the table. I walked down the hall thinking myself to be invisible until I came across Cale's room. I creep open the door to peer into it and noticed he wasn't there. I caught a glance at his alarm clock and noticed the time said nine instead of eight. I zoomed back to the diner, opened a rift to the ruins of Stellar High School. I grabbed a brick that rested against some ash and opened another rift back to the diner. I zipped back to Cale's room where I placed the brick in between so the door could not shut itself closed. I knew that once the door closed I would be locked into the room and grabbing a door stopper was the only thing I could think of. If Mr. Hamilton came marching into Cale's room noticing the brick I would simply open a rift back up to Las Vegas and port myself back.

I waited. No sign of Cale. I pondered about the last time I had saw him. I grew impatient and grumpy. "How could he do this to me?" I thought. "Why would he throw me away like a rag doll." I kept trying to remind myself that he had only the best intentions under his dark tactics and that I needed to be patient until he arrived where I would just talk to him. But a passionate bestial side of me wanted to pummel him as soon as he walked through the door. Footsteps alarmed me that someone was coming; I hid behind the door to make sure it was him. If it wasn't I prepared an escape plan to open a rift back to Las Vegas. The idea of the place lurked at the front of my head as the footsteps grew louder and more slowly. The door began to creep open and I watched diligently in stone until his face came poking into the room. At that moment a passionate instinct broke me out of my still stature and automatically grappled him into the room, kicking the brick out and shutting the door behind me.

"Tianna!" he gasps.

"How dare you push me!" I scolded, hiding the fact that I was just happy to see him.

"What are you?-" He starts saying, then his facial expression realizes what I was yelling at him about.. "Oh."

"Yeah! 'Oh' is right!"

"You are really angry."

"How'd you guess!"

"Keep it down!"

"Here." As he sits on the bed I threw the red i-pod at his lap. "It's a gift from Britney."

"She stole it?" he asked

"She charged it. The battery was dying or something."

"She took it just to charge it?"

"She's a techno-path. She controls technology. Anyways, she wanted to give you a card with it, but my dog ate it." I lied knowing that I left it back in New York where I substituted clothes.

"What's your dog's name?" he asks.

"I don't have a dog."

"Cale," he started to say, "I stole your i-pod to charge it, but I forgot to give it back. Follow Tianna through the rift so we can meet up. I'm looking forward to seeing you." An angry face grew on me as he read word for word what was printed on the card. "You read the card before your dog ate it didn't you?"

"Don't read my mind." I told him. "Now come on. Let's go."

"Where are we going?"

"Through the rift I opened in the dining room."

"Well good luck getting out." he said as he laid back against his bed putting his arms behind his head.

"He's so hot." I thought, catching myself knowing he would be able to read my mind so I quickly thought of an answer and faced him, too prideful to admit I had done something stupid by closing the door behind me. "I forgot."

He smiles crookedly and I feel actual butterflies nesting in my stomach. I was imprisoned in a room with the one person I wanted most in the world. "Might as well stop stressing yourself out by focusing on the rift." he yawns misreading my clenching mouth as a form of stress when I really was just hiding back happiness.

"But how will we get back?" I asked actually not caring, all I really wanted was to stay in the room with him for a while longer.

"Can you open a rift to somewhere different?" he asked.

"I don't know. I haven't tried. I'll give it a shot." Preparing to open another rift after closing the other rift in the diner I made as an escape route for us by leaving my focus from it to form a new one.

"Good luck." he said at my back. I turn around to find his eyes closed like he was getting ready to go to bed.

"What do you mean?"

"Can't use your powers in here. I've tried before."

"What will he do if he finds me here?"

"Let's hope its Brett that comes knocking then, eh?"

"Cale, this is serious."

"And I'm being serious."

Frustrated, I sit on the bed realizing there was no point in arguing with him. He was so stubborn and yet I was enjoying his kick-back mood even though I so desperately wanted to get him out of here. I let some silence pass before I quietly ask, "Why did you avoid me?" as I look to the wall. He doesn't answer me right away. "It's like…"I start to say, but I don't realize where I was going to go until he interrupts the pause.

"I don't want to talk about it." he grimaces.

"Well we're stuck here, might as well-"

"No."

"You so stubborn!" I yell standing up off the bed.

"Oh and you're not?" he exclaims mimicking my movement to tower over me.

"At least I'm willing to sacrifice some of my pride to communicate with you!"

"Yeah? Well it's kind of hard to communicate with someone who doesn't know what they want."

"At least I'm not broken!"

"Broken?" he asks astonished

"Yeah! Broken!" I sound out every syllable of the word. "You know, I don't even know why I came back for you!"

"It's because you're infatuated with me."

"Well I'm glad to see your ego isn't broken!"

"You haven't the slightest clue, okay?" he says, sliding over the bed and aggressively starts to hover over me menacingly. I couldn't let him know his threatening stance was working.

"I know! That's exactly it!"

"What do you want from me?!"

"All I want is you!" I yell with vigor as I punch him in his solid chest. It didn't seem to phase him.

"Oh yeah?! Well I want you too!" He yells back with vigor in his voice as well. My heart began to twitter at his confession, praying that every syllable was true.

"Prove it!" I yell.

"*You* prove it!" he yells back, and before he could finish yelling I grab him by the collar of his white v-neck and seal my lips up against his. How badly I wanted him to pull my hair as I pressed up against him. He lifted me up with his brawny arms and I couldn't help but bite him on the neck as an adolescent vampire in love. I couldn't resist him even if I wanted to.

I could barely stand the passion until he abruptly releases himself from me.

"Why'd you stop?" I ask as he backed away from me to sit down on his bed. I started to wonder if I did something wrong.

"Because…" he starts to say. I quietly sit down next to him and wait patiently for him to finish. "Because, Tianna. I love you." he was unable to look at me as my face lit up like a poor man winning the lottery. I knew I was in love with him the day I met him, I just avoided him because it made me weak. In middle school I was told that you were supposed to be mean to the other boys and they would like you back. But not Cale. It didn't work on him. He wasn't like most boys. I remember him from day one, it just scared me to think how weak I felt when I was around him. As crooked as people make love out to be, I knew my feelings for him were love, just as sure as I was about the sun setting in the west. I placed my hand in his carefully. Like a puzzle, his hand fit perfectly with mine. He turned to face me. He gazed into my eyes with a surreal look I would have never expected from him. I begin to wonder if we would have ever met if things were the way they were back when school was our only enemy. I've dated, but I've never felt anything remote to this moment in time. He had me star struck with happiness and yet my pride would refuse me to show it to him. It was a blessing and a curse what happened to our lives. An evil side of me would almost allow whoever did destroy the city to do it again if I could feel this way once more. If this was a dream, then I didn't ever want to wake up.

"Ouch." I yelped in shock. I felt something bite me on my hand that was grasping tightly onto his bigger hands. I looked down and my eyes grew with amazement. On my hand written along the lower top where my thumb sprouted out from was the word 'Forever' written neatly in boyish, but neat handwriting. I looked back up at him with a fortunate serendipitous look. I loved it. It was a tattoo, but I was confused on how it happened.

"I'm- I'm sorry, I didn't- I'm sure I can erase it somehow." he stutters.

"I thought you couldn't use your powers in here?" I asked.

"I can't. Watch." he say as he pushes his hand against the air towards the door. Nothing happens. And he turns back to face me. "You see?"

Knock, knock, knock. My eyes widen with fear before Cale directs me to hide underneath the bed. I hear someone come into the room who unmistakably was David Hamilton. "Hello Cale."

His voice reminded me that I needed to tell Cale about the White Crows. A conversation carries on between them as I try to remain in stealth and ponder about how I was going to get Cale out of here.

"Very Well. I shall expect you there in five." Hamilton says before exiting the room. I use his exit as my entrance cue by climbing out from under the bed with the help of Cale's unbearable strength the nearly yanked my arms out from their sockets.

"You have to get out of here. Go back." He orders.

"I'm not leaving you." I insist.

"Please. You have to trust me. My incubus wanted you back here for some reason, and I don't know why. I can't risk you getting caught."

"My incubus told me to come to you no matter what it takes." I lied trying to get him to come with me any way possible.

"I thought you said you didn't believe in your incubus?"

"I don't." reminding myself how the make believe dog eating his card story ended up.

"So why'd you listen?"

"My incubus also told me never to leave this place or I would suffer. And when you forced me through my own rift, I- oh! I almost forgot! There's something you need to know-"

"Not now Tianna! I have to go."

"But it's important!"

He grapples me with utter seriousness. "Open a rift back up, to that same place in Las Vegas. Go through it and as soon as I can, I will come find you." He doesn't let me speak as he pushes me out the door.

I'm pushed out of his room in frightening shock of what was lingering over me. Mr. Hamilton was holding the brick I had used as a door stopper. "I assumed this brick didn't belong here." he says in an evil tone. I hear the words *Run* in Cale's voice echo in my head, and I take off sprinting towards the diner like I had no control over my body. There were no free will cards in my hand that I could use to stay with Cale. I had to do what his voice had said in my head, and there was no stopping myself. "Stop her!" Mr. Hamilton ordered from behind me as I zoomed down the hall and opened a rift that took me back into the dressing room in New York. Another girl was changing in the room and screamed when I came out of nowhere.

"Hi." I said with a twitch in my eye, and grabbed the pair of white clothes I had left behind on accident before I focused on the dorm Shawn had us stay in, when I opened another rift and disappeared into it after witnessing the girl faint. I leave behind a chuckle before I step through to the other side.

When I expect to be surrounded by a bunch of snoozing teenagers, I find the room is empty and the door has been broken. I hear grunting and sounds of violence thresh together in harmony as I make my way out. What looked like a school fight appeared to be happening. Everyone circled around the vicious fighting noises, fighting with each other for a front row seat. I hurried myself over to the circle and pushed my way through to find Jonah and Shawn wrestling with each other. I enter the ring to try and stop them when A girl who must have been a White Crow stops me and shouts, "She's breaking the rules! The deal is off!" and she charges for me, tackling me to the ground without another warning.

I notice everyone begins fighting and wrestling with each other as I hurl the girl off of me making her soar through the air. I had no idea what was going on. I'm stricken in the face by an unfamiliar boy and all the fury in the world gathered itself in my head as I was sure my eyes were glowing red. Jonah leaped at the boy that hit me breaking his neck before I could. With a feral roar, Jonah had everyone collapsing over themselves as he commanded the ground to quake. Jonah's focus was broken as a boy twice his size tussled him to the floor. Shawn began to cowardly flee out of my sight as I tried pulling Riley off of poor Baley, but she proved herself a compatible opponent as she tossed a boy choking Marcus against the wall. The riot carried on and I continued to fight a supernatural battle I had no knowledge of its chronicles until something painful hit me in the back of my head, and I was sure I was going to die as my vision suddenly faded to black.

The headache throbbed in my head as I wondered how long I had been out. I awoke and Cale's friend Beef was at my side rubbing a chilled ice cloth against my forehead. It's dark outside. I can see the moonlight through a window. I realize I'm lying in a room that I have never been in before. I try to lean up, but he tells me that I need to lie down and rest. I try to murmur, "What happened." But fail to find the strength in my throat to sing the words.

"They've gone mad." He says. "Most of us have." His words were sad and full of solemnity, like something had been torn from him. "I'm sorry Tianna." He apologizes. I feel too weak to ask him why, but he answers himself, "I hit you on the head." I wanted to punch him for the misery my ache felt but couldn't. "It was an accident. Honest. I thought you were attacking Baley…" I almost laugh because he tries to avoid all eye contact with me. Beef was big teddy bear. He had a big heart and he continued to prove himself a loyal friend to Cale. "I carried you in here when I realized it was you…Just don't tell Cale okay? He'll kill me." I smirked and felt my lazy eyes slowly blink. "You've been out for a day. I hope your okay." He comforts. "Hey that rhymes!" he says to himself to the side and I couldn't help but laugh. Somehow the laughter cured the pain in the back of my head and I was able to sit up straight. "They said laughter is the best medicine. But at times like these… I start to think that there isn't enough jokes in the world that could bring things back down to normal again."

I slightly smile and whisper as far as my throat would let me, "Normal is overrated."

Some silence passes before he asks, "Where were you yesterday morning?"

"Visiting someone."

"Well. I hope it was important because not to point any fingers but they were fighting because of you."

"What?" I asked regaining more consciousness.

"Jonah couldn't find you and he already was getting ready to betray these White Crow people, so he blamed Shawn for your absence and they got into this fight because Jonah thought they had kidnapped you and you were lying dead somewhere. The guy's nuts. Jonah said that these guys were the ones who blew Irvine up, but I don't buy it."

"Where is everyone?" I ask paranoid.

"Gone. fled towards the city. I couldn't keep track with all the chaos that was going on, but everyone's gone. Britney got like kidnapped. Jonah got trapped in some kind of painting Baley drew, Marcus told her too. And then this guy named Paul told everyone to blend in with the world and everyone else just sort of scattered. It's like a bad soap opera. Jonah got his revenge on Shawn and somehow kept saying that they needed to find Paul who is the last leader of the White Crows I guess."

"Weren't there three?" I asked, bewildered for answers.

"The third one tried killing us remember? Jonah pointed that out before he got into the whole brawl with Shawn. He convinced most everyone, even some of the White Crows to rebel against Shawn and his loyal guys and Jonah just flat out killed 'em." Beef shrugs.

"Beef, everyone and their mother has been shooting, scratching and trying to kill us. Who is the *third one* you are talking about?"

"I dunno. Her name was like Kaley I think. Kaley Cohens or something."

"Hayley Owens?" I ask remembering the ring of the name as I read it on a label back at that weird science lab before we all escaped here into more trouble.

"Yeah that's it! How'd you know?"

I remembered the girl that tried killing us before Cale and the others came back. Her face matched perfectly with the one on television. I recognized Shawn's face almost right away the night we met. Hayley was unmistakably the other White Crow leader and this Paul guy must be the last. A memory of the past swooped past my mind as I saw a flashback play through my mind of the girl in the tank. Although more deformed than her picture on the news, the girl in the tank was Hayley Owens as well. I pondered on how she could still be alive after Jonah had buried her. She must have somehow been found and revived in that science lab. "I have to tell Cale." I said, realizing Beef was looking at me funny as I hid inside my mind seeing the flashback in my head.

"You're gonna go back?"

"I have to bring him back."

"He won't come back." Beef said, almost depressed.

"And why not?" I defend Cale.

"Because I know him. He's like a cat. He doesn't come when he's called. Only when he feels like it. There could be a fire and the entire United States army at his door and if he wanted, he would be able to avoid the situation no matter what kind of riot erupted." Beef began walking away as if Cale had died.

"Well, for his sake. Let's hope your right. But I'm still going."

"Everyone leaves Beef." I hear him whisper to himself.

"Stay here. I'll be back with him soon." I say opening a rift. I hear him mumble something else but I am already through the other side before I could understand what he said.

I tiptoe out of the diner I emerged in. Excited to see Cale, I tear a piece of my red shirt I stole that I intended to pay back off from the sleeve before I slowly enter Cale's room with severe quietness for my sake. I fold the piece of shirt I tore off so it is a little block before I place it in between the gap where the lock on the door is supposed to be inserted.

Something grabs my wrists before I can even turn around and Cale is staring me down. "Tianna?" he says. "What are you doing here?"

"I've come to take you back with me." I say sturdy.

"What's wrong? Are you alright? Is Beef okay?" he demanded.

"Yes. Me and Beef are fine. But the others, they've all gone missing."

"Just stay where you are. I'll be fine here. Look you can't come back here."

"I won't have to if you come with me!" I hiss. "Why are you so hesitant to come with me?"

"It doesn't matter, you've locked yourself out again." He says as he falls on his bed.

I didn't understand him. Here I was giving him a free ticket to run away with me and he refused. He apparently didn't notice that the green light on the door was not flickered on which meant the door was still open thanks to my sleeve. I lied, "Yes, and now you can either leave with me or I dorm with you."

"Looks like we're rooming then." Thinking I forgot about when the door being closed would extinguish our powers.

I played along, enjoying his company. I sat down on his bed. He put in his headphones and rested his head down putting his arms behind his head, obviously ready to relax. I snatched the crimson i-pod off of his chest to take a look at what he was listening to. *Creep 'acoustic'* is all I could read before he snatches it out of my hands and lays back down. "Radiohead" I thought. "Good choice."

"I know." He says out loud obviously hearing me in my head.

I glance down at my hand. I look at the words and can't help but biting my lip and laying down next to him. "Did you mean it?" I thought.

"Mean what?" he says with his eyes closed.

"When you told me...You know. That you loved me." I state in my mind as I turn my head to face him. He opens his eyes, keeping his relaxing position but turning his head to me and I hear his voice inside my head say *To the syllable.* I couldn't help myself but hurl my arm around his chest and breathe him in. It felt so right to be near him. So much warmth and emotions wrapped into one bodily structure. I just didn't understand why he wouldn't run away with me.

Cale sits up, takes out his ear phones, presses pause on the i-pod and turns his body on his side so his right arm and elbow held him up as his palm rested against the side of his face. "I would love nothing more than to run away with you." He admits obviously listening in on my thoughts. "Any guy would be stupid not to run away with you. But I just can't Tianna. Trust me okay? This is the best way."

I didn't understand, but I didn't want to anger him. I wanted to savor him. I wanted to take what I could with me. I would settle for now if he didn't come back with me, but I would return. And If he continued to be stubborn I would return another day. I was determined to catch Cale Valens. I nod my head like I understand, and he puts an earpiece in my left ear and the right earpiece in his. I lay on my left side so I could face him as he presses play on his i-pod. I listen to the lyrics of the singing man playing an acoustic guitar and it was as if Cale was trying to tell me something through the music. It was poetic and deep. It was as if the song was written for us. We sat there in silence as we stared at each other discovering every freckle on our face. There was nothing to say and nothing to think. We were merely lost in time. And it was perfect. The man with the guitar sings in my left ear, "She's running out again…" and Cale starts to, at a snail's pace, lean closer to me. I meet him halfway where I almost cry as he gives me the perfect kiss. My left eye waters the most as he slowly presses his lips against mine, and pulls away leaving me breathless.

He holds me through the night. I couldn't sleep, and neither could he. We said nothing. I thought nothing. I was happy. I was where I was supposed to be.

"Is the door open?" he asked and my eyes grow as I realize I had forgotten to tell him it was.

"Yes." I admit.

Cale releases his arms from around me and sits on the edge of the bed as if he had done something wrong. "You must go." He said.

"But-"

"No. Leave this place now. Get out." He interrupts calmly. I hated seeing him angry at me, so I sucked the sore feelings in deep down and stored them away knowing they would explode on him sooner or later.

I left his room, snatching the piece of red shirt out of the door. I whispered in my head, "I'll be back soon." Promising myself I would come back as many times as I needed to. And I know he heard me. But something in my head told me that the next visit would not be so pleasant on my part as I walked through a rift I created in the hallway back to the room where Beef took care of me.

Beef was snoring on the floor with a blanket and a pillow when I walked back in. I decide to curl up next him for the remainder of the night as I tried to think of something other than Cale. "Nada."

The next day, Beef had informed me that Baley and Marcus had run away somewhere carrying Jonah's prison canvas with them. He said the rest of them just simply followed the idea of blending in and scattered through the city.

"So are they still in Las Vegas?" I ask.

"They might be. Max said he was sick of everyone getting in his way. He's the only one I heard who was headed to New York."

Beef and I shuffle down a dirt path at normal speed towards taller buildings in the distance that I could only assume was the strip of Las Vegas. "So what's on the schedule for today?" I ask trying to get my mind off of Cale.

"Job." Beef states. Reminding me that I needed to pay back that shop in New York where I had stolen the outfit I continued to wear.

Days pass as we live from hotel room to hotel room without paying for them. I simply opened a rift that would lead us into an empty hotel room I had seen from the window and we would stay there for the night. I never asked what Beef's powers were, because he never talked about the subject. So I figured it was best to just leave the subject alone. Beef ended up getting a job at a pet store next to a local movie theatre where I was employed. We waited for Cale. But he never showed.

"I'm going back to get him."

"Don't."

"Why not?"

"Okay bring him this then." He says as he hands me an envelope. "Don't read it though." He sat on a hotel bed as I prepared myself to visit Cale.

"That's it? You're not going to tell me that it's a risky idea and you're not going to tell me he's not going to come back?"

"I'm not going to argue with someone who knows they are already going to win." He says.

"The future mostly comes to me in dreams."

"Mostly." He points out. He was right, sometimes I could sense things that were about to happen, but I usually catch the signs and decode them when it's already too late and the future has passed itself into the past.

"I need to get better at that." I thought. "Well then. I'm off to bring him back. Cross your fingers." Beef crosses his fingers while turning on the television in the hotel room and I open a rift into the diner again.

I crept into Cale's room where he sat straight up like he had been waiting for me. He takes out his headphones and says, "Don't close the door."

"Come with me." I say.

"No."

"Why not?"

"Why must you always ask *why*? Can't you just accept that I have my reasons?"

"Because I want to know."

"That's not a good enough reason."

"I'm not going to argue with you Cale." He bites his tongue. I stood uncomfortably holding the door open. It became awkward so I grabbed the folded linen I had tore from the red shirt I was no longer wearing but had paid for with my first check and placed it in the locks way just as last time. He pouts by looking away from me as I walk around to sit on his bed next to him while secretly placing Beef's letter on his dresser. "Will you talk to me?" I ask politely, but he doesn't answer. "What is the matter with-"

"What's the matter is that you don't listen!" he yells. "You just don't get it! I ask you to trust me and all you do come back with more questions! We can't be together because of me okay? It's just not going to happen, alright?"

"What are you talking about?-"

He rolls his eyes and starts to explain, "Listen. I have super powers. I am tricking you into thinking that you like me but really, you don't. This is all just a fake feeling that you are feeling and it's all my fault! I'm controlling you and you don't even know it because that's my ability! This is my curse!"

Like ice, my heart felt itself shatter. I tried to remain calm.

"So I need you to erase my memory of you. Or at least erase the last two times you came into my room trying to get me to leave, because guess what? I'm not going anywhere."

"You want me to erase your memory?" I asked, hurt at his request.

"Yes. Erase it. And don't come back again."

The repressed feelings I had been saving up started to boil in my blood. "How dare you." I scorn. "Who are you to tell me that *my* feelings are fake. You don't have the power to make me fall in love with you Cale, you arrogant- ugh! You don't care about anything or anyone else but yourself! And you have the audacity to order me to erase your memory because it will help *you* get over this quicker. What about me? What about this?" I show him my hand where the words printed 'Forever' are written. "You aren't controlling me Cale, so stop feeling sorry for yourself because no one is going to be there for you if you shut them out." He doesn't even look at me. My eyes start to glaze over with water and I reach my hand out onto his head taking back the memory of my last visit and this one just as my incubus taught me how. I had never done it before, so when Cale passed out afterwards I had hoped he would be okay, but I left him just as he asked. I tried holding back the tears and succeeded even as I closed his door behind me. I marched into the diner where I created another rift back to the hotel room. I couldn't fight the tears any longer because I knew this would be the last visit I made to see Cale. I knew before I stepped through the rift that I was leaving my heart behind, broken into a million pieces.

20. Evanescence

Tianna Lecher

I am nothing. I am dying. Slowly…I fade. Time passes me by. I go to work. I steal hotel rooms. But nothing has any color inside of it. Can't sleep. Can't eat. There is no reason to live. This feeling is indescribably unbearable. The only thing I knew is I would wish death upon anyone first, before this torture of utter pain.

21. Escape from Alcatraz

"Don't worry, it was only a tranquilizer." I hear Brett's voice say. "A horse tranquilizer. I wasn't sure if I needed to get you with another one, so I gave it to you just in case you were faking."

"I hate him so much." I thought. I had no energy to fight with myself but I knew the other side of me good or bad agreed with one thing. That Brett Gooding was a tool. I feel myself being dropped on a bed and my eyes finally open to see that I'm in my room back at the base. I can't really move but I somehow am able to adjust myself so my head could face the door.

"Where did he say Paul was headed?" David Hamilton's voice projects very angrily.

"To the clock tower in Las Vegas where the others escaped to." Brett says.

"Then it is time. We'll send all we've got to finish them off."

"What of the others that escaped earlier?" Brett asked as if he already knew the answer, he just wanted me to hear it.

"We kill them too. I have no use for them, I already sapped their blood samples."

"What of Cale?" Brett asked in the same tone as the last.

"I swear I'm going to kill him, clone him, kill his clone and then visit the place I bury him every day of my life just to pee on it."

"He's not going anywhere. We'll kill him when we get back. Make him sweat." David Hamilton deviously says before she shuts my door knowing that I would be unable to use my powers to escape.

An hour or two passed when I finally got most of my strength and consciousness back. Paul and the rest of his clan were going to be ambushed in Las Vegas today. I had no way of warning him. I was buried under the sea, who knows how deep, stuck in a exit-less room where I was to await my execution the next time the door opened. I plotted and escape plan for when they opened the door next, but the thought that Paul was being ambushed by Brett at any moment kept badgering me. It frustrated me to the point that I began slamming myself against the door. There must have been some kind of steel that was even stronger than my strength, because I didn't even leave a dent in the door when I grabbed my small dresser and nailed it against the door.

Anger flooded through me I didn't even notice there was a letter on the floor where my drawer was until after I demolished my bed in trying to escape. I quickly pondered on how the letter got here when I opened up to immediately recognize Beef's handwriting.

"Come back with Tianna." I read in my mind, *"Miss you man. She needs you more than you know. Don't be stubborn Cale. I know you. We'll be where you said you would come find us. Keep your end of the promise. Love you man. You don't need to say it back. I know you do too. Swallow your pride. Come back. Beef."*

There is silence in my head. I was confused on what he meant by coming back with Tianna. But I was overlapped with the worry that not only was Brett and his corrupted band of super heroes going to end the existence of the White Crows, but if they found Beef, they would surely snuff him too.

Anger, rage, fury, and wrath fused together in my head as I clenched my fists. Something within me released itself and the walls to my left, right and front are bulldozed down by an invisible crane of power that I seemed to be harnessing. I make sure I grab my i-pod before I start to walk out towards the room of relinquishment, where I was sure there was an exit. I took care of guard after guard as the alarm cried for help. Walls began crumbling down to rubble as I walked past them. The men and women that tried stopping me became deceased by a simple snap of the neck that the air seemed to do for me at the thought of it. I fought my way out with barely any effort until I reached the stairway where I climbed up to the very top. There was a doorway that flew from its hinges just before I even approached it and took out two men that were standing outside of it.

I walked out of the prison that was now a museum mark for failure. The old prison failed to keep a simple prisoner captive because it underestimated the intellect of the criminal mind, just as David Hamilton underestimated mine. I escaped Alcatraz in the same combat suit I had been wearing, except it was torn and ripped from battling against Hayley and Brett. I was on my way to Las Vegas where I would somehow stop Hamilton and his army of Pedigrates, even if it meant my demise.

22. Homeward Bound

People stare at me as I walk down the streets of San Francisco, but it didn't phase me. I was used to it. I watched a policeman park his cop car on the sidewalk as he began interrogating someone who was just passing along. I snatched his keys without having to touch them while I stood at the front of his car. I entered the cop car while the officer threatened me to get out of the vehicle. I don't listen. Instead I turn on the ignition and speed off, turning on the siren watching him fail at aim as I swerve down a crowded one way street going the opposite direction as all the other cars.

Out of the city I speed down the freeway dodging every car like they were falling shapes in the game of Tetris. I drown out the sound of the constant honking of the other cars by plugging in my headphones and turning the dial on my i-pod to "Let the flames begin" by Paramore.

Police cars imitate the siren I have on as they race behind me. I make them crash into one another with a simple head bob and the thought of the steering losing control. I exit off the next exit and turn the siren off. I forgot that they could track police cars wherever they were. I ditched the cop car once I ran into a beautiful maroon Audi parked alongside a curb.

"That is so mine."

"Wouldn't the owner be a little angry?"

"Eh, who cares." I thought to myself as I jumped out of the police car letting it roll down the street as I purposely leave it in neutral. I walk up to the maroon Audi and I wink to make the car unlock itself and open the door for me. "Thank you." I say to no one as I step inside the car. A pair of sunglasses dangle from the rear view mirror. I slap them on my face smoothly before I create a key that would fit perfectly in the ignition, press on the engine and drive.

On the road, still driving like a mad man, I realize that the owner of the car would be disappointed of his missing car and would surely become a tattle tale as he reported to the police of a stolen vehicle. I imagine the license plate to change its non-orderly fashion of numbers and letters to read 'Riot' instead, because I realized that that's what I was. A hero creates a villain to balance the opposition of a hero's existence. And once the villain was created, it was a race for control as any game of chess. I couldn't determine at this point whether Brett Gooding was a hero, or if he was the villain, but either way I was on neither side. I was the child in the play pen that took away the toy from another to give it to another kid who didn't need it, just to watch the newly toy-less child cry and beg for it back from the kid who suddenly grew attached to it. I was the neutral, wild revelry of a violent display of the disturbance of thousands fused together as one. There was no point in choosing a side or choosing a label. A label would only put up boundaries. Boundaries I would eventually break.

"You've got to be kidding me." I complain to myself.

"What?"

"Ron Burgundy needs gas."

"Who?"

"That's what I named my new car. Like it?"

"Actually, I love it." I agree with myself as I exit the next turn off the freeway. I pull up to a gas station and I jam the nozzle into Ron Burgundy's tank and prepare to give him his liquidated food that would allow me to travel to Las Vegas. With a snap, I think of money and a wad of fifty dollar bills appear in my hand as I march up to the store to pay for

my gas. Knowing I could easily create a pack of cigarettes I ask for a pack anyways and a red lighter.

"May I see some identification? The man behind the counter asks.

"No." I said rudely, knowing I was old enough to purchase them anyways.

"Okay." He said putting his head down in shame.

"Good boy. Now sit." He sits on the floor. "Roll over." He rolls over his back on the dirty ground. "Pant." he pants as a dog. I take the cigarettes and the lighter. "Put fifty on three." I command and he gets up types something into the computer that would allow gas to flow out of the third station. I have the fifty out and ready to go for him, but when he reaches for it I snatch it back, changing my mind about paying. "Gas is free today." He nods and starts panting. "Now play dead." I say as I walk out the automatic doors chuckling inside my head.

Something stops me dead in my tracks as I walk towards Ron Burgundy. He stood in front of my car like he had been running without rest for days. His fur shun of gold and his tail wagged with happiness. Buddy had found me.

Although he seemed happy enough, Buddy kept his distance from me as usual. I opened the passenger seat for him and he hopped in and into the back. When I was finished pumping the gas, I hung up the nozzle, screwed on the lip to Ron's tank, closed it, got in, buckled up, and sped off.

Buddy stared out the window. I rolled it down and he barked excitedly then threw his head out the window without thinking twice.

"Dumb mutt." I murmured.

He pulled his head back in just to bark at me, then posted it back outside the speeding car.

"Oh so you understand me? Well. Beef will be happy to see you."

Buddy barks nonstop when I say Beef.

"Alright shut up before I take you to the pound instead."

He whines.

"Good mutt."

Zooming past every car on the freeway, I innately knew there was a battle between good and evil going on and I was currently 50 miles away and couldn't do anything about it. So I floored it and tried to be optimistic. I noticed to best part of Ron Burgundy was that there was a chord that charged and hooked up to an i-pod.

"Sweet!" I thought as I plugged everything in, still going at lightning speed down the highway and played a song called "Paper wings" by Rise Against. Buddy brings his head back in and howls at the song in torture. "What?" I yell, turning down the music. He doesn't stop barking when I change the song to a random next and "Be my escape" by Reliant K comes on only making Buddy howl even more. My face grows indifferent at his disproval of my music. "You know you're awfully picky for a stowaway." I change the song and "What's up" by 4 non blondes comes on. I change it right away and Buddy barks even louder than before. "Good God! What do you want from me?" I yell in frustration, trying to maintain my speed and focus on the road. Buddy hops up in the front seat and presses his paw on my i-pod rewinding the song choice to "What's up" I swerve around a truck and maneuver in front of a blue minivan dangerously while the song plays and Buddy is quiet. "Really?" I asked sarcastically. "This song shuts you up?" Buddy barks at me for interrupting the song and somehow manages to intelligently raise the volume with a swift swipe of his palm. "Oh excuse me your highness." I mutter.

Out of the corner of my eye I see Buddy swaying his head to the beat of the song. "Why do I even have this song?" I say as buddy looks at me with puppy eyes. "You're not even real. I created you." Buddy barks. "Yeah yeah, just listen to your song." The fever of the chorus takes hold of my throat and I begin to softly sing at the beginning of the second chorus. Mysteriously my voice began to gradually sing louder as I got more into the song. Buddy sang along with me as we belted out the rest of the song. When it's finished, I threaten Buddy, "You tell anyone about this and I'll tell you how they make hot dogs in the Philippines." Buddy tilts his head to the side and whines.

I didn't know how Buddy found me, but I specifically remembered telling him to find me the day we were abducted. It had been weeks and I had forgotten him. Buddy brought out something in me as much as I didn't want to admit it. I kept the fact to myself that I enjoyed his presence and I was glad he was with me. *"Just a little bit."*

23. Destiny

When I finally found what I had been searching for, it was over. I could smell the stench of Brett's vulgar breathe as it passed through the wind. Patches of fire burned themselves out as I could only assume Amanda was here as well. They had come and gone from this place. This was nothing but a deserted clock tower surrounded by rubble. I was too late. I nearly fell to my knees at the sign of my own failure. Buddy remained silent. The torn open clock tower was ready to collapse. I walked into where the fray of battle had scarred the earth. Bodies lay strew and about. I didn't have the stomach to see their faces. If I even caught a glimpse of Beef's face I would have debated suicide. I turn to Buddy. *Go.* I order silently. *Go be happy.* And he takes off running down the dirt path I drove up towards the strip of Las Vegas. I look around me and I sense something barely moving on the gravel. I turn my head slowly to see what was moving and his familiar face gawked at me with blue eyes. *"Paul."* I thought as I walked over to him.

"Cale." He whispered in a raspy voice. I don't answer him, embarrassed at the fact that I had exploited his whereabouts to my arch enemy. "Don't let them find you." He warned as I knelt down. "Don't let them win." He coughs and gasps for air. "There must always be a balance." He repeats himself one last time before he lets out his final breath. Everyone I had ever cared about was dead. There was an emptiness building inside of me. A void in my heart. There were no final farewells I could make for Glenda, Beef or a boring past life I so longed for now as the world seemed to flay before me. I was alone.

"Just the way you wanted right?"

"Just the way I wanted." I lie to myself.

It has been quite a while since I've been here, almost a year. Ron Burgundy waits for me out in the parking structure but every day I continue to stay in my room. I've seemed to have lost all my senses and I've forgotten how to use my powers. My memory begins to fade as time goes by and I slowly realize I'm becoming more and more like my roommates. The doctors try to tell me what I am by saying fancy words around psychologists that run in and out of the area, but I was only this way because I chose to be this way. I was brainwashing myself as any other *lunatic* does. We are simply bliss in human form. *"We never really learn to grow up."* I thought as I watched the loonies around me plague each other with their awkward thoughts. *"We just learn how to* act *in public..."* The doctors hold their nose high as they judge us with unclean fingers.

I've made three doctors cry, and four others quit their job. No other doctor will see me. Doctor Winslow tried to tell me that what I was feeling inside was wrong and that the normal and healthy way to live was to express my feelings through art. I made her weep as I brought up the sodomy she had committed with another doctor in the work area. I told her how pathetic and hypocritical she was to tell me that my internal instincts were wrong, but her cheating wasn't. Doctor Charleston hanged himself after quitting abruptly after his first session with me. The chart goes on, but they continue to enforce the fact that *I* am the crazy one because they are scared and they don't feel anything.

From cannibals to serial killers, we were all kept in our designated rooms left to rot. They fed us waste and pills that were supposed to allegedly simmer us from our *violent, hyperactive* minds.

"I don't buy it." I tell myself.

"It's like the pills just make you more insane."

"The constant repeat of the swallowing becomes as natural as air."

"It's like a drug they use to keep you here. Locked away. Forever."

"And ever." I drift from my mind, almost forgetting the reason why I had checked myself into this asylum. David Hamilton was either still looking for me, or was convinced that I was dead. Either way was not a healthy relationship for me to be alive at the moment. So I had convinced myself that I was safe even though I felt like a baby in a straightjacket as the pure white straightjacket I wore sucked me into a cocoon making me feel claustrophobic. I just sat there with apathy. I calmly remained as still, frozen in time as an undisturbed lake, breathing lightly only enough to stay alive.

The guard opens my door and I still show know reaction, I just blankly gaze at the empty grey wall in front of me. The doctor is going to come in and feed me three pills. I cooperate as he sticks the pills down my throat and double checking after every entry to make sure I wasn't hiding them in my mouth somewhere so I could spit them out. He calls me a good boy and I can feel thoughts of violence ignite in my head. The doctor's eyes squint as he squeezes his forehead clearly showing he was in pain. The guard asks if he's alright. "I'm fine." He lies, clearly feeling the agony more thoroughly.

"No he's not." I deviously utter under my breath imagining the how painful his headache might be feeling. It seemed to grow harsher when I spoke as he releases a small cry for help. The guard says some words into his walkie-talkie as the doctor falls to the floor, seizing. A bit of blood flows out of his ear as more guards come in to carry him out of the room. The door slams shut and I am left alone to the pallid walls and one window of my room again.

It begins to rain. The water rapped against my barred window and I break my statue-like pose to inch my head towards the left to watch the drops of rain dance on the clear cut glass of my window. They waltz down smoothly, each one taking a different pattern then the last. None of them were in order. All of them were catastrophic with no sense of control. I watched as the drops on top gradually slide down to what I imagined their demise at the very base of the window seal.

My door swings open, but I continue to focus on the raindrops. A woman's voice announced, "Cale. Are you ready to see your new doctor?"

"This'll be fun." I thought, still continuing to watch the rain outside.

"What's it this time doc." I say bluntly as I hear him step into the room and the door close. "Another broken man seeking some sort of fetish desire to pick at the wounded, or perhaps another man seeking redemption from God for a terrible crime he had made in the past in thinking that visiting the insane will make up for his sins…"

"How about an old friend." The voice commands my attention as I recognize his voice. My head leisurely turns away from the raindrops to see Mr. Rusenkell standing by the door. Dusty as my memory was already, I had forgotten him. He disappeared the day we were abducted and I haven't heard word from him since. I figured he was dead. "Hello Cale." He grins warm heartedly. There was nothing to say to him. "I'm sure, you have a lot of questions." He says sophisticatedly.

"Actually, I've learned to just sort of go with it." I thought.

"But I am here to ask you something." I look at him and wait patiently for the question to brand my brain with a burning desire to come up with a lie if the question should be personal. "Why are you here?" he asks after a pause.

There was no answer to that anymore. I looked and looked for a file somewhere in my brain that could even remotely answer him, but I sincerely could not understand his question. *"I am here, because I want to be. Because I can be."*

"You are here because you have nowhere else to go." I argue, noticing I wasn't agreeing with plain self any longer.

"I am here because this is where Paul told me to go."

"Are you sure it's not because your just chicken and afraid that if you were to be caught again that they would kill you? Because you don't follow orders, remember."

"Cale?" Mr. Rusenkell comforts, bringing me out of my head. "Why are you here?"

"Because it's safe."

"You can find refuge in better places, Cale. You can be safe-"

"No. Safe for everyone else." I state. Mr. Rusenkell is silenced by the eerie comment. "Explain to me." I demanded.

"What would you like to know?"

"Everything."

He takes a deep breath in before he confesses, "I took Cameron Dark hostage because I knew he could turn invisible. I told him he needed to follow me for everyone else's sake and he did. I'm a leech. I needed him to stay with me so I could use his power to remain invisible for when they came to take you."

"You knew they would kidnap us."

"Yes." He admitted. "And if they would have found me, they would have surely killed me. I needed to stay alive, because I know more about David Hamilton then anyone in this world."

"How so?" I ask indecently, still focusing on being angry at the fact he knew we were going to be kidnapped.

"Because David Hamilton is my brother. I took my father's name, but David refused to forgive him after he killed our mother in a fit of jealous rage. I know my brother better than anything. If he knew I had supernatural abilities, his jealousy would tear this world in half. The man is obsessed with power and control. I'm guessing you've already visited the room of relinquishment?" I nod, catching some memory of my incubus. "Do you know why it is called that?" I shake my head. "Because the room is computer programmed to use your own powers against you. It's a mere test of faith when he uses your own image against you, but it's the perfect form of manipulation. No one can brainwash you more than you brainwash yourself. The *incubus* relinquishes your faith in morals and lifestyle to allow you to see things differently. These White Crows that have been exploited all over the news are nothing but experiments that realized they had strings attached to their limbs being controlled by the marionette David Hamilton himself. David wouldn't risk a group of wild renegades patrolling the states. He wanted them under his command or he wanted them dead. Those who couldn't be controlled were killed. Unfortunately, when I unleashed this bane against Stellar High-"

"Pandora did. Not you."

"Who?"

"Pandora. Amanda Robesun."

"No. It is my fault for even bringing such a catalyst in your lives in the first place. I take full responsibility, but he used the deaths of Irvine as a cover up story in his favor to blame a group of terrorists called the White Crows which consist of every runaway super being that resisted David's snake charm. When I was informed of everything that had happened in the last year, I went searching for you. And I found you here."

"Who told you about the massacre?"

"A spy of mine. Hayley Owens."

My brain spins in circles at the name. "She's dead." I told him "She couldn't have told you."

"Hayley is very much alive Cale."

"I watched her die."

"That's because that wasn't Hayley."

"What?"

"The real Hayley Owens is my niece. David's niece as well. He had enough of her blood to clone poor Hayley twice before she escaped with Paul and the others like I had warned them to. Both of the clones are presumed dead thanks to your friend Jonah and Paul. She was desperately in love with Paul, so I saw how empty she was when she found out he died. She said that she could somehow feel each other even over great distances. She said that they were so in love and attached to one another that they could even feel each other's powers at times and in that moment, she knew that love was a power of its own."

"Spare me." I murmur.

"Well are you ready to check out of here? I've got to get you someplace better than this."

"Why? You're not my father."

"I know that but-"

"So stop pretending to be interested in my welfare! I'm fine here! Now get out and don't ever come back!"

"But Cale you-"

"Get out!"

"Cale! I-"

"Get out!" I yell at the top of my lungs scaring Mr. Rusenkell away. The guard opens the door at my yelling and I somehow manage to hear Mr. Rusenkell say something along the lines of 'Don't give up, keep fighting Cale.' Before he leaves my room.

The night comes and a thunderstorm ignites the black sky outside my window. I can hear the other lunatics howl like werewolves to the crashing of nature's violent storm. I sit there in complete stone staring at the grey wall in front of me. Lighting flashes it's blinding light into my room and darkness returns in less than a second. Someone appears from nowhere, sitting in a chair right in front of me as the lighting fades away. The shadow in front of me lights up a cigarette and I can see from the ember in his hand that the thing staring back at me is the image of me in a white suit. "Not you again." I said rolling my eyes.

"Good to see you too, Cale."

"What do you want?"

He takes a drag. "I personally don't want anything. I'm only here in the interest of you."

"I don't need any charity."

"I wasn't offering any."

"Then vanish."

"I will. But you see, unlike you I don't hide from who I am. I'm a messenger and that is my destiny. I fulfill my destiny with pride, because that's what I was created for. And you know what? I'm friggen happy. So I'm going to deliver this message to you and you are going to listen." The image of me vanishes from sight and ends up right next to me hovering over my right side whispering into my ear, "Go find her." I turn to see me but I see that the image of me has vanished from my room. The words echo in my head over and over again as I lay down in my straightjacket, trying to sleep through the symphony of the hurricane outside.

I awake to a rooster crowing, carrying the dream I had into my existence of consciousness. I had dreamt that very soon, David Hamilton would find me and slip me the cure when he got the chance. In the dream I talked with Beef, and somehow I was convinced that he was still alive. But the one thing that I remembered most vividly were actually in fact memories. Memories that I had forced Tianna to erase. Somehow it all came back to me like a feral bash to my mind. I could feel her. I couldn't explain the feeling, but I knew that right as I awoke, she did too and I knew she could feel me as much as I could sense her. I remembered every moment I spent with her and how badly I wanted to take them all down on paper just so I could read it nonstop in a book. She was alive. I was definite about it. I couldn't explain it but I somehow managed to sense her powers and caught a glimpse of what I instinctively knew was the future. It was me and her, standing on a hillside watching the sunset in the distance from what looked like the top of the world. We shared a pleasant conversation…

Autumn leaves seemed to be falling all around us, but I had no natural idea of where they were coming from since we were on top of the world where there were no trees.

"Here we are." Tianna sighs.

"Here at the end of all things." I say morbidly. The sun begins to set behind overlapping, giant mountains in front of us. It's a long way down from where we stood. Three steps forward and we would surely be free falling down to what looked like a never ending plummet. I had no idea where we were, but I couldn't help but wonder if both Tianna and I were dead. It felt like heaven. The lavender sky meshed with the last of the crimson sun. Twilight took over and time seemed to have stopped. I knew Tianna had paused it for us.

"Not the end." She whispers, turning my face to look at her. She leans in closer to my face and I can feel time pick up again as the sun really begins to dim. A full moon takes its place in the midnight sky along with her diamonds scattered through the night. "This is the beginning." She whispers before sealing her lips against mine. I didn't have to look, but I could feel the shooting star soar through the cobalt sky above us as the last of the light fades away. I was near positive that wherever we were, it had to be heaven, or somewhere where we would share an eternity of forever with each other.

I was convinced that by the end of the day that's where we would be. Before sunset I would find her and my best friend. I sit up straight, my arms secured to my sides. I peer outside and see a bird—one I could have sworn looked like a phoenix at first—symbolizing the very essence of my rebirth, was crowing on the barbed wire fence.

"Malicious bird." I thought. *"All a twitter like everyone else in the world is a morning person."*

"Go to hell, bird!" I bellow.

I watched as the bird let out a spiteful siren, singing it with all of its heart. *"Beautiful."* I whispered in my head.

"There is nothing beautiful about a worm eating pest waking everyone up just out of pure spite!"

"Or is there…"

"What?'

"Just look at him." I tell myself as I watch the rooster balance himself on the fence while screaming at the top of its lungs. *"No one's telling him to do that. No one is controlling him to scream of dawn. He does it because he is born to do it."*

"Okay zookeeper, the only thing that's a problem is the fact that no one has shot that thing yet. Go back to bed!"

I continue to watch the fowl sing as the horizon behind him shows the starting point of a new day. The straps on my straightjacket start to loosen and I inch myself more and more to freedom. Visions of the disastrous past fly by my mind as I realize it was time for a new beginning. It was time to fulfill my destiny. Although scattered, I knew the remaining survivors of Stellar High School would be presumed dead by David Hamilton. I would spend the rest of my existence a secret with Tianna Lecher and my best friend Beef. Although odd, destructive events would follow me leaving trails, I had decided that I would evade the hunt. It would make my subtle life more interesting. Somehow I knew I was sharing the same thoughts as Tianna when I felt the memory of her throb in my heartbeat. She was my destiny. Tianna and I were meant for each other. And no form of scientific affliction would tear at the fabric of our destined, star-crossed bond.

"*What are you doing?*"

"*I'm getting out of here.*"

"*Thought you wanted to stay here forever.*"

"*I've had a change of heart.*"

"*One little rooster inspires you to leave this place, but here I've been talking to you for an entire year and you stubbornly sit as stone ignoring me?*"

"*No one tells the rooster to crow in the morning, no one brainwashes him to awake at the certain time before dawn. He just does it. It's innate. He's not the good guy, nor the bad guy. He is just a malicious fowl calling out to the world that he is here now at the dawn of a new day.*" The locks on my straightjacket snap off by themselves as I grow more and more impatient about escaping.

"*On second thought…maybe you should stay here.*" I tell myself, clearly antagonizing my new theory on life, by subtly calling myself crazy, in which how everything we know is all a form of brainwash. "*You could probably use the help.*" I antagonize, but I ignore myself and break free from my straightjacket like a monarch butterfly being set free from a cocoon. As I nearly bended reality with my will, I found my ruby ipod and headphones assemble itself on to me while my straightjacket flayed off of me into black dust. Like my ipod had a mind of its own that was somehow linked to mine it selected the very first song that came to my head, "Anna Molly" by Incubus. One snap of my fingers and in between the friction of my right index finger and thumb grew a cigarette. I smoothly blow my breath on the end that needed to be lit and a small ember ignited just before I took a drag. A memory of lying in ash with Tianna while a butterfly flew overhead crossed my mind as I imagined myself improved and with wings now. My head swarmed with passion and determination to find Tianna and live my life in bliss as ignorant as possible to every form of control. I was now and forever free from being controlled.

"*I'm here.*" I thought as I commanded the door to be blown off from securing me in. I walk out into the dark hall with silent havoc in my steps opening every locked door in the facility with just a wink connected to a thought. Every bulky, locked door of steel is crushed by an invisible force that obeyed me as I slowly and deviously made my way towards the entrance, pulling the fire alarm on my way out.

To be continued…

Havoc
The Lifeblood Within the Wolf

The anticipated sequel of the Riot Saga

About the Author

Isaac Tago grew up studying movies, stealing his parents video camera to capture a storyline his imagination fabricated in order to pursue his dreams. He picked up a pen at the age of seventeen to write his debut book Riot: The Fowl of the Crimson Dawn, putting his career dreams in motion. Always knowing hard times, it has been a struggle to keep fighting for what he believes in. Life has attempted to erode his beliefs, but as resilient as his spirit is, he strives for greatness and vows to do so even if it means the death of him.